"She's panicking."

The woman lets out a sharp, terrified scream and tries to curl deeper into what little space she already occupies. Her knees come up to her chest. Her arms wrap around her legs. "Go away! Leave me alone!"

This is not easy. It might be the most horrible thing Summer has ever done in her life.

The woman thrashes the air with one free arm, as if she's trying to ward off a vexatious fly. "Please! Just go!"

Summer gives her another nudge. If she wanted, she could easily put all her energy behind it in one huge thrust, and within seconds the woman would break into flames. Spontaneous combustion is how it would be explained. But Summer would know what had really happened. And Hunter would know, too.

"Summer?" Hunter's voice demands again.

You don't have to do this.

This idea comes to her with a startling clarity she nearly rejects out of hand.

You could simply fail.

Hunter would know, though. He would know and he would—

He *would* what? *What could he do?*

He *could have me killed. . . .*

THE
FAMILY

Book One: Special Effects

—

Kevin McCarthy
with David B. Silva

DAW BOOKS, INC.
DONALD A. WOLLHEIM, FOUNDER
375 Hudson Street, New York, NY 10014

ELIZABETH R. WOLLHEIM
SHEILA E. GILBERT
PUBLISHERS

DAW TRADEMARK REGISTERED
U.S. PAT OFF AND FOREIGN COUNTRIES
—MARCA REGISTRADA.
HECHO EN USA

PRINTED IN THE U.S.A.

*"Between the idea and the reality,
between the motion and the act,
falls the shadow."*
—Thomas Stearns Eliot, 1925

PROLOGUE

*"I know indeed what evil I intend to do,
But stronger than all my afterthoughts is my fury,
fury that brings upon mortals the greatest evils."*

—Euripides

1

For Hunter, it was the first time in his life he felt at home. Truly at home. It wasn't just the anticipation of what was going to happen in the next few minutes, though that certainly played its part. From this point on, there would be no turning back. The dice would be rolled and even craps wouldn't stop the next round of bets from hitting the table. No, he felt at home because here they knew who he was, what he was, what he was capable of doing, and it still didn't make any difference. It was what they wanted and it was what no one else could give them.

As far back as he could remember, he had been aware of the darkness growing inside him, a seed that had blossomed in his teens and now, at age twenty-seven, was nearly insatiable. It had escaped the notice of his parents. But his grandmother, a woman who knew her seeds well and what they could grow into, had told him once that she'd had an *itch* about him almost from the day of his birth.

"You've got a dark soul, Samuel. I know it's there. So do you. Some people, they learn to overcome such things the way you overcome the hurt when your parents don't love you. Some people, they just learn to hurt others."

She had died before he had come to that particular "Y" in the road. He was grateful for that. She was the only person in the world who could see beneath his facade, into the darkness.

2

From the beginning, Michael Hastings had argued against the experiment, claiming it wasn't necessary to take it to such an extreme. He contended that once the kittens—only two days old, and still blind, pink, and hairless—were removed from their mother, it would only be a matter of time before they grew hungry and started crying out for her. The electroencephalograph would record the mother's reaction, assuming there was a reaction, and the researchers would have their answer. The psychic connection existed or it didn't.

But that was too simplistic a conclusion, Hunter insisted. They needed to demonstrate through concrete, scientific evidence that a psychic connection not only existed, but that it could be manipulated to the benefit of both the project and the Agency.

Hunter had prevailed.

3

In the corner, out of the way, Michael Hastings displayed his displeasure as the lab technicians removed the kittens from their mother and placed them in a basket. The basket was carried down three flights of stairs to a small, windowless room bathed in fluorescent light. Cameras were mounted in all four corners of the room, high on the walls. Hastings watched the monitors as the kittens were removed from the basket and placed in a square, metal box about the size of a sofa cushion. There were no blankets. No bedding. Tiny cries escaped the wide-open mouths of the kittens as they stumbled blindly over one another, confused and disoriented in the harshness of this sudden new environment.

Hunter turned away from the window, where he had been staring absently down at the complex parking lot. He nodded. One of the two remaining technicians began to attach a series of wires connecting the mother feline to a nearby electroencephalograph.

"This is sick. You don't have to do this." Michael Hastings uncurled himself from the corner, then started for the door, unwilling—*unable*—to watch any more.

"Maybe. But it's more dramatic this way, don't you think?" A slanted grin cast a dark shadow over Hunter's face. "Leaves a lasting impression."

"You already know how it's going to turn out."

"Ah, but I'm not the one we're trying to impress. It's the guys upstairs."

Hastings stared at him a moment longer, his disbelief long ago replaced by his disdain for Hunter. He shook his head, then opened the door and left the room.

Amused, Hunter took a pack of Winstons out of his jacket pocket, tapped it against his hand, then pulled out a cigarette. Before the pack was back in his pocket, he had snapped the cigarette in two. He tossed the filtered half at the ashtray sitting on the windowsill, then struck a match to the remainder. He took a long, pleasant tug on the cigarette, releasing the smoke as if he hated to let go of it.

He nodded at the lead technician.

A switch was flipped.

An electric current went dancing through the metal box housing the kittens.

Hunter focused on the nearest monitor.

The muscle contractions were immediate and pronounced. A series of ripples sailed down the back of the tiniest kitten in the litter, forcing its hind legs to give out as it collapsed into a helpless ball in one corner. Its mouth opened and closed. A grimace curled back its lips. Valiantly, it managed to struggle back to its feet again, and blindly find its way back into the huddle with its brothers and sister.

Hunter gave another nod.

The flow of the current was immediately disabled.

A chorus of pules rose above the hum of the air conditioner.

Ten seconds had elapsed.

In short, faintly-registering waves, the thin wire arms of the electroencephalograph began to move across the graph paper. Hunter crushed out his cigarette, took one last glance at the mewling kittens in the monitor, then crossed the room for a closer look at the mother's response.

He watched the wave pattern gradually intensify, then expand its arc across the graph paper, as he had expected it would. There were no surprises here. Only a warm, tingling sensation that moved sinuously down his spine in the pleasant realization that from this point on, his life would never be the same again.

"She knows. She knows her babies are hurting."

Once the mewling died down and the kittens found new comfort in huddling together near the middle of the box, the agitation of their mother appeared to subside as well. The electroencephalograph fell idle again, except for the calm, rather banal movement of the needles along the edge of the paper.

"Incredible, isn't it? She knew. Three floors away and she knew. Absolutely incredible." Hunter's eyes were bright with renewed zeal. He placed a hand on the shoulder of the nearest technician, gave him a pat, then grinned. "Let's do it again. Step up the current and do it again."

"How much?"

"As much as it takes."

The tech glanced at him, the expression on his face unchanging, though Hunter could feel the muscles tighten in the man's shoulders. The room was in a hush. There were moments in interpersonal communications when letting the silence speak for you was more powerful than anything you could possibly say. This was one of those moments. Hunter let the silence expand.

Finally, the tech turned away. "Yes, sir."

"That's what I like to hear," Hunter said. He gave another hearty pat to the man's shoulders. "We'll goose the kittens a little, see how high we can make those needles jump, and it'll all be over faster than you can say Rumpelstiltskin. Trust me."

He was wrong, though. It took longer than that.

The current sent the kittens stumbling around the metal box like a horde of drunken sailors, their mouths wide and twisted, their cries stuck somewhere so deep in their throats that it seemed as if they were choking to get them out.

The mother feline reacted immediately. She backed into a corner of the cage, arched her spine, and let out a horrible wail that sounded like the screech of metal against metal. The needles of the electroencephalograph took off on a wild ride across the graph paper.

The tech glanced at Hunter, who squeezed his shoulder with reassurance. "Don't stop now. We're almost there."

On the nearest monitor, the kittens had gone into violent convulsions. Dark spots began to appear on their bodies, like patches of bruised fruit, and soon the pink flesh turned completely black. Charred lappets peeled away from the underpinnings of bone and cartilage. A flurry of sparks erupted. The kitten in the farthest corner collapsed and fell nose-first against the metal floor, its body still jerking. Then a second one followed, and a third.

The electroencephalograph turned frantic. The graph paper blackened beneath a series of long, violent lines stretching from one edge of the paper to the other, resembling a child's scrawl.

Again, the tech looked to Hunter for the okay to cut the current.

Hunter nodded.

Almost immediately, movement in the metal box ceased. The kittens were dead. Their mother, who had backed herself into the corner in a rage, stood paralyzed, her body twisted into a grotesque unnatural shape. Her eyes were huge white orbs. A rictus grin, too big for her face, exposed a full mouth of teeth.

Hunter knelt next to the cage, fascinated. His hands curled around the bars.

The feline swayed drunkenly for a moment before

her legs finally gave out. She collapsed in the corner, dead.

The fury of the electroencephalograph dissipated. The needles fell still.

Hunter stared in silence, then grinned. "I guess now we know, don't we?"

"What's that?"

"Mind over matter. We can make it work for us."

4

Two years later, Michael Hastings was dealing with the dread of paperwork when a knock sounded at the door. He looked up from the small area of his desk illuminated by a single lamp, not ungrateful for the interruption. Days always seemed longer when they were spent on paperwork. He rubbed his eyes, then focused on the office door. "Come in."

It was James, one of the recruits. He was a strikingly good-looking young man, a light-skinned African-American who reminded Hastings of a young Denzel Washington. James pushed his dark-framed glasses up on his nose. "Bad time?"

"As good as any, I suppose." Hastings motioned to a chair. "Turn on the light on your way in, will you?"

James stepped through the door, into the office, as if he were carrying the weight of the world on his shoulders. He was a serious kid at eighteen, thoughtful, with a sense of humor (when he was in the mood for it) that relied heavily on sarcasm. The day Hunter had introduced them, Hastings had been wearing his white lab coat. Hunter, who enjoyed sarcasm himself, had referred to Hastings as his chief lab technician. "I see by your outfit," James had said as they shook hands. It didn't appear as though there was going to be much humor today, though. James sat across the desk from Michael, looking uncommonly ill at ease as he took in the surroundings. Three walls of bookshelves. A window to the courtyard, where long afternoon shadows had given themselves completely to the darkness of the evening. It was neither particularly interesting, nor was this the first time James had seen it.

"I would think this would be the last place in the world you'd want to be during your off time."

"Guess I'm just a glutton for punishment."

The project had advanced dramatically since that first, early experiment with the kittens. Hunter had recruited three new subjects: Summer Mann, a fifteen-year-old who seemed to have a natural talent for telekinesis; James Powell, who was now sitting across the desk from Hastings, and along with his sense of precognition, was fascinated with the idea of becoming an agent for the CIA; and Kate Mimeaux, a little older at age twenty-two, but no less psychically talented. Three young loners. By nature. By circumstance. Four loners, if you cared to include Hastings, who had been grasping for something to hold onto ever since the deaths of his wife and daughter.

"So what's on your mind?"

"I don't know," James said. "It's just not what I expected."

"And we're talking about?"

"This. The project. The CIA. All of it."

Ah, well, you aren't alone there, Hastings thought.

It was no longer what he had expected either. Before Hunter and the PSI Project . . .

Doesn't matter, he reminded himself. *You can't change history.*

"Why don't you tell me what you *did* expect?"

"Code breaking. Strategic planning. Working with agents in the field."

"Anything but this?"

"Don't get me wrong . . . I know what you're trying to do here. The remote viewing and all. Trying to find new ways to gather information without risking agents in the field. It's just that it's . . ."

"Boring?"

A broad smile crossed his face. "It is. It's boring."

Boring had been Christy's favorite word before she had died. She was twelve, only a couple of months away from her thirteenth birthday. Twelve-and-three-quarters she would say when someone asked her age. Almost thirteen. Almost a teenager. Hastings didn't imagine those teen years would have been nearly as joyous or wondrous as her first twelve, but he hated never having the chance to find out.

"Not much I can do about boring," Hastings said.

"My dad used to say only boring people get bored."

"There's a certain truth to that, I suppose." *Loners by circumstance*, Hastings thought. James had lost his parents in a tragic house fire, the result of faulty Christmas tree lights, when he was sixteen. By outward appearances, he had covered his pain well, though Hastings suspected that the boy's sarcasm was—if not directly, then at least indirectly—attributable to the tragedy.

"You don't suppose Hunter would let me transfer into a different section, do you?"

"You know him, what do you think?"

"I think he's a tight-ass."

They laughed, James with a smile that was bright and beautiful against his black face; Hastings with the added knowledge that the room was probably bugged and eventually Hunter would be hearing this little conversation through a set of fat headphones that would put him right here in the room with them.

"What's with that guy?" James added.

"He just likes to keep a tight rein on things."

"He needs to lighten up once in a while. Get a life outside the office."

"His life *is* the office."

The laughter was short-lived, coming to an end that was neither abrupt nor lingering. It was true ∴ . . the PSI Project was Hunter's life, and it was also true that James was not going to find an easy transfer out. Sometimes, when you found yourself in a maze, you had to face the fact that all the exits were blocked. Hastings didn't know if James had reached this conclusion on his own yet or not, but he was a sharp kid and sooner or later the realization would settle in. It had settled in for Hastings a long time ago.

James nodded. The conversation had gone from awkward to comfortable to jovial, but now it was back at that awkward place again. "Yeah, well, I guess I should let you get back to your work."

"What did you really come here for?"

He stared down at the floor a moment, letting out a hiccup of a laugh as if he were scoffing at himself for being such a wuss. "I don't know. I guess I just wanted to talk to someone who wasn't bullshitting me."

Hastings nodded, then pushed aside the paperwork on his desk. He got up, went to the handcrafted wood pedestal that sat in the far corner of the room, and brought back an Aztec onyx, black-and-white chess set. "You play chess?"

"Only to win."

"Good. That's the way I play."

He set the board on the desk between them, then took up two of the pawns—one black, one white—held them behind his back a moment, then presented them in two closed fists. "Your choice."

James tapped his right hand.

He opened it. White. "You go first."

5

It had been a bad day for fifteen-year-old Summer Mann. Hunter had been waiting for her outside the high school. The temperature had reached the low nineties, the humidity miserable as usual. Summer came out with a sweatshirt tied around her waist, a style that was unchanging no matter the time of the year or the shift in weather. At five-six, she wasn't tall enough to be a model, nor would she want to be, but she had mesmerizing blue eyes, blonde hair that turned honey-blonde in the winter, and the slim, graceful body of a model. At a time in her life when she would have preferred to go unseen, too often her appearance drew the attention of others. It was for this reason that she had turned to the sweatshirts and loose clothing.

She spotted Hunter sitting in the Ford Explorer, the engine still running, but pretended not to notice. None of the kids liked Hunter; Summer liked him even less than the others did. "Sometimes he smiles at you, you know, like he's trying to be nice and all? But there's nothing nice about him. Nothing. He's all darkness."

You can't psych a psychic.

Hunter honked, then motioned to her.

Summer shifted the books to the crook of her left arm, glanced at the waiting bus at the other side of the parking lot, and knew she had been made. The jig was up, as the saying went. There was no pretending she hadn't seen the Explorer or heard the horn or noticed Hunter waving. So she took the long stroll across the concrete walkway, stretching out the inevitable with the shortest steps possible. She opened the passenger door and leaned in.

"What's up?"

"Get in. We've got a test this afternoon."

"There weren't any tests on the schedule."

"Sometimes things come up unexpectedly."

"What kind of test?"

"Get in the car, Summer." He stared across the seat at her, not needing to say another word.

Summer quietly did as she was told. She strapped herself into the seat belt, held her books pressed against her breasts, then stared longingly out the passenger-side window at the flood of kids still emerging from the high school. She had been here less than a month now. It had been Michael Hastings who had gone to bat for her, insisting that Summer wasn't like the other two, that she was still young and needed a normal environment (or as close to normal as possible) to add some stability to her psychology. Otherwise, Hastings had said, she would be difficult to control. It had been one of the few arguments with Hunter she had ever seen him win, and she would always be grateful to him for making the effort.

"So . . . how was your day?"

"Okay."

"You want to elaborate?"

"It was like every other day. Nothing special. All right?" She watched as they passed Tony Peters, sitting on the curb with a few friends, playing guitar. Through the window and over the whine of the tires, the music was a murmur, almost too faint to hear.

"Don't pull that routine with me. You hear? When you talk to me, you keep it courteous and polite, with respect. You owe me that much. You owe me a little common courtesy and respect. At the very least."

Summer closed her eyes. Sometimes it felt as if she could hide behind her eyelids. Disappear. Close them and drift away, wherever the thoughts and pictures took her.

"Hey! Look at me when I'm talking to you."

"That wouldn't be a good idea right now."

"Are you threatening me, missy? Because if you are—"

"Just let it drop. *Please*." The picture that had come to mind had not been a pleasant one. Summer didn't want to give it any more power than it already possessed. Once the simmer turned to a boil, it would be nearly uncontrollable. "*Please*."

Hunter, in one of his rare moments of good sense, turned his attention back to the road. They spent the rest of the thirty-minute trip back to the ramshackle buildings that housed the classified, special CIA project in silence. Hunter did a little simmering of his own. He fidgeted relentlessly in his seat to control it, twice flicking on the radio only to turn it off again almost immediately. He wasn't used to having less than full control and it did not sit well with him. Not at all.

Summer allowed her thoughts to drift. Eventually, with the drone of the tires in the background, they swept her away from the confrontation, into a peaceful corner of her mind. She let herself relax again. Her breathing deepened. Colors floated past . . . yellows and pinks, purples and reds . . . like fields of flowers. She nearly fell asleep, only to come out of it when Hunter finally parked the Explorer and slammed the door as he climbed out.

"Come on. Let's get going. I want to get this finished up as soon as possible."

"What did you say we were doing today?"

"I didn't." Back in control again. No doubt feeling the thrill of victory.

Summer climbed out of the vehicle, her books still pressed against her chest, because that minor effort somehow made her feel safer. They entered the building from the back, the shadows long behind them. Down the hallway, Summer trailed along several steps behind him, then through a door, past a small open area with a worn linoleum floor and no furniture. Hunter stopped and punched out a code in a keypad that opened the next door. The other side was a three-room restricted area that had always smelled a bit like a dentist's office to Summer.

Hunter pointed to a bench. It was a familiar spot for Summer. She had spent hours sitting on this particular bench, waiting for him to give her the okay to enter the lab. "Sit and wait. Oh, here, give me your books. You won't be needing them."

"I thought I'd do some studying."

"We won't be that long." He took the books.

Summer drew in a deep breath, then let it out slowly, trying to force herself to relax again. She didn't know what the test was going to be—she rarely received advanced knowledge of test parameters—but she knew it was unusual for Hunter to pick her up from school, and unusual for him to deviate from the schedule.

Hunter returned within minutes. "Okay, let's see how good you really are."

She followed him into the lab, unhappy with his choice of words and wondering what exactly he had meant. Inside, the lights were dim. There was a mirror along one wall, which everyone knew and accepted as a two-way mirror used for observation. Hunter always stood on the other side. Who stood with him, though, was something Summer had never determined. Maybe no one. Maybe he was like the Vampire Lestat and he stood alone.

She sat in the reclining chair, similar to a dentist's chair except it was roomier and upholstered in leather. The chair faced the mirror. She glanced up at her own reflection, then at Hunter, who looked dark under the poor lighting. He reminded her of a scruffy-faced carnival barker, leading the way into a seedy sideshow tent with the word "Freaks" painted in huge red-and-gold letters over the entrance.

She was, after all, exactly that: a freak.

They all were.

Hunter handed her a sealed manila envelope. "This is something different we're doing here today. I want you to take it all the way. No holding back."

"I can't do that."

"That's what we're going to find out."

"I'll hurt someone."

"The target's expendable."

Summer stared at him a moment, unsure of what she had just heard. Then she started to pry open the envelope. This was the first time anyone here, including Hunter, had talked about taking it all the way. They knew the dangers. You don't set a fire just to see if the fire alarms work.

"Leave it alone," Hunter said evenly. "You know the protocol."

"I want to know who it is; what he looks like."

"Who it is, is none of your business." He gave her the *look*—eyebrows angled, mouth tight, a scowl on anyone else's face. But on Hunter's face it was a warning, a sign that he had reached the end of his patience. Push any harder and accept the consequences. "It's standard procedure today, missy."

Summer hated being called missy.

Almost as much as she hated Hunter himself.

She dropped the envelope to her lap, then closed her eyes and tried to relax again. Hunter began the routine of attaching the sensors to her head. Standard procedure. Except this was the first time she could recall Hunter doing it himself. Normally, there were several lab tech types around to hook her up to the electroencephalograph.

"All set."

Summer opened her eyes. She thought Hunter looked different today. Uneasy. Like a man carrying a secret he feared might get out. Under the poor lighting, his face was a Picasso of shadows.

He handed her the customary blindfold. "Sit tight until I give the okay."

The next time she heard his voice, it came through the speakers mounted above the door. "You can open the envelope now."

She pulled back the clasp and removed the contents. The target photo, which was the top sheet of paper, was of a woman in her mid-to-late sixties with thinning gray-white hair pulled back from her face in a rather nondescript bun. She had dark eyes and wore a ruby lipstick that was too bright for her pale complexion. She looked like every little girl's dream of a grandmother.

"She's a woman," Summer said.

"Yes, she is."

"We've never done a woman before."

"There's a first time for everything," Hunter said over the speaker.

"Who is she?"

"That's not for you to know."

The back of the photo was blank. Sometimes you could catch a snippet of information there. A name, perhaps. Or an age. Or an ID number. Not this time. She turned it over again and stared into the woman's dark eyes.

"This is personal, isn't it?"

"Just do your job, Summer."

The second sheet of paper was a target map. The state: Virginia. The city: Fairfax. The address: 888 Jasper Lane. An "X" had been drawn in thick red ink just above the address. Not an exact location on the map, but an approximation. It was as much as she would need.

"I thought, you know, like we didn't deal with anyone here in this country?"

"Sometimes things spill over," Hunter said. "Are you ready?"

"Give me a minute." She needed to look at the photograph again. It was not the picture of a woman who posed a threat. Not in Summer's mind. Tracing the outline of the woman's face only brought up the gentlest of thoughts.

"Summer?"

"Okay. All right. You're in a rush. I get it." She had never heard this kind of urgency in Hunter's voice before. It made her all the more curious. Who was this woman? Why did he want her killed? Dangerous questions. "Just a nudge, okay? A hot flash. Maybe a low-grade fever for a few hours."

"It's all the way today, missy. This isn't a test. It's serious. Lives are at stake." He paused, then took a deep breath that the speaker amplified. "Ready?"

Summer nodded, though she would have preferred more time, more details, an opportunity to try to put it all into some sort of meaningful perspective. She didn't want to look back in ten minutes or a week or a year and regret what she had done simply because she hadn't been strong enough to say no. But she knew she wasn't strong. She had never been strong.

"Okay. Here we go."

The previous sessions had all started with a mix of sounds and music and this one was no exception. Over the speakers, Summer could hear two very distinct noises. The first, which seemed to completely surround her, was something that sounded very much like a clock ticking. Only it was ticking in double-time. Maybe even in triple-time. Quite fast. Behind the ticking, came a sound similar to a tennis ball exploding off a racquet. A steady, heartbeat rhythm that sounded as if it were coming from inside her head.

Summer closed her eyes, slipped on the blindfold, then settled back into the chair.

Her breathing, of which she was only distantly aware, ebbed.

Three . . . four . . . five minutes passed.

She fell deeper into the sensation of relaxation. Complete relaxation.

It was a state where she easily could have drifted off to sleep, let what dreams may come do just that, and find herself wherever. But on the verge of this nirvana, an alarm went off. The alarm, which lasted only seconds, was followed by the deep, hollow vibrations of something that sounded like an Australian didgeridoo. The vibrations were overlapped with a combination of wind chimes and what sounded like the wild screeching of a family of monkeys in fear of danger.

The room resonated with the noise.

Summer shifted in her seat. The photo and map—and the envelope they had come in—were in her lap now, and no longer necessary. Behind her eyelids, the woman's face came into perfect focus . . . the smile just at the edge of her lips, the eyes like depthless pools of water, the grandmotherly bun in the woman's hair.

Calm, hollow sounds took her deeper into herself.

"Where are you now?"

"Still relaxing."

That part of her—the logical, analytical, what's really going on here part of her—gradually slipped farther and farther into the background. With it, it took her uneasy awareness of Hunter's presence. Her sense of him behind the two-way mirror, watching her, monitoring the electroencephalograph, anticipating the first signs of the psychic connection now underway, was gradually cast adrift on a paper boat across the surface of her imagination until he no longer existed. There was no room in here to worry about Hunter, even when she heard his voice. . . .

Deeper.

Into a vague landscape of shadow and light, of soft whispers and words just beyond reach.

Deeper.

Bodiless now. A free spirit, as the expression goes. Floating. Unaware of her surroundings, her bearings.

Deeper.

"Describe it to me, Summer."

"Free now. Floating."

The sounds so far in the distance that they are murmurs now. Not whispers. Not music. But murmurs of emotion. She feels awash in emotion, her consciousness, swept up in the tide, carrying her away... away... away... until nothing else exists in the physical, every muscle stilled, every breath peaceful, every twitch far, far away.

Drifting.

The hollow vibrations of the didgeridoo swimming through her now, mingling with the consciousness of her cells, then letting the current carry them away.

Drifting.

No time. No minutes, no hours, no days. Only now. Only the simultaneous moment. No space. No objects to hurdle. No miles to cross. Only a boundless extension of herself.

Drifting.

Until the photograph goes floating past, dancing to the current like a falling leaf dancing to the wind. The sight rattles her. She feels a tug at her emotions that spins her around, then she discovers herself in pursuit, following the image because it has a connection to her, because it has a pull, because it is why she is here in this—

Instantly, Summer finds herself floating near the ceiling of a bedroom she's never seen before. There are huge double doors behind her, an armoire to one side, next to a long, ornately-carved dresser. All of these are done in rich, antique rosewood. Across the room, the curtains are drawn on a long line of French windows. There's a makeup area to one side, with a stool pulled out from the marble counter, and a mirror edged with small incandescent bulbs. Beyond the makeup area is the bathroom.

"Where are you now?"

"In her room, her bedroom."

Immediately, Summer becomes aware of the king-size bed, where the woman from the photograph is resting. She's dressed in black slacks and a white blouse. Simple, yet elegant. Her earrings, clip-ons, and glasses are on the ledge of the expansive headboard set behind her. Her legs are crossed at the ankles. She has kicked off her shoes, a pair of pumps, which lie on their sides on the floor next to the bed. She has one hand draped over her forehead, keeping what little light there is from penetrating her eyes.

Who is she? Summer thinks.

The woman clears her throat and rustles in her sleep, though she is not truly asleep. She is trapped in a strange state of limbo, just below awakened awareness, just above slumber, a meditative state not dissimilar to Summer's. Unlike the photograph, the woman is not wearing lipstick. Her complexion appears healthier, richer.

Summer has to remind herself why she is here. *Rule Number One: never allow yourself to identify with the target.* This thought, in the form of Hunter's voice, crosses her mind and sends a shiver through her. She is here to do something she has never done before in her life. She is here to kill. It is something she had known would someday be expected of her. But someday had always felt so far off in the distance as to be nonexistent.

Only now it is here.

And Summer doesn't know if she can do it.

She doesn't *want* to do it.

"Tell me what's happening."

"I'm trying to focus."

The woman stirs in her rest again, uneasily, then suddenly sits up. She sits up, her eyes wide open now, and she stares up at the ceiling, almost directly at Summer. Her eyes are dark. The expression on her face is a mix of surprise and confusion. Summer wonders if the woman can see her. Nothing has ever happened like this before. No one has ever been even remotely aware of her presence before. But this woman—

The woman's glance follows a road map of criss-crossing angles across the ceiling, pausing briefly here, then moving to the next place and pausing there. She can't see Summer, but she can sense her, like a movement just beyond the edge of her vision.

Summer finds this extremely unnerving.

She nudges the woman to distract her, to occupy her senses with something new to think about. The woman blinks, as if something is caught in her eye, then looks away and brushes a hand over her face. She does not appear frightened, as Summer might have expected. Only confused now. Still disoriented from her rest.

Summer nudges her again, because she just wants this to be over now. She has already rejected the idea of trying to deceive Hunter. It would be easy enough to convince him that she has been here and that she has done what she was supposed to do. But the deception would not last long. It would only be a matter of a few hours before he realized she had lied. Maybe less than that.

And you didn't want to get on the man's bad side.

He could be deadly.

The woman reacts dramatically this time. She jumps off the bed, visibly shaken. Her eyes are wide, her breathing rapid. She looks as if she has just realized she's in danger and can't quite determine how to respond. There's the bathroom, of course. Off to the left, past the makeup room. But she chooses a different escape and makes a dash for the double doors, which are open.

I'm sorry, Summer thinks as she pushes hard.

The doors close and lock before the woman can reach them. She stumbles back against the bed. Her legs buckle beneath her and she sinks to the floor like a beaten animal. It makes Summer's heart sink. It has always been a game in the past. See how much discomfort you can inflict without causing any real damage. And the targets have always been volunteers. But this . . . *this* is serious.

The woman breaks into tears.

Summer nudges her again, just a gentle push that raises the woman's body temperature a bit. A menopausal hot flash.

"Describe what's happening, Summer."

"She's panicking."

The woman lets out a sharp, terrified scream and tries to curl deeper into what little space she already occupies. Her knees come up to her chest. Her arms wrap around her legs. "Go away! Leave me alone!"

This is not easy. It might be the most horrible thing Summer has ever done in her life. She can feel the muscles of her body, however many miles away, tighten, as she, too, tries to curl into a smaller, more protective space. She feels this, then she wonders about the woman's reaction. *How does she know? How does she know someone is in the room with her? Does she know who it is? Does she know it's me?*

The woman thrashes the air with one free arm, as if she's trying to ward off a vexing fly. "Please! Just go!"

Another nudge.

Just a nudge. Nothing more.

If she wanted, Summer could easily put all her energy behind it in one huge thrust, and within seconds the woman would burst into flames. Spontaneous combustion is how it would be explained. One more mystery among all the other mysteries of the world. But Summer would know what had really happened. And Hunter would know, too. And while she would have to live with the guilt for the rest of her life, Hunter would walk away pleased, another paranormal theory proven to his satisfaction.

But this is a nudge. Enough to raise her temperature a degree or two. Enough to give her a slight fever for the rest of the night, maybe through tomorrow. But no more than that. Nothing painful. Nothing permanent. Nothing deadly.

"Summer?"

"I've given her a nudge."

Perspiration breaks out across the woman's face. She wipes the back of her hand over her mouth, swallows hard, then flaps the collar of her blouse to stir up the still bedroom air and cool herself off. It does little to help. Still, the woman does not look up. She does not cry out. And Summer is drawn to the possibility that she is already approaching that fine line between defiance and surrender.

There have been times in her life when Summer has found herself at the brink of that line as well. But at this particular moment, she stands at the brink of a very different line. She is near the point of no return now. Another nudge, slightly magnified, and it will be beyond her ability to pull back. The floodgates will open and the roar of her emotions will be set free. She knows this, because she has been here once before, a few years back, before the CIA and Hunter found her. She was unable to put the stops on then, and she fears she won't be able to put the stops on this time either if she doesn't do it soon.

You don't have to do this.

This idea comes to her with a startling clarity she nearly rejects out of hand.

You could simply fail.

Hunter would know, though. He would know and he would—

He would what? What could he do?

Summer's thoughts begin to revolve around Hunter, obsessively, the way she sometimes thinks about cheesecake (though she's one of the lucky ones and doesn't carry an ounce of fat on her fifteen-year-old body; where it goes is anyone's guess). This, of course, is a different kind of obsession. Less desire than fear.

He could have me killed.

That's the truth of the matter, the bare truth: he could have her killed.

The realization triggers a shudder that travels through both bodies simultaneously: her own and that of the woman. The response is swift and immediate, as if her emotions were strings connecting puppeteer and puppet. A dramatic tremor travels down the woman's body and flips her onto her back. Her eyes roll up into her head, exposing nothing but white. Then the seizure takes hold of her as if she is made of cotton stuffing and rattles the teeth in her mouth so violently that a tooth is broken. The chip pops out like a kernel of corn and lands on the plush white carpet several feet away.

"Summer?" Not Hunter's voice, but the voice of Michael Hastings. "Break it off, Summer. Break it off and come back."

Summer's body is taken by a seizure of its own. She can feel the sudden urgency to get back, tugging at her as if she were at the far end of a broken rubber band, only a *snap!* away from finding herself back in that darkened room again. She's afraid of that room. She's afraid of the man behind the two-way mirror. She's afraid she's fallen into a tar pit and she'll never be able to climb out again. It's all over for her.

It's over . . .

Over . . .

"Summer? It's over, Summer. Come on. Wake up. Pull yourself back."

Her body was rigid, her head thrown back against the rest, her fingers dug so deep into the upholstery of the chair that it would take nearly an hour before the impressions finally disappeared.

Hastings stood over her as her eyes opened. His hands were on her shoulders, where he had been trying to shake her free of her paranormal state. He released his grip, then gazed into her eyes, trying to see past the huge pupils.

For her part, Summer couldn't seem to bring herself to move. Hastings had watched her body go through some sort of horrendous spasm where she appeared completely out of control and in danger of hurting herself, but now that her muscles had seized control again, they had her in a knot.

"Come on, Summer. Take a long, deep breath for me," he said. "Slow and easy."

She looked at him without moving her head, her neck a solid rod, her eyes huge and white. Hastings had seen fear before—not often, but once or twice in his life—*real* fear, the kind you see in the face of someone confronted with the reality of his own mortality. As a boy, he had witnessed it on the face of Jimmy Walters, who was a year older than him, and who had stepped out in front of an old Chrysler after a baseball that probably would have been a home run no matter what he had done. Just before the Chrysler's front grille slammed into his midsection, Jimmy looked up and an unmistakable realization crossed his face. It was not dissimilar to what was on Summer's face at this very moment.

"Summer? You need to do me a favor now. You're going to be all right, but you've got to help me out a little here. You've got to do your own fair share here. I can't do it all myself." Hastings knew she was inside there somewhere, her eyes had followed his movements. But he didn't know if she could hear him, and he didn't know if she had the strength to fight through the temporary paralysis. "You need to get some air into your lungs. You need to take a nice, easy breath and get some air in there. Can you do that for me?"

Her jaws relaxed. She swallowed with the kind of effort that generally comes after several days with a particularly nasty sore throat. Then she took that long, deep breath he had been asking of her.

It was one of the most satisfying moments of his life.

6

The session had taken its toll on Summer. She climbed out of the chair on wobbly legs that barely got her to the door. Her hands were shaking as Hastings led her out of the lab area, through the restricted area, and into the main building.

"My God," she said, her voice weak and trembling.

"Shhh. Not now."

The hallway was empty. Against the worn linoleum, their footsteps made the lonely, hollow sound of two people who suddenly understood that they had only each other. Outside, the long afternoon shadows had given themselves to the twilight. Hastings took Summer by the hand. They crisscrossed through the parking lot, then found themselves out on the old county road that bordered the property. Summer had gotten her legs back and was walking on her own power now, though still a bit unsteadily.

"I can't believe what I almost did back there," she said.

"It wasn't your fault."

"I could have killed her."

"But you didn't."

"I could have."

"I wouldn't have let that happen," Hastings said. He put his arm around her shoulders.

"Yeah, and what happens next time, when you're not there?" A weak bravado had slipped uneasily back into Summer's voice. She slipped out from under the comfort of his arm, that old, self-protective wall immediately going up again. She was only fifteen, but she had grown up with a neglectful, alcoholic mother.

The experience, if it had taught her anything, had taught her how to appear tougher than she really was.

"Then you find your own strength to resist," Hastings said.

"Easy for you to say."

"He's just a man."

"No, *you're* just a man. He's a monster." She had been keeping a close eye on the uneven surface as she walked, but she looked up now, surprised and shamed by her own words. "Sorry. I didn't mean anything. It's just that you haven't seen inside him the way I have. I know what's in there."

"Does he scare you?"

"He scares the daylights out of me."

A car came up the road, its headlights on bright as it passed them. There wasn't much traffic out this way. The road was a patchwork of gravel and asphalt that came to a dead end some three miles ahead. Most of the traffic could be attributed to a couple of small cattle farms that you would never know were there if you weren't looking for them.

Summer watched the car pass, then turned and stared until it disappeared into the evening darkness as if she were making sure it posed no threat. She turned back, smiled uneasily, then cast her gaze back at the rough surface underfoot.

In one way or another, the kids had all had rough backgrounds. It was one of Hunter's primary prerequisites for participation in the project. These were kids who were outsiders, who were without family ties, who had learned to survive in a harsh world with their wits, their temperaments, and their talents. They were strong individuals on the one hand, and yet they were still young enough to mold and manipulate. Summer was the youngest.

After a long period of silence, Summer said, "Is that why he brought us here?"

"You mean what just happened back there?"

She nodded.

"That was never the original intent of the project. Not to my understanding. The PSI Project was designed to explore the use of remote viewing as a way to gather intelligence. That was all it was supposed to be about. Gathering intelligence. Nothing else."

Summer smiled crookedly.

"What?"

"You can't even say it, can you?"

"Say what?"

"You know."

What? Assassination? It wasn't that he *couldn't* say it, he didn't *want* to say it. He didn't even want to believe it. "I didn't know it was going to get this far out of hand. I never knew that. If I had, I never would have allowed him to recruit you."

She nodded without saying anything.

Hastings kicked at a rock, and surprised himself when it went rolling across the road to the other side. It disappeared down the dirt embankment. They were walking south, against traffic, the horizon so far in the distance that it meshed seamlessly with the evening shadows. When Hunter would let her, Summer often walked alone out here. It was her way of reminding herself that there was more to the world than the PSI Project, she said. Sometimes she seemed wise beyond her years.

"Ever wonder how you got here?" she finally said. The last of her upset seemed to have gone by the wayside. She was calm again. Her hands had stopped trembling, her gait had grown more determined and self-assured. "You know, like right here at this particular place in time?"

"As opposed to . . . ?"

"As opposed to where you would have ended up if you had done something—*anything*—a little different? Like if you had broken up with your first girlfriend a month later than you did, or if you had a gotten a 'C' instead of a 'B' in your high school history class. Would you still have ended up right here? Right now? Or would it have changed everything in your life?"

"Are you talking about fate?" asked Hastings.

"I guess." She shrugged. The evening shadows had turned her blonde hair to light brown, and it was becoming nearly impossible to read her eyes now. "Sometimes it seems like no matter what I would have done, I still would have ended up here."

"Is that a bad thing?"

"It could be better," she said with a smile. "Except for Kate and James. They're all right. And you, of course. You're cool."

Hastings kicked at another rock and missed. "Wow. No one's ever called me *cool* before."

"Well, you are."

The evening, except for the occasional distant protest from the cattle or the faraway drone of traffic, had fallen into a stillness that seemed to exclude the rest of the world. It was a peacefulness that Hastings seldom encountered in his life. He certainly would have enjoyed it if it had lasted longer, but some luxuries were seldom afforded. Behind him, he could hear the first, early sounds of tires kicking up gravel. He turned around, disappointed but not surprised, to see Hunter driving up the road in the Ford Explorer.

"Looks like someone's coming to check up on us."

"Oh, Christ. Doesn't he ever give it a rest?"

"Not in my experience."

Hunter pulled up next to them and rolled down the window. "A little late to be out walking, don't you think? Hop in, I'll give you a ride back."

"We can manage," Summer said.

"No, really, I insist." Hunter gave the left breast pocket of his jacket a quick pat, as if he were checking for a pack of cigarettes. Only it wasn't a pack of cigarettes that was under there. It was a gun. He had started carrying the thing six or seven months ago, telling Hastings you could never be too careful these days. But they both knew it wasn't about self-protection. It was about control. And in Hastings' view, it was one more demonstration of the dangerous mix of egomania and paranoia that possessed the man.

"It is getting a little dark," Hastings said.

Summer shrugged.

They climbed in, Summer first, Hastings right behind her. The trip back to the main compound was made in complete silence. Night swept away the last fringes of evening, leaving nothing visible but the small triangular patch exposed by the headlights. That was all right, though. Hastings had a lot to think about.

7

They were misfits. All of them—James, Summer, Kate, even Hastings himself. Individually, each had cut his or her ties to society, some by choice, some by circumstance. But they were drifting into dangerous territory now, potentially deadly territory, and Michael Hastings had become aware of the fact that he needed to do something before it was too late. Had she still been alive, Helena, his wife, would have said, *When someone's choking and you know the Heimlich . . .*

She would have left the sentence dangling there, leaving him to fill in the rest for himself: *you do what you have to do.*

Samuel Hunter had finally crossed the line. The PSI Project had been Hunter's baby from the very beginning. It was a well-kept secret, even within the confines of the CIA, run by a small fringe element that had grown more and more radical over the years. Hastings had watched it happen, almost from its inception. He had watched Hunter recruit Summer because of her psychokinetic abilities, then later recruit Kate and James, each of whom also had special abilities. He had watched their training, first in the little things—mental telepathy, lucid dreaming—then gradually more advanced training, which included remote viewing, expanded remote viewing, and then today . . . today Hunter had pushed Summer into remote mental manipulation. Assassination. Or as close to assassination as one could come without actually pulling the trigger. They were training a fifteen-year-old girl to commit murder.

It was the last straw.

Something had to be done.

Something dramatic.

With daylight behind him, Hastings sat at the kitchen table, under a single seventy-five-watt bulb and began making preparations to disappear with the kids. On a yellow legal pad, with a Bic pen he had brought home from the office, he wrote the word: *suicide.* Not a viable solution. If he were alone, faking his death or his suicide would deserve some honest consideration. Suicide was not an uncommon occurrence within intelligence circles, and it put an immediate end to most of the speculation. Case closed. But he was not alone, and there was no way in the world to fake four suicides.

No. This was going to have to be a disappearing act, à la Houdini.

A new note: *Are there any strings?*

By *strings*, Hastings was thinking attachments. Disappearing meant walking away from his life as it currently existed and never looking back. All his relationships—his family, his friends, his associates—would have to be severed, and they would have to remain severed permanently.

He thought of Helena. If she were still alive, this would be unthinkable. It would be choosing between life or death. For a moment, a flood of memories washed over him. Hastings put the Bic down and buried his face in his hands. Was this something he was really, truly prepared to do? Was it going to be in the best interests of the kids?

Maybe. Maybe not. But he knew one thing for certain: leaving them with Hunter was definitely *not* in their best interests.

He picked up the pen again. It was perhaps a sorrowful statement on what had become of his life, but Hastings thought he could do it. He thought he could walk away from all of it, never look back, and be no worse—maybe even be better—for whatever was left behind.

Could he say the same for the kids?

For Summer?

For James and for Kate? Kate was almost twenty-two now. Emotionally, she was the strongest of the three kids. Five-eight. One hundred and twenty-four pounds. Brown hair and green eyes that were like no other eyes he had ever seen. She had a quiet maturity about her, and though she was not a woman who could turn a noisy room quiet, she was quite attractive.

Neither Kate nor Summer had family ties worthy of concern. No friends either. Summer had never known her father, and had been turned over to Child Protective Services at the age of eleven after her alcoholic mother could no longer care for her. Kate, on the other hand, had cut all her ties at the age of seventeen, after growing up in a family that considered her unholy and a freak of nature because of her clairvoyant abilities. They had both survived, but their childhoods had left them isolated and outcasts. Hastings didn't believe either of them would have any qualms about starting life anew.

James, on the other hand, may have dealt with the death of his parents intellectually, but Hastings didn't think he had dealt with it emotionally yet. He was a young black man, still trying to understand his place in the world. Part of the lure of the CIA had been the idea of completely losing his identity and becoming whomever he wished to be. A "Man of A Thousand Faces," à la Lon Chaney. But emotionally, as he matured and became more comfortable with who he was, James was going to be tempted to reconnect with his heritage again. That could present a problem.

Not an immediate problem, though.

The immediate problem was Hunter.

Cash was going to be a problem, too. If he emptied his mutual funds, sold off his stock, closed his bank accounts and his brokerage accounts, he could put together close to a million dollars. That should be enough to carry them for a number of years. But he didn't want to live the life of a fugitive, either, moving from town to town just trying to stay a step ahead of Hunter. He had to devise a system for moving the money into a single account, then into another account under another name. He thought he could probably get away with moving the funds through a series of banks in a number of states, under various names, until eventually they would end up where he could access them without fear. But he had to be careful. Money could leave a conspicuous trail.

What about their final destination?

Hastings had already given this some thought. It had been in the form of a fantasy about where he would like to retire. But strangely enough, his prerequisites for the perfect retirement were much the same as those for a perfect fade. He had wanted to escape to somewhere with a warm climate, where the populace was such that he would be difficult to find (in case an emergency ever came up and the Agency came looking for him), where he had no obvious connections. It would have to be a place he had never lived before, a place where he had no roots, a place that was such a contrast with his basic human nature that even his closest friends would reject the idea out of hand.

His conclusion: Southern California, Los Angeles, Hollywood.

The more thought he gave to the idea, the more it solidified for him.

He would still have to change his name. Not a problem. He had learned enough during his years with the Agency that he could set up a new name, birth date, social security number, and driver's license within a matter of hours. But he also had the kids to worry about. Summer and Kate might be open to the idea, but he didn't think James would swallow it. A new identity for someone who was already struggling with his own identity would be dooming the whole effort before it even got underway.

And if he didn't give the kids new identities?

Hunter would track them down before they had time to find a place to live.

Hastings got up and went to the refrigerator. He wasn't really hungry, but he needed a break from thinking. On the second shelf, behind two tomatoes still sealed in the plastic bag he had brought them home in from the supermarket, was a plate with four slices of leftover meat loaf. The best meat loaf he had ever eaten. It was Helena's recipe. Well, actually the recipe belonged to Helena's mother, Ivy.

He took the meat loaf, along with a bottle of ketchup and a fork from the nearest drawer, back to the table with him. He had forgotten about Helena's mother. She was eighty-three, still living on her own in a small west-side apartment. Helena's father had died five years ago. Hastings was going to have to make some sort of arrangements to have someone look after her. Something to add to the list.

The cold meat loaf seemed to do the trick. He ate a couple of bites, then pushed the plate aside. Something else had just occurred to him: what if one of the kids didn't want to leave? What then?

They would have to leave him behind.

Note the use of the key word: *him*.

The ball always seemed to end up with James. Of the three kids, he was the one Hastings knew least, and what you don't know, you don't understand. So until the moment came when there was no turning back, when it was do or die, he supposed James was going to remain a question mark. There wasn't anything he could do about that. Not without jeopardizing everyone else.

Oh, and he had nearly forgotten: what about the fake IDs for the kids?

There was an ace up his sleeve, he supposed. Oddly enough, it was Hunter himself. Standard procedure would have Hunter sending out bulletins all over the country, alerting police departments and law enforcement agencies to be on the lookout for Hastings and the kids. But if he did that, he would risk drawing attention to himself, and by extension, to the project. Hunter was a man who thrived in the shadows. And Hastings knew that he had been working the past couple of years under the arm of a small splinter faction within the Agency. If Hunter let word get out and drew attention to the group, he was a dead man.

And there was another ace: Hunter's own arrogance.

He was the type of man who was hard to outsmart unless you let him outsmart himself. In this instance, especially in light of his need to keep a low profile, he would probably put out a nationwide bulletin on Hastings and skip the kids, figuring if he found Hastings, the kids would be in close proximity. And if the bulletin didn't pull any results within a few weeks, he would assume Hastings and the kids had changed their identities and he would focus his efforts elsewhere.

It was the *elsewhere* that Hastings was going to have trouble anticipating. Hunter was not a stupid man, and he almost always did the unexpected.

Which, Hastings thought as he sat back, *is exactly what I'm trying to do.*

8

The Great Escape, as they would come to refer to it, turned out to be rather anticlimactic. Several weeks earlier, Hunter had moved the research project, dubbed PSI—for Paranormal Sensory Intelligence—out of the old CIA building and into an old ramshackle tenement some distance away. At the same time, for security reasons, he moved the kids out of their safe houses and into makeshift rooms in the same compound. That move, coupled with Hunter's enlistment of Summer to go after a target with the intent of elimination, was what had finally brought urgency to getting the kids out from under his control. (Months later, Hastings would learn that the female target of Summer's psychokinesis was an ex-CIA agent and past superior of Hunter's. A woman he despised with a passion.)

Hastings went to visit the kids late in the evening.

It wasn't unusual for him to be inside the compound after hours. Often, on those nights when thoughts of Helena and Christy kept him awake, he would head into the office and spend a few hours going over research data or playing around on the computer, running simulations just for the fun of it.

He knocked on the door.

Kate answered.

Hastings placed a finger across his lips. Then, reasonably certain the room was bugged, he went directly to the stereo in the living room and turned on the music. James was already in the living room, reading a copy of Michael Crichton's *Timeline*. He looked up.

"Where's Summer?"

"She's in the back somewhere," Kate said. "I'll get her."

Within a minute, they were all gathered in the temporary living room, the kids sitting shoulder-to-shoulder on an old sofa pushed up against the wall like an afterthought, Hastings sitting across from them in a recliner with cigarette burns in the arms and an unholy squeal arising from the springs whenever he shifted. No one in this room knew the others well, though they all had one thing in common: they mistrusted Hunter.

"I'm going to get right to the point, because I don't think we have a lot of time to waste on discussion tonight. You've been around Hunter long enough to know he's a dangerous man. But what you might not know is that this project he's got you involved with, the PSI Project, is a well-kept secret, even within the Agency. It's run by a small fringe element, and Hunter . . . he's like a German officer overseeing a concentration camp during the war . . . he's just following orders, but he likes what he's doing."

"He likes it a little too much," Summer said. She glanced up, made a connection with Hastings, then stared down at the floor again. Her hands were folded and stuffed between her legs. She might be fifteen, but she looked like a frightened twelve-year-old.

"Yes, I'm afraid he does. And that's why I believe the three of you are in very real danger."

"What kind of danger?" James asked. His voice was dry and even, as if he had raised his hand and asked a question of one of his college professors in the middle of a lecture. It was a voice Hastings had heard before from James, slightly officious, sometimes off-putting, though it wasn't the eighteen-year-old's only voice.

"The kind that could get you killed," Hastings said, his own voice dry now. "There was a time when remote viewing was a hot topic in the Agency. That's no longer the case. Hunter, ever the pragmatist, wants to take advantage of the lack of supervision. He's not interested in having you gather intelligence for him, he wants you to kill for him. That's the real agenda he's set . . . to turn the three of you into assassins."

Summer stared quietly down at her folded hands, nervously picking at the cuticle of one thumbnail.

Hastings studied her reaction, which he thought was odd considering the circumstances. "You didn't tell them, did you?"

"Tell us what?" James said.

"I just wanted to forget it."

"What?" Kate said.

"Hunter already tried to send Summer after someone," Hastings said.

"When?"

"A couple days ago."

"Are you all right?" Kate asked, taking hold of Summer's hand. Hunter had discovered Kate in a New York psych ward after she had been picked up by police while roaming naked downtown. At the time, Kate had been nearly incoherent, simply repeating the words "Bomb" and "Murrah Building" over and over in some sort of self-flagellating mantra that no one understood or took seriously. Two days later, Timothy McVeigh had blown up the Alfred P. Murrah Federal Building in Oklahoma City. One day after that, while the FBI was busy releasing sketches of John Doe Number One and

John Doe Number Two, Hunter was busy taking custody of Kate.

Summer nodded self-consciously. Hastings could see she didn't like the attention.

"It's only a matter of time before he tries it again," Hastings said. "He's not going to stop with Summer."

If the conversation up to this point had seemed somewhat surreal, cold, stark reality suddenly set in. James glanced away thoughtfully. Summer stared down at her lap again, her breathing shallow. The long silence grew longer.

"I'm sorry," Hastings said eventually. He said it softly, and meant it. "I realize this is a lot to dump on you all at once like this. But you need to understand that Hunter is a dangerous man and it's a mistake to underestimate him. He doesn't mind using people, and he doesn't mind killing."

"A sociopath," James said.

Hastings nodded.

Kate asked, "And you think eventually he's going to kill us?"

"I think eventually he'll feel he has no other choice."

As objective as always, James asked, "What do you have in mind?"

Hastings did his best to be as direct and straightforward as possible. He spoke in a soft, even tone, as if he were describing a rather mundane day at the office. Though this was anything but mundane. He wanted them to give serious thought to doing something that might haunt them the rest of their lives. He wanted them to leave the Agency. It was the only way to escape Hunter's influence, he said. And here was the worst of it: they needed to make a decision tonight.

"Why tonight?" Kate asked.

"Because the arrangements have already been made and tonight's the night. Beyond that, just about the only thing we have going for us is the element of surprise."

"Oh, that sounds encouraging," James said.

"What arrangements?" Kate asked.

"Money and transportation to get us out of here and safely relocated to another area of the country."

"Any place in particular?" James asked.

"I can't tell you that. Not yet, at least. If one of you decides you don't want to go, it might put the others in jeopardy."

"What if none of us want to go?" Kate asked.

James stared at her wordlessly a moment, mild surprise on his face, then said, "Why the hell would you want to stay?"

"Hypothetically."

"If *you* stay, *I* stay," Hastings said. Though, from what he knew of Kate, her question had been anything but hypothetical. She had grown up feeling like an outcast, hating that she was so different from others and wishing endlessly that she could be just like everyone else. The irony was that here, with Hunter and the others, under these circumstances, she blended in. She was like everyone else.

"How do we know we can trust you?" she asked.

"We can trust him," Summer said quietly.

"Yeah, but how do we know?"

"You don't know if you can trust me. But you know you *can't* trust Hunter." Hastings looked at each of the kids expectantly. "It's all up to you what you want to do. I can't make the decision for you."

James sat forward. "It's tonight or never?"

"Tonight or never."

In the end, Hastings had been as surprised as anyone. James, whom he had thought might be the most resistant to the idea of leaving—if for no other reason than simply because he had originally wanted so badly to become involved with the CIA—turned out, instead, to be the most receptive.

"He's a dangerous man. We're in a dangerous position," James said, a slight forcefulness rising in his voice for the first time. "I don't know about anyone else, but murder wasn't what I had in mind when I came here."

"We leave," Kate said. "That makes him even more dangerous. We're talking about the CIA Tracking people down is what they do. What makes you think Hunter won't come after us?"

"Oh, I definitely think he'll be coming after us," Hastings said honestly. "It would be foolish to assume otherwise."

"So we'll be running for the rest of our lives?"

"I never said it would be easy."

Just above a whisper, Summer said, "At least we'll have lives."

"At least we'll *be* alive," James added.

All eyes suddenly turned to Kate, since she seemed to be the only one expressing reservations now. They were reasonable reservations, no argument about it, and Hastings wanted to be careful that he didn't back her into a corner where she felt the only way out would be to give in to the group.

"I know this is sudden, Kate . . ."

"We're all in this together," James said. "You aren't alone."

"If we go, we all go?" she asked. "I mean . . . we

stay together as a group? We don't end up scattered all over the country, everyone on his own?"

Hastings nodded. "That's the plan."

"And what about Hunter?"

"He doesn't get to come," Hastings said lightly.

Kate smiled. It was a sweet smile, innocent, a bright contrast to her sometimes fragile moments when she looked as if the world were closing in around her. She nodded. "Okay. I'm in."

"We're all agreed, then?"

James and Summer each nodded without hesitation.

"Good. Then we better get started." Hastings stood up, feeling a sense of relief mixed with the uncertainty about what lay ahead. Everything in their lives was about to change. Nothing would ever be the same again. Not for any of them.

"Oh, one last thing," he said. "I owe each of you an apology. I've known Hunter for years, known what he was capable of . . . I never should have let it get this far. I never should have let him involve you the way he has. I'm sorry you got dragged into this nightmare. I really am."

9

Once the decision was agreed upon, the rest went by in a flash. They packed the bare essentials; if you couldn't stuff it into a pocket or a purse, then it stayed behind. Hastings went out to the parking lot about ten minutes ahead of the kids, who exited the front of the building under the pretext of an evening walk. He picked them up on the street a couple blocks over.

They drove to Dulles International Airport, parked

in the Long-Term Lot on the North Service Road, then took the shuttle back to the main terminal. Inside, Hastings dumped his security ID along with his driver's license, in a trash can next to the automatic doors. Odds were they would never be found. But if they were, they would simply confirm what Hunter would have already concluded by then—that Hastings had changed identities.

They walked down the terminal to Hertz, where Hastings had already made arrangements for a new Jeep Cherokee under one of his new identities. From the terminal, they went out to the Hertz lot, keys in hand.

Hastings opened the driver's side door and . . .

and caught himself.

For a moment, he stared at the clean console, which looked something like the cockpit of an airliner, then climbed in and sat down. The air was rich with that smell that always seemed to accompany new cars. He closed the door, buckled himself in, and took a deep breath.

This was it.

From this moment on, Michael Hastings would cease to exist. His name was Kevin McConnell now. Still in his early forties, his brown hair graying at the temples, just over six feet and a few pounds short of two hundred, his physical appearance was unchanged. But these things were the only things that were unchanged. Nothing else in his life would ever be the same again.

ONE

Something had disturbed Henry Richards' sleep.

He wasn't sure what it had been. He raised his head off the stack of drawings on his desk, groggily aware that he was still at work and that he must have dozed off. It was sometime after midnight, Richards thought. Maybe a few minutes. Maybe more. It seemed his sense of time had gone the way of his dreams. It had deserted him. He swiped at his eyes with the back of his hand.

In the background, the radio dial was set to KCBS 93.1 FM, a rock 'n' roll oldies station with a bent toward the hits of the '60s. He listened to a few words . . . *one pill makes you larger* . . . recognized "White Rabbit" and fought off the final lingering effects of the nap.

Then the question came bubbling back to the surface again: what had brought him awake?

The huge warehouse could be a barren, desolate place in the middle of the night when you were the last remaining straggler. It was the hub of the Magic Wizard Effects complex, a Hollywood special effects studio where Richards had worked as an assistant for the past five years. A single fluorescent lamp sitting next to his computer mapped out a small rectangular area of the cubicle. It was the last light on in the building. A thick blanket of shadows had huddled around it.

The computer screen in front of him shifted from one geometric shape to a new kaleidoscope of brightly-colored lines. The screensaver was up. It must have kicked on sometime after he had dozed off. Which meant that no fewer than ten minutes had passed.

He had already known he wasn't going to make it home tonight, and that Annie was going to be pissed. For several months now, it seemed as if she had been on one nonstop pisser after another. He couldn't blame her much. This current project, a science fiction film called *Night Skies*, had devoured nearly all of his time these past four months. He had been working fourteen-, sixteen-, sometimes eighteen-hour days, and when he hadn't been here physically, he had been here in mind and spirit. Which was the part Annie hated the most. But then she had known he was like this before they had married. It hardly seemed fair for her to throw it back in his face now that they had been together for five years and had two children.

Richards swallowed hard, through the thick cottony dryness left over from his nap. He wiped away a string of spittle, then took a long, deliberate look into the surrounding shadows. The nap had left him tired and dragging. There was a lingering stiffness in his neck from sleeping wrong.

Still, something had awakened him.

He turned away from his desk, riding the swivel chair in a half circle that nearly cost him his balance. This was not a place you wanted to be at night, alone, if you were queasy about such things. Annie had asked him about it once, if it didn't give him the creeps being surrounded by all the masks and the severed heads and such. He remembered laughing and telling her that he never gave it much thought. But he was thinking about it now.

What had it been?

What had brought him up from his dreams?

He scratched at the five days of stubble on his chin, then stared into the shadows that lay in wait around the edges of the light. It was as if the world ended where the shadows began, as if beyond that line deep impenetrable pockets of nothingness had swallowed up the remainder of the universe. A perfect stillness had fallen over all of it.

"This is nuts."

Then something went scurrying across the corner of his vision.

Richards sat forward, frowning, a mix of unease and curiosity running through his veins. "Amos? That you?"

The night watchman, Amos Poss, was an old gent with a young face. Richards didn't see him often. When he was up to it, Poss made his rounds once or twice a night. The rest of the time you could find him curled up on the couch in the lobby of the office, adjacent to the warehouse. Sometimes he would bring in old Humphrey Bogart movies and play them on the VCR until he fell asleep. But it would be unusual to see him nosing around this time of night. Especially here in the warehouse, where he found the hodgepodge of masks and monsters mildly unsettling.

"Amos?"

A shadow beneath the shadows, off to his left this time. Something had moved there. He thought he had caught a glimpse of a black cat disappearing around the corner of a nearby cubicle. But if he were taking bets, he wouldn't have been willing to risk much. Not here, at night, still hazy after a nap. It could just as easily have been the back of a man's shoe. Or for that matter, it could have been nothing at all.

Richards grinned.

Annie was going to get a kick out of this when he told her about it. He had finally spooked himself.

"Are you sure you want to do that?"

Richards felt his body tense, then relax again as he realized what he had heard.

Annie's voice. On the computer. When he had told her it was so she would always be with him, even if only in voice, she had happily recorded a number of sound bites for the computer. The two phrases he heard most often were: "There's a message for you, dear," and the warning: "Are you sure you want to do that?" The latter usually came up when he was closing a window or a program. In this instance, he imagined the computer had run some invisible function beneath the screensaver. Still, it had nearly knocked him out of his chair.

Richards slid the mouse across the pad. The screensaver disappeared. Underneath, now exposed, the skeletal structure of one of the *Night Skies* aliens filled the screen. It was still in the early stages. The modeling was complete and the basic structure and design of the alien were in place, but the animating process was in the three-dimensional stage with another twenty minutes of screen time to be developed.

"Spooking easy tonight, aren't I, Bessie?"

Matt Levy had done most of the preliminary design work on the creature. It had been his idea to call the female alien Bessie. Short for Elizabeth, which had been the name of his ex-girlfriend. "Poetic justice," he said one day after work and just before his fifth Heineken. "The alien gets named for an alien."

Richards had never asked him to explain the comment. He had assumed it either meant that Matt had never really understood his girlfriend or that maybe she was an illegal . . . something that had become commonplace in the Los Angeles basin. Either way, it was none of his business . . . something else commonplace in the basin.

In the background, the radio station had moved through a couple of oldies he had stored so deep in his brain he had already lost track of them. Buddy Holly was standing at the mike now, doing his raw, edgy "That'll Be the Day" like no one had done it since.

Richards toyed with the palette of commands down the left side of the screen, absently passing the cursor over the list of options while his mind passed over a list of its own. It wasn't unusual to find himself the only one here late at night. Last week, he had spent Tuesday and Wednesday here, sleeping on a makeshift bed kept in the far corner of the building for just such circumstances. But tonight, tonight was the first time he could remember feeling uneasy about being alone here.

It's just foolishness, he told himself, without trusting his own words.

A good thing, too; because a moment later, he heard a noise off to his right, just beyond the edge of the line that separated the shadows from the light. It sounded as if someone had cleared his throat. A deep, almost guttural sound made all the more ominous by the depths of darkness surrounding it.

Richards stood and pushed the chair away.

"Okay, that's it. Who's there?"

He grabbed the fluorescent lamp next to the computer, turned back the metal shade, then watched the light seep into the darkness the way the moon seeps into a cloudy night.

"This isn't funny. Who's there?"

The light swept across the penumbrae, left to right, churning up the shadows. Richards felt the strange unease of looking into a deep pool of water and wondering what was swimming just beneath the reflective glare of the surface. Only there was no reflection here. No glare. Just the thick, impenetrable night.

He started his sweep back across the darkness again, right to left this time, then suddenly fell still at the rise of another sound. This one had come from behind him, somewhere beyond the stand-alone partition that separated his cubicle from the next one over. It had not been a guttural clearing of the throat this time. Instead, it had sounded as if something metallic had hit the floor, then lazily rolled across the concrete.

"Amos? Tell me it's you, Amos. Tell me you're just trying to put a scare into me tonight," he said out loud, without feeling anywhere near as ridiculous as he might have imagined. "Because it's working. Believe me, it's working."

As he spoke, he fumbled with the butterfly nut at the base of the lamp until it finally spun free in his fingers. He raised the long, spring-balanced arm into the air, casting a wide sphere of light around the cubicle. Shadows retreated ever deeper into the corners. The light fell across the outline of an overturned wastepaper basket. An empty orange juice container, some crumpled wads of paper, a straw, and what looked like a sheet of bubble wrap had spilled out onto the floor.

The cat.

It had to have been the cat.

But then he heard another noise, to his right this time, and the idea of blaming a cat suddenly seemed like little more than a desperate attempt to settle his nerves. Something else was going on here. Richards didn't know what it was, but he was willing to bet it didn't have anything to do with some damn cat.

He edged around the corner of the cubicle to the end of the electrical cord, then found himself stranded. If he wanted to venture any farther, he would have to do it without the light. This part of the building was dedicated to computer graphics. It encompassed a relatively small area, a set of eight cubicles, two rows of four, back-to-back. He was standing at the edge of his own cubicle. Matt's office was the next in line to his right. Beyond that was a span of open space, maybe fifteen feet or so, then the heart of the building with tables and shelves and walls lined with masks, posters, props, and models from various past projects. There was a makeup room off to one side beyond that, and another area to the other side where most of the molds were poured and processed.

All fascinating stuff.

Except Richards had taken this tour before, many times before, and it was not nearly as fascinating as it had once been. More important, at the moment, except for the table of Marshant Warrior masks and the cubicle area, the rest of the building was beyond the influence of the light.

It had been a long time since he had felt uneasy about the dark. But some fears, he supposed, were never truly conquered. They were like the family's crazy uncle. You didn't talk about him much, and you learned to tolerate him at family gatherings. But mostly, you simply did your best to avoid him. Throughout his life, Richards had done a fairly good job of avoiding the dark, to the point where he had rarely thought about it over the past few years.

But he was thinking about it now.

He clamped the fluorescent lamp to the panel, then crossed the floor, picked up the overturned wastepaper basket, and replaced the items that had spilled. He returned the basket to its home, against the far wall of Matt's cubicle, then gazed across the penumbra at the building's main bank of light switches just inside the entrance. It was the responsibility of the first person arriving in the morning to turn them on, the last person leaving at night to turn them off. From here to there, the distance was maybe sixty or seventy feet altogether. It looked and felt more like the length of a football field.

Which was stupid. Richards *knew* it was stupid. But that didn't make it any less real. He did *not* want to have to cross this open expanse, out of the light and into the strata of darkness that waited with open arms on the other side. Yet he knew if he was ever going to get any work done tonight, he would have to put his mind at peace again, and the only way to do that was to turn the lights on and have a good look around.

"Are you sure you want to do that?"

Annie's voice again. The screensaver had kicked on. *No*, he thought. *I'm not sure at all.*

He glanced at the computer, noted the screensaver had, in fact, gone on (*Thank God I didn't imagine that*), then started across the concrete slab floor. He wasn't sure exactly what it was that was making him so uneasy, but he thought it was more than just the dark. It wasn't the dark that scared most people anyway. It was what they couldn't see *inside* the dark. And Richards couldn't see anything.

At that same moment, in one of those rare ironies of life, the haunting introduction to "Darkness, Darkness" by the Youngbloods came up on the radio. It was as if some paranormal force had read his thoughts and answered them as directly as was possible, and it was an irony he could have easily done without.

He stopped himself in mid-stride, nearly halfway to the light switch, when something darted out of the shadows to his left and ran across the floor in front of him. His heart muscle tightened and cramped inside his chest. He held a breath, then allowed a startled, high-pitched sound to escape his throat. In turn, it birthed an echo somewhere in the distance, and he thought how hysterical it sounded, almost shrill, the way Annie's voice came out when she was visibly upset about something.

What he had seen was not a cat.

He didn't know what the hell it was, but he knew it was *not* a cat. It was too big for that, standing maybe eighteen inches off the floor. It had emerged out of the shadows, crossed the murky gray-black outer edge of the light, then disappeared again.

All in the matter of a breath.

There.

Then gone.

And it wasn't the size of the thing that was bothering Richards. It was the idea that he was almost certain it had moved on two legs.

Two legs!

What in the world, that size, moved on two legs?

From behind, he felt pressure across the back of his right calf, just below the knee. At first, he thought of the cat again; it had felt as if something had brushed up against him the way a cat might; but then the sense of pressure turned to a sharp, searing pain. He winced and grabbed for it.

"Jesus!"

The pain, which reminded him of a nick with a razor blade as the air rushes into the wound and catches your complete and undivided attention, was short-lived. The wound that caused it, however, he thought was more serious. There was a long, thin slit in the back of his jeans. Richards wormed his fingers through the opening, blindly discovered what lay beneath, and was greeted with another shot of pain that caused him to wince. When he held up his fingers to look at them, they were covered with blood.

"What the hell?"

What was happening here?

His instincts voiced concern—whatever was happening, he needed to get out of the building and he needed to do it now. Thirty or forty feet at the most and he would be outside, under the stars. Only another hundred feet or so and he would be to the main office, where Amos, awake or asleep, had a gun strapped to his belt.

Richards, though, ignored his instincts. He rose up and turned toward the shadows, searching instead for a rational explanation, anything that might dismiss the wild imaginings that had taken over his thoughts. Not a ghost, but a play of light. Not magic, but a sleight of hand. Not a two-legged creature, but a cat or some other perfectly normal explanation.

But apparently it wasn't going to be that easy.

Not nearly that easy.

Something hit him again from behind, hard enough

this time to spin him around. He gasped, producing a short, sharp noise that sounded as if it belonged to someone else. He stumbled to his right, trying to keep his balance as his legs nearly gave out. A gash opened across the back of his left calf. He could feel it. It was deep. Honest damage had been done. Serious damage.

Perhaps it was panic, perhaps it was the dimness of the huge warehouse, but he felt a moment of confusion, then a spin of brief disorientation before he finally started to hobble toward the back of the building. His mind stumbled ahead of him across the vast, dark space, trying to anticipate what he should do next.

He bumbled into a table that seemed to have appeared out of the shadows like a godsend, then waited for his feet to catch up with him. Another gasp escaped, feeling raw against the back his throat, and he thought momentarily about yelling for help. But what would be the point? Amos wasn't going to hear him. A gun could go off in here and no one outside these walls would ever know it. Besides, his lungs were beginning to burn as he pulled for more and more air.

Madly, he groped along the edge of the table until he reached the end. His muscles felt spongy under the burden of his weight. He broke out into the open again, slightly favoring his left leg, which had sustained the deepest wound.

Somewhere far away, "Darkness, Darkness" hit its last eerie note and gave way to more pressing sounds.

A low, guttural cacophony rose up from the surrounding shadows like a growl at the back of the throat of a rabid dog. Richards didn't know what it was, but he knew he didn't like it.

He felt himself slip deeper into the penumbra and darkness.

Then something clambered across the floor in front of him.

This time he found enough breath to let out a muted scream. It was a soft, unimpressive effort that reminded him of his childhood when he would sometimes lie in bed at night, not feeling well, and call for his mother so softly that it was impossible for her to hear him.

They were all around him now, everywhere . . . he could sense their presence. In and out of the shadows like rodents scurrying for cover. Only they weren't—

He began to stumble again. His left hip slammed into the corner of a table he hadn't noticed. The dull ache that followed burrowed all the way down to the bone. He favored it almost immediately, thinking with misplaced amusement that all those years of sitting in front of a computer screen had not been the best thing for him. He had put on weight. His muscles had gone the way of all his resolutions to start working out, with shame and a whimper. And now, when he needed them most—

He turned in a new direction, then slammed into another table and found himself face-to-face with the pasty-white mask of a zombie from the '89 horror film *After Death*. A scream caught somewhere near the back of his throat. Before he could shake it loose, he stumbled past the table, deeper into the belly of the building.

If he could get to the makeup room, there was a door . . .

Ahead of him, something darker than dark scurried across the outer fringes of his vision. The sight pulled him immediately out of whatever misplaced amusement was still left, and turned him cold from head to toe. Richards understood now, with complete clarity, the way you understand when you're backed into a corner and have no choice but to face an ugly truth: he wasn't going to make it. Not to the makeup room. And probably not home to Annie.

Not tonight.

Maybe never again.

He started across the floor with nothing left to lose now, his left leg dragging half a step behind, unable to do any better. There was a blood thirst in the air. Even he could smell it. Behind him, a thick red trail darkened the concrete.

In the surrounding shadows, an elemental vibration began to gather like a thick roll of thunder. *Voices*, Richards realized. The low throaty fearlessness you might hear when your enemies were gathering in the distance, preparing to close in for the final kill.

It wouldn't be long now.

Not long at all.

They caught up with him just as he made it to the arm of the sofa/sleeper near the far corner of the building. Too many to count. Scurrying out of the shadows like rats after the smell of blood.

A deep gash, across the back of his leg, severed a tendon and brought him down.

Richards fell helplessly against the sofa, then followed the shift of his weight off the edge and onto a ragged throw rug on the concrete floor. He rolled onto his stomach, into a fetal position, then covered the back of his head protectively.

Amazingly, with calm and clarity, he thought: *This is it. This is where they're going to find me.*

Something cool and sharp skated across his lower back where his T-shirt had pulled free and exposed the skin. It felt like a paper cut at first, more sting than substance. Then a trail of warm blood began to trickle out of the wound and down his back.

Richards swung wildly with his right arm, finding only air, before he covered his head again to protect himself. He pulled tighter into a ball, his face pressed against the throw rug. The pungent odor of months of accumulated dirt filled his nostrils. Worn edges of the coarse nap gnawed at his cheek.

Another wound opened across the back of his leg. He kicked out blindly, futilely, then covered himself again. He was bleeding profusely now. It felt as if his life force were emptying out of him, spilling out across the throw rug, soaking through to the floor beneath.

An odd, twilight sleepiness descended over him.

Shadows, vaporous and alien, danced across his vision.

Then the questions began to come, as if they belonged to someone else, someone standing off to the sidelines, completely detached from the proceedings. . . .

What are these things?

Why him?

Why were they after him?

Blood began to pool around the edges of the throw rug.

He weakly kicked out at the darkness again.

His eyes closed, the pain drifting now, like a cloud in the sky.

Far away, the radio once again made its presence known. The song was familiar, something by the Beatles, he thought, though he couldn't quite put a title to it. Things were slowing down. His *thoughts* were slowing down.

What was that song? Something so damn familiar

it was right at the tip of his tongue. He could almost taste it.

Don't let go of it, he thought. *Hold onto it now. Make yourself hold on until every single word is swimming around inside your head like some bored aquarium shark. Until nothing else exists. Just you and ... and the song. Let it drive you insane if you need to, just don't ... let ... go of it.*

It was all that was left to hold onto.

He rocked. A baby in a treetop.

New wounds opened across his legs, over his back, his neck. Hundreds of little scratches and nicks. Only a few deep enough to do their own damage. It was the cumulative nature of this attack that would take its toll. The hemorrhaging. The shock.

Shadows crowded in.

Whispering.

Scuttling.

And oh, the peace coming, the peace coming ...

Henry Richards' last thought: *Oh, yeah. I remember. I remember. "Helter Skelter." The song's "Helter Skelter." I knew that.*

TWO

The call came in around 8:00 A.M. The night watchman had discovered the body. Detective Lieutenant Daniel Kaufman arrived at the Magic Wizard building by 8:45. He was a big man, in his late fifties, with close-cropped hair that had gone white over the past five years. Marie, his wife, had made no secret of the fact that she believed it was the job that had turned his hair white. The guys at the station made no secret of the fact that they thought it was his wife who was the culprit. Kaufman figured it was a little of each, and counted himself fortunate to be married at all after twenty-five years of police work.

Outside, Magic Wizard Effects looked like just another dilapidated old warehouse, indistinguishable from the checkerboard of neighboring structures that were equally dilapidated. Windows were painted black. Corrugated tin panels sheathed the walls. Two huge dumpsters, painted brown, stood as sentinels on either side of the entrance, which was a set of nondescript double doors.

Kaufman climbed out of the car, a silver thermos of coffee in his hand. He rarely went anywhere without his coffee. He had never been a drinker like most of the cops he knew. Never acquired a taste for alcohol. The worst addiction he'd ever battled was Diet Coke, which, at one time, he had downed to the tune of ten to twelve cans a day. Never satisfied his thirst, though. Never. Always kept him coming back for more. And worse, the stuff had always left him hungry. Hence the switch to coffee. He had dropped twenty-five pounds over the past two years. Hardly noticeable on his six-three frame, though it was a start.

He ducked beneath the yellow crime scene tape, dangling the thermos at his side on the strength of two fingers. A young, uniformed officer nodded in recognition.

"Who's here?" Kaufman asked.

"Ident."

"How long?"

"About fifteen minutes."

"Any witnesses?"

"The night watchman. He's the one who called it in."

"Where—"

The officer motioned toward the building's entrance, where a blue-uniformed man sat in an office chair just inside the door, one leg folded across the other. The man looked lost and out of place, like a traveler in a foreign land.

Kaufman nodded. "Thanks."

Up close, the watchman turned out to be older than he had at first appeared. Maybe in his early-to-mid-sixties, Kaufman guessed. He noticed the obvious first: the man was as thin as a rail, with a turkey-gobbler neck and the face of a man in his early forties. Then he noticed the man's hands. A faint spattering of liver spots had begun to show themselves, and the lines were weathered deep across the backs, just above the pale outline of where he usually wore his watch. The man tapped out a steady but nervous beat with his thumb against his thigh.

Kaufman introduced himself. "You the night watchman here?"

"Nearly ten years now. Name's Amos Poss." He stood to shake hands. The office chair went rolling away behind him. "Pleased to meet you."

"You're the one who discovered the body?"

He nodded. "About an hour ago."

"You knew him?"

"Henry Richards. One of the computer whiz kids."

"How long he work here?"

"I don't know. I'd guess maybe four years."

It was Kaufman's turn to nod now, and he did so, trying to maintain the illusion that they were just two old friends who hadn't seen each other in quite some time and though it was a bit awkward, they were doing okay at getting reacquainted again. He had learned long ago that it was always easier to get answers when the questions seemed genuinely conversational.

"Special effects house, huh?"

"Magic Wizard Effects."

"Just like the sign says." Kaufman glanced past the man, into the warehouse, which was swathed under the bright glare of several banks of overhead fluorescent lights. Past the cubicles and computers, the tables lined with masks and props, near the far corner of the building, he could see the ident team busy at work. The body was back there somewhere, no doubt.

"No one pays much attention to who does the special effects," the watchman said, drifting off on a tangent all his own. He sounded as if it hurt him personally that his fellow employees weren't recognized. "The actors ... people remember the actors. And sometimes the director. Spielberg or Hitchcock or Coppola. When the name's big enough. Even the producers now and then. But the effects guys ..."

"I could name a few," Kaufman said.

And he could.

This was the third one who had been murdered.

THREE

Helena and Christy were dead. They had been dead for nearly three years now, though that fact didn't prevent Kevin McConnell from talking to his deceased wife when he felt like the last standing nail under the hammer. Helena had always been a good listener. He still missed her. He missed his daughter, Christy, no less. But it was Helena who had been his confidant, who had been the one person in all the world he knew he could trust.

He wondered what she would think of his changing his name to Kevin McConnell.

He wondered what she would think of him escaping the Agency.

He wondered what she would think of his new "family."

Kevin thought about all these things, as he had on numerous other occasions, without examining them too closely. What was done was done. He had accepted them, the way one accepts that brushing your teeth helps prevent cavities.

Three months had passed since the Great Escape.

Life was different now, saner, safer, certainly less stressful on the kids.

He flipped to the second page of the *Los Angeles Times* sports section, then glanced out the kitchen window at the backyard. It was sunny and warm, around seventy-five today, the kind of weather that made for jokes when you lived in Los Angeles. He wasn't completely accustomed to the jokes yet, and he wasn't completely accustomed to Los Angeles either. But he thought he was doing as well as could be expected in these new surroundings.

The house had been built in 1967 as part of the Buena Vista Estates. Back then, the Estates were considered one of Los Angeles' preferred suburbs. Well-manicured, gently-rolling lawns with flagstone retaining walls. Big, roomy houses. Clean, quiet streets. Not designed to accommodate children as much as to accommodate the facade of upper-middle class success, only a lucky break or two from Beverly Hills for those who were able to survive the Hollywood backstabbing. The neighborhood had retained its secluded, sometimes brooding personality, though success had long since moved on to other neighborhoods with more opulent houses and guarded front gates.

There were no front gates here. The house was a simple two-story stucco with a large picture window and a rather intimate clover lawn edged with a strip of redwood chips and an occasional rosebush to break the monotony. It was painted a light gray-blue, with an off-white trim a little darker than eggshells. The front door was stained oak, with three oval etched-glass windows.

Behind the front door was a wide entry, the floor an intricate oak parquet, the ceiling open and expansive, rising to nearly sixteen feet overhead. Directly beyond the entry, a warm, slightly-curving stairway rose to the second floor assortment of bedrooms. The kitchen, where Kevin was waging war with the morning newspaper and losing, was at the back of the house.

It was a little after nine. Kevin was still dressed in pajamas and a bathrobe, a little guilty at how leisurely he had become but not quite guilty enough to head back upstairs to dress. On the table in front of him, next to the sections of newspaper yet to be read, was an empty milk glass. It was a sign of his age, he supposed, but he liked to start his mornings with eight ounces of nonfat milk for the protein boost. Not that he didn't still enjoy his coffee. Next to the milk glass was a coffee cup.

He folded back the last page of the sports section—the Chargers, the only professional football team left in Southern California after the Rams and the Raiders had moved on, had lost another one—and Summer was standing in the kitchen doorway.

"Morning."

"What time is it?"

"After nine."

"Everyone still asleep?"

"Everyone but thee and me," Kevin said with a straight face. "And I'm not sure about thee."

Summer yawned, then leaned against the doorjamb, too hung over from her dreams to try to decipher what she had just heard. She was your granddaughter, the kid from down the block who hung around because she liked your wife's cookies, the girl behind the counter at the video store. Fifteen. Shy one moment, brash the next. Not yet a woman, but no longer a little girl.

"An old joke," Kevin said, making one last effort at returning the paper to its original state. "Hungry?"

"Think I'll just have some cereal. Do we have any real milk?"

"Top shelf. Behind the fake stuff."

She yawned again, then went about the routine of rounding up a bowl and spoon, a box of Frosted Flakes, and finally the milk. She sat down at the table across from him, added a little cereal and milk to the bowl, then used the spoon to play with it. Summer was not a big eater. She wasn't super-model thin, nor as bad as Twiggy had been in the sixties, but she could look rather emaciated at times when the light caught her wrong. A good deal of this, of course, was due to puberty and a recent growth spurt.

"It'll turn soggy," Kevin said. He put aside the paper for a moment.

"So."

"Unless it's oatmeal, most people don't like their cereal soggy." He looked across the table, and for a moment Christy was sitting there, four years younger, her hair in a ponytail, exasperation on her face. Sometimes, as in this very moment, she was still crystal clear in his mind. Other times, forming a picture of her was like starting from scratch.

Christy would have told him that she wasn't like most people. Summer was thinking the same thing, but she didn't need to say it. It was conveyed quite effectively in the annoyed glance she flashed in his direction.

"Starting to sound like a father, aren't I?"

A measured grin tugged at the corners of her mouth. "More like my kindergarten teacher."

"Your kindergarten teacher?"

"Um-hmm."

"She was a nag, I take it?"

Summer shrugged. "I don't know. I just remember she had a thing about cereal."

"Well, I guess it's nice to know I'm not alone in my eccentricities." Kevin checked his coffee cup, which had gone dry somewhere between the front page of the *Los Angeles Times* and the sports section. Nonetheless, every once in a while he would check it again, just in case he had been mistaken the previous some-odd times. Still empty. Surprise, surprise. He got up to get a refill.

"So tell me how you're doing," he said, making it sound as if it were an afterthought.

Another one of those glances, as if he were speaking a foreign language.

"Adjusting. To the new place . . . the new . . ."

"Okay, I guess."

Kevin finished filling his coffee cup, then leaned against the counter. "Yeah?"

"It's better than being a research monkey."

He laughed. "I never thought of it quite that way."

"It's true, though. Isn't it? I mean that's what we were. One step away from having electrodes attached directly to our brains?"

There was nothing he could say to this, nothing he wanted to say. It carried more truth than he cared to admit. Though if it had come out of Hunter's mouth instead of Summer's, he guessed it wouldn't have surprised him as much, or sounded so harsh. Coming from Summer it just felt a little too much as if the emperor had no clothes.

"So L.A.'s okay?"

"I don't know yet. It's too soon," she said, finally downing the first of her cereal. "I like the weather."

Too soon. It *was* too soon. They had put less than

three months between themselves and the Agency and Hunter, and sometimes it felt as if a long, elastic cord still connected them all. He wondered if that feeling would ever go away, if the cord would ever snap.

"You getting along okay with Kate and James?"

"They're okay."

Kevin grinned. He liked the sound of that. It was something she might say if she were talking about a sister or a brother. Love 'em all you want, but whatever you do, never admit to it. You shouldn't have to. Family was family. The bad came with the good, but in your heart you always knew they were there for you. That's what families were all about.

He sipped his coffee, ignoring the steam rising off the surface. It seemed like an awkward place to leave a conversation, a little like a starter with no engine. Given a little more time he would have felt it necessary to add something, *anything*, but the phone on the wall across the kitchen began to ring.

It was Daniel Kaufman—Detective Lieutenant Daniel J. Kaufman, Kevin reminded himself. His voice was as level and as straightforward as it always was.

"Kevin, I need to talk to you."

"Talk away."

"No, this would be better if we could do it in person. You have any spare time this afternoon when we could meet?"

Kevin told him the afternoon was free. Then, after agreeing to meet at Barney's Beanery in West Hollywood, he glanced over at Summer and got an idea. "Mind if I bring along Summer?"

When she heard this, Summer looked up with an expression of pure terror on her face. She mouthed the words: *No, please. Not me. I've got things to do.*

Kevin grinned, somewhat pleased with himself. "She's shaking her head at me, but I'd like to bring her along anyway, if it's okay."

Kaufman suggested a different restaurant in that case. He said they might as well try lunch at Hugo's, also in West Hollywood, since an occasional movie-type (as he bluntly put it) ate there. Maybe that would make it a little more appealing for her. "One o'clock?"

"No problem," Kevin said. "Do I at least get a hint?"

"I'd rather wait and give you the whole pitch at once," Kaufman said evenly. Then, with a trace of disgust in his voice, he added, "Christ, I'm starting to sound like a damn movie-type."

FOUR

"How come you've never asked?" Kevin had asked several weeks earlier.

They were traveling up I-5, just him and Kaufman, towing the Chevy behind them on their way to a classic car show in Quincy. It was a late Friday night, darkness closing snugly around them. The conversation that had been so spirited as they had left L.A. had gradually disappeared behind them, somewhere beyond the vanishing horizon. Kevin had spent the last ten minutes staring out the window at the lights of the distant farmhouses, his thoughts drifting aimlessly over the years since Helena's death.

"Asked what?" Kaufman said.

"About my past, where I've been, how I ended up in L.A. All of it." They had grown up together in a small Oregon coastal town nearly a thousand miles to the north, but their paths had parted shortly after high school. It had been their mutual interest in classic cars and a chance meeting at a car show that had brought them back together again.

"Ever own a dog?" Kaufman asked.

"No."

"When I was a kid—this was years before we met

in high school—I was maybe eight or nine, and we had this old dog named Duffy. He was a cocker spaniel. A little hyper at times, but a really sweet dog. Only he didn't trust anyone outside the family. If the mailman çame around, or a salesman, even a neighbor, he would growl. Never showed teeth. Never bit anyone. Just growled. My father used to say it was just the way he was. He was a dog and dogs were suspicious by nature." Kaufman had settled into the long drive with one hand hanging casually over the rim of the steering wheel. He glanced across the seat to see if Kevin was still with him. "I'm a cop. We're suspicious by nature, too."

"You checked me out?"

"That's what I do."

"How much do you know?"

"I know you were married and had a daughter, and they both died in an automobile accident about three years ago. I know you worked for the CIA. I know you've got three kids living with you, and that you're claiming they were adopted before your wife died."

"I've got the paperwork to prove it."

"I'll bet you do. And I know when you aren't around me, you go by the name of Kevin McConnell. How's that for a start?"

"Sounds like you haven't missed much."

"So who are you running from?"

"His name's Samuel Hunter," Kevin said softly. The words began to follow one another in a slow steady stream. He told Kaufman everything (no sense in trying to conceal the truth now) . . . his history with Hunter, the PSI Project, then Hunter's attempt to gradually, maliciously corrupt the kids. Kevin told him all of it, and when he was done, he felt as if he had shed an outer skin.

Kaufman nodded. The glare from a set of oncoming headlights passed across his face. He looked surprisingly stoic, his wide jaw set, his dark eyes squinting slightly as the headlights finally disappeared. "So suddenly you're father to three teenagers."

"Well, two teenagers, actually . . . Kate's twenty-two . . . but, yeah. I guess I am."

"Marie's going to want you all over for dinner."

"She knows?"

Kaufman checked the rearview mirror. "She's my wife. You're an old high school buddy. She needed to know. She had a right to know."

Kevin nodded.

Kaufman pulled into the inside lane, passed an old pickup towing a trailer with a pair of motorcycles, then pulled back into the slow lane. They were doing around sixty-five, though it felt much slower than that. Everything seemed to slow down as Kevin watched his friend closely.

"I'm sorry about your wife and daughter," Kaufman finally said.

"Thanks."

Night draped the last of its thick, black cape across the landscape and all that was left of the scenery was a spattering of lights in the distance. The white lines separating the lanes ticked off the miles.

After a while, out of the blue, Kaufman added, "The kids . . . they're really psychic?"

FIVE

Hugo's was apparently one of those Hollywood restaurants where those in the know, especially in the entertainment industry, liked to hang out. Kevin didn't recognize any faces, but he had heard about the place from somewhere. The air was rich with the scent of garlic and Italian cooking as the waiter escorted them to a table in the back. Kaufman was already seated and waiting for them.

"We late?" Kevin asked, as he waited for Summer to be seated.

"I'm early. I forgot they prefer reservations here, so I wanted to make sure we had a table." Kaufman nodded to Summer, who had immediately buried her head in the menu.

"She insisted on coming along," Kevin said.

"Did not."

"You never know," Kaufman said. "Brad Pitt could walk through the door anytime."

"Brad Pitt?" Summer said.

"He has to eat, too."

"Not here, he doesn't. Bet he has his own chef."

Kaufman laughed, with some amusement, then

turned his attention to the menu. "This is on me, by the way."

"Must be a write-off," Kevin said.

"You're fishing."

"Is it official business?"

Kaufman peered over the top of his menu. "Why don't we enjoy the meal first?"

Kevin ordered Pasta à la Mama, while Summer played it safe with an order of spaghetti and meatballs. His mind had been so preoccupied with why Kaufman had invited him to lunch that he hadn't noticed what his friend had ordered. When it arrived, though, it was some sort of pasta in a cream sauce. Pasta Alfredo, he imagined, without giving it much thought.

"Did he tell you that we went to school together?"

Summer, who seemed to brighten as the meal went on, pointed her fork at Kaufman. "High school, right? Up in Oregon? And you bought a car together."

"Hey," Kevin said, pointing a fork of his own. "That wasn't just a car. It was a '57 Chevy. The car of cars."

"A classic," Kaufman added.

"Just like you guys."

He looked at Kevin. "Oh, she's good."

"When she wants to be."

Kaufman told her about the Friday night they had driven out to Marina with a few friends from school. In those days Marina was still a rural area. Most of the homes sat on five-, ten-, fifteen-acre parcels, and the soil was all sand. "This was back in the early sixties, when your car was your manhood," he said, "and dragging was how you proved yourself.

"So we ended up on this stretch of flat land, maybe a mile and a half long, out in the middle of nowhere.

Kevin here, he was trying to impress Trudy Wither-
spoon." Then to Kevin, "You remember her?"

"Still dream about her."

"I'll bet you do."

"That's sweet," Summer said, though he couldn't
tell if she were being sincere or just taking a jab at him.

"So Kevin here, he's driving and she's in the passenger seat. I'm in the back with Sheila Morgan. And
these guys in an old Ford pickup, I think it was—I can't
remember exactly what the hell it was anymore—these
guys challenge us to a race. We know these guys.
They're a bunch of hammerheads from school. Just as
soon steal your car as race it. But this night, they'd been
tipping the bottle and they were feeling pretty good
and racing seemed to be all they had on their minds."

"Which must have been why they chose the pickup,"
Kevin said dryly.

Kaufman grinned. "So it's on. The big one. Pink slips
and the whole thing."

"Whoever loses, loses their car."

"Got it," Summer said.

"We start out and it's no contest; we're running two
car lengths in front and Kevin hasn't even put the pedal
to the floor yet. It's too easy. Almost enough to make
you feel guilty." Kaufman dropped his napkin onto his
plate and moved the plate aside. "So we're cruising
now. Everything's fine. We're halfway there already.
And the right front tire blows."

"Thought I was going to flip her."

"You almost did. The Chevy pulls sharp to the right
and heads straight for the dunes. That was it. We were
done. We were going to lose the race. We were going
to lose the car. It was over." Kaufman looked at Kevin.
"You remember all this?"

"Oh. yeah."

"You had me scared out of my wits."

"Kept control, didn't I?"

"That you did," Kaufman said. "I don't know how you did it, but somehow you managed to get her back on course. All I remember is my heart was kicking a hole in my chest about then, and Sheila was in my lap, her arms wrapped around me, saying a prayer as fast as she could get the words out."

"What about the Ford?" Summer asked.

"The Ford caught up with us. We were rolling along at about forty or so, and Kevin was fighting the steering wheel every inch of the way, trying to keep us neck and neck. I looked up and I could see the finish line ahead of us, marked by the headlights of some buddies. But our speed was dropping. The rim was digging a trench in the sand, and even with his foot to the floor, we were slowing down. So Kevin looks over and sees the Ford go by and he says, 'The hell with it.' And he reaches across to the glove compartment and brings out this little metal contraption. I don't know what the hell it was—it looked like something he might have made in metal shop—all I know is he points it at the Ford and *bam*!" Kaufman snapped his fingers. It sounded like a wine bottle popping. "The Ford's engine dies."

"You win?"

"We win."

"What was the box?"

"A rather crude little gizmo," Kevin said. "It interrupted the pickup's ignition system."

"So you guys won the Ford? I mean, isn't that like cheating?"

Kaufman laughed. "It's a lot like cheating. But we

never wanted the damn Ford. We just wanted these guys to be indebted to us. And after that they were."

"So . . . what? You made the box?" Summer asked Kevin.

"Guilty."

"Cool."

He stared down at the cup of coffee in his hands, nodding, pleased that she thought he had done something cool in his life. More than the Nobel Prize for Physics, more than his involvement with the Agency, the coolest thing he had ever done was to marry Helena. The second coolest thing was the birth of their daughter, Christy. These two events would always be the essence of his life, he imagined. His most profound contribution to the world. Though he hoped that someday he would be able to look back and feel similarly about his involvement with Summer and Kate and James.

"Time to get down to business." Kaufman said abruptly. He brought out a briefcase from under the table, opened it, and removed three thick manila file folders. To someone's casual glance, it might have appeared as if he were an insurance agent trying to convince a client and his daughter of the need for a new policy. But this was far less benign. Kevin could hear it in his friend's voice.

"Several months ago, I was assigned to a murder that took place at one of the big special effects houses in the film industry. You know . . . George Lucas, *Star Wars*, Industrial Light and Magic? That sort of place. This was a different company, but you get the idea." He opened the top folder and stared down at a black-and-white photograph. "The wounds on the victim were . . . well, let's just say they were unusual. A couple of months later, there was another murder. Same kind of wounds. Then last week, we had a third victim. All three of these murders involved someone from the effects industry. This is Hollywood. If the victims had been actors, every news agency in the world would be on us. But these guys were relatively unknown, so you haven't heard much about their deaths. Still, I don't need to tell you the kind of pressure that's starting to build from above. They want these murders solved."

"I'm not an investigator." Kevin said. "I wasn't a field agent when I worked for the Agency."

Kaufman looked up. "I know that."

"But that's what you're getting at, isn't it? You want me to help you on this thing?"

"Actually, I had something a little grander in mind. I was hoping I could get you *and* the kids interested in helping."

"Cool," Summer said.

Kevin glanced at her, unable to help himself. She smiled, with a bit of unease, then her gaze went from him to Kaufman and finally to the remnants of her meal. The spaghetti had disappeared, except for a single short strand stuck to the back of her fork. The last remaining meatball had been cut into fourths and moved to the outer edge of her plate, next to a sprig of parsley.

"I don't know," Kevin said.

"You don't have to make up your mind right now. Just give it some consideration."

"We left the Agency to get away from this kind of thing."

"No, we didn't," Summer said. "We left to get away from Hunter. Because he was a . . . *hammerhead*, like those guys from your high school, and what he was doing was wrong. This isn't like that. If we do this, we'll be doing something right. We'll be saving lives."

"And jeopardizing your own in the process."

"Wait a second," Kaufman said, putting up his hand. "No one's life is going to be placed in jeopardy. Give me a little credit, will you?"

"Is that a guarantee?"

"You want it in writing?"

"What I want is for the kids to have a chance at a normal life. That's what I want."

"What about what *we* want?" Summer asked.

The conversation, which had suddenly built to a near frenzy, abruptly halted. Both men looked at her. The startled silence lingered momentarily.

"We're old enough to decide for ourselves," Summer finally said.

"This isn't a date for the high school prom," Kevin said with immediate regret. He had not meant to sound patronizing, but that was how it had come out, and he couldn't seem to stop himself "He's talking about murder."

Summer stared at him. "I know what he's talking about."

Kaufman closed the file folder. "Maybe I was out of place here."

"No. you weren't," Summer said. She turned to Kevin. Her eyes narrowed. "People are dead. If we don't do anything . . . I mean . . . doesn't that make us the same as Hunter?"

It was something Helena would have said.

"Maybe you should talk it over with everyone first." Kaufman said.

Kevin nodded. "Yeah. If you don't mind."

SIX

Mimi Van Mears came out of the bathroom in her slippers and bathrobe, and shuffled down the apartment hallway to the study. She had been flirting with a cold for several days now and this morning the flirting had turned into a full-blown love affair. A half-empty box of Kleenex was stuffed under one arm as she sat down in front of her typewriter and tried to get comfortable. She placed the Kleenex box on the floor next to her, then reached for the glass of bourbon next to the typewriter. The bottle—Early Times Bourbon—sat nearby on the edge of the filing cabinet.

"Early times, late times, any times," she said with a swallow that bit.

It had been her grandmother who had first introduced her to drink. For medicinal purposes, of course. She had been twelve years old and fighting a bad case of bronchitis. Scotch had been her grandmother's drink of choice. Mimi, however, had eventually come to prefer bourbon. A more elegant drink, as she saw it.

She put the drink aside, then scooted up to the old Royal typewriter that was twenty years younger than she was. Computers were the rage today, of course. Especially in the newspaper business, Though very few people in the world would be inclined to consider the *National Insider* a newspaper. At times, it seemed too sleazy even for a tabloid.

HOLLYWOOD GOSSIP COLUMNIST BARELY GETTING BY.

You never saw anything about gossip columnists in the tabloids. No one cared. Why watch the trailer when you can see the movie?

In her early years, her heyday so to speak, she had written for *Variety*. For a time, she even had a nationally-syndicated column, "What Mimi Heard." Lavish premieres. Formal parties. Hollywood weddings. Bar mitzvahs. She had done them all. Toasted with stars like Cary Grant and James Stewart and Barbara Stanwick. Lunched with Howard Hughes and Shelley Winters, with the Hopes and the Newmans. It had been a different world then. Less cynical.

She typed the headline: WHO'S KILLING THE MAGIC MAKERS?

Another sip of bourbon. In the ashtray next to the glass, the last cigarette from a pack of Virginia Slims had burned its way to a quarter of an inch of the filter. She flicked the ashes, took a long drag, then coughed up a lungful of smoke. Damn cold. Then another sip of the bourbon.

It had been the alcohol that had killed her career. She couldn't even remember most of the seventies and eighties. They were one monstrous headache, and a long downward spiral that had ended in divorce, unemployment, and a two-week binge that landed her in the hospital after her ex-husband found her passed out in the bathtub. She had been lucky she hadn't drowned.

Everyone told her so. But Mimi had yet to be convinced that she had been lucky. She had felt soulless ever since.

She rolled the paper up three lines, stared at the empty white space she had created, then typed: *Sources within the Los Angeles Police Department are reporting that . . .*

SEVEN

Kevin knocked on the bedroom door, then waited until James said it was open. He leaned in, the knob still in hand. "Got a few minutes?"

"Sure, come on in." James was seated at his desk, next to the door. There was a single lamp on, its cast almost perfect over an open book on the desk. Outside, the sun had gone down and the temperature had dropped a few nearly-unnoticeable degrees. The curtains were open. The neighborhood lights seemed comforting somehow.

"What are you up to?"

"Just doing some reading."

Kevin sat on the edge of the bed, which was situated under the window so it wouldn't occupy any unnecessary wall space. The rest of the room was floor-to-ceiling bookshelves. James had been raised around books. His father had been a Professor of Literature at Duke University. His mother had authored a number of novels exploring the experience of black women in America. He had once told Kevin that he felt whole when he was in the company of books. And it was the only time he felt whole.

"Reading anything in particular?"

"*In Cold Blood*. Truman Capote."

Kevin nodded.

"It's one of the first nonfiction novels of modern literature," James said. "Spawned an entire subgenre. Very disturbing."

"A little like the Bible, huh?"

James seemed caught by surprise. He blinked, then nodded. "I guess you could say that."

"Didn't know you enjoyed that kind of thing."

He shrugged and pushed up his eyeglasses. "It's interesting."

Kevin glanced at the shelves to his left. *The Coming Plague* by Laurie Garrett. *The Ultimate Evil* by Maury Terry. Arthur C. Clarke's *2001: A Space Odyssey. Oswald's Tale* by Norman Mailer. *Paradise* by Toni Morrison. *The African Americans* by David Cohen. *Abandoned: The Betrayal of the American Middle Class Since World War II* by William J. Quirk. An eclectic collection.

"Have you really read all these?"

James nodded. "Uh-huh."

"I'm impressed."

"Reading's the easy part."

"What's the hard part?"

"Understanding what you read."

Three years ago, James had been living with his parents in a similar upper-middle class suburb of Durham. Two years ago, at the age of sixteen, not long after his parents had died, he had been a freshman in college, dabbling in political science and majoring in history. Then Hunter and the Agency had gotten hold of him, and now here he was, living in an unfamiliar part of the country, with people he knew only because they had shared a few brief months of his life with him. It was a difficult, confusing time for him.

"I don't know if I ever told you, but I first went to college at the University of Nevada in Reno. It's not a huge campus as universities go, you probably know that, but I was from a small Oregon town with a single high school, and for me, it was like landing in New York. Everything seemed foreign: the buildings, the curriculum, the professors . . ."

"*Stranger in a Strange Land*," James said.

"Exactly."

"You don't need to worry."

"Worry?"

"I'm okay."

Kevin nodded. "You sure?"

James sat back, then removed his glasses. "Have you had this conversation with the others?"

"No. I suppose I should, though. It's long overdue."

"This isn't a black thing, is it?"

"I don't know. Is it?"

"I hope not."

Kevin grinned. "We're all a little out of our element here."

"Only me a little more?"

"Not at all. Not unless you feel that way?"

"I don't."

"Good. Glad to hear it." Kevin nodded, then stood up.

"It's not the *Stranger in a Strange Land* that bothers me. It's the uncertainty, the wondering if today will be the day."

"The day?"

"When Hunter finally shows up."

"That worries you?"

"Shouldn't it?"

A fair question, and one they both knew the answer

to: sooner or later it was nearly inevitable that Hunter would track them down. It was just a matter of time and money. "Why don't you let me worry about Hunter, okay?"

"Hardly seems fair, you get to do all the worrying."

"Just one of the many perks of adulthood," Kevin said. He moved across the room to the doorway. "You know, though, if you ever need to talk about anything, anything at all . . ."

"I know."

"Good."

"So what's going on downstairs?" James asked.

EIGHT

It was after eight by the time Daniel arrived home. He closed the car door and trudged up the walkway to the front door, hungry and hoping Marie had left something in the oven for him. She was off to her accounting class at the community college tonight. He slipped the key into the lock, then noticed the reflection of the streetlight off the window next to the door. He couldn't remember the last time he had made it home before nightfall. All part of the job, he thought tiredly. All part of the job.

Marie had left a pan of lasagna in the oven, bless her.

By the time Dan sat down at the table, some of the weariness had begun to lift. It was impossible to draw a line dividing his job and his marriage, here he was a cop and *here* he was a husband. He was both, and they would always be intermingled, whether it made things more difficult or not. Still, when he was home, he did his best to give it his undivided attention. Some nights he was more successful than others. Tonight was not one of those nights.

Marie returned home before he finished dinner, an hour-and-a-half earlier than expected. The teacher, she said, had left a note on the classroom door canceling the class. She was irritated. Twenty to thirty minutes there, twenty to thirty minutes back.

"Someone should have called. It's just courteous."

"Was he sick?"

"I don't know. The note didn't say." She poured herself a cup of coffee, then sat at the table across from him. It was impossible to imagine life without her. She was the breath in his lungs, the beat in his heart. He was a fortunate man and he knew it. Even when Marie was upset, as she was now. "I just hate it when class is canceled. How am I ever going to learn this stuff? This is the second time this semester he's pulled this stunt."

Dan took another bite of lasagna, ate it slowly, and listened. Marie was working toward becoming a CPA. She was still debating whether she wanted to use it for income tax preparation or maybe to go into real estate. Whichever direction she chose, Dan knew she would be good at it. She was good at everything she did.

"I need all the class time I can get."

"Honey, have you pulled anything less than an A on a test?"

"It's not about As. It's about being able to use the material."

"I realize that, but don't you think—"

"It's an indication?"

"Exactly."

"I suppose. I just don't want to fool myself into thinking the classroom is the same as the real world." She stared down at her coffee a moment, silently worrying the way he had seen her worry so many times before. When she looked up again, there was moisture in her eyes. "I'm being silly, aren't I?"

"No. not silly. Just a worrywart."

Marie nodded, mostly to herself, then took a sip of coffee. "Your day go any better?"

"I had lunch with Kevin and Summer."

"How are they?"

"Fine. Summer's starting to come out of her shell. I think she's going to be a handful. I don't envy Kevin any. Three kids like that."

"They're lucky they have him."

"Yeah, they are." Dan finished the last of the lasagna and pushed his plate aside. "I asked them in on a case."

Marie caught his glance. "Both of them?"

"*All* of them, actually."

"You sure that's a good idea?"

"I don't know."

"The special effects case?"

"Yeah."

"They're awfully young," she said, referring to the kids again.

"And talented," Dan added.

"Tough case?"

He nodded. "I'm up against a dead end with it. It's driving me crazy. The best the M.E. can tell me is that she thinks they're all animal attacks. But she can't tell me what kind of animal."

"And you still don't have a motive?"

"Not even a guess at a motive."

"You think Kevin and the kids can help?"

"I don't think they can hurt any."

NINE

They gathered in the kitchen, which had become the central meeting place of the household. It was rare to find all four of them together at the same time—in that respect, they had become the average modern American family—but it was a good bet someone would be in the kitchen. Kate and Summer were already seated at the table when Kevin and James joined them. This was not the first time they had come together for a meeting since the night they had left the Agency, but it had been a while.

James sat at the table, next to Summer.

Kevin leaned against the nearby counter. "I don't know if Summer's said anything—"

"I haven't."

"Okay. Then let me try to be as direct as I can. You've all met Daniel Kaufman, and you all know that he works for the Los Angeles Police Department, that he's a detective lieutenant in the homicide division. Summer and I had lunch with him today, and he asked if the four of us would be willing to help him on a case."

Summer turned to James. "Cool, huh?"

"It's a murder case, of course. I don't really know

anything about it because I didn't want to get into the details before we had a chance to talk."

"You didn't want to get into it at all," Summer said.

"You're right. I'm not sure this is in the best interest of any of you."

"Why?" Kate asked.

"Well, for a couple of reasons. First, because of your experience at the Agency."

"Which is history," Summer said.

"No. It's not history. Now let me finish this, then I'll shut up and you can say whatever's on your mind." Kevin closed his eyes and took a deep breath. "You've all been through a little bit of hell. You're in a new setting, trying to get along with new friends, and I say it isn't history because we don't know what Hunter's up to. He may have already dropped his interest and gone looking for new recruits. Or he may still be looking for us, knowing that it's unlikely he'll ever be able to replace you. We don't know. And until we do, it's not history. Then there's the fact that this is a murder case. I'm not convinced that is the best thing right now. Not for any of you."

He shrugged. That was it. He had said his piece.

"Is it up to us?" James asked.

"*All* of us. Meaning myself included."

"Why us?" Kate asked.

"I would assume it's for the same reason that Hunter is interested in you—because of your talents."

"I thought cops didn't trust the paranormal? Didn't believe in it?"

"Dan isn't like most cops. He's willing to try anything to solve a case, and apparently this particular case has him stumped."

"Who was murdered?"

"I don't know. Like I said, I didn't ask for any details."

Kate shifted in her seat. "It would be nice to do something . . . I don't know . . . positive, I guess. Something to make up for what we did at the Agency."

"You didn't do anything at the Agency. Those were all tests."

"Something for what we *might* have done then."

"We could be saving lives," Summer said.

"It's the right thing to do," James said. "That's all that matters. isn't it? We can turn our backs and pretend it isn't our fault if someone else dies, or we can do what we need to do. It's not about us. It's about what's right."

Kevin stared at the floor, feeling a twinge of shame. James had put a fresh face on the discussion, one he had to admit he hadn't considered. "You think I don't want to do what's right?"

"I think you're shining the light on the wrong corner."

"Kate? You feel the same?"

"Yes."

"Summer?"

"It's time to start thinking about someone else besides ourselves."

"So you all want to do this?"

They nodded in unison, as if they were conjoined triplets and all of a single mind. Kevin still didn't like it. It left him feeling as if he were letting them down, that he should be strong enough to say "no" if it was in their own best interest. But that was the rub, because he wasn't sure that this wouldn't be in their best interest. It could bring them closer together. And it could give them a sense of purpose again. And as Summer had been so quick to point out from the very beginning, they might be able to save some lives.

"I'll call Dan tomorrow."

TEN

The message went into every major newspaper in the country. *The New York Times. The Chicago Tribune. The San Francisco Examiner. The San Jose Mercury News. The Los Angeles Times.* It went into the classified section, under personals.

The message read: Trying to find my way back to you and the kids. Can't get along without you. Home is where the heart is . . . come back before it's too late.

It was signed: The Hunter Seeks.

ELEVEN

You've got to check it out.

No matter how preposterous a tip might sound, you still had to take the detour to see where it led. Most of the time you found yourself at another dead end, looking back and wondering how you managed to get so far offtrack. But every once in a while, a detour would surprise you and you'd actually come out ahead of where you thought you were on the map.

Kaufman had arrived at work to find five new messages on his desk waiting for him. All five were tips on what he had come to think of as the Special Effects Murders. It sounded like the title of a bad mystery novel, or worse, a low-budget horror movie. But it was accurate and made for easy reference.

He was on the phone with an elderly woman who claimed that her dogs had committed the murders. An interesting theory. The medical examiner believed the wounds on all three victims might very well have been the result of animal attacks. Information which had not been released to the public.

"Now why would they want to do such a thing, Mrs. Tarrington?"

"It's that movie. With the rabid Saint Bernard."

Kaufman had to think a moment. "*Cujo?*"

"Yes. That's it. *Cujo.*" She paused, and Kaufman heard the soft, distinct sound of lips drawing smoke through a cigarette. "They didn't like that movie. Not one single bit. It made them angry; that's what it did."

"And why's that?"

"Because it made them look bad. There oughta be a law, you know. So you can't discriminate against dogs. They've got laws for the coloreds. They've got laws for the queers. But dogs—"

Kaufman covered the mouthpiece, then took a long, meditative breath. The tightness that had begun to circle his chest gradually released its icy hold. He raised the phone to his ear again. "I've got another call, Mrs. Tarrington. I'm sorry, but you're going to have to excuse me."

"Do you need my address or my phone number or anything?"

"I've got everything I need right here, thank you."

"Oh. Okay, then."

"I'll have someone follow up as soon as I can."

"Oh, you will?"

"First chance I get."

"Well, I'll be right here."

"I'm sure you will."

"You can call me any time."

"We're pretty swamped right now, Mrs. Tarrington. But we'll get to you as soon as we can. In the meantime, I think it might be best if you kept your dogs inside, so they can't hurt anyone else."

"Oh, well, they're always inside. I have to keep them inside. They're Pekingese and you can imagine how the other dogs pick on them."

"Pekingese?"

"Yes."

"Like I said, I'll have someone follow up as soon as possible, Mrs. Tarrington." Kaufman hung up without saying good-bye. It was the only way he was ever going to get off the phone. He wrote: *"Her Pekingese did it"* across the phone message, then dropped the message into a file folder overflowing with similar dead ends.

"Kaufman?" Captain Savino was on his way back to his office, a fresh cup of coffee in his hands. He motioned for Kaufman to follow him. "Give me a few minutes, will you?"

"Sure." He grabbed a pencil and a steno pad off his desk, then changed his mind and left them behind. The Captain was in the process of changing into a white dress shirt as Kaufman entered the office and sat in the nearest chair. "Problem?"

Savino, a man Kaufman largely admired because he let his men do their jobs with minimum interference, finished tucking in his shirt, zipped up his pants, and tightened his belt. He was a political animal, though he would deny it, and the politics had aged him ahead of his time. Gray had seeped into his eyebrows and sideburns over the past year, and though he carried a medium build, the flesh under his chin had begun to sag a little as well. These were the things you noticed when you started thinking about your own mortality.

The Captain nodded at a copy of the *National Insider* on the desk. "Have you seen that?"

Kaufman picked it up. There was a photo of Kathie Lee Gifford in sunglasses on the cover, with a teaser underneath that asked, in bold letters: IS IT OVER WITH HER HUBBY? Along the fold, there were two other photos, much smaller. One depicted a pentagram outlined in white candles. The caption: ARE YOUR

NEIGHBORS PRACTICING SATANISM? Beneath that, a photo of five black dots against a blue sky. This caption: ALIENS GATHER OVER AREA 51.

"Why?"

"Read the bottom."

Another teaser. This one read: WHO'S KILLING THE MAGIC MAKERS?

Kaufman felt something stick in his throat. He flipped to page eight, and skimmed half a dozen lines.

"How does she know?" Savino asked.

"It's been in the papers."

"We've never said anything about a connection between the cases."

"That's true, but a little research—"

"You sure you don't have a leak?"

"I'm the only one working the case," Kaufman said. "Remember? You were tight on manpower and you wanted to keep a low profile on this thing as long as possible. If she got it from the department, she got it from me."

The Captain motioned for more. "Yeah? So now you tell me how you haven't leaked a word to the media. And how you haven't said anything to anyone else, even your wife."

"You know me better than that."

"But I need to hear it from you."

"Not a word to anyone."

The Captain nodded. "Good enough for me."

"It's the *National Insider*, for Christ's sake. Nobody reads this crap anyway."

"*Everybody* reads it."

"They don't believe it."

"They *all* believe it."

Kaufman nodded reluctantly, knowing it was closer to the truth than not.

"Read it when you get a chance. Mimi Van Mears. She was a hotshot gossip columnist back in the old days. Sounds like she still has an ear to the business. Check it out if you think anything's there." The Captain slipped into his dress blue jacket, adjusting the length of his cuffs. "And I'd just as soon not see anything more showing up in the *Insider*. We in agreement on this?"

"Of course."

"Good. Glad to hear it." He grabbed his hat off the rack, tapped it on the edge of the desk, and grinned. "John Foley's retiring today. Big luncheon. All the brass. I get to play politics. You like politics?"

"Not particularly."

"Me, either. There's nothing worse than shaking hands with a guy who's so busy playing with himself he doesn't know there's someone else in the room. The size of the egos on these guys. Incredible. It's a miracle they can get through the damn door."

Kaufman didn't argue.

"There's going to be more victims," the Captain said bluntly.

"I know."

"It's going to get ugly."

"I know that, too."

"Let's try to stop it."

TWELVE

"Why us?" Kevin asked.

It was not what Kaufman had been expecting to hear from his friend. He had expected Kevin to say something along the lines of an apology. *Sorry, but we've decided to stay out of it.* Kaufman sat down at his desk and switched the phone to his left hand.

"Kevin?"

"Just answer that for me. Why us?"

"Do you remember the summer before graduation, when I was working at the bakery, mopping floors and cleaning mixing machines? You remember how much I hated that job? And how you kept after me to quit since I hated it so much?"

"Yeah."

"You remember what I told you?"

"You wanted a car."

"And I'd do whatever it took to get one," Kaufman said. "I don't even know if I believe in the paranormal and all this psychic sleight-of-hand stuff, but if it helps me solve this case and put a stop to the killing . . . whatever it takes . . . that's the bottom line."

There was a long, thoughtful pause that Kevin eventually broke on his own. "I'm not convinced that this is in the best interest of the kids, you know."

"Then don't do it. I've got other pokers in the fire."

"Any of them hot?"

"Not yet, but you never know."

"They want to do it," Kevin said. "The kids. They feel it's the right thing to do, the only thing to do."

"And what about you?"

"I guess I agree with them."

"You want to get together, then?" Kaufman asked carefully.

"Tonight okay?"

THIRTEEN

It is a world unto itself in here. A step back in time. A shadowy, self-made tomb where night is eternal. It has been this way for a long, long time.

The dull, never ending drone of traffic on the street outside is barely discernible beneath the *clickety-clackety* rhythm of film passing through the projector. A light mist of dust stirs in the air. The stale, musty odor is an old, familiar friend.

The flicker of the frames reflect off huge movie posters thumbtacked to the surrounding walls. These are science fiction and horror films from the '50s and '60s. Titles such as *It Came from Beneath the Sea*, *The Hideous Sun Demon*, and *The Monster of Piedras Blancas*. This movie, running through the sprockets at this very moment, is *The Fly*. The original. The 1958 Vincent Price version. A classic.

It is the nuances, the lighting, the background he studies. The grainy film only contributes to his appreciation. Time may wear away the film stock, but the images always remain fresh in his mind. They are as unsettling today as they were when the film was first released.

The ending approaches.

He hears that enduring line: "Help me, please, help me!"

The credits roll.

He checks his watch. He should be working, creating, but maybe one more movie would be nice. There is time today. There is always time these days. The sand in the hourglass never runs out.

He climbs out of the worn recliner, then feels the need to stretch and does so. It occurs to him that he has not eaten in quite some time and there is a slight ache in the pit of his stomach that finally demands his attention. He looks from the door leading to the kitchen to the mahogany cabinet in the corner, next to the poster of *Carnival of Souls*. The cabinet has been designed specifically to hold his film canisters, his treasures.

One more movie, he tells himself. *Then I will eat.*

His choice is *House of Wax.*

They don't let you enjoy a movie these days. Not the way they used to. You get a flash of this, a flash of that. Every scene is a sneaker commercial. They give you a headache just watching them. They make your eyes hurt. You have to work just to keep up with what's going on.

A shame.

A dirty little shame, the things they are doing to movies these days.

He rewinds the last reel of *The Fly*, then threads the first reel of *House of Wax*, and starts it rolling. It is hard to go wrong with Vincent Price.

FOURTEEN

They were gathered in the kitchen again, the second time in two days, only Detective Lieutenant Daniel Kaufman had joined them this time. He had brought a briefcase with him, and a cheap cardboard file box, which he placed on the tile floor at his feet. Kevin sat at the table with the kids. Kaufman stood near the counter, sipping coffee out of a Styrofoam cup, and looking like a man who would much rather be sailing, as the old bumper sticker used to say.

He finished his sip, then raised the cup in the air. "Thanks for the coffee,"

"There's plenty more."

"Good. I'll probably need it." He put aside the Styrofoam cup, then opened his briefcase and pulled out the top file folder. "We have three victims. They all worked in the movie industry. More specifically in the special effects side of the industry. They were all males. They were all young, twenty-eight to thirty-five. Two of them were married with children, one was single. They were all murdered on the job, working alone late at night."

Kate, who was taking notes, raised her hand. "So

it's their profession that ties all three murders together?"

"And the manner in which they were murdered."

"Which was?"

Kaufman glanced uncomfortably at Kevin. "I don't know how much of this you want me to share."

"What have you got?"

"The medical examiner's reports. Photos from each of the murder scenes. Autopsy photos. Some of it's pretty gruesome."

"We can handle it," Summer said.

Kevin stared at her. "How do you know that?"

"I just know."

"Well, I don't," he said. He turned back to Kaufman. "What do you suggest?"

"I'd probably put the autopsy photos away. Not much blood, but some of the wounds are a little ragged. The reports should be okay. And the photos from the murder scenes, I don't know. There's a fair amount of blood, but you're spared the really raw stuff." Kaufman paused. "It's your call."

"Let's skip the autopsy photos, then."

"And the rest is okay?"

"Sure."

Kaufman shuffled through the file folder, pulling out some murder scene photos and all three autopsy reports. He passed the photos and two of the reports to Kevin, who shared them with the kids. "All three victims were already dead by the time they were discovered. Nearly twelve hours had passed in the worst instance; approximately five hours at the other end of the spectrum. No gunshot wounds. Nothing out of the ordinary in the toxicology reports."

Kate, who had been thumbing through one of the reports, looked up. "Bites?"

"Yes. All three bodies had evidence of bite marks."

"It sounds like the medical examiner thinks these were animal attacks?"

"That's right."

James said, "Dogs, maybe?"

Kaufman leafed to the back of the report in his hands, under the section titled: Opinion. "It is my opinion that Henry Richards endured a vicious, extended attack by more than a single animal, resulting in multiple lacerations throughout the body, and two deep bites to the neck, severing both the jugular vein and the carotid artery. The cause of death was the wounds to the neck. The mechanism of death was loss of blood and shock. The manner of death was animal attack."

"That's it?" Kevin asked.

"Usually in an animal attack, you've got some sort of corroborative evidence. An eyewitness. Animal hairs. Droppings. A broken tooth. A bloody footprint. Something that will help the M.E. identify the offending animal. That hasn't been the case here. We've discovered a few unidentified footprints, and . . ." Kaufman took the top off the cardboard filing box, rifled through the contents, and pulled out a plastic evidence bag. "And this."

"What is it?" Summer asked.

He held it up for everyone to see. "It's clay."

"*White* clay?"

"We haven't been able to identify its origin yet. All we know is that this piece was discovered next to the body of our second victim, and we weren't able to link it with anything else in the building."

"So we're looking for Gumby," James said.

Summer laughed.

Kaufman passed the clay sample to Kevin. "We're looking for a murderer."

"I thought these were animal attacks?" Kate said. "You think someone is training animals to attack and kill on command?"

"I don't know. It's not unthinkable, certainly. People train Rottweilers and pit bulls to kill. And I doubt these animals, whatever the hell they are, picked their victims at random. Someone has to be directing them. And that means there has to be a motive. Someone does not like the movie business. Could be someone who got fired. Could be someone who got hurt, a stuntman or someone of that nature. Could be a fanatic who doesn't like all the violence in today's movies."

"So he kills to stop the violence?" James said.

"Read the papers. You've got antiabortionists blowing up clinics and ambushing the doctors. You've got the Unabomber. There's no shortage of fruitcakes in the world."

Kevin passed the evidence bag with the clay to James on his right. "What else have you got?"

"That's just about it."

"This clay . . . it's not modeling clay? The stuff they use for special effects design?"

"It doesn't match any of the commercial materials used at any of the three studios. The people we've talked with all say they've never seen the stuff before, they've never used it for their own work, and they've never seen anyone in the business using it."

"And you said you haven't identified it yet? You don't know what part of the country or where in the world it came from?"

"That's correct."

"You aren't leaving us with much to go on."

"I don't have much to leave you."

James passed the clay to Summer.

"So how can we help?" Kevin asked.

"Well, first of all, I want to be up front with you. The department would have my badge if they knew I was doing this. It has to stay between the five of us here in this room. I'll give you my pager number and you can page me if you need to reach me, but it's probably best if you don't call me directly at the office unless it's an emergency." Kaufman closed the file folder he had picked up for no other reason than to be holding something. He tossed it into his briefcase. "Kevin, you and I will need to get together once or twice a week just to touch base. So you can bring me up to date on things."

"You still haven't answered my question."

"I know," Kaufman said. "That's because I'm not sure. I guess I hoped you'd do some interviewing for me, follow up a few leads, and then ... well, you know ... pass along any *impressions* or *insights* you might pick up."

"You mean psychically?"

"Yeah, psychically."

"You know it doesn't come and go at will, right? It's not like turning on the TV to see what's on today. Sometimes you get impressions, sometimes you don't. It's like a loose connection that gives you static most of the time, but every once in a while, if you jiggle it enough. the static disappears and the reception is perfect. You never know when it's going to happen."

Summer passed the evidence bag to Kate, who held it up against the light. The clay had been worked. Kneaded. It was curled at one end, with a deep gouge down the back, as if someone had ripped the piece from a larger block. There was a soft sheen to it, something that reminded her of satin, and the white coloring was rich and creamy. This wasn't Play-Doh.

Kaufman said. "No, I didn't know that."

"I'm sure if the kids pick up anything. They'll be happy to pass it along, but there are no guarantees with the paranormal, and the impressions you get can be wrong. They're not infallible."

"I'm not asking you to solve the case for me—"

"No, I understand that," Kevin said.

"I was just hoping you might be able to point me in a direction I might have overlooked."

"Right."

"And that's possible, isn't it? You can do that?"

"I hope so. I know the kids—" Kevin never had a chance to finish what he was going to say. Something in Kaufman's eyes stopped him cold, and when he followed their gaze, it took him to Kate, who was sitting at the opposite end of the table.

At that very moment, a violent shudder quaked through Kate's body.

FIFTEEN

It happened in a breath.

Kate stiffened.

The evidence bag slipped out of her fingers and fell to the table.

Her eyes rolled back.

She saw a field of black dots against a white background, and the sharp, bitter odor of burned almonds filled her nostrils. For a moment, she held on, still distantly aware of sitting at the table in the kitchen. Then she felt a tug, and she was gone.

A murky darkness.

Cold.

She found herself in a cellar somewhere. No . . . a basement. Huge. A set of stairs, made of pine, not nailed together but assembled with screws and brackets, ran up the wall to her right. A continuous workbench snaked along three of the four cinder-block walls, capped by overhead cabinets. No windows. One door, at the top landing of the stairs, nearly indiscernible in the murky shadows. This was a place she had never been before.

She swayed.

The basement swirled.

Overhead, in the distance, a rhythmic *ticking* sound.

Tick . . . tick . . . tick . . .

Faster, though.

Tick—tick—tick.

Something familiar, though she couldn't quite place it.

Still cold.

It was cold in here.

The *feeling* was cold.

Tick—tick—tick.

And she was not alone.

This thought struck her hard. She spun around. What was it? What was here with her?

Click—click—click.

Not a *tick*, she thought in a completely different direction. A *click*.

Then back again: there was someone upstairs. Above her. She was not alone because there was someone upstairs.

No . . . that wasn't right.

It wasn't the source of the discomfort, the source of the . . .

. . . anger.

Yes. Anger. That was what she felt.

Anger.

Anger.

Anger.

All around her.

She spun again. Then again. Or was it the room spinning? Because she couldn't be sure. It felt as if she were trapped in a spiral, round and round, all around her the anger . . . savage anger . . . trying to get at her . . . to claw her . . . to bite . . .

A new sound now.

This was *not* a click. Not a *tick*.

Low. Guttural. From the back of the throat.

An animal?

This was another thought that struck hard. It sent a shock wave through her. Where was this place? *What* was this place? Why was she here?

Kate.

Kevin's voice. Far away. Out of place.

Another low, guttural growl, just below it.

It wasn't always clear . . . whether it was remote viewing . . . whether it was precognition . . . whether it was a dream . . . or it was real . . . or just imagination . . . and sometimes Kate felt too disoriented to know the difference. This was one of those times. She was trapped, surrounded by the angry, growling cacophony, and there was no way of knowing if she could get back to her body or not. They told you that you always made it back, but people had died while they were out of their bodies. Kate had seen it happen. So she knew better than to trust anything she had been told at the Agency. You learn not to listen when the man with the knife tells you he's not going to hurt you.

Kate.

Kevin's voice again.

Follow it, she thought. *Follow it back.*

The cabinets above the workbench.

That was where the anger was coming from. She was sure of that now. She could feel it. It was explosive . . . part of the room . . . more than the room . . . all around her . . . yet centered in the cabinets.

Kate.

The cabinet doors rattled. It . . . the anger . . . whatever the hell was behind the anger . . . was fighting to get out . . . fighting to get at her.

Kate, can you hear me?

An explosion, or something that sounded like an explosion, went off.

One after another, down one wall, across the next, the cabinet doors exploded open, as if a bomb had gone off. The basement filled with a deafening wail. Kate backed toward the far corner.

Come on, Kate. Come on.

Eyes.

Glowing, golden eyes.

In the darkness, the dankness, she could see the flicker of eyes, dozens of eyes, peering out from behind the open cabinet doors. This was evil. Pure evil. And it was everywhere.

Now, Kate! Right now!

She felt a tug back.

Thank God!

But she didn't know if it would be in time.

The eyes were moving.

SIXTEEN

Kate came up desperate for a breath. She opened her mouth wide and gulped air as if she were coming to the surface after holding her breath to the limits of her lungs. The chair tipped back. Kate nearly went with it, saved by James, who was standing behind her now.

"Kate?" Kevin had her by the shoulders. He forced one of her eyes open. The pupil was dilated. "Just try to relax. You're back now. You're okay."

She took another breath, this one shallower, and her eyes fluttered open. Her hands thrashed the air, as if she were trying to ward off an attack. An eerie, almost otherworldly groan escaped her throat.

"That's it, Kate. Welcome back. Just keep breathing slowly. One little breath at a time."

Summer was holding her hand, squeezing it as if she were squeezing her grandmother's hand to let her know she was there in the room with her. Kate looked at her, fright in her eyes, then smiled weakly.

"Where?"

"You're back home," Kevin said. "In the kitchen. Remember?"

Kate's eyes cleared. She leaned forward over the

table, resting on her elbows, then brushed the hair away from her face. It was a slow process of getting reoriented again, grounded. Finally, she said, "No. I was wondering where I had been."

Kevin sat down again. "We were hoping you could tell us."

"I was holding the clay . . ."

"That's what sent you out?" Summer asked.

Kate nodded. "I think so."

"Describe it for us," Kevin said.

Kaufman, who had never witnessed an out-of-body experience before and appeared slightly shaken, said, "Wait." He rummaged through his briefcase and brought out a small handheld tape recorder. "We might as well get this on tape in case we need it."

He handed the recorder to Kevin, who turned it on and set it on the table in front of Kate. "What do you remember?"

"It smelled . . . dank. Like the sun was never allowed in."

"Underground?"

She gave this some thought. Impressions were rarely perfect. They could be unclear, imprecise, even wrong at times. Like dreams, when you were caught up in the experience, they could appear vivid, almost real. Taste, smell, touch, all of a person's senses heightened. But later, when you tried to bring them up again . . .

"No," she said. "A basement. I think it was a basement. The walls . . . they were cinder block. And there was a workbench with cabinets above it."

"Sawdust?" Kevin asked.

"I don't think so. I don't remember any."

"Tools?"

"No. That's odd, isn't it? No tools?"

"Maybe it wasn't a workbench," Kaufman suggested.

"This was a very neat, well-kept place. It belonged to someone who was very meticulous. A place for everything and everything in its place." Kate closed her eyes again, concentrating. "There were drawers beneath the workbench. A long line of them. Clutter has its place, too. But not when it comes to his work. He likes to keep the surface of the workbench clean, clutter-free. A clean workplace is a clear mind."

"*He*. You said *he*. We're looking for a man?"

"Yes."

"Can you describe him?" Kaufman asked.

"Not physically. Not his age or his height or anything like that. I never saw him. He wasn't in the basement. He doesn't go down there very often. It's dark, and he doesn't trust the dark, even when the lights are on." Kate's eyes were open again. She looked puzzled as she stared off into the distance rummaging through the impressions that were still somewhat fresh. "No, I don't think that's right. He's afraid of something, but it's not the dark. Sometimes he actually prefers to keep the lights off. That way he won't have to face what scares him."

"What is it that scares him?"

"The anger," Kate said. "He's afraid of the anger."

"Who's angry with him?"

"No, not *who*. I don't think this is a person. This is something else."

"Maybe an animal?" Kaufman asked.

"I'm not sure. Maybe. It feels . . . wild, though. Undomesticated. Almost as if it were out of its place and time." Kate took a deep breath. She was completely centered now, back in the present. Her emotions, though still fresh, had stepped aside and she was functioning primarily on her intellect now, trying to put into words those feelings and impressions she had experienced. "It's almost as if it were primordial, primeval."

"How about prehistoric?" James said. "Something out of *Jurassic Park* or *The Lost World*? Or maybe *Carnivore*?"

Summer elbowed him. "Shut up!"

"I was just kidding."

"Well, it wasn't funny."

Kate looked at him, actually looked through him, still lost in her thoughts. "No, this is more elemental than that."

"Whoa, whoa, whoa. Wait a minute here. We're getting way the hell out there all of a sudden, aren't we?" Kaufman raised the Styrofoam cup, which was half-empty, in Kate's direction. "You went from anger to an animal to some sort of elemental beast in barely more than a breath."

"I never said it was a beast. I don't know what it was, exactly."

"She's just giving you her impressions," Kevin said. "How we interpret them and the conclusions we draw . . . that's another ball game altogether. Right now, we just want her to share what she can. Later on, we'll take a more critical look at it all."

Kaufman put aside his cup of coffee, only mildly appeased. "Already sounds like speculation to me."

"We're here on *your* invitation," Kevin reminded him.

"You're right. You're right. I'm sorry. I'll shut up."

"Kate?"

"The anger," she said. "It feels as if it has no focus, no direction. No reason. It simply is. It exists. That's its basic nature. That's why I have this feeling of it being elemental, because the anger is at the very core of this thing. Without the anger, it has no reason to exist."

"What else? Can you tell us anything about the man?"

Kate shook her head. "No. He's there, but he's peripheral. As if he were . . . I almost want to say *controlled* by the anger, but that's not true. He's afraid of it, yet he also admires it. He's like the father with a son who's gone bad. He can't condone the actions of his son—in fact, he finds himself appalled—but at the same time, he can't keep himself from loving the boy either."

"He's connected to it somehow? To whatever's behind the anger?"

"Yes."

"Maybe a relative, like you said? Or a friend? A guardian?"

"You're forgetting, the anger isn't human. The elemental force behind it isn't human. We're not talking about genealogy. The connection is an emotional connection. Something holds him to the anger, the way love holds a father to a son. But they are not father and son. They are not related." Kate swallowed. Her voice had gradually grown softer and softer. "They can't be related. One's human, and the other's . . ."

She let the sentence dangle there, and made no effort to finish it. She didn't need to. Everyone at the table knew exactly where she had been going. For a long, uncomfortable moment, they all fell silent. Kevin thought the silence served as a necessary breath, a chance for everyone to process what they had heard. It was a lot to try to make sense of, and it had come at them in a rush.

"Thirsty?" he asked.

Kate looked at him, then shook her head. "No, I'm fine."

"The clay triggered this?"

She nodded.

"What do you think connects the clay to the anger?"

"I don't know."

"There is a connection, though?"

"I don't know." She looked tired, which wasn't an uncommon aftereffect of this sort of out-of-body experience. It could be very draining, not only emotionally but physically as well. "There must be."

"Is there anything else you can tell us?" Kaufman asked. "Anything at all?"

"The anger . . . I think the man might be directing it without realizing what he's doing. Subconsciously. It's like a parasite that way. Drawing off the emotional energy of the man. Using it to satisfy its own needs and some of the needs of the man." She stared down at the evidence bag on the table. "This sounds odd, but it's almost as if this elemental force, this anger, feels as much loyalty to the man as the man feels toward it. Neither of them is whole without the other. They are both independent and dependent at the same time."

"I thought you said the man was peripheral to all this?"

"I did. By peripheral, I meant that he, himself, was not doing the killing."

"But it sounds as if he's directing it?"

"Not consciously."

"So he doesn't know what it's doing? That it's killing?"

"He knows. And he wants it to stop. But he doesn't now how to make it stop. Not without losing his connection to it." Kate looked up at Kaufman. "He needs this thing. In some way I don't understand, it's part of who he is. He's afraid to be without it."

The tape recorder, which had been running without notice throughout most of the session, suddenly came to the end of the tape. It made a loud *clicking* sound that repeated itself three times before the play button popped out and the room fell silent again. Kate winced.

"What is it?" Kevin asked

"That sound, at the end of the tape. that *click . . . click . . . click?* I think I heard something like that in the basement. It was coming from upstairs somewhere, from above me. It was rhythmic. Very steady. Like a metronome. Faster, though. And it never stopped. I had the sense that I was listening to a heartbeat. Metaphorically, of course. But a steady beat that kept the juices flowing in some manner."

"Like a pulse?"

Kate nodded. "Yes. That's exactly what it was like. Like a pulse."

SEVENTEEN

He doesn't think the *slapping* sound that has brought him awake has been going on long. He is usually a light sleeper, and there is no reason to believe this is not the case in this instance.

The screen is filled with bright, white light. The credits have rolled. The music has stopped. *House of Wax* is over now. The tail end of the film slaps against the projector as it makes its endless, continuous rounds.

He listens to the sound, not annoyed by it, but rather soothed instead. It is a familiar sound. From his childhood. Through his teens. Into his adulthood. Movies have been his lifeblood, his reason for existing. Not just the considered classics—*Citizen Kane* or *Casablanca* or *Gone With the Wind*, though all of these have their place in his heart as well. But also those movies that Roger Ebert likes to refer to as guilty pleasures. Movies like *King Kong* and *The Tingler* and *20 Million Miles to Earth*. These are the movies that he finds most thrilling, most life affirming. These are the movies that bring him up from his dreams each morning, that give him the strength to shower, the will to eat, the need to continue the struggle through one more laborious day.

Life does not always turn out the way you envision

it. He knows this well. Life is full of surprises and disappointments, defeats and victories. He has done his best to make a difference, but life has passed him by and now he is helpless to do anything about it. He is trapped in a spiderweb of yesterdays, long past the time for struggle, long past the time for salvation.

Life and death.

Contributions and failures.

Good and evil.

He has lived them all. They have woven themselves into his life, sometimes tragically, sometimes momentously, and it is has all been too quick to comprehend. How fast these pleasures pass. Here a taste, there a glimpse, rarely long enough to appreciate until it's too late, until they are part of his history, his memory, and no more.

But he has his movies.

And movies are timeless.

He reaches across the arm of the chair and flips the switch that slowly brings the reel to its final rounds. The *slapping* sound falls silent at last. He feels a moment of complete and utter loneliness. Outside, the traffic drones on mindlessly, unaware, unappreciative of his presence, his existence.

Still, he realizes, there are only so many hours in a day, and so many days in a lifetime. He cannot afford to feel sorry for himself. His work has gone ignored today and it is time to get back to doing what he must do.

There is a floor lamp standing next to the chair on his right, an antique passed down to him from his grandmother to his mother. He turns it on, taking that final step out of the world of movies, into the world of blinding reality. He does not want to spend any more time than is absolutely necessary away from his imagination. Human existence is all imagination, he believes. Reality is no more than a simple agreement among its participants that this is where we shall meet, and these are the rules that we shall abide by.

And the most basic of rules is this: one should strive to exercise his imagination at every given opportunity. Use it or lose it, as the old saying goes.

He removes his glasses, blended bifocals that have gradually grown thicker over the years. With the tail of his shirt, he cleans the lenses, taking great pains to do a thorough job. He is thorough at everything he does. Then he slips the wire frames back over his ears and climbs out of the chair.

Hi, ho. Hi, ho. It's off to work we go.

The drawing board is set up in the corner of his studio, beneath a hanging, overhead fluorescent light that he rarely uses. You can't trust fluorescents, he has come to believe. They trick the eyes. Make you see shadows that aren't there. Instead, he uses a halogen desk lamp, perfectly balanced so that it hangs above his work unobtrusively.

He sits in the armless, swirl chair, peels back the protective sheet of wax paper, then stares down at his drawing. It has been a long time in the making, this design. He calls it a Task Master. It is a biomechanical alien, genetically engineered to lead an army of Protectors which watch over a family nest. There are others in the series. A dominating male. A female. Several offspring. This particular Task Master is nearly complete now. The others, four identical creatures that are distinguishable primarily by their personalities, have been completed for several months now. Together, these creatures form the nucleus of an alien family unit, which will be at the heart of his next project.

Imagination has no limits.

Today's movies have no imagination.

Not like the old days.

Not like the classics.

But here, in his world, anything is possible.

EIGHTEEN

Kaufman arrived at the station a few minutes after eight. He took the stairs to the third floor of the Parker Center, sucking a little wind at the top landing before he entered through the fire door. A new stack of messages, written in hand on yellow message pads, sat in the middle of his desk where he would be sure not to miss them.

He peeled off his jacket, hung it on the back of his chair, then went for his first cup of department coffee for the day. By the end of an average day, he would be into the urn for as many as twenty cups. Marie had begun to worry that he might be doing the same thing with coffee that he had done with Diet Coke, that he was becoming addicted to the stuff. He knew she was probably right. And he knew he would have to do something about it eventually. But it would have to wait until he felt the coffee was more trouble than it was worth.

Currently, that wasn't the case.

Currently, there was only one case.

Kaufman was still reeling from the experience with Kate. Two days had passed, but if he closed his eyes, he could still see her pushed back in her chair, her body going through some sort of wild convulsion. On top of that, he could still hear that odd, foreign sound coming out of the back of her throat as if she were a wild animal.

In his years on the force, he had learned to view murder scenes through a detached, unemotional frame of reference. The old saying that you never got used to seeing a dead body, to seeing what man can do to his fellow man, simply had not proved to be true in his case. And he didn't think it was true of anyone else he had ever worked with in the department either. You *did* get used to it. You *had* to get used it. If you didn't, the job would eat you alive and spit you out. You'd be worthless.

One by one, Kaufman leafed through the messages. There was another call from Mrs. Tarrington. He wasn't in the mood to deal with that lunacy again. She was probably worried that her Pekingese had killed a neighbor. A call back from the night watchman at Magic Wizard Effects. (Kaufman wanted to run through it all one more time in case the man might have overlooked something that had since come back to him. It wasn't uncommon to have a witness remember some small, seemingly insignificant detail days after the actual incident. Sometimes it actually made a difference to the case.) The names and phone numbers on several of the other messages were unfamiliar. You never knew what you might get from a call that had come out of left field, so you always hoped. He leafed through them all, went through them one more time just in case he had overlooked something, then placed the stack on the desk next to the phone.

This was the first time he noticed the flyer. It had been sitting beneath the stack of messages, along with a handful of departmental memos, but now it was sitting in front of him in plain sight. The banner read: WANTED FOR KIDNAPPING. Beneath the banner was a picture of Kevin McConnell. Only the name was listed as Michael Jacob Hastings. Near the bottom was the warning: Dangerous: Do Not Try To Apprehend. Do Not Approach. Contact Agent Samuel Hunter at . . . and there was a phone number given. It was odd not to want a suspect in a kidnapping to be apprehended.

Kaufman picked up the phone, then thought better of it and put it down again.

Kevin had warned him that sooner or later the odds were in favor of a flyer showing up. Kaufman hadn't given it much thought at the time; but he was thinking about it now.

He glanced up, taking a long, slow survey of the room. Wanted flyers came through here by the hundreds every year. They were notoriously annoying, and they rarely garnered more than a quick glance before they were filed away. But this one was different. This one was personal. Kaufman was surprised by the schoolboy feeling of guilt that suddenly held him, as if he had just cheated on a test and now he had to endure the long wait to see if he was actually going to get away with it.

He crumpled up the flyer and tossed it into the wastepaper basket next to his desk.

Somehow, that seemed to relieve a small portion of the anxiety.

Then his pager went off.

He looked down at it. The message read: Call the Chevy Man. It was followed by an unfamiliar number. Kevin, the Chevy Man, was probably stuck in a phone booth somewhere. Kaufman needed to do the same thing, to step outside the building with his cell phone in hand and afford himself a sense of privacy.

He took a quick sip of his coffee, stood up, then grabbed his jacket off the back of the chair. On his way out, he tore a copy of the Hastings wanted poster off the bulletin board and tossed it in the nearest trash can. No one seemed to notice or to care.

Now he knew what it felt like on the other side of the law.

NINETEEN

"Chevy Man?"

Kevin laughed. "You like that?"

"My boss thinks I'm in the market for a new car." Kaufman glanced out across the boulevard. Los Angeles was a schizophrenic town of drones and late sleepers. The late sleepers hadn't fully awakened yet. When they did, the second wave of the rat race would be in full swing and it would be a madhouse on this corner.

"All for the best."

"So what's up?"

"Just wanted to let you know that Kate and I were planning on dropping by to see Mimi Van Mears today. That still okay with you?"

"It's as good a place to start as any." Kaufman had suggested Van Mears because he was curious about some of the details she had included in her *National Insider* piece. He wanted to know where she had gotten her information, who she had been talking to, and if she knew anything else. He figured she wasn't likely to say much to a cop—journalists, even the slime balls who wrote for the tabloids, loved to wave their First Amendment rights in the air the moment a cop asked a question—but she might be willing to open up to someone in a less official capacity.

"Play the fan," Kaufman suggested. "That's probably your best bet."

"That's not a role I play all that well," Kevin said. "I'm bringing along Kate, though. Maybe she won't mind."

"Good. I don't know how much this Van Mears knows, or if it'll turn out to be worth a second of your time, but it's a good starting point. Maybe she can give you a few leads into the business."

"We'll see what she has to say."

"Kate's okay with this?"

"I think she's actually looking forward to it."

"Good," Kaufman said. Someone had left a half-empty bottle of Budweiser sitting on the concrete walkway a few feet away. He stared down at it as he spoke. His natural curiosity wondered who had left the beer behind, and how long it had been there. No bottle cap, he thought absently. Then he turned away. It was the only way to bring his thoughts back to the conversation. "I appreciate this, Kevin."

"No problem."

"Hey, there's something else you should know."

"Yeah?"

"I got a flyer in this morning."

"Let me guess. I'm famous."

"Are you ever," Kaufman said in agreement. "A nice big photo with about a week's worth of stubble. An ID plaque and a nice-looking height chart on the wall behind you. Makes you look like the scum of the earth."

"They probably doctored an old ID photo."

"They did a nice job of it."

"What's the charge?"

"A 6AD. Felony warrant, armed and dangerous. For kidnapping."

Kevin let out an audible sigh. "So how much trouble am I in?"

"Hard to say. The flyers aren't much of a problem. They get filed or tossed almost as fast as they come in. But you're going to be in the database now, in the computer."

"The name on the warrant is Hastings, right?"

"Yeah. Michael Jacob Hastings. You've got that going for you. As long as you don't get booked for anything, you should be all right. Once they run your prints, though, there's no getting around it. You'll be made."

"Guess I'm going to have to behave myself."

"Sorry, man."

"Hey, we knew it was coming. It was always just a matter of time."

"You going to tell the kids?"

"I don't know," Kevin said. There was a moment of complete silence, and Kaufman could imagine his friend staring off to the horizon, wrestling with what would be best for the kids under the circumstances. "Maybe I'll let it slide for a while. They've got enough on their minds. I don't want them having to worry about Hunter on top of everything else."

"It's your call."

"Why? You think I should tell them?"

Kaufman chuckled. "This parent thing's got you second-guessing too much. Way too much. Just trust your instincts, for Christ's sake."

"Helena had all the instincts. Me, I haven't got a clue." There was another pause, then Kevin asked quietly, "So, how come you and Marie never had children?"

They had talked about it almost endlessly before their engagement, and the topic had spilled over into the first few years of their marriage, but in the end they had both agreed that it wouldn't be fair to the children. "I'm a cop. I work long, erratic hours. It's a high-risk profession. There's no guarantee I'll come home alive tomorrow. We made the difficult choice."

There was another silence, uncomfortably long, and there seemed to be nothing else to say on the subject.

TWENTY

Mimi Van Mears answered the door dressed in a purple satin bathrobe with a white feather boa, and a glass of bourbon in one hand.

"Welcome," she said throatily.

"Mrs. Van Mears?"

"*Miss*, my dear. It's Miss Van Mears."

"Hello. I'm Kate. I spoke to you earlier." Kate had called ahead, to be sure the woman would be there, and to ask if she could stop by and visit. She said she was working on her college newspaper, hoping to become a journalist after she got her degree, and wanted to do a profile of one of the best-known gossip columnists of her day.

"Yes. Yes. Please come in."

Kate stepped across the threshold of the doorway, into the apartment, and Kevin was right behind her. "Oh, and this is my editor, Kevin McConnell."

"Pleased to meet you, Kevin."

Mimi escorted them into the living room, which was like stepping back into an old Victorian parlor. The carpet was dark brandy, plush, soft underfoot. Drapes hung ceiling to floor across one wall, dark and brooding. Kevin imagined it had been a long time since sunlight had graced this room. She directed them to a chesterfield sofa, upholstered in rich velvet, then sat across from them in a bergere chair upholstered in a similar fashion. There was a strong odor of cigarettes in the air, mingled with the staleness of someone who has lived alone for a good many years.

"I'm sorry, how rude of me. Can I get something for you to drink?"

"No," Kate said. "Not for me. Thank you, though."

"You're quite welcome," Mimi said with a slightly uneasy smile.

"This is a beautiful room. Have you lived here long?"

"Nearly twenty years now." The hoarseness behind her voice reflected the deep lines of her face. She had led a hard life by appearances. Or perhaps it had only been a wild life. "I moved in after my divorce. I can't imagine living anywhere else. It's so much me."

"I can see that," Kate said.

Kevin nodded in concurrence. "You have an office away from the apartment where you do your writing?"

"Oh, no. There's a small office just around the corner. I do all my writing here at home. It makes it convenient. I can write any hour of the day, any day of the week, whenever the fancy strikes."

"I see."

Kate brought a pad of paper and a pencil out of her purse. "What first got you interested in Hollywood gossip?"

"I was still a teenager then. It was in 1948, I believe. Or somewhere right around then. Anyway, it was when Robert Mitchum was busted for smoking marijuana with that young starlet. I can't remember her name now, but it didn't really matter who she was. What mattered was that Mitchum was this godlike movie star back then, and he was married, and here he was playing around on his wife and smoking reefer. That's what they called it in those days. Reefer. There was a huge scandal. And it was the first time I realized actors actually had lives away from Hollywood."

"What was your first job?"

"In the business?"

"Yes."

"I started out working in the subscription department of *Confidential*. You remember *Confidential?* Today it would probably be thought of as just another tabloid. But back then, they called it a scandal sheet, and there was nothing else like it around." Mimi leaned forward, the drink still in her hands, and whispered. "They printed a big-time story about the kidnapping of Marie MacDonald, who was considered a B-actress back then, and it turned out to be nothing more than a publicity stunt."

Mimi laughed and took a sip from her drink. The ice cubes clattered, sending out an odd shattered sound that was quickly absorbed by the furnishings. "Oh, did they look bad. So bad."

"You weren't involved in that one, were you?"

"Not me, thank God. That would have been the end of it right then and there. You could have tossed my career right out the window."

"Were you still working there at the time?"

"No, I paid my dues at the *Confidential*, but they never let me do any writing." She smiled reminiscently, regretfully. "So . . . I moved on."

"It's a tough business," Kevin said.

"Hollywood's a tough town. Very few people come away from it unscathed." She rolled the ice cubes in her glass, then stared down at them. "Did you know that Spielberg was twenty-five when he made *Jaws*? The same age as Orson Welles when he made *Citizen Kane*. This town loves its youth."

"Just don't get old," Kate said softly.

Mimi glanced up at her. There was a flash of coldness in her eyes. Coldness or anger, Kevin couldn't be sure. Either way, there was no mistaking the personal affront behind it.

"That's the trick, isn't it?" Mimi said.

"I'm sorry," Kate said. "I didn't mean to imply . . ."

"How long have you been writing for your school newspaper?"

"This is my first year."

"Well, there's a secret to becoming a successful writer, young lady. It doesn't matter if you want to write poetry or short stories or recipes for the Home Section of your local Sunday newspaper. The secret is this: you better learn to develop a thick skin. 'Cause you're going to be turned down and turned away and outright rejected until you feel like shit. Trust me. I'm not that sensitive." Mimi climbed out of her chair. The glass was empty now, except for a few ice cubes. "Now if you'll excuse me, I think I need a refill."

She started out of the room with her feet barely lifting off the carpet. It was like watching a death march, Kevin thought. The sound of her slippers slapping against the heels of her feet marked each and every step of the way.

Questioningly, Kate looked to him.

He touched his finger to his lips, encouraging her to wait until the woman was out of the room. As soon as the sound of Mimi's shuffle had quieted beyond notice, he turned to Kate. "What is it?"

"I don't know how to get her to where we want her."

"You're doing fine. There's no need to rush her. Just let her talk. Sooner or later, she'll get us there all by herself." There was the clatter of ice cubes against the inside of a glass, and Kevin glanced expectantly in the direction of the sound. When nothing followed, he spoke softly. "Let her do most of the work."

"You sure?"

"Interrogation 101. Keep her relaxed and talking."

"Oh, I think she's plenty relaxed."

Mimi Van Mears returned with a full glass of bourbon, the clanking of ice cubes, and a new sad smile on her face. She sat down as elegantly as a woman balancing a drink in one hand might, then crossed her legs and adjusted her bathrobe to keep them covered. "Are you sure I can't interest either of you in a drink?"

"No, thank you," Kate said.

Kevin shook his head.

"More for me, then," Mimi said, tipping her glass. "Did you know Marilyn Monroe and Shelley Winters were roommates once? I can't imagine how those two could have ever gotten along. Looks for one, brains for the other. They must have been after each other all the time."

"Did you ever meet Marilyn Monroe?" Kate asked.

"Once. At a dinner party. Shortly after her marriage to DiMaggio. He wasn't pleased to be there, as I remember it. I think he was basically a very private man, and here he had this woman on his arm who could light up a room just by smiling." Mimi took a sip of bourbon and tipped her head back, helping the alcohol slide slowly down her throat. "Now *there* was a real tragedy. Marilyn's death. One of Hollywood's greatest stars and she kills herself."

"I thought it was supposed to have been an accident?"

"It was an overdose. Barbiturates, I believe. But then downers are an accident waiting to happen if you ask me." She took another drink, and chuckled, mostly to herself.

Kate turned a page in her notebook. "I understand you're working for the *National Insider* now. Is that right?"

This was not a question that was greeted positively. Mimi glared at her a moment, saying nothing. The entire mood shifted from frivolity to tension in the matter of a few short seconds. She sat back in her chair, suddenly less concerned with the propriety of her legs showing.

"You think that's because I'm all washed up now? Is that it?"

"No. No, that's not what I meant at all."

"Well, I'm not." She swirled her drink. "I used to write for *Variety*, you know. I used to have a nationally-syndicated column. I'm as good today as I ever was then. Even better. You better believe it, too, honey, or this little conversation of ours is over. I don't need this kind of harassment."

Kate shook her head. "That's not what I meant."

"It's all still up here," Mimi said, tapping herself on the side of the head. "I may have misplaced a few synapses here and there, but I've still got more facts stored away in my brain than you could look up in an encyclopedia in a month. Just ask me something. Anything about the movie business. Your favorite star. Anything. Just go ahead and ask."

Kate glanced at Kevin, who offered little help. He had watched her dig herself into this hole and now he wanted to see if she could dig herself out of it again.

"I'm not a big moviegoer," Kate said.

"Everyone goes to the movies."

"I have a friend who likes Mel Gibson."

"Not many people know this," Mimi said, her eyes narrowing. "But before Gibson became a star, he was notorious for bar fights. You remember *Mad Max*? He was still recovering from a fight when he auditioned for that movie. As it happened, director George Miller liked the look of the bruises on Gibson's face, so he gave him the part."

Mimi laughed. "Ask me another one. Anything."

"Like I said . . ."

"I heard that *Psycho* wasn't Hitchcock's favorite movie," Kevin said.

"True. His personal favorite was *Shadow of a Doubt*." She sat back in her chair again, and seemed to relax. "Now there was a man who knew exactly what he wanted when he made a movie. He used to claim he didn't care what his movies were about, all that interested him was how well he could manipulate the audience. He could make a matchstick frightening if he wanted. Did you know he used chocolate syrup for the blood in the shower scene of *Psycho*?"

"No," Kevin said. "I didn't know that."

"I think it filmed better in black and white. Made it appear more realistic."

"Anything on Jack Nicholson?"

"Not many people know that Nicholson actually replaced Rip Torn in *Easy Rider*. And that was the role that turned out to be his big break."

"Lucky break."

"Hollywood's made of lucky breaks," Mimi said lightly. She stared down at her drink, swirled the ice cubes again, and sighed. "So who are you really?"

The blood emptied out of Kate's face. "A journalism student. Like I said."

"There isn't a journalist worth her salt, student or not, who would bring her editor to an interview. So let's cut the charades, okay? You're here for a reason. What is it?"

Kate turned to Kevin for help. He cleared his throat, then sat forward. Sometimes these things happened. It didn't always go as smoothly as you would like. He looked Mimi directly in the eyes. "Actually, you're right. Kate isn't a student journalist, and I'm not her editor."

"So who are you?"

"We've been hired by the family of Henry Richards to investigate his death."

"The guy from Magic Wizard?"

"Yes, ma'am. Our clients feel the police aren't doing everything they can, so they hired us to see if we could answer some of their questions."

"And you came across my piece in the *Insider*."

"Yes, ma'am, we did."

This seemed to bring her a degree of amusement. She grinned and nodded, then took a short, quick drink from her glass. "It's true."

"What's that?"

"That the murders are tied together."

"And what makes you think so?"

"It doesn't take a genius to figure that out. Three murders. All in the space of a couple of months. All involving someone who worked in the movie business, particularly in effects."

"So your article was primarily speculation?" Kevin asked.

"Did you read it? I cited sources."

"Unidentified sources."

For the first time, she put aside her drink, leaving it on a small, cockleshell-carved end table next to the chair. From the same table, she picked up a pack of cigarettes and pulled one out. "Naming sources is stupid business. You only get away with it once. After that, you no longer have a source."

"So there was a source?"

"Of course."

"And this source of yours was able to confirm a link between the murders?"

"Beyond a doubt." She put the cigarette between her lips, and left it unlit. "Listen, I can't give you any names, but I know how hard this has to be on the families. So let me tell you this much . . . you would do yourself a favor by asking around in the medical examiner's office."

Kate started to write the information down.

"And let me give you another tip, honey. Don't be so quick to write everything down while you're asking questions. It makes people crazy. If you have to . . . make a note or two. Write down a key word if you're worried about forgetting everything. And the rest of it . . . leave the rest until you get out the door."

"Actually, she's my secretary," Kevin said. "She's used to taking dictation."

"Even in interviews?"

Kevin smiled guiltily. "Well, she's never done an interview before."

Mimi found herself another chuckle, then finally touched a match to the cigarette in her mouth. She took a long, serious drag, The smoke came out of her in a huge cloud accompanied by a lengthy sigh of relief. "Aren't very good at this, are you?"

"Apparently not as good as we thought we were."

"Well, check with the medical examiner's office, like I told you." She took another satisfying drag off the cigarette. "You talk to anyone in the business yet?"

"The movie business?"

"Anyone working in effects?"

Kevin shook his head.

"Let me give you a few names. You can talk to them if you want. They probably won't be able to shed much light on the murders themselves, but I can tell you they're knowledgeable. They might be willing to help."

"That would be nice of you."

Mimi Van Mears left her glass of bourbon on the table and her cigarette in the ashtray. She left the room with her feet a little lighter this time, her head a little higher. When she returned, she handed Kevin two business cards. One had a phone number written in pencil on the back. Both were well worn and bent in the corners.

"This one here," she said, pointing. "Use the number on the back. The company moved across town about six months ago."

"Thank you. I'll call them both. I promise."

"You tell them I sent you. Tell them Mimi Van Mears sent you, and ask them this question: Who was the man in the monkey suit in the 1976 remake of *King Kong*." She laughed, her voice as throaty as when they had first arrived. "They'll get a kick out of that. And they'll know you aren't lying to them."

TWENTY-ONE

Kevin stepped out into the sun and shaded his eyes. He had liked Mimi Van Mears—dark Victorian apartment, too much booze, and all. He had also felt saddened for her. She had struck him as a woman who was painfully unhappy with the doorstep where life had finally left her.

"So what do you think?" Kate asked.

"I think someone in the medical examiner's office is making a few extra dollars on the side."

"You going to tell Mr. Kaufman?"

"Don't you think I should?"

"Yeah, I guess."

"You *guess*?"

"I don't know. It just seems like her sources are all she has left. If we take those away—"

"He needs to know," Kevin said.

They walked along the sidewalk toward the car. He had bought a Ford Taurus shortly after they had arrived in California. He had bought it because it was basically nondescript, and yet popular enough that you saw them nearly everywhere. He unlocked the passenger-side door and held it open for her.

"You liked her, didn't you?" Kevin asked as he closed the door and went around to the driver's side.

"She's had a hard life."

"Yeah, I think that's probably true."

"And she's lonely."

"Is that an impression?"

Kate looked at him. "Just an observation. That's all."

"Any impressions?"

"No. The alcohol gets in the way. It makes everything fuzzy."

TWENTY-TWO

Stupidity reigns supreme, Samuel Hunter thought.

Greene, who was sitting behind an elaborate oak desk nearly the size of a formal dinner table, had his hands folded over his belly like a football fan after a satisfying win and the best half of the pizza. But he was not a man to underestimate. And he was not a man to cross. He stood nearly six feet and carried an extra thirty pounds that had been added in just the last two years. That was the price one paid for a cushy desk job, Hunter imagined.

"You're the one who left the barn door open," Greene said.

"Please . . ." Hunter said, stopping himself before he said the rest of what was on his mind: *spare me the country bumpkin euphemisms*. He had been sitting here, listening to Greene rake him up and down in that soft, understated voice, for nearly half an hour now. His anger was long past the boiling point. Still, Hunter was not a stupid man. Greene was a military beast as well as a political beast, and that combination was a dangerous one. To top it off, he didn't mind throwing his power around when he felt it was to his benefit. And he was always looking to grab more power.

"I know the error was mine," Hunter continued, "We both know the error was mine. So now that we've assigned the blame, let's do something to fix the problem."

"Such as?"

"Getting the kids back."

"And how do you propose to do that?"

"We find Hastings, we find the kids."

"You're forgetting. Hastings is one of us. He's not going to be an easy man to find."

"I know that."

"Then let me fill you in on something you might not know," Greene said. "I'm not about to compromise everything we've accomplished up to this point because you can't handle a group of adolescents. The PSI Project stays down until the problem is resolved. Is that understood? No more recruiting. No more tests. It all comes to a standstill until Hastings and the kids are either neutralized or returned."

"You want me to find them, I'll need the manpower."

"Use your contacts. Rely on your wits. Do what you have to do, but you damn well better keep a low profile on this. You understand?"

"What about—"

"I don't want to hear anything else out of you. If you can't get it done, then do yourself a favor and disappear. Because if this thing doesn't get settled quickly and quietly, it puts us all in jeopardy. And if *we're* in jeopardy, you're the first person who gets to fall on the sword. Am I making myself clear?"

"Secrets come with owners," Hunter said cryptically.

Greene leaned forward. He placed his hands on the desk and folded them. His eyes narrowed. "More important, they come with consequences. If you want to

sign your own death warrant, you're well on your way,
my friend. I don't care much for threats."

"Neither do I."

Greene swallowed and let the moment stretch. "You
find Hastings. You bring him back. And you bring back
the kids with him. It's that simple. That's the only way
out of this quicksand. Anything else and the PSI Project is buried. And you're buried with it. That's as plain
as I can make it. I don't want Hastings coming back
to haunt us."

"He won't be."

"Good. You make sure of that."

TWENTY-THREE

"It's someone in this office," Kaufman said.

George Dutton sat safely behind an executive desk cluttered with piles of reports, file folders, departmental memos, projected budget numbers, etc., etc., etc. He was an officious little man, who seemed to love the bureaucratic jungle that came with his job. He pushed his black-rimmed glasses higher on his nose and shrugged. "So what do you want me to do?"

"I want you to find out who it is and put a stop to it."

"I've got a staff of seventeen working here. Some of these people, *most* of them, are recently out of medical school. They work long, stressful hours. They get paid a pittance. The work is unrewarding, often demanding, and always—"

"We could try obstruction of justice charges."

Dutton sat back and stared silently across the desk. "Against who?"

"Personally, I like to start at the top and work down."

"I didn't know anything about this, and you know it."

"Three people are dead. They were all young. Two of them were married with kids. The lives of everyone they knew have been changed forever. Nothing will ever be the same again. Their kids are going to grow up fatherless." Kaufman lowered his voice. "I don't want this happening to anyone else."

"I'll ask around," Dutton said.

"You do better than that. You find out who did the leaking, and you get rid of him."

"I can't do that. I'm a civil servant here. I can't just fire someone. There are procedures. Rules and regulations. I'll have to do a written reprimand first, then start a file. I'll need evidence of an ongoing problem. I'll—"

"Spare me the bureaucratic nightmare, all right?"

Kaufman had heard it all before. He had heard it from Captain Savino. He had heard it from the District Attorney's Office, from the Department of Motor Vehicles, from the desk sergeant, from too many sources to remember. It was the anthem of the '90s. *Sorry, there's nothing I can do.* Worker's rights. Defendant's rights. Attorney privilege. The buck never stopped anymore. It just got passed to the next guy in line. And the line went on forever.

"You're the one I'm holding responsible. *You.* No one else. If anything else on this case gets out, you're the one I'm going to come looking for. It's your tail I'm going to nail to the wall. Enough said?"

Dutton lost color. He nodded.

"Then we understand each other?"

"Yes. Perfectly."

"Good." Kaufman stood up and offered his hand. "Then I hope we'll never have another conversation like this again."

TWENTY-FOUR

Garrett Davenport was surprised to find himself in this position. It wasn't like him to be running behind on a project. He liked to have everything planned out, each step of the process broken down by the number of hours required and the projected day of completion. And he liked to give himself a window of at least a week to fall back on in case things weren't going as planned, which they rarely did. But he had already used his one-week window on the design and the armature of the film's *Rangda*. He couldn't afford to lose any more time, or he would be in danger of causing delays in the film's shooting schedule.

And *The Fear Mongers* couldn't afford any delays. It was operating on a shoestring budget as it was. The producers, who had started up their own little production company less than two years ago, had come to Davenport because he was in a similar position. He had started Garrett Davenport Productions with a few thousand dollars left to him after the death of his grandfather. While he was still a small company, he had built a reputation for delivering topnotch puppets on a tight budget. He didn't want to jeopardize that reputation. Which was why it was well after midnight, and he had been working since eight yesterday morning, and he wasn't going to stop until the *Rangda* was fully articulated.

Davenport tightened a screw on the armature mechanism that was designed to allow the creature to grimace and growl. This was not as sophisticated as moviegoers might find in a big-budget production, but the techniques and the engineering were still respectable and far beyond anything being done even ten short years ago. It was going to look convincing on the big screen, he was confident of that.

He was about to test the result, using a small handheld control device that was connected by a cable to the armature, when he heard a jarring noise in the main warehouse. It sounded as if something had fallen off a shelf onto the hard, concrete floor. With the control box still in his hands, Davenport looked up and listened.

The silence was complete and lingering.

But he had heard something. He was sure of it.

Davenport stood up.

He listened again.

Still nothing.

Sometimes Debbie would come down to the warehouse when he was working late, maybe bring a little snack with her, or just hang around to keep him company. She didn't like being at home alone at night. He didn't blame her. He didn't like being *here* alone at night. But sometimes—

He heard it clearly this time. Something in the warehouse had fallen over. It had sounded like a can of spray paint. First, there was that hollow, tinny echo. Then right on its tail was the sound of the marble or the steel bearing or whatever the hell it was they put inside the can to help stir the paint when you gave it a good shake. The sound had stopped now. Davenport, though, momentarily put aside his concerns about the armature. His attention shifted to the other room.

He placed the control box on the workbench, then moved out into the hall.

The makeup room was across the hall. The light was off. The door was closed. The next room over was the art room. One wall was covered with storyboards for how the *Rangda* was going to be used in various scenes. There were two huge drawing boards along the adjacent wall, and then floor-to-ceiling cabinets with some of the art supplies. The only light source was from the luminous digital clock on the far wall.

He moved past the last room and stood in the doorway of the main floor of the warehouse. Across the way, he could see the dim red light of the smoke detector above the outside door. In front of him, the floor was cast in a dirty-gray shimmer from the light at his back.

Davenport stood there a moment, listening, then flipped the switch that brought a flood of light to the entire main floor. To his left, stood a maze of eight-foot-high open-shelf storage racks, holding everything from paints to plasters, foam latex to gelatin. On the floor, against the wall, was a long line of steamer trunks. The lids were open for easy access to the contents, which included eyeballs and hair, hands and masks, plus a large selection of spare parts from past projects. At first glance, nothing appeared out of place or out of the ordinary.

He started across the floor to check the front door. It wasn't unusual for him to leave the door unlocked when he worked late; he'd never had reason to be concerned. But for his own peace of mind, he thought he'd better lock it now. Just to be on the safe side.

His footsteps echoed off the distant wall to his right. That part of the warehouse was almost entirely open space. There was an area for test filming, an area for miniatures, and an area for the design and construction of larger puppets. He glanced that way, and again noticed nothing out of the ordinary.

But something was wrong.

Davenport could feel it.

The hair on the back of his neck was charged. His mouth was dry. He didn't like the tightness in his stomach, as if someone had threatened him and his muscles were anticipating the first blow.

He checked the door, which he had left unlocked, made sure it was closed securely, then set the dead bolt. That might have been enough to settle the issue for him right then and there, had he not heard something else.

He whirled around.

"Who's there?"

No answer.

It had sounded—and this was crazy, and he knew it was crazy—but it had sounded like claws scuttling across the concrete. Like rats. Big rats. Scurrying to find safety in the shadows.

Davenport felt his heart step up its tempo.

He moved along the outside wall, peering down the aisles formed by the storage racks on either side. This was a time when he wished he had listened to Debbie and kept a gun for protection. There wasn't much here he could use as a weapon. Though he noticed the rod leaning against the end of the nearest rack. It was a blue-screen rod, used for manipulating puppets. Thin, about four feet in length.

Davenport crossed the span and picked it up.

Not much of a weapon—lightweight, hollow—but it would have to do.

He peered around the corner, down the aisle.

Nothing.

He moved to the next aisle.

Nothing.

To the next.

Nothing.

Then the last aisle.

His hand tightened around the rod. He took a deep breath, held it, then jumped into the opening. The long, narrow aisle stretched to a horizon of steamer trunks in the distance. Between where he stood and where the open trunks stood, there was a single can of spray paint lying on its side on the concrete floor.

And that's all there was.

Nothing else.

Just a can of spray paint.

Exactly what he had first thought he had heard. Someone had left it on the edge of the shelf or left it lying on its side, and it had shifted slightly (the way things do sometimes) and had ended up on the floor.

He lowered the rod.

"Jesus. Scare yourself to death, why don't you."

The tempo of his heart continued to keep double-time, but he felt the air empty out of his lungs and the tightness relax in his stomach. He moved down the aisle, feeling a little easier now. It was funny how active the imagination could sometimes be, how easily it filled in details that were never really there.

Davenport stopped and picked up the can. Flat

black. He used it on the backdrops mostly, though sometimes he used it as an undercoat for a puppet. The marble rolled around inside the can as he returned it to the shelf. It felt as if it might be nearly empty, which might also have played a role in how it had ended up on the floor.

He shouldn't have let it spook him.

He smiled, then flipped the rod in the air and caught it at the opposite end.

And that's when he saw them for the first time.

TWENTY-FIVE

Summer came out of her bedroom carrying a bathrobe, slippers, and a towel on her way to the bathroom. It was well after midnight now. Kate was coming upstairs after spending a few minutes getting a small snack before heading for bed.

They had gone to a late movie together, just the two of them. Their first girls' night out. The film had been a small independent production called *Sister Paths*. It was about twin sisters who were separated at birth and who found each other again in their mid-thirties. Even though Summer had felt it was on the long side and at times almost unbearably tedious, she had also felt that in some ways the film described the way she felt about her relationship with Kate. Sometimes it seemed as if they had known each other all their lives, as if they were more than just acquaintances or even friends, but actually sisters who had been separated and now had to rebuild their relationship all over again.

Kate smiled. "You're going to fall asleep in there."

"I hope so."

"Just don't drown."

"I won't."

"Enjoyed the movie with you tonight."

"Me, too."

Kate stood at her bedroom door a moment, looking like she wanted to say something else, then said a polite, "See you in the morning" instead and disappeared.

"Good night," Summer whispered softly, barely loud enough to be heard. She closed the bathroom door behind her, then did a quick two-step off the cold tile floor and onto the pink bath mat. When they had moved into the house, the girls had claimed the bathroom as their own territory. They took responsibility for decorating it, which had resulted in a flower motif with a white-and-pink color scheme. They also took responsibility for making sure it was clean, as long as the guys promised they would keep the toilet seat down. Of course, the girls had kept their end of the Faustian bargain. And no one had been terribly surprised, least of all Kate, who had predicted it from the very beginning, when the guys had quietly gone back to their old nasty ways. Men could be such inconsiderate pigs. If they only weren't so damn cute.

Summer undressed, folding her jeans and then her shirt, placing them on the white marble counter, next to the sink. She sat on the edge of the tub, ran the water, and added some bubble bath.

She felt more peaceful and quiet tonight than she had felt in a good many years. It had been nice getting out of the house with Kate, just the two of them. Sometimes it felt as if the only things they had in common were the Agency and Hunter and their current circumstances. But tonight, at least temporarily, all of that had been put aside and they had been friends for a while. No history. No paranormal nonsense. No worrying about tomorrow. Just friends.

She climbed into the tub, immediately succumbing to the warm caress of the water.

Her eyes closed.

She leaned back.

It had not been an easy life. Her mother had been a bitter alcoholic who had given birth out of wedlock, then tried to raise Summer alone. Summer had never known her father. At the age of eleven, she was turned over to Child Protective Services after a neighbor called to complain that the house was a filthy mess and that Summer's mother spent most of her time passed out on the living room couch. Both of the accusations were true, though by no means had that made things any easier. It was the only home Summer had ever known, and they came and carted her away as if *she* were the one lying on the couch with her head floating in booze.

Within twenty-four hours they had placed her in a foster home. Mrs. Carmichael was the woman who ran the home. She had two kids of her own and two other kids, young sisters, who had been placed there by Child Protective Services shortly before Summer. Mrs. Carmichael did not drink. She did not smoke. She did not cuss. But she *did* have a thing for keeping a perfect house, and she *did* seem to derive a peculiar sense of pleasure from taking a ruler to the bottoms of the young sisters.

Summer tolerated less than a month there. Then one day, after Mrs. Carmichael had walloped on the girls because they had gotten dirt on their clothes while in the backyard playing, Summer reached her limit. Mrs. Carmichael had an afternoon nap routine, when everyone in the house had to lie down for an hour. It didn't matter how old you were or how sleepy you were. For one hour, every afternoon, you were confined to your

room, in your bed, to nap. After witnessing the pad-
dling of the two young ones, though, Summer went to
Mrs. Carmichael's room that afternoon.

She was angry, and she had intended to tell the
woman that if it ever happened again, she was going
to call the police. But Mrs. Carmichael had argued and
screamed and things had gotten out of control.

Summer still wasn't sure exactly what had happened. All she knew for certain was that at that very
moment she had hated the woman beyond description.
She remembered a blackness falling over her, and her
body beginning to tremble. Then the next thing she remembered was looking up to find the bed on fire.

Mrs. Carmichael, who had remained in the bed,
under the covers, as they had argued, screamed bloody
murder. Her face turned bright red. Her eyes grew
wide with terror. She looked up at Summer, wearing
a strange, twisted expression that seemed to be stark
realization. The scream trailed off, though her jaws remained locked in a wide, canyon-sized yawn.

Summer, who had been caught in a hypnotic, apparently psychokinetic state, shook herself free. For a
moment, as she realized what had happened, paralysis held her. Then, without thinking, she folded the
flaming bedspread in half and tore it off the bed. A
thick cloud of unbreathable smoke rose into the air. It
huddled near the ceiling in a thin noxious layer.

Within minutes, the oxygen-starved fire burned itself out.

Hours later, Summer was removed from Mrs.
Carmichael's foster home and shipped off to a group
home. Two days later, Hunter and several associates
arrived to interview her. The rest was history.

TWENTY-SIX

Two of them stepped out from behind the storage racks in front of Davenport. Two others appeared behind him at the far end of the aisle. Four creatures, standing eighteen to twenty inches high, unlike anything he had ever seen before.

The blue-screen rod nearly slipped out of his hand. He tightened his grip around it, then glanced up and down the aisle again, assessing the predicament in which he suddenly found himself.

The creatures stood on two double-jointed legs that appeared much the same as the hind legs of a dog or a horse. Their shoulders were high, their necks long, their heads low. They were solid muscle, with slightly-humped backs and a line of spikes down the contour of their spines.

Reptilian, Davenport thought.

For a moment, there appeared to be a standoff. No one moved. It was a game of Red Light, Green Light, and the color was red. What troubled Davenport was what would happen when the color turned green. He loosened, then tightened his grip around the rod in his hands, afraid moving a muscle even that slightly might trigger an attack.

Then suddenly the light turned green.

One of the creatures between him and the hallway took a run in his direction.

The sudden movement startled Davenport. He panicked and backed into the nearest rack, then raised the rod and rammed it into the creature's chest. The beast staggered back a step, stunned. He jabbed at it again. The creature snarled, then swiped at the metal rod with one huge, four-fingered paw that nearly tore the rod from Davenport's grip.

They were small, but powerful.

Then the second of the twosome attacked.

The end of the rod struck this second beast on the snout, just above the nostrils. The creature growled, bared its teeth, then took a swipe that caused Davenport to immediately pull away.

At his back, the two remaining creatures made their way more cautiously down the aisle in his direction, apparently willing to wait and see how things were going to unfold. Davenport glanced over his shoulder at them, feeling a claustrophobic box closing in around him. To keep them at a safe distance, he swung the rod wildly, slicing a chest-high swath through the air. The warning set them back on their heels, retreating half a dozen steps or more.

He barely had time to bring the rod back under control, when he was struck ferociously from the backside. The creature hit him low, across the ankle. Its razor-sharp claws slashed through the fabric of his jeans, leaving behind four long, thin slits.

Davenport reeled backward again, into the racks, caught off guard and stunned by the speed with which the creature had struck. Half a dozen cans of spray paint rolled off the open shelves and clattered to the floor. He looked down. Blood had started to flow. The sight, which scared the living daylights out of him, was shortly followed by the first sensation of pain.

He screamed, then struck out at the attacking creature. The rod landed squarely across the side of the beast's head, sending a glob of white, gelatinous material flying across the aisle. It splattered across the footing of the metal storage rack. The creature tumbled backward in a somersault, landing on its rump. It struggled unsuccessfully to climb back to its feet, then shook its head and let out a deafening wail.

Davenport never saw the next attack. He felt something sharp across the back of his leg, then his knees nearly collapsed out from under him. The pain bit deep into the muscle. He grabbed for it, worrying that a tendon or a ligament might have been severed.

Cut them low, he thought. That was how they brought down their prey. Cut them low and let them collapse under their own weight.

For a moment, he found himself supported by one of the metal shelves on the nearest rack. The frame swayed slightly, letting out a series of short, sharp complaints under his weight. When the creature approached for a second attack, he shifted to his weak leg and managed to land a solid kick to the belly of the beast. It was sent flying through the air like a stuffed teddy bear. It landed hard against the wall, then fell, stunned, into a trunk full of eyeballs.

At least they could be hurt. There was that little shred of hope to hold onto.

Davenport turned in time to see the two remaining creatures take a run at him. They lowered their heads, then split the aisle, one moving down each side. Their eyes narrowed into small, round, silver-gray marbles, and for a moment, Davenport thought he could see an intelligence behind them. These were more than savage little mutations that had blindly stumbled into the warehouse. They were here with a purpose in mind.

He already had a fairly good idea what that purpose was and he did not intend to help them accomplish it. He shifted his weight again, this time to his good leg, then wrapped his hands around the frame of the nearest storage rack, and brought it down, across the aisle, over the heads of the approaching beasts.

The warehouse exploded in a cacophony of echoes.

Tubs of latex, cans of spray paint, cables, screws, machined armature parts . . . all went scattering across the concrete floor.

Davenport stumbled back, regaining his balance, just as he was hit again. The creature struck low once more, just above the ankle. This time, though, it didn't use its claws. Instead, it sank its teeth into his calf muscle and locked its jaws.

He screamed.

God, how he screamed.

It hurt like a mother.

The creature held on until he slammed it up against the overturned storage rack, then it released its hold and fell to the floor. Blood colored its teeth an ungodly red. It staggered back a few steps, stunned.

Davenport started toward the back rooms, his left leg dragging behind him.

In front of him, to the right, the creature who had earlier slammed into the wall was now climbing out of the steamer trunk. It plopped down on the floor, still shaken, then lumbered drunkenly to one side before catching itself and standing tall again. Its eyes narrowed. It lowered its head and started after him.

He met the creature halfway. The blue-screen rod was still in his hand. He swung it, missed, and lost his grip. The rod went flying through the air, landing forty feet away, next to a miniature downtown set that was still under construction. It made a loud, hollow metallic sound as it struck the concrete, then bounced three or four times and fell silent.

Davenport stopped and stared down at the creature.

It stared back at him a moment, then went for his legs.

He sidestepped in an effort to avoid it, but the beast moved with him. It struck hard against his thigh, then wrapped around the muscle and dug its claws deep into his flesh.

Davenport screamed.

The creature held on tenaciously.

Behind him, another creature emerged from beneath the rubble of supplies. It teetered on its heels, struggling to regain its balance, still mildly stunned.

Davenport didn't have much time.

He wrapped his hands around the animal attached to his thigh, then tore it lose with another agonizing scream. As he went to toss it, the beast bit down again, this time on his forearm. It ripped a chunk of flesh the size of a meatball away from the bone. Davenport slammed it against the metal corner of the nearest storage rack, dropped it to the floor, then took off running for the back rooms.

He never looked back.

That would have been a mistake.

Instead, he hobbled to the nearest wall, using it to support and guide him around the corner and down the hallway.

Behind him, he heard the banshee-like rise of angry wails.

Before they caught up with him, though, Davenport fell into the design room, where the armature for the *Rangda* sat waiting on the workbench. He slammed the door behind him, leaned against it, locked it, then pushed a two-drawer lateral file across the entrance.

Exhausted, he slid to the floor, fighting to fill his lungs with air.

His leg was bleeding heavily now. As was his forearm. The pain was there, too, though it had already begun to retreat into the background, leading him to wonder if maybe a state of shock was soon to follow.

Have to stop the bleeding.

At his back, the creatures began to ram the door. Each solid hit rumbled through the hollow metal structure, the lateral file, then finally through Davenport's body.

Boom.

He reached down with one hand and painstakingly removed his shoelaces.

Boom.

He tied the first one around his calf, just above the wound. He tied it loose enough so that he wasn't in danger of completely cutting off the circulation, yet tight enough to dramatically slow the flow of blood.

Boom.

He tied the second one around his forearm.

Boom.

Then Davenport closed his eyes, and let his mind drift away.

Boom.

Boom.

Boom.

TWENTY-SEVEN

Steam drifted off the surface of the bathwater, fogging the windows and the mirror over the sink. Warm water dripped rhythmically out of the spout, singing a soothing, crystal-clear note each time a drop struck the surface. Summer adjusted the washcloth she had placed over her eyes to block out the light, then took another breath and fell deeper into relaxation.

She was tiptoeing along the edge of sleep now, drifting peacefully.

On the horizon, though, something didn't feel right. She noticed it the way you notice a broken fingernail long after the damage is done. Almost absently, with a degree of surprise. Once it's noticed, however, it becomes nearly impossible to set aside again. The feeling tugged at her, persistently, until finally she followed.

It took her to a small, lonely room, a place of fear and isolation.

Something ugly, something *angry*, resided just outside this place. It was something that was struggling to get in, and it was something that frightened her.

She filled her lungs with a long, deep breath, then

tried to move beyond it. She thought of afternoon rain, of warm sand beneath her feet, of falling autumn leaves, and robins in the trees. She thought of ocean breezes, the taste of fresh peaches, the feel of satin late at night. She thought of laughter, of children, of the last time she held her arms in the air and tossed her head back and felt the warmth of the sun against her face. She thought of . . .

. . . of a man.

This odd image came to her in a flash. It sent a jolt vibrating through her body. The man was on the floor, slumped against a barrier, bleeding and frightened. His eyes were shut, his breathing shallow. He was, she thought, on the verge of surrendering himself to some unseen force. The image came in pieces, in glimpses, in shattered glass and thick morning fog.

Behind him, Summer sensed yet another presence. *Presences.* Plural. More than one.

A disturbing image flashed behind her eyes.

She heard a faraway, muffled scream.

She sat up. The washcloth fell away from her face. A cold chill rattled through her body. Her teeth chattered. She wrapped her arms around herself to keep warm. A sense of vertigo swirled around her. She felt light-headed, drugged, confused.

Faraway, she heard what sounded like someone knocking on wood.

Then a voice: "Summer?"

The sound swirled around the edges of her consciousness.

"Answer me. Summer. Are you all right in there?"

I don't know. I don't think so.

"Summer, please."

The voice . . . it sounded so familiar . . . it sounded like . . . like Kate's voice . . . yes . . .

The bathroom door exploded inward. She heard it slam against the spring doorstop, making an almost-laughable *boing* sound.

She closed her eyes again.

Kate's voice called her name. "Can you hear me?"

Yes.

Another chill passed through her. She shivered and started to slide back into the warm water. Someone held her up. Summer looked around the periphery and focused on Kate's face. She smiled, drunkenly. "I'm cold."

"Just sit there a moment; I'll get you a towel."

Farther away, another voice said, "Bet it's an OOBE. Bet she's been out of her body."

"Is that it?" Kate asked, as she knelt next to the tub and wrapped the towel around her. "Were you out?"

Summer nodded.

"One of Hunter's targets?"

No.

The feeling of vertigo, of being lost and confused, was beginning to subside now. Summer shuddered, then shook her head. Her teeth had stopped chattering, but goose bumps were still marching up her arms in waves. Finally, she was able to focus on her surroundings. "Th-th-the m-m-murders, I think."

Kate wrapped a second towel around her, then glanced back at Kevin and James, who were both standing in the doorway. "Why don't you wait for us downstairs. I'll see if I can warm her up, and get her dressed."

Kevin nodded.

The door closed.

"It's all right now," Kate said.

It felt all right now.

It felt safe again.

Twenty minutes later, Kate and Summer finally made it downstairs. Kevin had a cup of hot chocolate waiting for each of them. Summer had warmed up gradually, and now, dressed in pajamas and a bathrobe, she felt almost one hundred percent better. She sat down at the table, feeling the press of concerned stares upon her.

"I'm okay now."

"You gave us a scare," Kevin said.

"I gave myself a scare."

"So what happened?"

"I'm not sure," Summer said. She took a sip of her hot chocolate. It felt warm and calming going down. "I saw this man . . . felt him . . . I think he was hurt. And it was like he couldn't get out of this room . . . like he was trapped there . . . 'cause there were these *things* that wouldn't let him out."

"Things?"

"I don't know how to describe them. They were like something you'd see in the movies. You know, like an alien or something like that."

"You said something about the murders. You think there's a connection?"

"That's what it felt like."

James, who had finished his own hot chocolate and was washing out his cup at the kitchen sink, said, "You think we should call Mr. Kaufman?"

"And tell him what?" Kevin asked.

"He wanted our impressions, didn't he? She saw something, didn't she?"

"*Felt* something, actually," Summer said.

Kevin, who always seemed to have a difficult time whenever they started talking about psychic impressions and stuff, sat down at the table. "Was that what it was? An impression?"

She shrugged. "I guess. It felt like it. You know what was different this time, though? It was like I was there, but I wasn't there. Like I was dreaming someone else's dream. It's never been like that before."

"Was this something similar to remote viewing?" Kevin asked.

She shrugged again. "I don't know. Maybe."

"I guess I'm wondering if you think it was actually taking place as you were experiencing it? Simultaneously? In real time?"

"It felt that way."

"Why?" James asked. "You think we've got another murder on our hands?"

"Possibly." Kevin scratched his forehead, then folded his arms again. "I'll give Dan a call tomorrow. There's no sense bothering him tonight. Even if it just.happened, we still don't know exactly what happened or who was involved or where it transpired. Maybe by tomorrow, one way or another, he'll be able to confirm some of your impressions. But right now, I doubt there's much he could do with the information."

A thoughtful silence settled over the room.

Summer took another sip of her hot chocolate. She hoped it would help keep her awake most of the night. The idea of closing her eyes again, and possibly being carried back to that same place, facing one of those same horrible little creatures . . . she didn't want to even think about that possibility.

TWENTY-EIGHT

They return early in the morning, before sunrise. He finds them in the basement, all four of the Protectors, huddled together on the workbench. His greatest fear, that they have been out again and that someone has been hurt, is confirmed as he steps off the last step of the stairway and crosses the floor. They are covered in blood.

"Oh my, no," he says. "Not again, my little ones. Not again."

He turns on the overhead light, then pulls a stool up to the workbench. The creatures appear agitated, restless, much as they have after their other excursions into the night. He tries not to think about what they have done, about whom they might have hurt this time.

"Come. Let me take a look at you."

The one named Roland moves forward out of the pack, its tail slowly sweeping across the counter from side to side. It raises its head and a deep, sorrowful sound comes up from its throat. There is dried blood across its snout and above its eyes.

"What in God's name did you do?" the man asks gently.

He takes a rag from a drawer, wipes away the blood,

then checks to see if there has been any other damage. There has not, thank God. And there has been no damage to two of the others either. But the fourth one, the one named Silas, has not been so lucky.

"That looks serious," he says.

Silas has lost a good portion of the left side of his face. A hole has ripped open the thin latex covering. Underneath, the lightweight skeletal structure is exposed where a chunk of white clay has been torn away.

"You cannot keep doing these things. No. No. No. It's not right, what you do. And it is dangerous."

He unlocks a nearby cabinet and takes out a block of white clay. He unseals it, removes slightly more than he thinks he will need, then reseals the plastic bag again and returns the block to the cabinet. He pulls a small satchel of sculpting tools out of a drawer, unrolls it, then works the clay into the wound. The clay is moist and pliable as he applies it. It takes the steady hands and the patience of a perfectionist to shape and sculpt it exactly the way the creature was originally envisioned.

"Sit still. Don't make this more difficult than it already is, please."

The others have gathered around, watching curiously.

Silas closes his eyes.

"It's not so bad it cannot be fixed," the man says. He finishes molding the clay around the creature's cheek and jawline, then brushes the surface with sealer and sits back on the stool. Normally, a cast would be made after this step, with the armature placed inside. Then the cast would be injected with liquid latex to form the pliable skin around the armature in the shape of the original sculpture. But it is vital that the white clay remain part of the creature's structure. Without it, the creature is no more than a mere sculpture. As lifeless, as soulless as all the others he has created in his lifetime.

He adjusts the latex skin to try to cover the wound. It will be okay, he thinks. He will need to apply another latex skin, of course, but the damage has mostly been cosmetic. At least this time out, Silas is going to be okay.

"My Pinocchio," he says sadly. "My little Pinocchio."

Silas stares at him blankly, his head tilted slightly to one side.

How much do they understand, the man wonders. Do they understand at all? Yes. Yes. Of course, they do. They have to understand. Why else would they do what they have done? For him. It has all been for him.

This is not a thought that brings him comfort.

Bitterness, after all, is a man's reflection.

And now *his* bitterness has brought harm to others.

He does not find comfort in this at all.

Not at all.

TWENTY-NINE

Kevin was up a little after seven. This was a house of night people, though he himself preferred the mornings. They were what he liked to think of as his quiet times. No conversation. No music. No banging around in the refrigerator. Just peace and quiet and the morning paper.

He got up from the kitchen table, refilled his coffee cup, then sat down again and started in on the classifieds. More specifically, he started in on the personals. Old habits died hard, and so did Agency training, he supposed.

The personals were an easy way to connect with someone you dared not contact directly. They were also an easy way to send a message to someone you were looking for, someone who had made himself as invisible as he possibly could. Someone like Kevin himself.

He had started reading the personals the day he and the kids had arrived in L.A. He had been curious to see if Hunter was interested enough in tracking him down to go through the trouble of placing ads in all the large newspapers around the country. This morning, Kevin had received his answer: Yes.

The ad read: *Trying to find my way back to you and*

the kids. Can't get along without you. Home is where the heart is . . . come back before it's too late. The Hunter Seeks.

First, the wanted flyer.

Now, the message in the newspaper.

Hunter was stepping up his efforts. For a while, Kevin had indulged in the hope that his old boss might have decided to cut his losses and walk away. But he should have known better than that. Hunter was a man who hated to fail, who viewed failure as a sign of weakness. He had never walked away from anything in his life.

Kevin got a pair of scissors out of a kitchen drawer and cut the personal ad out of the paper. He didn't know what he was going to do, but he was going to have to do something. Sooner or later, Hunter was going to catch up with them. And then what? The thought of him ever having control of the kids again . . . well, Kevin simply couldn't let that happen.

He realized he had finished his cup of coffee and got up to get a refill. On the way, the phone rang. It was Kaufman.

"Don't you ever sleep?"

"We've got another victim," Kaufman said evenly. "He's alive. We've got him under protection down at Cedar-Sinai."

"Same kind of attack?"

"It looks like it."

"He say anything?"

"Not yet. We know his name's Garrett Davenport. And we know he runs a small independent special effects house. But he'd lost a lot of blood by the time he was able to find the strength to call 911. He's still fighting. Right on the edge."

"Married?"

"Yeah."

"Christ."

"I know," Kaufman said. "I was hoping you and the kids might be able to come down to the crime scene this afternoon, after everyone's cleared out."

"Of course," Kevin told him. They set a time. Kaufman filled him in on the location. Then Kevin brought up something that had nearly escaped him. "This happened last night?"

"Late last night, early this morning sometime. Why?"

"Because Summer picked up something last night."

"Anything we can use?"

"I'm not sure." Kevin had always found himself at odds with what he believed to be true, what he could scientifically *prove* to be true, and what he had personally witnessed. A suspicious undercurrent ran strong through his thinking. It went something like this: no matter how bizarre or crazy a situation might first appear to be, there will always be a rational, scientifically-based explanation.

For instance, spontaneous human combustion, which had gone unexplained for centuries and which many people believed to be a paranormal event, had recently been proved by forensic scientists to be nothing more than the wick effect. The human body, when ignited by something as ordinary as a cigarette, had the ability to burn like a candle wick, feeding off its own body fat in a slow, methodical process. Scientists had actually demonstrated the effect using a dead pig.

So if Kevin had learned anything in his time, he had learned never to jump too quickly to conclusions. "Any animal bites?"

"One deep one. On the thigh. Another on the forearm."

"Summer thought she might have caught a glimpse of one of the animals. She described it as something out of the movies. An alien or something of that sort. Something you might see in a science fiction film or maybe a horror movie."

There was a long pause on the other end of the line.

"Don't know quite what to do with it, do you?" Kevin said. He had felt the same way himself.

"No. I'm afraid I don't."

"Well, you aren't alone. Neither do I."

THIRTY

Gerald Greene pulled into the underground parking structure, parked, then took the escalator to the main floor of the open shopping mall. He strolled along the myriad of storefronts, past the Bold Boutique, the Sun Coast, the Radio Shack, in no particular hurry. It was slightly overcast, though not terribly cool, and he was enjoying the rare opportunity to be outside, under the open sky in the middle of the day. He was also running fifteen minutes early for the meeting.

He was not a stupid man—stupid men did not find themselves in positions with this kind of power—though he had been more than willing to let Samuel Hunter think he was stupid. It was always to your advantage when your opponent was naive enough to underestimate your strengths. And Hunter, while not necessarily an opponent at this point in time, certainly posed a potential liability somewhere down the road.

Greene stopped at a Doggie Delight cart, and bought himself a Coke and a large hot dog with onions. He sat on a nearby bench, watching the people pass by, the single women, the families, the teenagers with a few hours to kill. *This* was what it was all about, right

here. This was America. People free to walk about without fear, to do their business, to lead prosperous,
productive lives. This little snapshot of suburbia, du-
plicated a thousand times across the country, was what
it was all about.

The man in blue joined Greene on the bench just as
Greene was finishing the hot dog. They spoke softly,
without looking at each other. The conversation was
about Hunter.

"He's become a double-edged sword," Greene said.
"He can swing against us just as easily."

"Which way is he swinging now?"

"I think he's okay."

"That's good."

"For now. No guarantees, though. He's too unpredictable for guarantees."

"You set him straight, right?"

"I warned him of the consequences if things got out
of hand."

"And he listened?"

Greene crumpled the hot dog wrapper into a ball
and tossed it at a nearby trash can. "I warned him.
How much of it made it into his brain is something
else altogether. He's not a man who likes to be talked
to. You know what I mean? In the real world, he'd be
the nice-looking kid who's polite to his neighbors, while
he's got a dozen bodies buried in his basement. You
never really know what's going on inside the man's
head."

The man in blue nodded.

"I'd hate to have to scrap it."

"The project? We've got another track in place. We've
been running a parallel since the beginning. This is too

important to place solely in the hands of someone like Hunter. You saw what he tried to do to Molly Culligan."

"His old boss?"

The man in blue nodded. "Tried to turn the project on one of his own people. He's a dangerous man."

"We'll keep an eye on him."

"You make sure you do. If he becomes a problem . . ."

"I'll handle it."

THIRTY-ONE

Kaufman's car was already parked in the lot by the time Kevin and the kids arrived. On the outside, the warehouse was a rather unimpressive building, located in an old industrial park in the suburbs. The windows were painted black. A dumpster sat next to the entrance, the lid open, the bin overfilled with cardboard boxes, metal and plastic scraps, foam rubber appliances, and a myriad of other junk from the trade.

"This is it?" James asked.

"I think so," Kevin said. "That's Dan's car."

They got out and stretched. The drive over had placed them smack-dab in the middle of a bumper-to-bumper tortoise race on the freeway. An hour and fifteen minutes for what should have been a half-hour trip. They were all a little cranky. Kevin was particularly tired of being cooped up.

He held up the strip of yellow crime-scene tape as they each ducked under and entered the building. Kaufman was waiting for them at the far end of a row of supply racks. He waved.

"Almost gave up on you."

"Got caught in traffic," Kevin said. He followed the kids down the aisle, acutely aware of the smell, which reminded him of the chem lab from his old college days. "This is where they do their movie magic?"

"Garrett Davenport Productions. One of a number of small effects houses. From what I gather they mostly specialize in puppets and miniatures. They cater to low-budget, independent filmmakers." Kaufman motioned to an adjacent aisle, where one of the storage racks lay on its side. "We believe the brunt of the attack took place around there."

"Has the guy been able to tell you anything at all?"

"Not really. They've got him doped up pretty good."

"Cool," James said. He had wandered over to the steamer trunks and he was holding several of the plastic eyeballs in his hands. He held them up. "This stuff is great."

"The magic of Hollywood," Kaufman said with little interest. Then, to Kevin, "One of the employees found him passed out in the back there, in a small room. Apparently he had barricaded the door to keep out the attackers."

Kevin glanced at Summer. "That what you saw last night? A man trapped in a room?"

She nodded without saying anything. Under the bright fluorescent lights, her complexion appeared a little on the pale side. Her arms were crossed snugly over her chest. She shifted uncomfortably from one foot to the other. Looking at her, Kevin wondered if she might be coming down with something. But when he thought about it longer, he realized it might, instead, be that she was still haunted by what had happened last night.

"Are you okay?" he asked.

"This is the place. From last night. This is it."

"You're sure?"

She nodded, then glanced away.

"Can you tell me about the animal you saw?" Kaufman asked.

"It wasn't an animal. Not like a dog or cat or anything like that. It was like something you'd see in the movies. Ever see *Alien* or *Pumpkinhead*? It was like that."

"*Pumpkinhead?*"

"It's not what it sounds like," James said. "It was a horror movie in the late '80s, with Lance Henriksen. About this back-hills guy whose son is killed by these teenagers. He has the local witch summon up this monster to take revenge. A good flick."

"*Pumpkinhead*," Kaufman repeated, mostly to himself.

"Can you describe it? The monster?" Kevin asked of Summer.

She shook her head.

"It's important," Kaufman said.

"I don't want to go back there."

"Lives could be on the line," Kevin said. This was exactly why he had not wanted to get the kids involved. For all her experience and hard knocks, Summer was still a little girl. Far too young for the ugliness in the world. Yet here he found himself, doing his best impression of Hunter, pushing her to open herself to the evil.

She looked at him, silently pleading for a pass.

"I know it isn't easy."

"It's strong here. Stronger than last night."

"Just a description," Kaufman said. "That's all I need. A brief description."

"It's okay," Kate said. "You'll be all right."

Summer dropped the lid on one of the steamer trunks and sat down. She leaned against the wall and put her head back. Her eyes closed. Her breathing grew shallow. "It was small. Maybe two feet tall. Stood on two legs. It was scaly, like a lizard. Sharp teeth, pointed. Claws for hands. There were ... four digits on each hand. And a tail. And a ..."

"What?" Kaufman asked.

Summer shook her head. "It's not alone. There's more than one of them."

"How many more?"

"I'm not sure."

"What about the anger?" Kate asked.

"The anger's in the spirit."

"What?"

"The anger's in the spirit."

"What's that supposed to mean?"

"I don't know," Summer said. "It just came to me. It think it has something to do with ... I don't know ... something to do with their ... *souls?* Like there's something inside them, this kind of *ugliness,* and that's what makes them do what they do."

No one seemed to know what to say to that. Kaufman made some notes on a pad of paper he was holding in his hands. James sat down next to Summer and gave her a comforting pat on the leg. Kate nodded, as if she could empathize, though she didn't say a word. And Kevin didn't know what to make of any of it. Summer seemed to be implying that these things, whatever they were, had a psychological underpinning to their actions. They weren't acting purely on instinct as an animal might, but were inspired to action by what she had called a *soul.* It seemed to Kevin that the use of the word *soul* suddenly elevated these creatures above the animal kingdom. There was a *reason* for their actions. A *purpose.* And while at first that seemed a frightening concept to absorb, it also gave them a potential avenue for solving the case.

"Thanks," Kaufman finally said.

Summer smiled weakly.

"I mean it. I know that was hard for you." He clipped the pen to the cardboard backing of the paper pad, then nodded toward the area where the storage rack lay on its side. "Let me tell you what little we know about what happened. There's not much."

Summer and James got up and joined him.

"Apparently, Davenport was working in the back when he heard something and came out to investigate. His wife, Debbie, said he was working late, trying to catch up on a puppet that was running behind schedule. The framework for the puppet was on the workbench in the back room."

"The same room where he barricaded himself?"

"Yes," Kaufman said. "So we think he came out and turned on the lights—the lights were on this morning when the employee arrived—had a look around, then went to check the door. The guy told us it was rare for Davenport to lock the door at night when was he was working alone, and he found it unlocked this morning. But we're assuming the attacker, or attackers, had to let themselves out."

"So he checks the door and they jump him on the way back," James said.

"That's what we're guessing." Kaufman pointed down the aisle. "The struggle took place here. You can see the first signs of blood, then the trail heading down the hallway as Davenport apparently made his escape."

"Any signs of animal blood?" Kevin asked.

"It's too early to tell. We took samples, and we'll

have the lab check them against Davenport's, but right now, my guess is it all belongs to him."

"These things don't bleed?"

"We haven't found any blood at any of the scenes. So, yeah, I guess you could conclude they don't bleed. Or they haven't been hurt."

"With all that violence? You'd think one of the victims would have been able to do some damage."

"Yeah, you would," Kaufman said. "We did find some more clay, though."

"Same stuff?"

"Appears to be. Here, let me show you." Kaufman directed them around the nearest storage rack, down the aisle on one side and back up the aisle on the other. This was the same course it was believed Davenport had taken last night.

"Here," Kaufman said, pointing out an area that had been splattered in clay. Most of it was gone, carried off to the lab in a sealed evidence bag, but there was still some residue left, and a few clumps stuck to the edge of the rack, looking as if someone had spilled a pail of plaster of paris and had done a poor job cleaning up. "We found it right here."

Kevin dabbed his fingers in it and smelled them. He wasn't sure what he was anticipating the smell to be, maybe something like linseed oil, though it didn't appear to have any odor at all.

"They don't use this stuff on their puppets?" he asked.

"Not according to the employees we talked to. They all claimed they've never seen anything like it."

Kate picked up a couple of spray cans off the floor and put them aside. She kneeled next to Kevin. "I don't like this stuff much."

"I don't blame you." He showed her his fingers. "There's no smell to it."

"How much of this stuff did you find?" he asked Kaufman.

"Not much. Maybe a handful,"

"Can you spare some?"

"Don't see why not."

Kate said, "What are you going to do? Test it yourself?"

"I'm not really equipped to do that. But I would like to take a closer look at it."

Kate nodded absently, She pulled a clump of clay off the foot of the storage rack. Kevin watched her, impressed that her courage allowed her to so easily put aside her last experience with the clay. He shouldn't have been surprised, he supposed. She was a fighter, after all. A survivor. One of those rare people who never looked back because that was then and this is now and now was all that mattered.

She held the clay up to the light, took a closer look, rolled it in her fingers to get the feel of it. Then suddenly her body started to convulse.

It all happened so fast.

Her eyes rolled up into her head, her muscles stiffened, then she fell forward. On the way to the floor, her head struck the corner of the rack. A gash opened. Blood started to flow. Her arm swung across the nearby spray cans, scattering them in all directions, the sound shattering what had previously been a peaceful, quiet moment.

Kevin teetered for a second, mostly surprised but also disbelieving. *Not funny*, he thought. *Not funny at all*. When he finally realized it wasn't a joke, he immediately shifted into automatic. He checked her breathing (which appeared clear and normal), her pulse (strong and steady), then noticed the wound on her forehead and the profusion of blood. He grabbed a rag off the floor, pressed it against the gash, and held it tight.

Then Kevin looked up at Kaufman. "Better call an ambulance."

THIRTY-TWO

Kevin held Kate's hand in the ambulance on the way to the hospital. He had tossed the car keys to James and asked him to take Summer home, but they had both insisted on going to the hospital, too. James had been particularly adamant, reminding Kevin that not only were they no longer children, but they were a family now, and that Kate would need them to be there. He had been right, of course.

Once at the hospital, Kate had been wheeled into emergency and Kevin had found himself standing alone out in the hallway. He waited around until a nurse suggested that it would be best if he went upstairs to the waiting room. She promised a doctor would be up there to talk to him as soon as Kate was out of emergency.

Kevin had been around hospitals enough to know that sometimes a doctor would show up and sometimes you had to go find him. And waiting rooms . . . the world never seemed as bleak as when you were sitting in one. He went upstairs just the same, and it was only another fifteen minutes before everyone else showed up.

"How is she?" Kaufman asked.

"Haven't heard."

Summer leaned against James, who put his arm around her. Kevin was surprised by how young they looked. So often when he looked at them he would see adults. But at this very moment, they were children again, and he wished he knew how to take away their pain.

"Did they say anything?" Kaufman asked.

"Not a word."

"Have a seat and we'll be up to talk with you?"

"Exactly."

The wait was torturous, and though it was only an hour before the doctor arrived, it felt like an eternity. His name was Revell. He had a perfectly emotionless face, a handy attribute in his line of business, Kevin supposed. Especially when you were delivering bad news.

"How is she?" Kevin asked.

"She's stable." Revell said. He was a small man. slight, with a powerful handshake. "But it's serious. She's comatose."

"No," Summer cried.

"Can you tell me what happened?"

There wasn't much to tell, and Kevin didn't see any sense in talking about the paranormal or Kate's particular talents at clairvoyance or telepathy, or how her coma might be related. You start messing with a person's belief system and he'll tune you out altogether. So Kevin kept it straightforward and factual. Where they had been. Why they had been there. What Kate had been holding when the convulsion hit. What the convulsion had been like. What the aftereffects had been.

"Did anyone happen to bring along a sample of the clay?" Revell asked.

Kevin glanced at the others. "No, I don't think so. Why?"

"To be perfectly honest, we aren't sure what triggered this. We're all a little baffled. So maybe if we had a sample, we could run it through toxicology and see if we come with anything. It could be an allergic reaction or something of that sort. It's a long shot, I admit, but at this point we've got nothing to lose by exploring it."

"So you don't know what caused the coma?"

"No. There is the possibility that it may have come from striking her head. A coma is generally the result of damage to the brain. And damage can be from a head injury or an abnormality such as a brain tumor or an abscess or a hemorrhage. You mentioned she hit her head, and you were right, it wasn't serious. But you never know about these things. You just never know."

"So you did a scan?"

"We did a CT scan, and there's no evidence of a tumor or a hemorrhage or anything of that nature. In fact, there's no evidence of any brain damage whatsoever."

"So that's good, isn't it?" Summer asked, wiping away a tear.

"Well, yes. But it still doesn't mean we're out of the woods. And it still leaves us without an explanation of why this happened."

"How deep is the coma?" Kevin asked.

"Good question. There are varying forms of comas, and Kate has already shown signs that hers might be relatively mild. She's mumbled a few words and she's moved a little in response to questions. Both good signs. At this point, it's hard to ask for any better news."

"How long?" James asked. "I mean . . . is there any way to know how long she might be . . ."

"No. I'm sorry. There's no way for us to tell how long she'll be comatose. It could last hours. It could last years."

With that, a somber, pensive mood fell over the room. Revell answered a few more questions before he was paged, then he excused himself. On his way out, he passed a nurse who was on her way in. She informed them that Kate was now settled comfortably into Room 203 and they could visit her shortly. In the meantime, she said, someone needed to fill out the paperwork.

"That would be me," Kevin said.

She handed him the clipboard. "You can turn it in at the nurse's station at the end of the hall when you're done."

Kevin looked down at the forms. If it had all seemed a little like a dream up to this moment, reality had now arrived. It was the little formalities that made a person wake up. Kevin still remembered filling out his first income tax forms after Helena and Christy had died. Putting his signature at the bottom of the page had been the hardest thing he had ever done. It had been the period at the end of the sentence of their lives together. The finality. This was a finality of a different nature, but it was no less real.

Kaufman tapped him on the arm. "How 'bout I go back and get that sample for the doc?"

Kevin nodded numbly. "Sure."

"I shouldn't be long."

"Okay." He almost let him get away. "Hey, while you're at it, bring back a sample for me, will you?"

"Will do."

"Thanks."

Kevin looked down at the forms again, then from Summer to James. He was glad they were here. "I think I'll do this later. Why don't we go see Kate?"

THIRTY-THREE

Two days later, Kate was still caught in the grasp of the coma. There had been no change in her condition. She continued to respond mildly, with a small movement or a mumbled word, to stimulation, and the doctors continued to express hope. But Kevin had grown restless with playing the waiting game. He was convinced that Kate had tapped into the force behind the murders, and the key was the white clay. If he could determine the source of the clay . . .

"Still up?" James said.

Kevin looked up from the computer screen. He hadn't heard James come in, and he hadn't realized how late it had become. Through the window, the streetlights had come on, casting an eerie yellow-white glow over the neighborhood. "What time is it?"

"Almost eleven."

"Any change at the hospital?"

James shook his head. "Summer's going to stay with her overnight."

"You guys have been great. I want you to know I really appreciate it."

"No problem," James said. "Had one of the nurses ask how we were all related."

"People are curious. It's their nature."

"Told her you kidnapped us from a secret government project and we were all on the lam."

Kevin grinned. "You left out the part about the one-armed man?"

James stared at him a moment, that mock-serious expression on his face. They had talked about how they were going to present themselves as a family, and all three of the kids understood the cover story. They had been adopted, then Kevin had lost his wife, and now they were making a new start. "You were more fun when you used to be gullible."

"Me? I was never gullible."

Temporary as it was, it was a moment of release for both of them. They had had their laugh, taken their short reprieve from more serious thoughts about Kate, and Kevin thought it had probably been good for both of them.

"Oh. I almost forgot. Mr. Kaufman and his wife came by for about an hour. I think he's still feeling like it's his fault."

"What makes you think so?"

"I don't know, I guess just the way he seems so quiet when he's around her." James pulled up a chair. "What are you working on?"

"Just throwing darts in the dark. Trying to find something on the Internet."

The toxicology report on the white clay had come back with nothing notable. Not surprising. He had wanted to believe it could be something that simple, that easily explainable. But nothing seemed as black and white as things had once been in his life. Other people had handled the clay with no apparent reaction. Kate, on the other hand, had exhibited a strong response both times she had come in contact with the stuff. Of course, that could be attributable to some sort of allergic reaction. But Kevin was more inclined, under the circumstances, to believe that her reaction had been more psychic than physical.

"Having any luck?" James asked.

"Not really. Everything's too general."

"That's the Internet."

"Lots of information on commercial polymer clays, but this isn't a commercial clay we're dealing with. I spoke briefly with a guy from the police lab and he said it wasn't blended. It was pure, with a high level of alumina. That was about all he had, though."

"No idea where it might have come from?"

"Somewhere on the continent, he said. With no guarantee."

"Full of information, wasn't he?" James said. He gestured toward the computer. "Mind if I give it a try?"

Kevin didn't mind at all. He had been at it for better than four hours, since shortly after leaving the hospital around six. His eyes were tired, and the first early warnings of a headache were coming on. He stood up, gladly offered his chair, and stretched. "Have at it."

James sat down in front of the screen.

"I'm going to get something to drink. You want anything?"

"No, thanks."

There was no coffee made. He had forgotten to put on a pot after he arrived home from the hospital. So Kevin rooted around in the refrigerator and came up with some apple juice. He poured it into a glass and carried it back into the office.

"Tell me you found something."

"Don't I wish." James said without looking up. "Even I'm not that good."

Kevin sat down, rejuvenated from the short break. He didn't expect they were ever going to find any concrete answers on the Internet, but he was willing to stick with it a while longer. There was nothing to lose by poking around. And if he started feeling too tired, he supposed he could always put on that pot of coffee. Caffeine had kept him working through many a night in his time.

He took a sip of the apple juice, then placed the glass on the desk and picked up the plastic bag with the sample of white clay Kaufman had gathered from the warehouse. He held the bag up to the light. The clay was slightly off-white, but still only a shade darker than a handful of snow. Mother Nature certainly had a way with her colors. It was still moist and pliable, which was the one attribute Kevin found most fascinating. This stuff should have dried out while it sat in the open air of the warehouse overnight. Very odd.

He unzipped the bag.

"What are you doing?" James asked.

"Just looking."

"That stuff's dangerous."

"Only to Kate, apparently." He tore a small clump off and rolled it in his fingers. It was cool, with a soft gummy feeling, the way rubber cement feels after it's had a chance to dry out a bit. He offered it to James.

"No thanks."

"It won't hurt you."

"That's what you say."

Kevin laughed. He couldn't blame James; fear and distrust were vital human survival traits, but there was no reason to believe this stuff was dangerous. In the situation with Kate, the clay was the messenger. It was the message they needed to fear.

"Okay," Kevin said. He resealed the bag, tossed it on the desk, and continued to play with the bit he had torn off. Where in the hell had this stuff come from? How had it ended up at the murder scene? What relationship did it have to the creatures Summer had sensed? Questions. Questions. And more questions. Where were the damn answers?

"Check this out," James said.

"What is it?"

"Maybe nothing. Maybe something."

Kevin dropped the clump of clay on the desk and scooted forward in his chair. The room was bathed in the light of the computer screen, aided by the small, shaded desk lamp. He let his eyes adjust before reading again. "Okay. What have you got?"

"It's mostly about clay pottery. How it's been used in various cultures and societies since the beginning of time. But they talk a little about some African tribes that believed clay could actually hold the human soul."

"Didn't Summer say something about the soul?"

"I think so," James said. "What does *numinous* mean?"

"Numinous?"

"Yeah. It also mentions that some cultures believe clay contains the numinous. Is that the same as the soul?"

"No. Numinous refers to a supernatural presence."

"What? Like a demon or something?"

"A demon. A ghost. Any presence you might think of as being supernatural."

"Interesting."

"Definitely," Kevin said. "Do they mention any cultures in particular?"

"I don't think so," James said. He scrolled down the screen, skimming over half a dozen paragraphs, then farther down the screen. "Yeah, they do. A Native American tribe called the Minitu."

"That's something, at least."

"Then it talks about pots being the house of the spirit. And something about the ash effect, where a presence comes alive when the object is used."

"These are all Minitu beliefs?"

"Yeah, I think so." James scrolled up and reviewed the last paragraph. "No, I'm sorry. It all just runs together here. I think they're talking about different beliefs from around the world."

Kevin looked away from the screen, then rubbed his eyes. It was a small computer screen by today's standards, only fifteen inches. But it was also getting late, and he was tired, and the lighting in this room was rather dim. He reached for his glass of apple juice on the desk, and stopped in midcourse.

Something wasn't right. What was it?

The clay.

He had placed the clay on the desk, next to his glass, and now it was missing.

"James?"

"Yeah?"

"The clay. Did you move it?"

James took his eyes off the screen and stared down at the area next to the computer. The glass of apple juice was there, right where it was supposed to be, right next to the sealed plastic bag with the remaining clay, right next to a pencil and a spiral-bound notebook, right next to a paper clip and an old diskette.

But the little clump of clay that Kevin had torn off . . . *that* was missing. "You put it right there, didn't you?"

"I thought I did."

They both moved at the same time. Stood up, pushed back their chairs, and backed away, as if it was part of an old vaudeville comedy routine.

"Then where is it now?" James asked.

"I don't know."

"I told you that stuff was dangerous. I told you."

Kevin reached forward and took possession of the pencil. He slid the sharpened end under one corner of the plastic bag, raised it, and looked underneath.

"Anything?"

"Nope."

"This is creepy, man."

"I know."

"I don't like it."

"Neither do I." Kevin hooked the pencil through the wire spine of the notebook, raised it off the desktop, then dropped it to the floor. There was nothing underneath.

His attention turned immediately to the stack of books sitting near the edge.

"Maybe it rolled off somehow."

"It's not a marble."

"I know that, but . . . maybe . . ."

He gave the bottom book a nudge, poking the stack as if it were a dead rodent in the street and he wanted to see if it would move. Finally, the weight shifted. One after another, the books toppled off the edge of the desk. They hit the hardwood floor with a loud, repetitive *bang* that sent a jolt through him even though he'd had the presence of mind to expect the explosion of sound.

Underneath, the desk was bare.

"I'm starting to feel like an idiot." Kevin said.

Then something moved.

He caught a glimpse out of the corner of his eye.

"Right there!" James screamed. He pointed to the back right-hand corner of the computer, where one end of a large rubber band was suddenly out in the open and clearly visible. The white clump of clay had attached itself around the middle like a parasite, and the rubber band was writhing as violently as if it were a nightcrawler someone had dropped onto a hot plate. "See it?"

"I see it. I don't believe it, but I see it."

"What do we do now?"

Kevin glanced around the room. "We need something to put it in. A glass jar, a small box, a tin can, something we can use to contain it."

James rooted through one of the desk drawers and came out with a small plastic index card box. He turned it over, dumped a rainbow of colored cards onto the floor, then handed the box to Kevin.

"Is there any tape in that drawer?"

"Some Scotch tape."

"Any rubber bands?"

"Yeah, a whole box."

"Get it out."

James did as he was asked, then closed the drawer, and backed away. Kevin placed the card file near the corner of the desk. He took the pencil, slipped it through the middle of the rubber band and dropped the band into the card file. It was still squirming, wormlike as he snapped the lid closed. James handed him the box of rubber bands. He pulled out three, then double-wrapped them around the card file and stepped back as if he thought the lid might explode open at any moment. He was surprised at how hard his heart was pounding inside his chest. It felt as if someone had slugged him right above the solar plexus.

"Now what?" James asked.

"I think now might be a good time to call it a night."

They didn't talk much about what they had witnessed. It was almost too much to comprehend at one time. James stayed downstairs and watched some TV for a while (after Kevin agreed to place the card file and the plastic bag in the four-drawer filing cabinet and lock the drawer). Kevin went upstairs and got ready for bed. He read a little, from a book called *The Holographic Universe*, then gradually drifted off to sleep.

His dreams were haunted by writhing rubber bands.

THIRTY-FOUR

The man has been waiting for this day for quite some time. He has finished the miniature set, and he has finished the design and construction of the creatures. Now it is time to put them all together for a test shot. If this works the way he imagines it will, it could revolutionize the way movies are made.

He moves down the line, opening the cabinet doors. One by one, the four Protectors and then the family members jump down to the workbench, then to the floor. The man is in awe of these creatures. From the drawing board to the construction to the animation, these are his babies, his *little ones*.

"Today, he says, as they all start up the basement steps ahead of him. "We film a test shot."

THIRTY-FIVE

Daniel hated finding himself at the end of a day. Even a good day, a day when he had closed a case or when an interrogation had gone unusually well, even *those* days were like getting off the bus at the last stop and having no idea where you were. He always felt lost. His mind was always one stop back, checking out the road signs, worrying that he had missed some little thing that might have held all the answers. There was a finality about the end of a day that scared him.

He rolled over in bed and watched as Marie slipped out of her dress and hung it in the closet. She had been quiet all the way home from the hospital, as he himself had been. For his part, he was still trying to deal with the guilt of what had happened to Kate. Kevin had insisted the guilt was not only unwarranted but unhelpful.

"The kids knew what they were getting into," he had said. "They didn't do this without understanding the potential consequences."

And maybe that was so. But it didn't change the fact that Kate had ended up in the hospital. She may have had her eyes open, but she had been looking in the wrong direction. And Dan should have been able to anticipate that possibility.

Marie went into the bathroom. The water in the sink began to flow. It was the only sound in the house. For her part . . . well, he wasn't sure *why* she had been so quiet all evening. She had been shaken when she first learned what had happened to Kate. Even more shaken the first time they had gone to visit her. But she hadn't been willing to talk about it, not yet, and that was out of character.

The water went off.

Marie came out in her bathrobe. She stood at the edge of the bed, stepped out of her slippers, shed the bathrobe, then climbed under the covers. She kissed him on the cheek, a kiss that felt obligatory and meaningless, then rolled away from him as if he were a stuffed animal sharing her bed.

Dan stared at the ceiling. "Are you all right?"

"Are *you?*"

"You've been awfully quiet lately."

"So have you."

"Guess I've got a lot on my mind."

Marie rolled over. "Then share it with me, would you? Because your silence is starting to drive a wedge between us, and I don't want the distance to get any bigger."

"*My* silence?"

"You're letting it eat at you, honey. You're closing me out; you're closing Kevin out; and you're letting the guilt eat away at you like a cancer. It wasn't your fault."

"I hate seeing her in the hospital that way."

"Me. too. She looks so fragile."

"Helpless."

"Yes."

"I never should have involved her and the others."

"That's not true."

"Yes, it is. With their backgrounds? I should have thought it through."

"They needed to help. They *wanted* to help."

"They didn't know what they were dealing with."

"Neither did you."

"But I should have known better. It's my job. It's what I do. I should have known how unpredictable things were . . . how *dangerous*."

"You couldn't have known something like this was going to happen."

Dan shook his head. "The worst part is . . . I'm not even sure what *did* happen."

Marie reached out and cupped his face in her hands. "She's a strong-willed young woman. She's going to come out of this all right."

"God, I hope so."

Marie kissed the back of his hand. Sometimes he would look across the room at her, while she was reading a book or talking to a friend on the phone, and he would give a silent prayer of appreciation because she had chosen to share her life with him. God, what a lucky man he was.

"You've been waiting on me, haven't you?" he asked. "That's why you've been so quiet lately?"

"You can lead a horse to water . . ."

"Is that what I am? An old horse you have to try to coax into drinking?"

"Not old. Just stubborn."

He laughed. It was a mix of relief and discomfort, and it felt good. It was true, he could be stubborn. And he could be silent, though he had always told himself

his silence was for Marie's benefit. Maybe that hadn't
been true. Maybe it had been for his own selfish benefit. Sometimes it was easier to say nothing than to
have to talk about how much this world scared him,
how he didn't understand the ugliness, and how just
the thought of waking up and not finding her sleeping next to him was paralyzing.

Marie gave him another kiss. On the lips this time.
With meaning. They held the kiss a long time. Dan slid
his hand down her shoulders and across her breasts,
where it lingered tenderly. Marie reciprocated, sliding
her hand down below his navel and across the bare
skin just above the elastic band of his briefs. She teased
him for a moment. They kissed again.

The foreplay was leisurely, neither of them in a rush
to end it, though gradually it stretched into lovemak-
ing. The touch of their bodies together felt as perfect,
as soft and as tender as it had felt the very first time
they had made love. And the chills it sent through both
of their bodies were as life-confirming, as passionate
as Dan could imagine.

He was a lucky man.

God, what an incredibly lucky man.

THIRTY-SIX

It was approaching eleven in the morning, and Mimi Van Mears had been up less than an hour. She hung up the phone after a long conversation with a friend who happened to work at one of the better known special effects houses, then immediately took out a cigarette. Before she had a chance to find a light, the phone rang again. It was that Kevin McConnell character who had stopped by a couple of days ago.

"Sorry to bother you," he said.

"No bother. No bother at all."

"I have to apologize. I've somehow gone and misplaced the names you gave me the other day. You remember? The two people who you said worked in the special effects industry? You thought they might be worth talking to?"

"I heard about the newest attack," Mimi said. She was curious to see what sort of reaction she might get. "Garrett Davenport? Garrett Davenport Productions?"

"Where did you hear that?"

"I've got my sources."

"I hope you take caution in who you consider a source."

"Are you trying to tell me I've got my facts wrong?"

"I'm trying to suggest that you can't believe everything you hear. Especially when it revolves around such a potentially ... *public* case as this."

Mimi smiled, appreciating the cautious choice of words on Mr. McConnell's part, She found a match, lit the cigarette, and took a long slow drag. It felt good. Sometimes, she didn't feel fully alive unless she had a cigarette burning and her lungs full of smoke. "I have a friend who heard the call over the police band. He recorded it for me. I followed up on it."

"With one of your contacts from the medical examiner's office?"

"No, I went straight to the horse's mouth this time. Spoke over the phone with Davenport himself. I've got an interview in person with him tomorrow, after he's released from the hospital."

There was a pause on the other end, and she could imagine him trying to choose his words again, with even greater care this time. "Just out of curiosity, what did he have to say?"

"You'll have to wait like everyone else, until next week's issue hits the stands."

"I can do that. I just didn't want to see him lead you down the path with information that isn't accurate."

"He's the victim," Mimi said, thoroughly enjoying the banter. "What possible reason would he have for giving me false information?"

"Fifteen minutes of fame."

"Are you telling me I shouldn't trust what Mr. Davenport has to say?"

"Not at all. I'm just saying that I might be able to confirm parts of his story."

"I think I'll take my chances, if you don't mind." The

old Royal sat in front of her, thinly veiled by the cloud of smoke that hung in the air. She placed the cigarette in the ashtray, then took a drink out of her glass of bourbon, and started searching through the desk drawer for her business card file.

"It's your story."

"That it is, Mr. McConnell." She found the file, brought it out, and started to thumb through it. "As for those referrals I gave you, I'll be honest, I don't remember which ones they were. But let me give you a couple of names that you still might find useful."

"Thanks, I appreciate it."

"Of course, I expect you to give me a call if it turns out they have anything to say that might shed some light on the case."

"Of course."

Mimi smiled. "You're such a smooth liar."

"I do my best."

She pulled out the first card. Victor Koenig. Many in the business considered him one of the best. He was a gentle man, in his early sixties, who had a reputation for innovation. The second card bore the name of Creston Arnot. Arnot was an arrogant little bastard, but he knew the industry inside out and was generally at the forefront of the newest technological advances. Mimi gave both names to McConnell, along with addresses and phone numbers.

"Don't lose them this time. You only get *do overs* once."

"Do overs?"

She laughed, that throaty laugh that came from smoking a couple of packs a day for most of her life. "I don't know where the hell that came from, but you know what I mean."

THIRTY-SEVEN

Summer was slouched in a chair next to the hospital bed, her eyes fighting to remain open, when Kevin and James arrived. She perked up almost immediately, even though she looked tired.

"How's she doing?" Kevin asked.

Summer climbed guiltily out of the chair and stood next to Kate's bed. "About the same."

"And how are *you* doing?"

"About the same."

He had made arrangements to meet Victor Koenig at his home this afternoon, and he wanted Summer to come along with him for the interview. James was still a little uneasy after what had happened last night, as was Kevin himself, and Kevin didn't want to push him into anything new right a the moment. Besides, people had an easier time talking when there was a woman to help ask the questions. They seemed more comfortable, less ill at ease.

He held Kate's hand. It was difficult to look past the feeding tube and the intravenous lines, but once you were able to do that, she looked well-rested and comfortable. The hospital had already initiated a regular routine of physical therapy to reduce the stiffness in her joints and to maintain her muscle strength. She had continued to instill confidence in the doctors by issuing an occasional whispered word or two, or by opening her hands sometimes when she was touched. Kevin thought he could feel strength in her grip.

Summer combed the hair away from Kate's face. "Sometimes when I brush her hair, she raises her hand an inch or so. Like she wants me to let her do it herself."

Kevin leaned down. "Hey, Kate. The whole gang's here."

"We miss you," James said.

"I've been leaving all the dirty dishes in the kitchen sink, saving them for you." Kate was notorious for leaving her dirty dishes in the sink, something that irritated Kevin to no end. Lately, he had been increasingly ragging on her about rinsing them off and putting them in the dishwasher. Though the past few days, every time he had looked and found the sink empty, he had thought of her and it had hurt a little.

There was a slight twitch at the corner of Kate's mouth.

"She smiled," Summer said. "Did you see that? She smiled."

"I think she did," James said.

"I saw it." Kevin squeezed Kate's hand again, wanting so much for her to know that they were here, that they were rooting for her, and that her signal to them, however slight it might have seemed, had been noticed.

"That's what I mean," Summer said. "Just all of a sudden, like. She'll just do some little thing like that, and it's like you know she's in there and she can hear you."

James nodded.

The doctors had told them that they couldn't be sure exactly what Kate was hearing and not hearing, though it was common for recovered coma patients to report that they had been very much aware of the conversations going on around them while they had been away. The more stimulation, the better, the doctors seemed to think. With that in mind, the three of them huddled around Kate's bed for better than an hour, talking about everything from the warm weather to the song, "My Little Red Book," which James had found on an old Love album belonging to Kevin.

They did *not* talk about the case or what had happened at the warehouse. Nor did they talk about what had happened at home last night. Summer was still unaware of the event with the clay and the rubber band, and for the time being, Kevin thought it was probably best to keep it that way. She did not need the added stress. There was only so much weight you could add to such slight shoulders, and Kate's condition was burden enough. As far as he was concerned, the card file was securely locked away in the filing cabinet, and the clay was safely out of reach. He would dig it out again once he had decided what to do with it.

James finished up with his official proclamation that "My Little Red Book" was worthy of a listen, even if only for a few laughs.

"Your turn is coming," Kevin warned him. "Just you wait and see. It'll happen before you know it. You'll wake up one morning and your kids will be down-stairs thumbing through *your* old CDs, and they'll make *you* feel like you were born in the Triassic Period."

"I'll still be younger than you."

"If you live that long."

James grinned, a little mischievously, and was about

to say something else when a woman in her mid-thirties arrived at the door. She was a petite thing, wearing glasses and a dark-gray pleated skirt that showed below the hem of her white hospital coat. She introduced herself as Maria Santos, one of the hospital's social workers. She handed a business card to Kevin, who accepted it without thought, momentarily taken by the surprise of her sudden appearance.

"A stay at the hospital is always stressful," she said. Her hair was raven black, her eyes brown, her smile both warm and reassuring. "I'm here in the event you'd like to talk to someone. We have stress management courses, and we offer group support for the entire family if you feel it might be helpful. Anything we can do . . ."

Kevin glanced down at the card in his hands. He had never thought about counseling for the kids. Neither for all the trauma they had gone through in their early lives, nor for the grief Hunter had put them through at the Agency. He had not even thought about how it might be helpful for them to talk with someone about Kate's condition. That made for a sudden rise of guilt. It was a feeling he tried not to let show as he introduced the kids.

"Thank you. This is my son, James."

"Black face, white dad," James said with a smile. "In case you're wondering, they equal adopted."

"I was wondering," Maria said without a flinch.

"And this is Summer."

"Also adopted," Summer added.

"Nice to meet you." She turned back to Kevin. "And Kate? Is she adopted?"

"Yes."

"And is there a Mrs. McConnell?"

"She died a few years ago."

"I'm sorry." She made some notes on the clipboard she had brought in with her, then looked up, a combination of concern and hope on her face. "How's Kate doing?"

"The doctors are cautioning us, but we think she's showing signs of improvement."

"It's the little things that give us hope," she said, as if she had gone through a similar experience.

Kevin nodded, then a silence fell over the conversation. It was broken when one of the nurses, a diminutive older woman, came in to check the drip. She glanced at it without comment, then turned around and marched out much the same as she had marched in ... as if it were all so routine by now that it was simply obligatory and little else.

"I guess I should leave you to your time with Kate," Maria said, almost apologetically. "Please don't hesitate to let me know if I can do anything to help."

"I'll do that," Kevin said.

"Nice to have met you."

She walked out of the room, and Kevin watched her disappear down the long corridor before he turned back and realized how late it was becoming. Room 203 had a nice view of the parking lot, and beyond that a rather smog-tainted view of the city. But with the curtains open, the sun came through, casting a wide slant across the foot of the hospital bed that seemed to brighten the mood. Kevin glanced at the clock.

It was approaching midafternoon.

"We need to get going," he said. Then to Summer, "You want to come along?"

"What about Kate?"

"She'll be all right," James said. "I'm staying,"

Kate rarely spent a moment alone. They had stood in the hallway outside Room 203 after their first visit, and—unanimously—they had agreed that if at all possible one of them should always be with her. Summer had carried the brunt of the load so far. James had done more than his share as well. It was Kevin who had been remiss. He explained himself by arguing that he would be of more use trying to determine the cause of Kate's coma. But he knew it was a deflective argument. The truth of the matter was this: ever since Helena and Christy had died, he'd hated everything about hospitals. He hated the cool, bland colors painted in the waiting rooms. He hated the smell that got into your clothes and went home with you. He hated the hours of waiting and worrying. Most of all, though, he hated the utter helplessness he felt here.

"I'd like you to accompany me on an interview," Kevin said. "After that, I'll take you home so you can catch up on your sleep."

Summer agreed, though it was less than enthusiastically. She was tired, of course, and that could easily have accounted for it. But Kevin thought it was more likely that she simply didn't want to be away from Kate that long. The situation had not been easy on any of them, but it had been particularly hard on Summer.

THIRTY-EIGHT

Captain Savino said. "So there's no question about it?"

"None," Kaufman answered.

"That's a break, isn't it?" The Captain was a man who liked order in his life. When you looked at his bookshelves, the books were alphabetized by subject. When you looked at his in box, the stack of forms and memos and general mail never stood taller than half the height of the box. He was a man who believed in dealing with matters when they arose. Put things off, and they're always milling around, waiting for you. Face them head on, and you put them behind you, fading in the rearview mirror. But he was also a pragmatic and patient man.

"'Definitely," Kaufman said. He'd had an opportunity to interview Davenport yesterday afternoon for the first time. The man was scheduled for release tomorrow. The doctors had insisted on keeping him an extra day in light of the animal bites and the potential for rabies. They had started administering the vaccine the first day and the injections were scheduled to continue for several more weeks. Though, as Kaufman was surprised to learn, the injections were no longer administered into the stomach, making the process much easier on the patient.

Davenport had told him plenty. He had survived something normally reserved for the movies and he was almost giddy with the chance to tell everything he had seen. There had been four of them, he had said. *Them*, in this case, referred to some sort of small reptilian creatures that walked on two legs and looked a good deal uglier than any rodent Davenport had ever seen in his life. He gave Kaufman a thorough description, which was remarkably similar to what Summer had claimed to perceive. But better than that, Davenport had been able to draw him a picture of one of the creatures.

"Looks like something out of a science fiction movie," Kaufman had said when he had first held it in his hands. It bothered him that Davenport, who worked in the movie business, had come up with something that seemed so perfectly suited to his profession. It wasn't that he didn't believe him. He had no reason to suspect Davenport would lie. It was just that sometimes victims could fill in the blanks in a quite innocent effort to make everything fit properly in their own minds. Kaufman wanted to feel confident that the blanks in Davenport's memory were not giving way to his own imagination. He hoped, once Summer had seen the drawing, that she might be able to confirm its accuracy.

But aside from the drawing, Kaufman was pleased to have the other details. He now knew that Davenport had, in fact, left the door to the warehouse unlocked. That meant the creatures hadn't found entrance through the use of a key or some other means that would imply they were closely connected to the business. He knew that Davenport had never seen these creatures before, and that he had no idea about why they had targeted him in particular. He knew he was dealing with more than one creature, and that the creatures were acting in concert. That seemed to imply a degree of intelligence. It might also imply the existence of some sort of community where these things gathered. He knew that the creatures could be hurt. Not only had Davenport felt he had hurt one of them, he was sure that the splattered white clay was the result of the damage he'd done.

Kaufman also knew that if he told the Captain any of this or showed him the drawing Davenport had done, his days on the case would be numbered. Generally, Savino was willing to go out on a limb for the men in his department, but he wasn't foolish enough to go out on a limb that was conspicuously cracked. This case had a crack in it you could see from a mile away. If word ever got out Kaufman was seriously considering mysterious little creatures as the perps, all hell would break loose. No, at this point in the investigation, it was smart to stick to the animal theory. No foul. No harm. Everybody's happy.

"We got off lucky," Kaufman said. "Davenport survived. And as soon as I have a chance to talk with him we should have a much better idea of what we're up against here."

"You haven't talked to him yet?"

"Only briefly," Kaufman lied. "He's still a little rattled."

"I want to hear about it when he talks. I want to know what he has to say." The Captain picked up the phone, effectively announcing the end of their conversation, then glanced up as Kaufman climbed out of the chair. "No leaks this time?"

"I think I've effectively plugged that hole."

"Glad to hear it." He nodded again, to put a punctuation mark at the end of their conversation, then went about dialing the phone number.

Kaufman returned to his desk. He had received information from one of the management types at Magic Wizard Effects about an employee who had recently been fired. Apparently, the man was more of a traditionalist, schooled in the art of stop-motion animation. His name was Lyle Henderson. He had been with the company a little more than four years, but recently they had grown tired of his constant grumbling about modem computer technology and what he termed as the lost "art of the soul." They had fired him nearly six months ago. From what management had told Kaufman, Henderson did not go gently into the night. Instead, he had gone vowing to exact revenge.

A visit with Henderson was definitely warranted.

THIRTY-NINE

Victor Koenig was a soft-spoken man, short in stature, a few years older than Kevin had expected after talking with him over the phone. He walked slightly hunched over as he escorted Kevin and Summer through the house to the living room.

"Please, sit down, be comfortable. Can I get you something? Water? A soft drink?"

"Nothing. Thank you."

"So," he said, sitting across from them in a recliner covered in a wool, knitted afghan. The room was small. The curtains at Koenig's back were open, inviting in the bright afternoon sun. "How did you say you came to call on me?"

"Mimi Van Mears gave us your name. She said you were the person to talk to if we had any questions about the effects business."

He grinned humbly. "Mimi is a very unique individual, isn't she? That was most generous of her to say. I don't know how true it is, I'm not really in the business these days, but it is most kind of her."

"What are you doing these days?" Kevin asked.

"Relaxing," Victor said. "I'm retired now. It's a business for younger men than myself. The changes these past few years . . . it's remarkable what they can do on the screen. Over my head, I'm afraid. Too far over my head."

"Computer enhancement and all that?"

"Oh, it's more than simple enhancement. Let me assure you of that. Take a movie like *Dragonheart* . . . did you see that? The dragon is completely designed and manipulated on the computer. They program in all this information and pretty soon they've got what they call a wire-frame, three-dimensional dragon. Then they give it muscles. Then they add the skin. Then they tell it how to move. These things . . . we did all these things by hand in my time."

"Stop-motion animation?" Kevin asked.

Victor Koenig's face brightened. "Yes. You're familiar with it?"

"*King Kong*, 1933. Willis O'Brien did the effects. My father took me to a special showing when I was ten."

"I studied under Willis O'Brien. A true master of his craft. Very precise and patient. If stop motion demands anything of a man, it demands precision and patience." To Summer, he said, "You've seen *King Kong*, too?"

"No, I'm sorry."

"There's no need to be sorry. Not many people have seen the original. And not many would appreciate the craft that went into it if they had."

"So your specialty was stop motion?" Kevin asked.

"Well, I am also a patient man. Twenty-four frames a second. You snap the picture. Click. Then you move an arm or a leg or whatever. Then click. And you do it all again. Twenty-four times for one second of what you see up on the screen. Very precise. Very demanding."

"You designed the puppets as well?"

"Yes, of course. You were expected to do everything in those days. I would sketch a design, then handcraft the armatures for the puppet's joints so they could be positioned in nearly any manner I desired. That was how the puppets moved so seamlessly. And then . . . well, then you had the clay sculpture, and the cast, and the painting of the skin. It was all very detailed work. It could be quite rewarding when you saw it for the first time up on the screen."

"And you did it all yourself?"

"From beginning to end."

Summer said, "I saw *Jason and the Argonauts* on TV once. With those skeletons? Is that what you do? Make things like those skeletons?"

"That's exactly what I do. Though it was a gentleman by the name of Ray Harryhausen who made those particular skeletons."

"They were great."

"Mr. Harryhausen learned from Willis O'Brien, also."

"What about some of your movies?"

"Let's see . . . did you ever see *Prehistoric World*? 1957? Or *Attack of the Red Ants*? 1961? Or *The Star Creatures*? 1964?"

"Science fiction, right? About these aliens that look like starfish? They start showing up on the beaches all around the world, and kids are taking them home for pets?"

"You did see it."

"Definitely fun," Summer said.

"Good. Good. I'm happy to hear that. You made an old man's day."

"You're not old."

"Tell that to my aching joints every morning." He laughed gently. "So here you are, and you still haven't told me how I can help you."

"Do they still use stop motion?" Kevin asked.

"Well, not so much anymore. Not so much with all the computers they have now. They started using *go motion*, which was, I suppose you could say, a sort of bridge between stop motion and computer animation. In fact, Harryhausen's stop-motion classic *Clash of the Titans* was released the same year as *Dragonslayer*, which was the first film using go motion. That was 1981, I believe."

"Oh. then it's been a while?"

"Since stop motion was used in its purest form? Yes. A long while, I'd say."

"So someone such as yourself, you not only moved the puppets and snapped the frames. you did all the design work yourself? The modeling and everything?"

"Yes," Koenig said quietly. "As I mentioned, it was a craft."

"It showed on the screen," Kevin said. "There was another movie I remember as a kid. *20 Million Miles to Earth*? With this alien, dinosaur type creature that starts out as an egg, then hatches and grows into adulthood?"

"That was Harryhausen's work. 1957."

"A great movie."

"Yes. Yes, it was."

Kevin nodded, reminiscently. He had intended to ask about *Mighty Joe Young*, because he had heard that a remake had recently been released, but instead he became aware of the plastic bag in his pocket and was reminded why he was here. He pulled the bag free and held it up. "I almost forgot. I was wondering if you might know of anyone in the business who has ever used this stuff on their puppets?"

Koenig held it in two hands, turning it over several times. "For modeling? White clay? No. No. This is not something you would use for sculpting a model. This looks as if it's right out of the ground."

"So you've never seen this type of clay in use before?"

"No. You need a good blended clay. A commercial clay."

"Then this wouldn't work for modeling?"

Koenig squeezed the bag, leaving a deep impression in the sample. "It might. Good texture. Good moisture content. Probably a kaolin clay, which means it was found in the place in the earth where it was formed. Who knows? It might work. I've never seen anyone use something quite so unusual, though. I would imagine it would be difficult to find. Commercial clays . . . you can order them from any art supply house in the country. But this material . . ."

He shrugged, wearing an expression of apology, and handed it back. "I could show you what I use?"

"Would you mind?" Kevin asked.

"No. No. Not at all." He climbed out of his chair. "Come."

They went through a short hallway into a huge, open room that you might not have even noticed from the front of the house. The ceilings were twelve feet high. The floor was covered in linoleum instead of carpet. There were no windows. Koenig flipped on a light switch. The wall at their backs was decorated with posters and movie props. There was an original poster of *Frankenstein, the Man Who Made a Monster*. Another of *Attack of the 50 Ft. Woman*. A model of the spacecraft used in *The War of the Worlds*. One of the swords from *Jason and the Argonauts*.

Koenig directed them to the other side of the room, where a floor-to-ceiling cabinet stood against the wall. He opened the nearest double doors, and with an effort, pulled down a twenty-five-pound block of brown clay.

"This is Wed clay," he said. "Very popular in the business these days. When you work it, you have to keep it moist with a spray bottle. It's water-based. Dries slowly. But it smooths out very nicely. Cleans out of the molds with little trouble."

"The standard for the industry?" Kevin asked.

"You could say that, I suppose."

"On another note, I was wondering if you had ever met Henry Richards at Magic Wizard Effects?"

Koenig shook his head. "I know of the company, yes. But a Henry Richards . . . I don't recall that name."

"How about Garrett Davenport?"

"Is he with Magic Wizard as well?"

"No, he runs his own effects company."

"No, I'm sorry. I don't know either of these names."

Kevin glanced at Summer to let her know he was ready to wrap things up and to see if she had any last questions she wanted to ask. Her response was a blank stare, rather faraway and dreamy. Her long night at the hospital was finally catching up with her. She needed to get home to bed.

He thanked Koenig for his time and apologized for their intrusion. Not much had come from the meeting, though Kevin had definitely enjoyed reminiscing about *King Kong* and some of the other classic movies that had made his childhood an imaginative wonderland. No matter how old you grew, there was something magical about the movies. They could take you anywhere in the imagination, to any time in all of history, make you laugh, make you cry, make you sit up and pay attention. Kevin considered himself fortunate to have had an opportunity to speak with one of the great talents in stop-motion animation.

FORTY

The phone was ringing as they came through the door. Kevin tossed the keys on the table and picked up the receiver with Summer only a few steps behind him. The exhaustion was finally catching up with her. She had drifted in and out of a nap during the ride home after the visit with Victor Koenig.

"He's cute," she had said about Koenig.

"He's older than me."

"So? You're cute, too."

Ill at ease with that surprising response, Kevin changed the subject. "Besides being cute, what did you think of him?"

"I liked him."

"Any impressions?"

"Like what?"

"Like anything."

"He's lonely."

"What makes you think that?"

"Wouldn't you be?"

Summer had closed her eyes and settled back into the seat. Sometimes she was a little girl; sometimes she was a wise, perceptive woman.

Loneliness was not a stranger to Kevin. It had vis-

ited often after Helena and Christy had died. There
was still an emptiness inside him where it came to re-
side on those nights when he woke up out of a bad
dream and found himself alone. Yes, in response to
Summer's question. He would also be lonely.

Summer pointed toward the doorway now and
mumbled the words: *I'm going up to bed.*

Kevin nodded.

It was Kaufman on the phone. "Thought you might
like to come along. I just got an interview set up with
a guy by the name of Henderson. Apparently, he was
fired from Magic Wizard a few months back. He was
not a gracious ex-employee."

"When?"

"Tonight. Around seven."

Kevin said that sounded fine. He needed to talk to
James, though, to make sure it was okay with him.
Kevin was thinking of taking the shift tonight and giving Summer a break. In fact, both of the kid probably
needed some time away from that hospital.

"We talked with Victor Koenig this afternoon,"
Kevin said.

"Who's he?"

"An old effects master. Mimi gave me his name."

"Mimi? What did you think of her?"

Kevin laughed. "I don't know. She has a certain
charm, I suppose. She smokes too much. Drinks too
much. But I did enjoy talking to her. I got the impression she's someone who got dealt a bad hand, but she'd
prefer to forget about it."

"And what about this other guy?"

"Koenig? Nothing new. I showed him a sample of
the clay."

"And he's never seen it used in the business."

"Right."

"Well, someone's using it."

Kevin paused and let himself think about what he wanted to say next. Up to this point, he had managed to avoid saying anything about what he and James had witnessed last night. But it felt a little like not telling your father about the dent in the rear panel of the family car. Sooner or later, he was going to notice, and then what?

"What do you think we're really dealing with here?" Kevin asked. "Your gut feeling?"

"Truthfully? I feel like we've stepped into an episode of *The X-Files*. I don't know what we're dealing with, but I'm willing to bet it's something I haven't dealt with before." Kaufman paused, then added, "Not much help, am I? I wish I could make the leap from some lunatic with a knife and a big bite mark to a team of little alien creatures out for revenge. It's just so . . ."

"Unbelievable?"

"Yeah. That's as good a word as there is, I suppose."

"I'm afraid I've got something else to toss into the stew."

"Do I want to hear this?"

"The sample of the clay I took home . . ."

"Yeah?"

"I saw it wrap itself around a rubber band. James was there, too. We both saw it."

"What do you mean? Like it was alive?"

Kevin had refrained from using that word for a very good reason. He did not want to grant that much of the life force to something as inanimate as clay. Things were not always what they appeared to be. Sometimes a person could misinterpret what he saw. Sometimes personal beliefs could get in the way. You had to be

careful not to make leaps of faith, to let your assump-
tions go unchallenged. Having considered all this, he
went on to describe exactly what had happened, as he
remembered it, doing his best not to use any words
that might be misrepresentative.

"Christ," Kaufman said when he was finished.

"We don't know what it means yet. I haven't had a
chance to take a closer look at it."

"Wouldn't the lab have come up with something if
this was living matter?"

"They should."

Kaufman was quiet for a moment. "What does this
mean exactly?"

"I don't know yet."

"Could the clay be the thing that's giving life to
these creatures?"

"Possibly. Or it could be a component of their structures, their flesh or their blood or something vital to
the very nature of their genetic makeup. We just don't
know at this point."

Kevin leaned back against the wall. He wondered
if the clay's silicone content might have somehow reacted to being in close proximity of the computer. He
wondered if maybe there had been a magnetic field
surrounding the clay that might have interacted with
the electrical current running through the walls. He
wondered if there might have been some sort of chemical reaction between the clay and the rubber band.
These were all stretches of the imagination, of course.
Hypothetical shots in the dark. But there was no question in his mind they were preferable to the alternative.

FORTY-ONE

If you can't find the needle in the haystack, then you figure out a way for the needle to find you. Samuel Hunter believed that was precisely what he had done.

Walking away from your life was not as easy as most people imagined. Even if you had the smarts and the connections to make it happen, there was still a strong psychological consequence to completely giving up your past. Taking on another identity and abandoning your previous life required incredible self-discipline. You had to be willing to walk away from all the relationships of your life. Your parents. Your sisters and brothers, uncles and cousins. Sometimes even your wife and children.

Most of these relationships did not apply to Hastings. There were no siblings. His parents were both dead. His wife and daughter had died in an automobile accident. But there was one relationship that he still held in high regard, and that was his relationship with his mother-in-law, Ivy Hough.

Shortly after Hastings' disappearance, Hunter had put a tap on the phone lines at the small westside apartment where Ivy lived. Nearly a month passed before Hastings finally made the first call. He was not a stupid man. He knew Hunter would be listening. With that in mind, he routed the call through a dozen different countries so it couldn't be traced. Hastings had done the same with all his subsequent calls as well, and at the end of his last conversation with Ivy, after he had said good-bye, he had added, "And my best to you, Hunter. Hope you're sleeping better these days."

Last night, Hunter had never slept better. It had occurred to him that he had been using his bait all wrong. Instead of using Ivy as a way of leading him to Hastings, he had decided to use her as a way of bringing Hastings to him. This morning, he had made arrangements to move Ms. Ivy Hough out of her apartment and into a safe house, where her personal care could be watched more closely.

The next move belonged to Hastings.

FORTY-TWO

Lyle Henderson was a fast-talking, bitter man to whom Kaufman took an immediate dislike. Being a cop, by its very nature, forced him into contact with all sorts of people he would otherwise have never met. Some of them, Kaufman liked enormously, despite the fact that they were guilty of some truly atrocious crimes. Others, he hated with a passion, even though they had never done anything wrong in their lives. And for still others, it all lined up perfectly: he couldn't stand them or their despicable crimes. It was too early to tell where Henderson was going to fit into this spectrum of possibilities, but he already had one foot firmly planted on Kaufman's bad side.

"I haven't done anything," Henderson said as he blocked the doorway of his house. He was tall, over six feet, hadn't shaved in a week (though the gray stubble nearly blended into the man's pale complexion unnoticed) and hadn't showered in nearly as long. "What do you want?"

"We'd like to talk with you about your recent firing from Wizard Effects."

"Recent? That was better than six months ago. Besides, when was it made a crime to get fired from a job?"

"Actually, Mr. Henderson, we're investigating a murder. Could we come in?"

He glanced over his shoulder, back into the house. "The place is a mess."

"We promise not to call *House & Garden*," Kaufman said.

He opened the door and waved them in, clearly not happy to be doing so. "Straight ahead. First room to your left. Just toss the papers on the floor."

The sofa was covered with old newspapers. Kaufman noticed the headline of the *L.A. Times*, an issue from several weeks back: MAN KILLED IN SAVAGE ATTACK. It was a story about Henry Richards' death. One of Henderson's previous coworkers.

"You like to save your old papers for recycling or something?" Kaufman dropped them in a stack next to the sofa, then added a pile Kevin had passed him.

"I use them for papier-mâché molds when I get low on materials. It's the life of the unemployed."

"Still haven't found a job?"

"The way of the dinosaurs, man. I'm extinct."

"Meaning what?"

"Meaning there isn't any room left for someone like me. Everything is computer graphics these days. High-tech animation. It's not a craft anymore; it's an assembly line. How big can you make the explosion, and how fast can you do it. The back end is all that matters." Henderson leaned against the television set, his arms crossed, his eyes darting between Kaufman and the sliding glass doors that opened into the backyard. "Me, I'm obsolete. Fifty-eight and all washed up. Nobody wants a guy who's not a whiz on a computer."

"The way I understand it, it was as much your attitude as anything else that got you fired."

"This is about Richards, isn't it? You guys think I went back and *offed* the guy. That's nuts. If I was going to off someone, it wouldn't be Richards. He was just another grunt, man. An ignorant little monkey who learned to jump through their hoops for bananas. No, if I was going to go after someone, it wouldn't be Richards. I'd go after one of the big guys. Archer. Or maybe McGuinnis. One of the guys at the top. Those are the fuckers who don't have a clue about which end of the film goes first."

"You know when he was killed?"

"Richards? Yeah. I read about it in the papers."

"Where were you that night, Mr. Henderson?"

He motioned to the surroundings, and scoffed. "Where do you think? Right here. Paradise in a box."

"Can anyone confirm that?"

"Sorry, I slept alone that night. Me and the missus broke up a couple of years ago. I don't get as lucky as I did when I was in my twenties. What else you want to know? What I wore to bed?"

"You still creating models?" Kevin asked.

"Yeah, sure. It's what I do."

"Ever use white clay?"

"For sculpting models? No. Never heard of anyone else using white clay either. You see guys using an oil-based clay sometimes. Something like a Roma Plastilina. But most of the guys who know what they're doing use Wed clay. It's water-based. Dries real slow. Real easy to work with."

"Where do you work?"

"In the basement. I've got a nice little setup down

there. All my tools, my supplies, my work away from work."

"Can we see it?"

"Do you have a warrant?"

"We can get one."

Henderson laughed. "You do that. You go on down to the judge and convince him you need a warrant so you can see what's in my basement. And when he asks you what you've got and you tell him that I was fired from Wizard Effects a while back and now you've got a dead body, do me a favor and time how long it takes before he stops laughing. Because he's going to know, right off the bat, what I already know—that this is all a big joke."

"You think it's funny Richards is dead?"

"No. I think it's funny you're trying to pin his death on me." He stood up and motioned toward the doorway like a ground operator trying to direct a 727 into its dock at the airport. "The interview's over, guys. Time for you to go."

"I've just got a couple more questions," Kaufman said.

"And I've run out of answers. You know where the door is. Use it."

FORTY-THREE

Kaufman and Kevin climbed into the car.

Kevin glanced at Henderson's house. "So what do you think?"

"I think I'm going to run him through the computer and see if anything turns up."

"What about a warrant?"

"He's right. I'd never get it past a judge."

"You think he's involved?"

"God, I hope so. I'd love to slam the door on that skinny little ass of his."

Kevin laughed. "But only if he's guilty, right?"

"If he's guilty, I'll slam it a little harder."

FORTY-FOUR

Mimi was in good spirits when she called. At first, Kevin thought she had been hitting the bourbon a little early, but it wasn't long before he realized the source of her giddiness was something else altogether. "Guess who I spoke to this morning?"

"Who?"

"One Garrett Marshal Davenport. He of the latest attack."

Kevin sat down in the nearest chair. He closed his eyes. This was something he really did not want to have to deal with. "How is he?"

"Sore," she said. "The doctors said he had two very severe animal bites. He'll be receiving rabies shots for several weeks to come."

"He's back home, right?"

"Being spoiled rotten by his wife, Debbie."

"He earned it."

"So how would you like me to write this up? My guess is El Chupacabras."

"Why are you asking me?"

"Because I'm not a complete idiot, Mr. McConnell."

"Which means?"

"Which means I checked you out. I'm not sure who

the hell you are, but you're no private eye, and you aren't working for the Richards family."

"You don't miss much, do you?"

"So who are you helping out? Someone in the department?"

"If I say yes, will we still be friends?"

She laughed. "Only because I like you."

Kevin thought about it a moment, deciding there wasn't much to lose at this stage of the game. "Okay, let me tell you what I can. You're right. I'm working with a friend of mine, off the record, on the side. And, yes, he works for the department. But he's a good cop. He just wants to get this thing solved before anyone else gets hurt."

On the other end of the line, Mimi took a long drag off her cigarette. She let the smoke out slowly, running out the suspense, he suspected. "So how would you like me to write this up?"

"You said he was receiving rabies shots."

"You're kidding, right? You want me to call it a dog attack? Have you talked to Davenport? This wasn't any domesticated animal that went after him. These things walk on two legs, for Christ's sake." He listened to her take another long drag off her cigarette. "Just so you should know . . . this is one incredible story. But if you want, I can slant it for you."

"Is that why you called, Mimi?"

"I called because I thought between you and me, we could work out a little arrangement."

"And what kind of little arrangement did you have in mind?"

"I could go ahead and write the story, using what Davenport gave me. Or I could slant it toward our monster of the month, El Chupacabra."

"What on earth is an El Chupacabra?"

"The goatsucker of Latin America. It's suppose to be some sort of cross between a kangaroo and a gargoyle and heaven only knows what else. Very big news in New Mexico and across the south lately."

"It walks on two legs?"

"That's what they say."

"Is this an *Insider* regular? Like Bigfoot and alien babies?"

Mimi laughed. "See? I knew it. I knew you read the tabloids."

"Only the *Insider*," Kevin said. "And only your column."

"You little flatterer."

He grinned. "You're trying to do the right thing, aren't you, Mimi?"

"We tabloid writers aren't as heartless as we're made out to be. Besides, it's not purely humanitarian. There is a catch."

"Which is?"

"I want the inside exclusive when the case is solved. I'll slant my story at El Chupacabra and focus it solely on Davenport. Nothing about how the attack ties in with the others. That should buy your friend in the department a little extra breathing room, and it should make my editor happy, since he's a big fan of El Chupacabra."

"I'll have to clear it."

"You do that."

Kevin grinned. "So why all the generosity?"

"Please don't put it that way. And please keep this to yourself. You'll ruin my hard-earned reputation as the Queen of Sleaze."

"My lips are sealed."

"You're good people, McConnell."

"So are you, Mimi."

"Now, solve the damn case and get me my exclusive."

FORTY-FIVE

Kevin hung up the phone and smiled. They had caught a lucky break. Kaufman had been concerned that the press might jump on Davenport's story and start a feeding frenzy. If that had happened, Kaufman would have had Captain Savino on one side and the press on the other. The case would have become overwhelmed by all the pressures. But the mainstream press had concluded that Davenport was either a nut case or the perpetrator of a wild hoax, and had totally ignored the incident. And now Mimi had come through with her own little surprise.

Yep, a lucky break.

Kevin got a glass from the cupboard, filled it with water out of the tap, and carried it with him into the office. He flipped on the computer, then sat down. As the computer booted and the operating system loaded, he stared at the filing cabinet. The cabinet had remained locked since he had buried the rubber band at the back of one of the drawers. It had remained that way because Kevin was uneasy about opening it. Originally, he had been convinced that it had been her psychic abilities that had sent Kate into her coma. Her psychic abilities teamed with whatever power was behind the white clay, plus the fact that she had hit her head. The only thing he was sure of now, though, was that the clay was dangerous.

It was also the key to the case.

He heard the opening wav file play on the computer as he stood up and unlocked the cabinet. He took out the file box, placed it on the desk, then sat down and stared at it. The box was made of plastic. It was black. The three rubber bands were still wrapped securely around the outside.

One by one, Kevin removed the rubber bands.

He flipped the latch, then raised the lid. Inside, the rubber band lay dormant in the corner. The white clay had attached itself to the inside of the box near the back, something Kevin had, for some reason, never even considered as a possibility.

He closed the lid, then placed the box on top of the filing cabinet.

It had occurred to him that the clay might actually be discriminating. That it might be able to participate in a process of preferences and choices. Following that train of thought, other questions began to come to mind. Was it possible that it could serve as a fundamental building block of the creatures' makeup? Were the creatures actually inanimate without the clay, the same way the rubber band was inanimate? And had the clay attached itself to the creatures the way it had attached itself to the rubber band? Or had the creatures sought out the substance as something necessary for their existence? And was it possible that the clay itself was inanimate? Possessed by an even more elemental organism?

No, he thought to this last question. If that were true, then the organism most likely would abandon the clay the way the clay had abandoned the rubber band. No, the clay itself was quite capable of changing its host. It was similar to a parasite in that manner. Though it did not appear to draw anything from its host, the way a leech draws blood. Instead, it seemed to function more similarly to a hermit crab, merely borrowing a convenient shell for its own use.

Kevin cleared an area of the desk. On one side, he lined up a handful of items from around the office: a paper clip, a glass paperweight, a leaf off the spider planet that sat on top of the filing cabinet, an art gum eraser, and a bottle of Wite-Out.

He opened the file box, then set it on its side across from the line of items.

He sat back, took a drink from his glass of water, set the glass aside, then waited.

It wasn't long before the clay emerged.

The sight of it snailing its way over the black plastic lid and onto the desk sent a chill through him. He had never witnessed anything quite like this before. This was inanimate matter, lifeless, mindless matter that was moving with purpose from one place to another. He watched, fascinated, as his mind raced through—and rejected—one rational explanation after another. This was not possible within the realm of his personal experience, nor the extent of his acquired knowledge. This was . . .

What?

Preternatural?

Displaying an absence of interest in the leaf of the spider plant, the clay moved past the organic material, then climbed the side of the art gum eraser where it finally came to a rest again.

That answered at least one of his questions.

The eraser began to quake.

That answered another one.

He picked up the paperweight, the Wite-Out, and the paper clip, and put them aside. In their places, he tore three more leaves off the spider plant. Then he did something that would strike him as extremely careless, looking back on it later. He peeled the clay off the art gum eraser and dropped it back into the file box.

The art gum eraser went into his pocket.

In its place, he substituted a pencil.

He sat back and waited.

Again, the clay snailed its way out of the plastic file box. It passed over the first leaf, then the second, and as Kevin had suspected it would, it attached itself to the pencil.

Whatever force or power was contained within the clay, it was primarily attracted to inanimate matter. A living host was not of interest.

Kevin carried the pencil, clay and all, out to the kitchen. One-handed, he fished a plastic freezer bag out of one of the drawers, then dropped the pencil into the bag and sealed it. He carried the bag back into the office, tossed it back into the filing cabinet, then locked the cabinet drawer.

It was time to call Kaufman.

FORTY-SIX

Kevin caught him at his desk.

"Has the lab been able to tell you anything else about the clay?"

"Nothing worthwhile. I talked to them this morning," Kaufman said. "The basic makeup of the stuff is hydrated silicates of aluminum. Toxic if it's mishandled over an extended period of time, but otherwise hardly notable."

"Nothing else?"

"Why? What were you hoping for?"

"I don't know. Something that might explain its properties, I suppose."

"No signs of living matter, if that's what you're asking."

"Actually, I think this stuff is drawn to inanimate matter," Kevin said. He explained what he had done and how the clay had reacted and what he had gathered from that, however unscientific the observation. "There's some sort of power or life force within the clay. Something within its basic structure. If we can determine what that source is, then maybe we can understand the basic workings of this stuff and how it influences the objects it comes into contact with."

"If it's only attracted to inanimate matter . . . how does that explain the creatures that Davenport encountered?"

"It's conceivable that the creatures themselves are inanimate."

There was a long pause that seemed to expand the distance between them. Kevin knew that what he was saying sounded a bit like science fiction, but it made an odd sort of sense under the circumstances.

"You're saying without the clay the creatures would be lifeless?"

"Possibly."

"Like puppets without string?"

"More like bodies without a soul or a heart."

"Then where did the creatures come from?"

"I don't know. If I had to hazard a guess, I suppose the first thing I'd consider is where we live. This is Hollywood, after all. Land of make believe. You can bring extinct dinosaurs back to life, or sit in a bar next to alien beings from other planets. And it all appears perfectly real."

"Movie monsters?"

"Makes sense, doesn't it? All the victims worked in the business."

"What's the motive?"

"I don't know. Revenge maybe?"

"You know, I still haven't found anything that connects all the victims. Besides their profession, I mean. Beyond that, and a couple of them meeting briefly at a convention and a couple of the others working on the same movie, there's nothing. These guys may have known each other only by reputation, and maybe not even by that. Richards was a computer whiz kid, but outside of Magic Wizard, I haven't found anyone who knew him by his reputation. Davenport is a little better known, but not much. These guys aren't the Stan Winstons or the Rick Bakers or the Tom Savinis of their profession. They're good, but not that good."

"Motive's your department," Kevin said evenly.

"Thanks."

"I've got one more name that Mimi gave me to follow up on, and I'm thinking of talking to an anthropologist when I get a chance. Maybe someone who specializes in Native American cultures. It's probably a toss of the dice, but I thought we might be able to find something about clay in the mythology."

"What brought that to mind?"

"James and I did some poking around on the Internet and found a few things on clay pottery in African lore. There was also a mention of a Native American tribe in Northern California that believes white clay can contain the spirit or the soul. I figure it's worth a toss."

"I checked out Henderson," Kaufman said.

"Anything?"

"Not much. He's got a temper, apparently. He's been picked up a couple of times for bar fights, the last time about ten years ago. The rest is just petty stuff. Public drunkenness. One D.U.I. Threatening an officer."

"Sounds like a real prick."

"Well, we pretty much knew that after we met him. It would have been nice to have found something more on him, but basically, I think you called it. He's a prick, and that's about all he is."

"Too bad."

"Something else will come along."

"I just hope it comes along before anyone else gets hurt," Kevin said.

"Me, too," Kaufman said quietly. "Me, too."

FORTY-SEVEN

The black file box was open.

James found it on the kitchen table, on its side, waiting for him. Nothing else existed beyond the chairs and the table and that little plastic box. A consuming blackness hovered around the edges like the faceless bystanders that gather around an accident. A white light sharply framed the scene, dust particles floating in the air, a fine line dividing black and white.

He sat at the table, then placed his arm across the cool surface, palm up, offering it for sacrifice.

White clay emerged from the file box.

It moved like a caterpillar, spinelike striations rolling down its form, front to back, front to back, continuously. Down the open lid. Across the surface of the table. Onto his upturned index finger.

There was no pain.

He had been anticipating pain—great pain, in fact—the kind of agony that comes from the death of the soul as he imagined it.

But there was no pain.

The white clay climbed onto his index finger, then moved along the crevice between the two fingers until it climbed the last hurdle onto his palm. James watched unemotionally, with a strange detachment, as it made this journey, but now he was suddenly alarmed. The clay had left a trail across was his fingers and the palm of his hand which had bleached all the pigmentation out of his skin. It was as if vitiligo had eaten away at him . . . eaten away at his blackness . . . turning him white right before his eyes . . . white, then whiter . . . even albino . . . not a black man anymore but an albino . . . not a black man but . . .

but . . .

James opened his eyes.

For a moment, he was still lost. The lights were turned down. It was night outside. Through the window, the landscape of city lights glittered brightly, familiarly. Then he noticed Summer, asleep in the chair across from him. And he noticed Kate, lying motionless in the hospital bed.

He looked down at his hand, turned it palm up, and studied it closely.

As black as the night.

Oh, my Lord, thank you.

It had been a nightmare. That's all. Just a stupid little nightmare.

James stood up and stretched. There wasn't a muscle in his body that wasn't sore, but it was his neck that seemed to bring him the greatest discomfort. He rolled his head on his shoulders, loosening the muscles, then went to stand next to Kate.

He had been sixteen and spending his first semester away at college, only a few days away from going home for the Christmas break, when the fire had broken out at his parents' house. His father, who had been trapped in the upstairs office, had died on the scene, but the firemen had managed to rescue his mother.

Third-degree burns covered nearly eighty percent of her body and she was holding on for dear life by the time James had made the trip home from college and had arrived at the hospital. She never recovered consciousness. In fact, he had stood by her bedside, holding her hand, for only a few moments before she finally passed away. It was as if she had waited for him, and with his arrival she had finally allowed herself to be set free.

That wasn't going to happen to Kate.

He wasn't going to let it.

He held her hand, coldly aware of the lack of response. "Hey, Kate. I know it's the middle of the night and you're probably off checking out the cosmos, but I'm right here, holding onto your hand. How about a little squeeze for me? Just something to let me know you're paying attention?"

"I don't think she is," Summer said.

James turned around, momentarily startled. Summer had fallen asleep with a blue hospital blanket in her lap. She dropped it on the floor and stood up. He continued to be impressed with how dedicated she had become in her vigil.

"Sorry, I didn't mean to wake you," he said.

"You didn't. I was already awake."

"Oh."

"So, did she squeeze your hand?"

"No."

Summer came over and stood next to him. It was difficult to look at Kate without thinking of her smile, her sometimes vulnerability. She lay on her back, her head slightly tilted to the right. The gentle curls had gone out of her reddish-brown hair. Her mouth was open; it was always open. The fingers on both hands curled toward fists. She had never looked more vulnerable.

"I think she's getting worse," Summer said. "She won't squeeze your hand anymore. She won't smile. It's like she's given up."

"The doctor doesn't seem worried."

"The doctor stops by for five minutes once or twice a day. He doesn't have a clue."

"You really think she's getting worse?"

"Yes," she said, troubled.

He didn't like the way she said it, and he didn't like the idea that she might be right. Kate had not been responding the same as she had even as recently as two days ago. James had noticed it, too. But he had chosen to believe it wasn't so much a step back as just a temporary plateau in her climb toward a full recovery.

Summer picked up a brush off the bedside table. There were no tears in her eyes as she began to brush the hair away from Kate's face, but there were tears in her voice when she spoke. "I like her. I don't want her to die."

James put his arm around her shoulders. "She's not going to die. Don't even think that way."

"I can't help it. It just feels like she's drifting away."

FORTY-EIGHT

It just feels like she's drifting away.

Kate heard this. The voice was a soft, distant murmur. She thought it belonged to Summer, and she was pleased to know Summer was there with James, watching over her. She wanted desperately to reach out to them, but Summer had it right. Like a sailboat without a sail. Kate had begun to drift aimlessly away, and she felt helpless to do anything about it.

It was a dream here.

Ethereal.

Sometimes she could feel a breath against her face or a chill across her back. Sometimes she could smell jasmine or lavender. Sometimes she could hear the soft murmur of familiar voices. But most of the time there was no time. No time, no sense of place, no sense of orientation. It was a dream within a dream, a fog so thick nothing else existed, a night so silent it was lonely. And sometimes . . .

Sometimes she could see the demons.

There were several of them. Smoky, loosely-defined tendrils she had noticed floating around the edges of her perception. They had been there from the very beginning, and now, looking back on it, she thought they seemed remarkably familiar.

Familiar?

Yes. Kate recalled when she had first held the plastic bag with the clay, the strong sense of something cold . . . dark . . . *angry* . . . that had overwhelmed her. This was the same feeling.

The demons.

They were gathered around the edges, watching her, wanting to get to her but held at bay by . . . by their own preoccupation with something else . . . with some-*one* else . . . with the man she had sensed above her. They were . . . not spirits in the sense of ghosts . . . not souls trapped in an endless limbo between realities, but *demons* . . . pushing against the bubble that protected her . . . lithe and shifting forms . . . white ragged outlines . . . glowering red eyes . . . angry, ancient beings. . . .

Just don't talk that way.

The voice of James this time.

Kate wanted to move toward it, but she continued to drift.

The voices were growing fainter, moving farther away.

The demons . . . they were coming.

FORTY-NINE

Creston Arnot immediately reminded Kevin of Henderson. He wasn't as ill-tempered as Henderson, but he had the same arrogance. Kevin was beginning to believe it was a natural personality quirk of those in the profession. Arnot was a hyperactive sort. Long hair, swept back in a ponytail. Dark eyes that never settled long in any one place.

Kevin met him on a sound stage at the Warner Brothers Studio in Burbank, where Arnot was working on a science fiction movie called *Excursion*. Arnot, who had been standing in front of a television monitor, studying the camera's perspective of a spacecraft miniature, seemed satisfied with what he saw.

"So how is Mimi?" he asked.

"Last we spoke, she was excited about an article she was working on."

"Cool. Glad to hear it. She's got a heart, you know. She doesn't like you to know it, of course—that would spoil her image—but she'll push you out of the way if she thinks you're going to get trampled by the Hollywood rumor mill."

"She push you?"

"Yeah. Once. When there was an accident on a set

and fingers started pointing my way." Arnot walked around the miniature, which was better than twenty feet in length and suspended by wires from an overhead beam. He sat down on a director's chair next to Kevin, then motioned toward the spaceship. "What do you think?"

"It's very impressive."

"It's an enemy ship. In a week it'll be toast."

Kevin took a long look at the miniature. "Seems like a shame."

"After all the work that went into it, you mean? Yeah, I suppose. But I'm still a kid at heart. Blowing things up gives me a tremendous sense of satisfaction."

"Is that your specialty? Blowing things up?"

"I don't really have a specialty, so to speak. I'm sort of a jack-of-all-trades type. On this film, I'm just supervising. Making sure everyone's on the same page."

"Ever done puppets?"

"Animatronics? Sure. There isn't much I haven't done."

"Used modeling clay?"

"Wed clay? Sure."

"Ever use white clay?"

Arnot shook his head, absently. He had become distracted by one of the technicians, who was setting up a black screen not far from the miniature. "Rick? Drop it down about six inches. It's too high."

"What's the screen for?" Kevin asked.

"To keep the glare from the lights off the camera lens."

Kevin pointed out the huge green screen behind the miniature. "I thought they only used blue screens?"

"Depends on what you're filming. Green's a better contrast against the silver-blue ship."

It was a fascinating scene: the miniature suspended in the air, the huge green screen behind it, the steel dolly track on the floor with the camera mounted on a mobile crane. Off to one side there was a bank of machinery and computers for controlling everything. The floor was littered with cables and extension cords. Chaos appeared to rule supreme here, yet every minute detail was planned and purposeful. Fascinating.

"Ever work with Henry Richards?"

"Is that what this is about? Richards' death?"

"You knew him?"

"We worked together once. He did some morphing for me, through Magic Wizard. Nice guy. A wife and kids. I read about what happened."

"How about Garrett Davenport? Ever work with him?"

"Nope, don't believe so. He does miniatures and animatronics, right?"

"I think so."

"Nope. Sorry. Never worked with him."

"Do most of you guys have specialties?"

"I wouldn't call them specialties so much as preferences. You start out doing anything you can, anything they'll let you do, and after a while you find you like doing pyrotechnics a little more, or maybe makeup, or computer graphics. Like Rick Baker's the guy I'd go to if I needed a gorilla. He can do much more than that and he does. But he's the one I think of first for that particular skill. It just depends on your interests."

"Anyone in the business especially good at aliens?"

"H. R. Giger's had a huge influence on alien design. You know, the look and feel. He did the original designs for the creatures in *Alien* and in *Species*. Very influential. But he doesn't really work in the business. He's primarily an artist."

"Anyone else?"

"Everyone's done an alien, or an alienlike creature at some time in their career."

"It's that common, is it?"

"Stock of the trade."

Kevin watched a man climb to the top of a ladder, where he peered through the camera lens at the huge miniature of the spaceship. He wondered what this was all going to look like when it was finally up on the theater screen. "Ever work with Lyle Henderson?"

Arnot grinned. "Now there's a man only a mother could love."

"Didn't like him much?"

"Didn't like him at all. He's one of those people who finds fault with the way you tie your shoes. Not just a perfectionist, but an angry, martyr type. And he's nervous. He's worse than me. Never stands still for more than a few seconds. There isn't enough room for two nervous types on a movie set. We only worked together once."

"That was enough?"

"Any more and someone was going to get hurt." Arnot watched the man at the top of the ladder until he couldn't stand it any longer. "Sammy? How does she look?"

"Cherry," Sammy said. "Absolutely cherry."

"That's what I like to hear."

Without the benefit of the camera, Kevin studied the miniature spacecraft again and he had to agree—it did look cherry. "Amazing what you guys can do these days."

"It'll just keep getting more amazing, believe me. Technically, we could resurrect Humphrey Bogart or John Wayne and build an entire movie around him."

"I've seen the commercials they've done."

"Or we could build a movie around an actor who never existed. All computer generated."

"Like *Toy Story* or *A Bug's Life*?"

"Exactly. All CGI. No more potatoes for asteroids or pie tins for alien spacecrafts," Arnot said with a laugh. "And we aren't even talking about the other side of the business. No more projectors. Everything will be digital. Sent right to the theaters via satellite. And the theaters will be more interactive. Your seats will be mounted on hydraulics. Very exciting stuff. Movies will all be three-dimensional, almost holograms, they'll look so real. No limits. Lots of fun."

"Holograms?" Kevin asked.

"Absolutely."

"Is anyone using holograms today?"

"Only on a small scale."

Kevin nodded. He had never considered holograms. Of course, they couldn't explain the injuries that occurred to the victims. But they could explain what Davenport had seen. Some sort of holographic image? Was that possible? Was it workable?"

Arnot excused himself, saying he really did have to get back to work. Kevin thanked him for his time and trouble, and wished him good luck on the film. On the way back home, he went out of his way to drive by the Hollywood sign. For no particular reason. Just to see it. Just to remind himself where he was and how different his life had become.

He had read somewhere that the sign had first been erected in 1923 to publicize a housing development, and that originally it had spelled out Hollywoodland. The last part of the sign had been removed sometime in the mid '40s, and the remainder had stood as a monument ever since.

Hollywood.

World of illusions.

Maybe his new life wasn't so different from his old one after all.

FIFTY

Ivy had never owned an answering machine.

But she had one now.

Which would have been grand if Kevin had heard her voice on the message. But it wasn't her voice. It was Hunter's.

"Hastings, you old fool. How could you leave your poor old mother-in-law without an answering machine? What if she wasn't here when you called? How would she ever know you cared?"

"Christ," Kevin muttered.

"So . . . the bottom line is fairly straight and simple. I've got Ivy. You've got the kids. We can make a trade or . . . well, I'll let your imagination run with you. You know how to reach me."

The machine beeped.

Kevin let a moment slip away. "We need to talk. The kids and I scattered less than forty-eight hours after we left the complex. We figured if we split up and you tracked down one of us, you'd still have no way of finding the others. I couldn't bring them to you if I wanted. I don't know where they—"

The machine beeped again.

A moment later the line went dead.

Kevin replaced the receiver and stared absently out the window, across the street. Hunter wasn't going to buy it. Nothing to lose by trying, but Hunter was definitely not going to buy it. He was not a foolish man.

Damn.

FIFTY-ONE

Captain Savino dropped the newest issue of the *Insider* on Kaufman's desk without saying a word. Kaufman picked it up and scanned the headlines. GHOSTS IN THE WHITE HOUSE? PSYCHIC DOG SAVES FAMILY. EL CHUPACABRA LOOSE IN HOLLYWOOD. RAVES THAT KILL. Nothing terribly noteworthy except the word Hollywood. He flipped through half a dozen pages to the article, then scanned down the lines until he saw Davenport mentioned. He glanced at the byline. Mimi Van Mears. Then he started reading.

Kevin had told him about the conversation with Mimi, but he hadn't said anything about El Chupacabra. At the bottom of the article, Kaufman grinned, then took a look at the sketch of the supposed El Chupacabra. It was a goofy-looking creature. No mistaking that. But Mimi had definitely come up with a winner. It walked on two legs, had sharp claws, and was carnivorous. He had to remember to drop her a thank you card for this one. He had to remember to take this home to show Marie, too. She would get a kick out of it.

He picked up the phone, dialed for the Captain, and asked, "Can I keep this?"

"Consider it yours. Though you might not want to walk around with it tucked under your arm."

"I'll keep it hidden."

"Nice touch, that El Chupacabra crap."

"We have Van Mears to thank for that. It was her idea," Kaufman said, just as his beeper went off. He checked the message. From the Chevy Man. Definitely Kevin.

"Great fiction."

"She wants an exclusive when the case is solved."

"Don't tell me about it. Just do it."

That was fine with Kaufman, and he said so. He hung up, spent another moment looking appreciatively at the drawing of El Chupacabra, then tucked the *Insider* into the middle drawer of his desk. By the time he made it outside the building with his cell phone, ten minutes had passed since Kevin had beeped him. He dialed the number.

"What's up?"

"I need to see you."

"You onto something?"

"No, this is personal."

It was personal, and by the sound of Kevin's voice, it was serious. Kaufman suggested the Griffith Park Observatory in forty-five minutes. Kevin said that would be fine and thanked him.

It took Kaufman longer than he had expected. Kevin was waiting for him, leaning against the concrete ledge next to one of the telescopes. Kaufman stood next to him, both of them staring across the smoggy L.A. cityscape.

"They've got Ivy," Kevin said.

"Helena's mother?"

He nodded. "Hunter's got her."

"What does he want?"

"An exchange for the kids."

"How can I help?"

"I still have friends in the Agency. I can still call in a few favors. But I can't arrange both the intelligence and the rescue. Not without exposing myself and putting the kids in jeopardy." Kevin spoke evenly, unemotionally. It was not a side of him Kaufman had often seen, though he could recall once in high school just before an English midterm exam Kevin had been worried about passing and for twelve hours straight he never cracked a smile or changed expressions as he studied. There was definitely a serious side to the man. "Can you help with the intelligence?"

"This is in Washington?"

"Washington. Virginia. He'll have her somewhere in that general area."

"I'll see what I can find out."

"Everything has to be covert. Nothing can trace back to you."

Kaufman nodded. He was going to have to call in a few favors of his own.

"All I need to know is where he's keeping her."

"You can handle the rest?"

"One way or another."

He didn't need to say any more than that. Kaufman could already imagine a scenario where Kevin would have to return to Washington to finish the rescue himself. "If worse comes to worst, you know Marie and I will do whatever it takes to help out with the kids."

"I appreciate that."

"Just wanted to make sure you knew."

Kevin nodded without saying anything.

FIFTY-TWO

James walked down the hospital corridor to the elevators, on his way to the first floor where the cafeteria was located. Summer had just returned from dinner, and though James wasn't hungry, he was thirsty. He pressed the down button and was surprised when the doors opened and Kevin was standing there.

"Sorry I'm late," Kevin said. "I got caught up in a conversation with the doctor."

"Yeah? What did he say?"

"Not much. All we can do is wait and see."

James changed his mind about the drink and accompanied Kevin down the corridor to Kate's room. "Summer thinks she's getting worse."

"Getting worse how?"

"She doesn't seem to be responding like she was. She won't squeeze your hand anymore."

"Revell didn't say anything about that."

They arrived at Kate's room.

Summer was sitting in a chair next to the bed, reading a paperback book. The curtains were open, and outside the lights of the city had come on. The L.A.

night life was emerging from its long sun-washed slumber.

Kate, on the other hand, was still buried deep in her coma. Kevin held her hand. Not only had her fingers begun to curl slightly, her whole body seemed to have closed in upon itself. Not dramatically. Not into a fetal position. But definitely noticeable.

"Hey, Kate. How are you doing?" Kevin asked.

"She's slipping away," Summer said.

Kevin seemed to be caught off guard by the remark, and for a moment he seemed unable to say anything in response. James watched him with a fair idea of what was probably going through the man's head. He was probably hoping Summer was wrong, probably *praying* she was wrong. But it was true. Kate did not appear to be squeezing his hand the way she had in the past.

"Well, let's not give up on her yet."

"I'm not giving up on her."

"No, I know," Kevin said. "I just meant that Kate's a strong girl. We've got to trust in her strength."

James leaned against the wall, watching Kevin as he spoke softly to Kate. He had quit hearing the words. The words didn't matter. It was the way Kevin held her hand and kept his voice low and encouraging. James had begun to wonder if the man had really cared; he spent so much time away from the hospital. But that concern disappeared now as he watched Kevin hovering over her.

"I'm going to get something to drink," James said finally. "Anybody want anything?"

No one did.

FIFTY-THREE

The drive back to the house had been quiet. Summer had decided she wanted to stay overnight with Kate, so there was only the two of them. After spending last night at the hospital, James was looking forward to sleeping in his own bed again. Kevin was eager to play around on the Internet some more. He wanted to see if he could find anything more on the clay. He was caught between his worry for Ivy, his deep concern for Kate, and an unsettling sense that all he had been doing lately was spinning his wheels.

The unanswered questions were mounting: What exactly were the creatures? And what was the role of the white clay? For that matter, what was it that animated the clay? And if it wasn't the clay that was keeping Kate comatose, what was it? And who, if anyone, was the presence behind the creatures? What was his motive? New questions just kept coming and coming.

Kevin parked in the driveway. He turned the engine off, and for a moment, neither he nor James moved. Finally James asked, "Do you think she's going to be all right?"

"If there's anything we can do to help her, we'll do it."

James nodded. He had majored in political science during his short period of college life, before the Agency had got their hands on him. He was a smart kid. Smart enough to know that what Kevin had just said, especially in political terms, would be considered a non-answer by some. Or maybe more appropriately, a non-denial denial. And he would probably know it for what it really was: Kevin's attempt not to address a question that was difficult and carried unimaginable consequences if the answer was not what they both hoped it would be.

"It'll work out," Kevin said unconvincingly.

James climbed out of the car. He waited for Kevin to catch up with him and they moved up the walkway without saying anything more. Kevin unlocked the front door. James went through first. He flipped on the light and started up the stairs. Kevin closed the door behind him, dropped the car keys on the table, and headed for the office.

He turned on the light, crossed the room to the computer, and turned it on. Before he had a chance to sit down, though, he felt a long, sharp pain slice across the back of his right calf.

FIFTY-FOUR

Night has come, and the man has given himself to his dreams.

They are the dreams of his fears, nightmarish, disturbing.

The room is buried in complete darkness, the blinds pulled, the curtains closed, only the soft glow of the dial of the electric blanket visible. The man rolls over, onto his back. He clears his throat and places an arm across his eyes.

His dreams take him deeper.

Above the bed, the demons begin to gather. Ethereal beings. Ghostlike shapes that struggle to take form. Smoky. Vague. Hovering. Slipping in and out of the physical reality.

He has brought them here. Not purposely, but innocently. And they are his now.

He opens his mouth, fills his lungs, then swallows hard.

The demons move closer.

He takes another breath, deep, and the ethereal beings follow the breath into him, past his lips, down his throat, into the very soul of his being.

He coughs.

His dreams take him deeper.

FIFTY-FIVE

James went barreling downstairs to see what the commotion was all about. He found Kevin in the office, cornered. He was backed up against the desk, confronted by two of the creatures that Davenport had so aptly described. Slightly shorter than twenty inches high, walking on two legs, they were some sort of a reptilian/alien biological combination. Unlike anything James had ever seen before.

Kevin motioned to him to stop. "Wait! Davenport said there were four of them. I don't know where the other two are."

"What are they doing here?"

One of the creatures turned and looked at James. It tilted its head, curious, but not terribly interested. It turned its attention back to Kevin.

"What do you want me to do?" James asked.

"I want to capture one if we can. See if you can find a blanket or a pillowcase, something we can throw over them."

James nodded and was starting out of the room when he noticed the blood streaming out of a slit in the right leg of Kevin's jeans. "You're bleeding."

"I'll be all right. Just get the blanket."

Then James had his turn.

The creature struck from behind him, slashing the back of his calf. The cut was long and shallow and sent an immediate wave of alarm through his body. James let out a sharp squeal, then grabbed for the injury. In an instant, he found himself face-to-face with two more of the creatures. They were small. Short, powerful arms. Claws that looked as if they had been designed to kill. High shoulders. Dark eyes.

James stood and backed into the wall. "I think I've found the other two."

"I see."

"What now?"

"Are you all right?"

He nodded. He had never been so scared in his life—the muscles in his legs were twitching uncontrollably—and he could see that Kevin, whose knuckles had turned white they were so forcefully wrapped around the edge of the desk, was equally upset.

"Let me—" Kevin took a single, sliding step toward his left.

One of the creatures took a swipe at him, its claws brushing across the surface of his jeans. It did not rip through the fabric as the previous swipe had, but Kevin quickly took his step back.

"Be careful," James said.

"Touchy, aren't they?"

One of the creatures turned and looked past James at its buddies. It opened its mouth, made a strange clicking sound as if it were trying to communicate, but its throat was dry, then raised its head and let out a guttural, almost painful howl.

"What do we do?"

"I don't know," Kevin said.

Another howl rose from one of the other creatures. It seemed agitated about something, the howl almost an admonishment to its companion. It raised its head, howled again.

They were definitely communicating.

"They're getting restless," James said.

"So am I."

"Maybe we should make a run for it?"

"On three?"

James nodded.

Kevin didn't count out loud. Whether he was worried that the creatures would understand him, or he was worried that his voice might upset them, he chose to countdown with his fingers instead. He raised the index finger of his left hand.

One.

James tried to regain control of the muscle spasms in his legs. He had never been what you might think of as an athletic type. He enjoyed shooting a few hoops as much as the next guy, but he had never been all that good at it. It was something to do when he needed to relax a bit, do a little thinking.

Two.

Kevin stood away from the desk. James shifted his weight onto his back leg.

Three.

The next few seconds passed with no thought. Or with very little thought.

Before Kevin had fully extended his ring finger, James exploded off his back leg. He swung hard and his foot connected squarely with the chest of the nearest creature. It let out a horrible squeal, then went flying through the air, backward. It landed against the hallway wall, hard, visibly shaken.

The second creature lashed out immediately, opening a wound across his shin. James not only felt it, he acknowledged it with a quick, sharp scream.

Kevin screamed too, though it sounded more like a painful groan, and James didn't have time to turn around and see what had happened. He kicked at the second creature, knocking it aside, then made a mad dash down the hallway.

Behind him, he could hear the clatter of the chair against the edge of the desk and books slamming against the floor. He imagined Kevin had done the smart thing and climbed up onto the desk, though in reality he had no idea at all what was going on back there.

He took the stairs, two steps at a time, reaching the top landing just as one of the creatures had reached the bottom. He paused there a moment, staring down. The creature paused, staring up. Then it let out an angry wail and started up the stairs.

James headed for his bedroom.

He slammed the door behind him, locked it—though the locks on these door were useless, any kid could pop them—then backed into the room, unable to take his eyes off the door.

Seconds later, one of the creatures ran up against the other side. It made a loud *bang!* Then a moment or two of complete silence followed, and after that, the doorknob began to jiggle.

James glanced around, his mind racing. *Think. Think. Think.* The desk lamp. Yes. He unplugged the desk lamp, fumbled through the middle desk drawer until he came up with the X-Acto knife, then cut the wire near the base of the lamp. He split the wires, stripped the protective covering, then plugged the cord back into the wall.

The doorknob jiggled again.

James touched the wires to the metal. There was a loud *pop!* Sparks flew. A wail rose from the other side, followed shortly by a thud as he imagined the creature falling back to the floor.

Then the doorknob jiggled again.

Another wail.

Another thud.

The doorknob jiggled again.

The room was bathed in darkness, only the faded, yellowish cast of a streetlight through the window offering any illumination at all. He unplugged the cord, then stripped the wires another three inches and wrapped them about the knob. He plugged the cord in again.

Another pop.

Sparks.

Another wail.

Somewhere downstairs, it sounded as if it were directly beneath him, he heard something crash against the wall. The bedroom window rattled. A tremor passed through the floor beneath his feet. He thought of Kevin. Then he remembered what Kevin had said. Something about capturing one of them, tossing a blanket over one of them.

Think.

The blanket was easy. It was right here on the bed.

Another pop.

Another wail.

Think.

He would need more than a blanket, though. He needed something to secure it, something that would effectively subdue the creature, render it harmless. Rope. Or cord. Or maybe . . .

James dropped to his knees and dug through the bottom drawer of his dresser. He pulled out the two belts Kate had bought for him shortly after they had moved in. He didn't wear belts, never had, but he hadn't had the heart to tell her.

He tossed the belts on the desk, then took a book down from the shelves, which he also tossed on the desk. Next, he tore the blanket off the bed, doing a short battle with the connection to the electrical cord and eventually winning.

Another pop.

He unplugged the wires wrapped around the doorknob.

Another wail.

Then the knob started to jiggle again. This time, when he heard the *pop!* he knew it wasn't the sound of electricity surging through the metal. It was the sound of the lock popping.

James raised the blanket.

The door flew open.

The creature rushed through the opening. The skin had been burned off its right hand, exposing white clay that glowed in the darkness. Underneath the clay, the glow from the streetlight reflected off something shiny. James noticed this in a flash as he backed farther into the room.

"Come on, you little bastard. Come on."

The creature quickly took in the strange surroundings and focused on James. It raised its head, letting out a guttural unhappiness as it advanced. James took his last step back, then braced himself. His eyes fixed on the precise spot where he wanted the creature to be.

The moment it stepped into that space, James tossed the blanket.

The creature ducked too late.

The blanket came down all around it, not the parachute full of air James had feared it might be, but the proverbial wet blanket tossed over a party to smother it.

The creature wailed, and threw an instant fit.

James grabbed the book off the desk. He swung it hard at the outline of the creature's head and when it hit, almost immediately the outline collapsed under the folds of the blanket.

The wailing halted.

James held the book high in case he needed to use it again. Everything in the room fell momentarily still. He tossed the book aside, took possession of the two belts, then knelt next to the blanket.

It began to move again. Less frantically now, though James feared that it was only a matter of moments before the movement turned violent and he would have his hands full again. He scooped the blanket around the bundle where he believed the creature's legs to be, then wrapped the belt around and tightened it. He wrapped the second belt around the creature's waist, clamping its arms against its body

There.

Done.

It wailed again, struggling against the bindings.

He didn't believe there was much chance it could tear itself free.

For the moment, he was the victor.

Then he glanced up, and standing in the doorway was the silhouette of another creature, the hall light at its back. James was grateful he couldn't see the creature's face. Imagining the savagery there was unsettling enough.

Slowly, he climbed back to his feet.

The creature under the blanket rolled into his legs. He kicked it aside.

Then the second creature attacked.

It closed the distance between them in a flash that James could barely comprehend. One second, it was standing in the doorway. The next, he felt a stinging sensation across his left shin like air across a razor cut.

He kicked at it blindly, caught nothing but air, then retreated a step and studied the darkness. Everything around him felt perfectly still. There was no movement of air. There was no sound. The creature under the blanket gave up its struggle. Far away, he thought he could hear a guttural cry rise from downstairs. But that was another place, another time, too far away to even comprehend. Right here, within these four walls, the silence was deafening.

He felt his heart hammer a little harder against the inside of his chest.

He felt his lungs burn for more air.

Then a movement.

To his left.

He backed into the wall, his spine pressed against the corner of the window frame.

Then a noise.

Again to his left, near the bed. A rusty, squeaking noise that sounded as if the creature had bumped into the metal frame that housed the box spring. This brought a rise of hope to James. It told him that the creature's vision was no better than his own. Two blind mice, see how they run.

Then suddenly the creature struck again.

It hit him across the left side of his leg, deep enough that he thought he might be seriously injured this time.

Though it wasn't very deep, he felt immobilized. He flinched, then panicked and made a dash for the door.

His shoes pounded out a heavy beat across the carpet, then one shoe caught on the blanket and James went skidding across the floor on his belly. Before his momentum had completely ground to a halt, he felt another screaming pain across the back of his calves.

He crawled out into the hallway, turned around, and sat with his back up against the wall.

In front of him, the bedroom door was open wide, all the way to the stop.

Beyond the doorway, except for the diffused glow slipping through the window, the room was a patchwork of shadows and night.

James pulled himself higher up the wall, then glanced down at his legs. He was bleeding. His jeans were ripped, already frayed in several places, and edged in red in several others. The pain had been at its worst as the wounds were opened. Now the lingering burn felt as if it were settling deep into the marrow of his bones.

He wiped his hand over one of the wounds, felt a sudden stinging rush, then looked at the blood on his fingers. The sight scared him, but not as much as he had imagined it would, and the scare did not last long. When he looked up, the second creature was coming at him.

Reflexively, James raised his leg and kicked.

His foot caught the creature just below the chin, across the neck. The force sent it reeling backward into the shadows, where James lost sight of it.

James climbed back to his feet and started down the stairway.

FIFTY-SIX

He dreams he is watching a movie. The projector is running.

Click ... click ... click.

Each frame of film passes in front of the lens like a soldier marching past the podium at a military ceremony. A white cone of light carries the images through the darkness to the screen, some twenty feet away, then makes them real.

The film is a familiar film, one of his own. There is an alien family, lost and confused in a hostile, foreign landscape. There are the four Protectors to help insure the family's survival. There are the humans, who don't understand, who make quick and panicked judgments, whose fears leave them no options but to destroy the aliens. It is a particularly poignant film as the roles are reversed and the sympathy of the viewers goes to the aliens instead of the humans. That is perhaps what he likes most about the story.

The aliens huddle in the temporary safety of a tenement building. The floor is littered with discarded fast-food wrappers, old beer cans, wine bottles, the refuse of a world that is accustomed to tossing out what it no longer has use for.

The humans come around the corner in pursuit. They are many, and they are well equipped to kill. The aliens flee deeper into the long-abandoned building, dodging the onslaught of bullets as best they are able. One of the Protectors catches a slug in the back, beneath its shoulder blade. Another Protector injures its hand on a sharp metal door frame. A third Protector goes down and fails to get up again.

The humans remain in hot pursuit.

Then suddenly, the screen explodes inward into the room. The man is so startled by the implosion, he falls back in his chair and ends up on the floor. As he climbs to his knees and peers over the edge of the base of the overturned chair, he is met face-to-face by the aliens.

Behind them, on the screen, military personnel continue their floor-by-floor sweep of the tenement building.

But the aliens are nowhere to be found.

FIFTY-SEVEN

The office had become a battleground and it looked the part.

Kevin stood on top of the desk, next to the computer, his back against the wall. The spider plant was on the floor, the potting soil forming a black puddle on the carpet. Strewn all around the plant were various books, a pencil sharpener, a wall clock, two bronze bookends, a tray organizer, and everything else he had been able to turn into a weapon during the brawl. So far, he had managed to keep the creatures at bay, but he was already feeling the strain of battle, and there were several deep gashes in his legs.

One of the creatures wrapped its claws around the edge of the desk and raised its head above the plane.

Kevin gave it a swift kick to the chin, connecting solidly.

It fell back, head over heels, landing in a ball against the wall.

The other creature, which had inflicted the last wound to Kevin's leg and ended up with a book across the side of its head, stood up, still dazed.

Kevin went down on his knees, pulled out the middle drawer of the desk, then sifted through the contents until he came up with a letter opener. It was made of plastic, the edges somewhat rounded, but at least it had a point at one end. He pulled it free of the drawer just as the second creature mounted the chair.

The beast took a wild swipe at him.

He leaned away, and felt the rush of air cross his face. The creature's claws had missed him, but not by much, and now, for a brief moment, the creature was in an awkward twisted position, with its side open and exposed. Kevin buried the letter opener into its flesh, just below the left shoulder blade.

It let out an agonized wail.

The creature tumbled off the chair, onto the floor. Still wailing, the sound mournful, even heartbreaking, it struggled to reach the letter opener and pull it free. It turned in a complete circle, up on its toes, trying unsuccessfully to grab the plastic shank, to find a way to release the sudden and intense pain that had taken hold of its body. It bounced blindly into the filing cabinet, then fell onto its side, still struggling.

Kevin watched with a mixture of fascination and astonishment. That should have been enough to kill the thing. Or if not kill it, then certainly enough to render it helpless. But while it was clearly in pain, it did not appear to have been seriously injured, and a very unsettling thought came to Kevin's mind. Was it even possible to kill one of these things?

The first creature climbed back to its feet, still a bit groggy, then crossed the floor to help its companion. It wrapped both hands around the letter opener and pulled it free.

The room filled with a loud, painful wail.

Kevin stood up again. He had hoped it was over, but clearly that was not the case.

The letter opener was tossed aside, streaks of white clay covering the shaft.

The second creature managed to get back to its feet. It stumbled clumsily to its left a few steps, then straightened its body. As it regained its sense of surroundings, it was obvious that the creature was favoring its left side, where the wound had occurred.

They were vulnerable after all.

Kevin took great relief in this discovery.

He leaned across the four-drawer filing cabinet, grabbed hold of the curtains, then ripped them away from the window, bringing down a mix of hooks and the nearest end of the curtain rod all in one full swoop. Both of the creatures stood together now, while one appeared to attend to the injury of the other. It was the first time since the attack had begun that they had stood in close proximity to each other. Kevin took advantage of the opportunity.

In one huge sweeping motion, he sailed the curtain out over the creatures. It dropped heavily to the floor, burying them under its thick fabric. Kevin took to the air, landing on his feet at the far edge of the curtain. He had made it with relative ease, though immediately upon impact his knees gave out on him.

He rolled into the door, then scrambled to his feet and stumbled out into the hall.

Behind him, the office filled with angry, frustrated wails.

Kevin did not look back.

He barely had a moment to realize he had made it out of the office safely when James came flying around the corner. James looked up at him, his eyes wide, a harried yet determined expression on his face. "Got one right behind me."

Together, they stumbled down the short hallway into the kitchen. James immediately went after the chairs around the kitchen table. One by one, he tossed them aside, then turned the table onto its side and shoved it up against the doorway. Behind him, Kevin opened the door that led to the side yard.

"What are you doing?"

"Giving them an alternative."

One of the creatures slammed into the table and howled.

"I don't want them in here."

"Neither do I. It's just in case."

James leaned against the back of the table. "What kills these things?"

"Nothing."

"There must be something."

"I'm open for ideas," Kevin said.

"Heat?"

Kevin started tearing through the kitchen cabinets. He didn't know what he was looking for, not specifically. In fact, he was open to suggestions, inspirations, anything. He slammed the nearest doors, then moved to the next set. "It might melt their flesh, might even cause them some pain, but it won't affect the clay underneath. Not at any temperature we could generate."

"We have to destroy the clay?"

"That's my guess."

The kitchen table started to tip forward into the room. James placed his full weight—which wasn't much, he was a thin kid, maybe 140 pounds—against the back. Over the top, he watched two more creatures coming down the hall. "Your friends are coming."

"Can you hold them?"

"I don't know."

Kevin joined him on the kitchen side about the same time the other two creatures joined the ruckus on the hall side. He looked down at them. They were in a frenzy now, clawing at the table the way a dog claws at the earth when he can smell a gopher. The table was made of particle board and surfaced in laminated oak. It would not hold long. Once they tore through the thin oak veneer, James would have to back away or risk contact with those deadly claws.

"Any suggestions?" James said.

"Give me a moment to think."

"I'm not sure we have that long."

The frenzied sound of the claws *clicking* against the tabletop was maddening.

James braced himself with one leg against the tile floor.

Kevin said a silent prayer that the table would hold longer than he feared it would. Again, he glanced around the kitchen. If they couldn't kill these things, they at least needed to *discourage* them . . .

He went back to the cabinets, across one side, down the other . . .

Vinegar. Olive oil. Crisco. Salt. Food stuffs.

Down the line of drawers . . .

Silverware. Utensils. Plastic wrap. Tin foil.

"Kevin!" They had broken through the underside of the table at one end. James moved to the opposite end, repositioned his weight, and tried to keep well out of harm's way.

"Hang on."

The bottom row of cabinets . . .

Pots and pans. Dishwasher detergent. Comet. Oven cleaner.

Oven cleaner.

Kevin snatched up the aerosol can. "Here!"

He tossed it.

"Try it!"

James shook the can, popped off the lid, then leaned over the top of the table. His first targets were the two creatures clawing at the spot where they had already broken through. White foam splattered in layers across their backs, down over their heads, coating their arms.

Both of the creatures let out sharp. annoyed squeals, then raised their arms in protest. They backed away from the table momentarily, rubbing at their eyes, then squealed again and went back at the table with renewed determination.

"It doesn't seem to bother them much."

"Just keep spraying!" Kevin ripped open the cabinet doors above the stove. On the bare wood shelf, next to the sheet metal stove pipe, sat a small fire extinguisher. He pulled it down, glanced at the label. A carbon dioxide extinguisher.

A wail suddenly erupted from the hallway, just beyond the overturned table.

"Oh, Christ," James said excitedly. "I don't believe this. I think it's working."

Kevin carried the extinguisher with him across the room, stood next to James, then peered over the top of the table. It was difficult to tell exactly what physical effect the oven cleaner was having, but it appeared, through the foam, that the flesh of the creatures had begun to disintegrate.

One of the creatures took a halfhearted swipe at him.

James emptied the last of the can, shook it, tried to get more out of the container, and couldn't. "It's out."

The creatures had stumbled away from the table, wailing in agony. They appeared confused now, disoriented, as they pawed at themselves in an effort to scrap away the acidic foam. One of the beasts fell backward on its rump, rubbing wildly at its eyes to remove the oven cleaner.

Kevin imagined it hurt something awful.

"Let's see if we can herd them out of here," he said. He pulled the ring on the fire extinguisher and handed the canister to James. "Here. Use it if you need it."

"What are you doing?"

"Offering them the alternative. That's all."

He stepped up to the table, hooked his fingers around the edge, then slid the table away from the door frame. He made a concerted effort to preserve the table as a barrier between James and himself and the creatures.

James raised the extinguisher.

It was a surprise, maybe not to James but certainly to Kevin, when the three injured and demoralized creatures actually took advantage of the opportunity. The first one stumbled toward the open door, rubbing at its eyes, weaving rubber-legged, until it finally found the opening. It fell out into the side yard, then silently disappeared into the night. The other two followed not far behind.

An eerie, long overdue silence fell over the house.

Kevin dropped his grip on the table and made a dash for the door.

James followed close behind.

The sounds of the door slamming into the jamb

and the lock clicking into place were the sweetest sounds Kevin had ever heard in his life. He leaned against the nearest wall and slid to the floor, exhausted.

FIFTY-EIGHT

The man wakes up in a sweat.

The dream follows him out of his sleep, and for a moment, until he becomes aware of his surroundings, he is still haunted by the aliens. But he is fully awake now and the room, *this* room, is his bedroom. It has only been a dream.

He throws back the covers, sits up, and wipes the last of the dream from his face. They have done it again. He can feel it.

He works his feet into the slippers that always sit on the floor next to the bed, slides one arm into the sleeve of his bathrobe, then the other arm into the other sleeve, and makes his way out into the hall. For a long time after Dorothy died, the house seemed empty without her. He was a ghost, walking its passages, lost in past memories and gradually disappearing deeper and deeper into his own little world.

It is still a lonely house.

He is still a lonely man.

But they have saved him from complete self-destruction.

He makes his way past the workroom, through the kitchen, and opens the basement door. There aren't many basements in Los Angeles. Not many at all. But the people who built this house, back in the early '60s, designed the basement as a fallout shelter. Thick cinder-block walls. A generator. Plenty of bottled water. Survivalist food packs. They were different times then. People lived in greater fear. The generator still sits in the corner, though he hasn't started it up in years and has no idea if it still works. The bottled water and food packs disappeared years ago. They used some, but the rest eventually made their way to the garbage cans.

He flips on the light switch, and stands on the landing, peering down into the belly of the basement. The creatures are milling around on top of the workbench. The family is all there. Three of the Protectors are there. But Roland . . . he can't see Roland.

"What is it now? What have you done now?" he says, starting down the stairs.

Whatever they have done, they have done it for him.

FIFTY-NINE

The phone was ringing.

Kaufman wasn't sure how long it had been ringing, but as he came awake, he glanced at Marie and
was pleased to see that the sound hadn't disturbed her.
He rolled onto his side and grabbed the receiver in
mid-ring.

"Hello?"

"Dan?" It was Kevin.

"Yeah?"

"You gotta get over here."

"Where?"

"The house."

"What time is it?"

"I don't know. Near midnight, I think."

"Can't it wait until morning?"

"Not this. You aren't going to believe this."

SIXTY

Kaufman was not a night person. It was a quarter past one by the time he arrived at Kevin's place, and he still wasn't fully awake.

Kevin opened the front door and hurried him in like a kid eager to have his father watch him take his first dive off the edge of the swimming pool. "Back here," Kevin said. "We moved it into the kitchen."

Kaufman followed along behind him, replaying the word "it" in his mind, and not quite knowing what to make of the word choice. That all changed, though, the moment he entered the kitchen. Instantly, the sleep that had dogged him on the trip over here disappeared, and he came fully awake. He stood in the doorway, thinking that it had to be a joke. That was the only rational explanation he could find for what was strapped to the kitchen table.

"You guys are kidding, right?"

"Does it look like a joke?"

"What the hell is it?"

"One of your suspects," Kevin said with a laugh.

The creature was on its back. James and Kevin had used rope to strap its arms and legs to the table, each separately, and duct tape to strap down its head, chest, and thighs. It looked remarkably like the sketch Davenport had done. It howled, then struggled futilely against its bindings.

"Incredible, isn't it?" James said.

"Yeah, but what exactly is it?"

"Latex. clay, and a metal armature," Kevin said.

"What?"

"It's a puppet. A creation of Hollywood."

"You mean it's not real?"

"Oh, it's real, all right," James said.

"Let's not jump to conclusions." Kevin added evenly. "We don't really know if it's real or not. We don't know what's animating it. All we know is that it's got a thin latex skin, and under the skin is clay, and inside the clay is an armature."

"Remote control?" Kaufman said.

"Possibly."

"There's no power source. No transmitting device," James said.

"We don't know that. We haven't been inside it yet. Not from head to toe." Kevin motioned Kaufman over to the table. "Come here and take a look at this."

Kaufman, who had been leaning against the door frame, with one hand in his pocket, crossed the room and stood next to his friend with a bit of reluctance. He didn't like this one little bit. It was going to make for one huge problem with Savino and the rest of the department, and he couldn't even vaguely imagine how he was going to explain it.

Kevin peeled back a lappet of latex skin. "It's latex. That's all. If you look close, you can see the paint that gives it its coloring."

Kaufman held the latex between his fingers without saying anything.

"And underneath, you can see the white clay that's been showing up at your crime scenes." Kevin used a bread knife to scrap the clay away from the underpinnings. Underneath, a dull, metal rod was exposed. "And then there's the armature."

"A puppet," Kaufman muttered. "A damn puppet."

"Exactly," Kevin said. "Now, normally, from the way I understand it, the designer would have first sculpted the creature in clay. Part of the process would be allowing room for the armature, then making a mold of the sculpture. Once the mold is made, then the clay sculpture has served its purpose and the puppet is actually built around a model using the mold. But for some reason, in this case. the sculpture also serves as the actual model."

"It's the clay," James added. "That's what I think."

"What do you mean?"

"It's the clay that gives the thing its life. That's why the puppet is built around it."

Kevin nodded noncommittally. "Well, that's something to consider."

"What makes you think it's the clay that gives it its life?" Kaufman asked.

"Did he tell you about the rubber band?" James said.

"Yes."

"That did it for me."

"There's something else," Kevin said. He had been using the creature's left forearm for the anatomy lesson. Now, he peeled the latex skin back from the wrist all the way to above the elbow. He began to scrape away the white clay, one layer at a time, down to the armature.

"How come it doesn't clog up the works?"

"That's another reason I think it's the clay," James said.

Kevin didn't look up. "I don't know. But look at this." He had peeled away nearly all the clay along the forearm and an interesting thing had happened. The arm had become less and less active. "You see how it's not moving as much?"

The creature snarled at him, and continued to fight against the restraints. But it was fighting with much more strength and much more of an effort with its right arm than its left arm. The claws on its left hand continued, however, to scrape across the surface of table in an annoying, unsettling effort to free itself.

"What about the left hand?"

"I haven't removed any clay from there."

"So without the clay, this thing's—"

"A puppet without strings."

"See?" James said. "It's got to be the clay."

"Well, for all we know, the clay is some sort of conductor. The silicates could be reacting to a magnetic field or the current running through the house. Or someone could have tampered with the ions. For that matter, there might actually be some sort of remote control function embedded in the armature that's activated by contact with the clay. It's unlikely, but we don't know anything for sure at this point."

"We know that the clay definitely appears to be the power source, don't we?"

"There appears to be a direct correlation between the clay and the animation of the creature, yes," Kevin agreed cautiously.

"Could you tiptoe a little lighter, please?"

Kevin grinned. "I just don't want us jumping to any quick conclusions."

"It's the clay," James insisted stubbornly.

"It might be. We just don't know for sure."

Kaufman continued to stare down at the animated creature, finding it hard to believe this wasn't part of a dream. He leaned forward and took one of the claws in his hands, studied it, and dropped it back to the table. "We still don't know who designed it, or who's behind it."

"No, we don't. Though it's a fairly safe bet it's someone in the effects business."

He nodded absently, his mind busy working through a mishmash of other thoughts that had begun to puzzle him. A special effect, a puppet, whatever it was, the creature looked as real and as dangerous as anything he had ever seen. "How did you end up with it?" he finally asked.

"They were waiting for us," James said. "When we got back from the hospital."

"*They?*"

"There were four of them," Kevin added.

"Davenport said there were four."

"Well, there's only three now," James said with a grin.

Kaufman nodded, lost in his own thoughts again. "Why you? Why did they come after you? It's always been someone in the business up to now. Why would they suddenly be interested in you guys?"

"Someone knows we're nosing around," Kevin said.

"The three of us know. Summer and Kate, they know. Marie, I've told her. But that's it. No one else has the faintest idea you and the kids even exist."

"Except the people we've already talked to."

"You thinking of Henderson?"

Kevin shrugged. "It's possible, isn't it?"

"Why would he come after you?"

"Because we hit a nerve, I suppose."

"Why not me?"

"Because going after a cop carries greater consequences than going after some schmuck without a name," Kevin said evenly. "Plus you get two birds with one stone. One guy gets eliminated, the police get a warning."

Kaufman looked at him without saying a word, then moved away from the table and stood near the refrigerator. It bothered him, standing next to the creature as it struggled to free itself from the bindings. It felt like an intrusion, like a window into hell had opened and this was what had climbed out.

He nodded toward the creature. "So what do you want to do with it?"

"First, let me show you something."

Kevin pulled the fire extinguisher out from the cabinet above the stove. The ring had already been removed. He raised the nozzle, held it a couple feet away from the creature, then fired off a blast of carbon dioxide. A snowy white cloud plumed into the air. Almost immediately the creature's frantic movements became labored. Every moving joint seemed to lose its fluidity, its naturalness. Suddenly the creature seemed as if it were little more than a crudely-built toy with sticky gears.

"It doesn't care much for the cold, does it?" Kaufman said.

"The clay stiffens. It has to work twice as hard."

"You going to freeze it?"

Kevin nodded. "I thought we could strip the clay, seat it in some Tupperware, and toss it in the freezer. Then you can take what's left down to the lab."

"Not the whole thing. I can't take the whole thing down to the lab. Wish I could, but they'd laugh me out of the department." Kaufman thought about it a little longer. "But I'll take the skin. Maybe if I show it to the guys in the lab, they can come up with a trace of blood from one of the victims."

Kaufman stared down at the creature.

It howled again, reminding him of a lonely wolf in the night, longingly calling out to anyone who could hear.

SIXTY-ONE

"This was serious this time," the man says. "You cannot do this anymore. No more. It's too dangerous. You've hurt others, and now you've hurt yourselves."

Roland is missing, and while the other three Protectors, including Silas, have all returned, they have returned with severe blisters covering their latex skins. He can only guess at what has caused the blistering—some sort of chemical agent, he supposes—though whatever it is, he knows that none of this is good. None of it.

He picks Silas up around the waist, then sets him down on the workbench on his back. The creature opens its mouth without letting out a sound, then opens its eyes wide and stares at him as he fishes through a nearby drawer and pulls out an X-Acto knife. The man makes a long incision down the length of the creature's body, from just below its neck to just above its groin. He peels back the latex covering. No damage appears to have been done to the internal workings.

"You are lucky," he says. "You are very lucky. It could have been much worse."

He pulls up the stool, sits down, then begins to work

the rest of the skin free of the white clay beneath it. He does this in a haze of guilty thoughts. It has all gotten out of hand, too far out of hand, and he doesn't know what he can do about it now. After the first killing, when the creatures returned covered in blood, and the paper carried a short article two days later, he finally made the connection in his mind, but his heart disavowed it. It was too much to believe, too incredible to comprehend. Then the second killing occurred, and his pretext of ignorance became nearly impossible to maintain. He understood then, as he understands now, that they neither killed randomly nor did they kill for pleasure. They killed for him. Their victims were *his* enemies.

But he did not want anyone to die.

He never wanted anyone to die.

He harbored a bitterness toward the effects industry in general, toward the bright young men who used their computers to make digital monsters, to do their morphing, to build their special digital effects without caring about the craft that had paved the way for them, without leaving room for the masters who had been painstakingly doing it by hand for years, twenty-four frames per second, without even considering for a single moment that he might still love his craft and want to continue.

But he never wanted anyone to die.

That has never been his intention.

He peels the last of the latex off the creature's frame, then stands Silas up against the back wall of the workbench. It raises its head and lets out a soft, satisfying sound. Its tail sweeps across the surface, stirring up a swirl of dust.

"You'll be all right. I'll fix you up, and you'll be all right."

Tomorrow and the day after tomorrow, he will have to sit down at the table with the newspaper and read each and every page. He is already dreading what he might find. No doubt a story about another attack, maybe even another death, maybe even more than one death...

He never wanted this.

Never.

SIXTY-TWO

It was nearly three o'clock by the time Dan arrived back home. He left the car in the driveway, not wanting the garage door to wake Marie. The fog of exhaustion that had lifted in Kevin's kitchen as he had first set eyes on the creature was back again, so heavy now he could barely drag himself down the hall.

He hung his jacket in the closet, used the bathroom, then sat on the edge of the bed and peeled off his shoes and socks.

"Everything all right?" Marie asked.

He twisted around, briefly, to look at her and give her a pat on the leg. "Sorry. I didn't mean to wake you."

"You must be exhausted."

"That I am."

"Kevin and the kids all right?"

He nodded, and slipped out of his shirt.

"Something to do with the case?"

He shed his pants, then climbed under the covers. She curled into his arms. He never felt as safe as he did when he was with her. What an odd thing. He had always thought it was supposed to be the other way around. Marie was supposed to feel safe, and he was the one who was supposed to provide that sense of safety. Big L.A. cop and, oh, how much he needed to be here next to her.

"Kevin and James encountered a little trouble tonight."

"Are they all right?"

"They captured one of the creatures."

Marie pulled back and looked him in the eye. "What?"

"They caught one."

"I didn't think they were real."

"I don't think I did either," Dan said softly. It had been a theory and now it was reality. He wasn't sure exactly where the line had been crossed, but it *had* been crossed and he knew he was standing on the *Twilight Zone* side now, and he was going to have to make the best of it.

"It's a crazy world we live in."

He closed his eyes.

Sleep swept him away on a long overdue cloud.

SIXTY-THREE

As tired and as drained as he had felt, James couldn't bring himself to go right to bed. After he had helped Kevin bandage his wounds, he hung around downstairs in the kitchen and helped strip the last shreds of clay off the creature. By the time they finished, the freezer was filled to near capacity, and the creature . . . well the creature was no longer something to be feared. It lay on the kitchen table like the main course at an autopsy. All that was left were the inner mechanical workings—the armature, as Kevin continued to refer to it—and the thin outer layer of latex, which lay bunched in a pile like the discarded skin of a chicken.

Kevin sat down at the table to study the armature further, and James finally excused himself to go to bed. He was beyond exhaustion now. In the excitement of the evening, he had forgotten about the battle that had gone on in his bedroom, and when he stood in the doorway, surveying the damage, he realized it would be a while before he could finally climb under the covers and close his eyes. He couldn't steep with the room like this. He couldn't wake up to it like this.

He picked the books up off the floor and reshelved

them, closed up the dresser drawer he had left open, got a new blanket out of the hall closet, and remade his bed. The desk lamp was a throwaway now. He left it in the hallway, just outside his bedroom door, along with the severed cord. There was still a single lamp that sat on the nightstand next to the bed, and when he finally turned it off and climbed under the covers, the room fell into a blackness of solitude that felt both peaceful and lonely at the same time.

He folded his arms behind his head and stared at the ceiling.

The image kept coming back to him . . . Kevin running the knife down the creature's arm and peeling back the skin. The white clay underneath, like a ghost staring out into the night. And underneath the clay . . . the *mechanics*. Nothing but mechanics.

James looked at his own arm, which was barely visible in the dark. There was no white clay underneath the skin, no white meat on this body. But he wondered fleetingly how much of his soul had turned white over the past few years.

A stupid thought. He wasn't sure where it had come from or why it had shown itself at this particular time, but he didn't like it, and he pushed it a little deeper into his subconscious.

He had thought he was going to die tonight.

He had thought Kevin was going to die.

They were both lucky.

He closed his eyes.

Sleep came quickly.

His dreams were restless.

SIXTY-FOUR

Kevin didn't like sleeping late, but sometimes it just worked out that way. This was one of those times. It was nearly ten o'clock by the time he first opened his eyes. He checked the clock on the nightstand, then rolled over and tried to go back to sleep, but his mind wouldn't let him.

Gotta get up.

Gotta get going.

Too much to do today.

The first thing he wanted to do was call Mimi and see if she could tell him anything more about Victor Koenig and Creston Arnot. Even though he had visited with each of the men and nothing particularly odd or out of the ordinary had struck him, he hoped Mimi might be able to offer some additional insights, something that she may have overlooked previously.

That was first on his list of things to do. He showered, shaved, and got dressed, then went downstairs to the office, where he thought he would make the call. One look at the mess left over from last night's encounter, and he closed the door and went down the hall to the kitchen.

The creature, what was left of it, was still strapped

to the table. The latex covering sat in a pile off to one side. The metal skeleton of the creature lay on its back, spread-eagle, the bindings still in place. He untied the ropes, stripped the duct tape, then moved the armature off the table and onto the floor. He picked up the cordless phone, then sat down at the opposite end of the table from the latex skin.

Mimi was home, she always seemed to be at home, and he thought he might have caught her in the middle of a drag off a cigarette because she coughed out a throaty *hello* that sounded as if she had a cold. The cold cleared up rather quickly after that. Then Mimi asked what he had thought of the *Insider* article.

"I'm sorry; I haven't had a chance to pick up a copy yet."

"Well, you go down and get yourself a copy today. I think you'll be pleased. El Chupacabra makes a damn good story, even if it is a bunch of bullshit."

"I'll do that," Kevin said, meaning it. "Can you do me another favor, Mimi?"

"Depends on what the favor is and what you'll do for me."

"I was wondering if you could tell me anything more about Koenig and Arnot."

"Such as?"

Kevin caught himself staring across the table at the pile of latex. Try as he might to put it aside, he continued to question himself about what exactly had happened last night. He had learned enough about Hollywood effects to know that something similar to the creature was certainly possible. The design and construction were both within the current capabilities of the business. But to make it move with such fluidity, such naturalness . . . that might require as many as seven or eight people with control boxes, all working in perfect tandem. And if the creature hadn't been controlled in that manner . . .

"I'm not sure exactly."

"Something else happen?"

"You could say that."

"You aren't going to tell me, are you?"

"I can't. I wish I could, but if I did I would be putting myself and Kate and several other people in jeopardy."

"And I'm not going to get anything out of this, am I?"

"You'll still get your exclusive," Kevin said. He turned away from the pile of latex and stared out the window. "I don't think anyone's going to believe it, and I'm willing to bet that my friend's going to ask you to keep his name out of it, but the exclusive's still yours for the taking."

"Like I said, I'm not going to get anything out of this, am I?" She took a drag off a cigarette and this time there was no mistaking it as she exhaled long and slow. Her voice immediately turned gravelly. "Koenig was one of a handful from the old school. You had people like Dick Smith and Ray Harryhausen and Willis O'Brien, these guys were doing incredible things with stop motion and makeup. They were the groundbreakers of their day. Koenig was in the same circle."

"What happened?"

"Times change," Mimi said with a throaty laugh. "Technology changes. People get put out to pasture."

Kevin heard this and realized with surprise that she was talking as much about herself as she was about Koenig and the others. "Was he bitter about it? He didn't seem bitter when I met him."

"Koenig's a German name. Germans aren't known for wearing their emotions on their sleeves. He lost his life's work. Wouldn't you be bitter? One day the phone quits ringing and it's like you're the only one not invited to the party. How could he *not* be bitter?"

"Bitter enough to kill?"

"You think he's the one behind this?"

"I didn't say that."

Mimi took another drag on her cigarette. "Have you seen the remake of *Psycho*?"

"No."

"The remake of *Mighty Joe Young*?"

"Sorry, I haven't had much time to go to the movies lately."

"Willis O'Brien and Ray Harryhausen both won Oscars for the original *Mighty Joe Young*. Why do you suppose they bothered with a remake?"

"I don't know. Why?"

"Because they could," Mimi said flatly. "That's what this town is all about. Color is better than black and white. Bigger is better than smaller. Newer is better than older. That's the way the people in this town think. That's what drives them."

"And Koenig got buried in the traffic."

"Everyone gets buried sooner or later. For some, it hurts a little more than for others. But no one gets away without a few tire marks down their back."

It sounded not terribly dissimilar to his experience with the Agency.

"What about Arnot?"

"Arnot's still on the rise. He hasn't peaked yet. It'll be years before he's sporting tire marks."

"So there's nothing you've heard that might set him off on a killing spree?"

"I'm not the guy's shrink," Mimi said bluntly. There was some playfulness in her voice, though, and Kevin thought it sounded as if she was thoroughly enjoying herself. "And I lost my Tarot cards in the '60s. It's just me and the old Royal these days. I write what I hear when I hear it, but I don't hear everything. People don't come to me to confess their sins. They come to me when they want to get even with someone or when they want to make a few extra bucks in exchange for a little juice."

Kevin grinned. "How do you sleep at night?"

Mimi laughed. "Like a rock, thank you."

"And no one's been whispering in your ear?"

"Not about Arnot."

"Or Koenig?"

"Or Koenig," she said. "Not much help, am I?"

"Not true. You've been a big help."

"Save it for the suckers," she said. She took another long drag off her cigarette and Kevin thought she must have sucked it down to the last shred of tobacco. Either that or she had swallowed the thing. There was a moment of complete silence, then with some effort she added, "Okay, before you go and hang up on me, here's an easy one for you, because I know you're a Jack Nicholson fan."

"Who isn't?"

"In what film did he make his debut?"

"*Easy Rider?*"

"Don't I bet he wishes," she said with a laugh. "Actually, one of his first roles was in a Roger Corman film called *Little Shop of Horrors*."

"The original?"

"That's the one. Remember the guy in the dentist's office? The masochist? That was your Nicholson."

"You know I'm going to have to go out and rent it now."

"Trust me. It's him."

Kevin wasn't sure of that, but he thanked her just the same. Both for her help with Koenig and Arnot, and for the trivia quiz. Anytime, she said. Then he hung up and sat at the table for a while, staring across at the mangled hole the creatures had clawed into the surface last night. Mimi had been right. She had not been all that much help.

He tapped his finger on the edge of the table, nervously, then picked up the phone to call Kaufman.

SIXTY-FIVE

Kaufman had been expecting to hear from him.
After his beeper went off, Kaufman stepped
out into the stairwell to make the call. They agreed
to meet at the Griffith Park Observatory again. The
last visit to the park had been the first time Kevin
had seen the copper-domed observatory. He had been
taken not only by the architecture, but also by the
view.

"An hour?"

"Works for me."

Kevin was waiting in the same spot. He had
brought the creature's latex skin with him, sealed in
two one-gallon freezer bags inside a brown paper
grocery bag. He handed the package over. "There's
no visible blood, but you never know."

"We'll see if the lab can come up with anything."

Kevin nodded. "Got the clay in the freezer. Seems
to be doing the job. The rest of it's just sitting in the
corner, against the wall."

"Did you figure out how they got in?"

"Through the office window. I left it open a crack."

"Bet you keep that one locked from now on."

"You better believe it."

Kaufman was quiet for a while, enjoying the view across the city. He didn't get a chance to stop and relax much in the day-to-day grind of the job. It was nice here. "I still can't close my eyes without seeing that damn thing strapped to the table."

"Me either."

"What do you think we've stumbled into?"

"I don't know."

"Something . . . I don't know . . . supernatural, maybe?"

Kevin shrugged without looking up.

"Help me out here, will you? I've been stumbling around like a damn wino, trying to figure this thing out."

"What do you want me to say?"

"You've worked with the kids. You've seen things. Is there really anything to this supernatural stuff? I mean, is it possible that's what we're dealing with here? Something supernatural?"

Kevin swallowed once or twice with some difficulty, as if he were trying to clear bile that had suddenly risen to the back of his throat. "I sat behind a two-way mirror once—this wasn't all that long ago, less than a year, I'd say—and I watched Summer focus on this water bottle sitting on the table in front of her. This was a little plastic bottle. It held maybe twelve ounces when it was full, but it was empty in this case. I watched her move that bottle around the table like it was a kid's top. You know, spinning in the air. She never touched it. Never came close to touching it. But that bottle danced for her. It danced."

Kaufman didn't say a word.

"Now, I don't know how she did it. If she were someone I didn't know very well, then maybe I could have chalked it up to a parlor trick and felt a little better about the whole thing. But this was Summer. You know her. She's a sweet kid. Very honest, very direct. There's not a deceptive bone in her body." Kevin turned and looked him in the eye. "So you tell me, was it supernatural, what she did? Because I don't think I know what's natural and what's supernatural anymore. I honestly don't."

Kaufman nodded.

"It is what it is. Simple as that. Whether we understand it or not."

"I'm not sure if I understand anything right now."

"I know. I feel the same way."

For a time, they stood shoulder to shoulder, leaning against the cement wall, gazing out over the landscape in complete silence. Kaufman thought about Marie for some reason. Maybe it was because she was the only person in his life that he had ever truly understood, the only person that had ever kept him grounded. The world was too big these days. Too fast. Like Kevin had said, whether we understood it all or not, it was what it was . . . sometimes mysterious . . . sometimes ugly . . . sometimes graced with the beauty of someone like Marie.

"I'm going to pay another visit to Henderson," Kaufman said eventually.

"Yeah?"

"Nothing to lose, I figure."

"I talked to Mimi this morning. To see if she could tell me anything more about Koenig or Arnot. She didn't have much to say, but I think I might stop by and see Koenig again. She thought he might still be bitter about the business."

"How's Kate doing?"

"About the same. Saw her this morning for a few minutes. Summer and James are with her."

"Marie and I are planning on stopping by tonight."

"She'll like that," Kevin said, referring to Kate.

They didn't talk much longer. Kaufman lost himself in thoughts about Kate, which led him to thoughts about the case, and eventually to the bag he was holding in his hands. Running the latex skin through the lab was purely routine. If it showed anything, it would show what he already knew: that all the crimes were connected. What he really needed to know was who was behind the creatures, and that part, at least for now, appeared to be a dead end.

Kevin said something about stopping by UCLA.

"Yeah, and I suppose I still need to see if I can get in touch with Henderson today." Kaufman checked his watch, then held up the bag. "Thanks for the sample."

"No problem."

"Oh, I almost forgot." He stuck his hand in his pocket and brought out a business card. On the back side, printed in block letters, was an address. Above it was the name: Ivy Hough. He handed the card to Kevin, who took it and immediately turned it over. "I can't be positive she's there. No one's actually seen her. But I think this is probably your best bet."

"What makes you think she's here?"

"It's an old crack house. Been abandoned the past year and a half or so. The neighbors started complaining to police last week, saying it looked like there was some activity going on there. When they checked it out, they were met by a guy who flashed a CIA ID. Said the house was being used by the Agency."

"Spying on the citizens again."

"Exactly. There was no reason for them to be there."

"Thanks," Kevin said. "I really appreciate this."

"Hey, it's the least I could do."

SIXTY-SIX

Time had a way of standing still for Kevin. especially when he was working intently and the work was all-absorbing. It also had a way of disappearing out from beneath him when he was least expecting it. The next several days disappeared in a flash.

He spent a good portion of them at the hospital. Kate's condition was not improving, and though the doctors continued to keep an optimistic tone to their outlook, Summer was not nearly so certain. It placed Kevin in an awkward position. He was, after all, a scientist by nature. Science was at the heart of all his reasoning. And modem medicine, as it was practiced in the hospitals of the western world, was one of the purest forms of science. On the other hand, he was also well aware of Summer's intuitive nature, and he was not one to easily disregard her feelings. Either way, there was little he could do about the situation. James and Summer continued their vigil, talking to Kate regularly, helping with the physical therapy, holding her hands. As helpless as it felt, there wasn't much more they could do but wait and see.

Dan and Marie dropped in at the hospital for a few hours one night. Marie brought a loaf of homemade zucchini bread and invited everyone over for dinner the next night. It was a welcome break, especially for Summer and James, who had both spent long hours at the hospital.

She cooked a huge meal: pot roast, with asparagus tips, mashed potatoes, whole wheat buns, a nice green salad, and a blackberry pie topped with vanilla ice cream for dessert. For the first time in several weeks, the constant pall of worry lifted for a few short hours. After dinner, they sat down at the table and played a couple of games of Shanghai Rummy.

It was a therapeutic night for everyone, Kevin thought. Long overdue.

The next day, he was finally able to make a connection with someone in the Anthropology Department at UCLA. They spoke briefly, the man was late for class, and didn't have time to talk. He was familiar with the Minitu, though, and he said he'd be happy to share whatever he knew, so they made an appointment to meet.

Off the phone, Kevin booted up the computer and checked for an anticipated e-mail message that still hadn't arrived. He was awaiting word from an old friend who walked a fine line just outside the mandates of the Agency, a man who had agreed to help him with Ivy's rescue. It was still a little soon to hear back, Kevin had passed the address to him only two days ago, but there was a growing a sense of urgency surrounding the situation. Helena's mother was not a young woman. Kevin had no idea how well or how long she would hold up in a strange environment, isolated from her friends.

To his disappointment, there was still no word.

He leaned back in the chair, trying to ignore the

helplessness that once again was hovering over him like a hungry vulture. It was getting late. The house was quiet. He was tired. There wasn't much more he could do tonight.

Kevin turned off the computer, then stood up and stretched. The office was still a mess after the attack. He glanced at the surroundings and for a brief time seriously considered taking on the chore of cleaning up before going to bed. But outside of his work, he had never been a terribly orderly person, and this could wait. It did not carry the same urgency as the situations with Kate and Ivy. It simply wasn't important enough to address right here and now.

He dragged himself upstairs and climbed into bed with a copy of Tom Clancy's *Rainbow Six*. It was a book he had been meaning to start for more than five months now. Time had a way of disappearing out from beneath him when he least expected it.

SIXTY-SEVEN

Benjamin Dougherty, Ph.D. was an Associate Professor in the Department of Anthropology at the University of California, Los Angeles. The departmental curriculum focused primarily on the four traditional fields: archaeological, biological, linguistic, and sociocultural anthropology. Dougherty's specialties were cultural anthropology and American Indian languages. He was dressed in a black turtleneck with a brown corduroy jacket and a pair of well-worn Levis. Kevin met him at the Institute of Anthropology at the northern end of the campus, near Royce Hall.

They shook hands, a firm shake that Kevin admired.

"Thanks for sharing your time."

"My pleasure."

They sat in a small back office, Dougherty on one side of the desk, absently toying with a rubber band, Kevin on the other. Dougherty was a middle-aged, a pound-or-two-a-year man with a round face, a receding hairline, and a black mustache that stood out on his face the way a pimple might—you just couldn't take your eyes off it.

"You were a bit vague when you called. You're interested in the Minitu?"

"Yes, well, that's as good a place to start as any, I suppose."

"And is there something in particular you want to know?"

"They're a Northern California tribe, is that right?"

"Yes."

"You said that you've studied them?"

"Yes. Actually, there was a study done by another anthropologist, a woman by the name of Elaine Rasmussen, and I had the opportunity to study her records and conduct a series of interviews with various members of the tribe. The study itself wasn't mine."

"Could you tell me what the study covered?"

"Well, it was a cultural study. So it covered just about everything. Knowledge and beliefs. Recreation. Housing. Religion. Politics. The whole gamut."

"I guess I'm most interested in the cultural beliefs, particularly as they pertain to the soul or the spirit."

"The *loitcet*. The spirit of the dead."

"Yes."

"What is it you want to know?"

"I read somewhere that they believed the spirit could be contained in clay?"

"In the earth?"

"Not just the earth, but clay in particular. White clay."

Dougherty, who had intense blue eyes, shook his head. "Clay pottery, maybe. Though that sounds like a mythology more attributable to African tribes."

"No, this was the Minitu, I believe."

"White clay. *Luru'qi welog.*" He nodded. "Yeah. I remember something about a clay burial ground, up near Hayfork, if my memory serves me. This was a place where the Minitu buried warriors who had disgraced the tribe in some manner. Cowards. Thieves. Warriors who had murdered outside of battle. The place of shame, they called it."

"This was white clay?"

"Yes," Dougherty said absently. His eyes narrowed slightly as he seemed to fall deeper into his thoughts. "They believed the clay would bind the souls to the earth and prevent them from advancing to higher spiritual planes."

"You ever go there?"

"No. I read about it in the study Rasmussen did, though. And I remember, in one of my interviews, a woman brought the subject up briefly. We didn't spend too much time on it. What I've told you is probably all I gathered on the subject. But you might want to talk to her. She was an interesting woman, a shaman in training, so to speak. I'm sure she could tell you more than I could."

"You have a number for her?"

"Not with me. It's back in my office. Can I call you later with it?"

"That would be great." Kevin shook hands with the man, and excused himself. He stood outside the Institute of Anthropology, surrounded by the Dance Building, Royce Hall, the Anderson School, and feeling a long lost sense of appreciation for academia. College had been one of the most exciting times of his life. It had been his first experience living away from home, away from a small town. Intellectually, emotionally, politically . . . everything about the campus had seemed charged with energy, excitement, challenges, limitless potentials.

UCLA was a much larger campus, of course. The University of Nevada had grown over the years, but it was still comparatively small. Yet. the feeling in the air was the same. The enthusiasm, the idealism, the hope. Even after all these thirty-odd years later, he could feel the hope in the air.

Kevin took a long, leisurely walk around the campus. He enjoyed every moment of it.

SIXTY-EIGHT

Kevin stood in the office doorway, surveying the damage, close to turning around and walking away. He wasn't much in the mood for housecleaning. It was a few minutes past midnight. James and Summer had both returned home for the first time since Kate had fallen into her coma. Summer had said good night as soon as she was inside the door, then had gone upstairs to her room. James had wandered around in the kitchen for a while, fixing himself a chicken burrito in the microwave before heading upstairs to his own room.

The downstairs belonged to Kevin again.

It felt lonely tonight.

Nights always seemed to feel lonely without Helena and Christy. He had not been with them the night of the accident. Christy had started taking piano lessons six months earlier and it was her second recital. He had promised to be there, but at the last minute Hunter had called him into his office and handed him a field report of a Russian Psi program he wanted distilled and analyzed for a meeting the next morning. Kevin had called Helena and apologized and promised to be home after the recital so he could hear all about it.

The rest of the story came courtesy of the Highway Patrol. The road was wet and icy after the first big storm of the season. The car, a Volvo—Helena insisted on driving a Volvo, claiming, "It's the only safe car on the road"—blew its right front tire and went into a skid. It sideswiped a tree, crossed back across the highway and struck an overpass pillar head on. There were no witnesses. It was a lonely stretch of road and no one was quite sure how much time had passed before someone stopped to help. Helena and Christy were both pronounced dead at the scene, and the autopsy report concluded that they had most likely both died immediately upon impact. There was that small blessing.

It was the only blessing.

Death had played a dirty little joke on Kevin. It had taken his wife and his daughter, the two people he loved more than anything in the world, and it had left him behind to suffer the guilt. If he hadn't worked late . . . if he had gone with them . . . if he had been driving . . . if he'd had the tires checked during the last 6,000 miles . . . if he hadn't let them go alone after the storm . . . if

. . . if

. . . if only he had died with them.

That was what haunted him most in the months that followed.

Why hadn't he died with them?

That was the way it should have been.

They belonged together, the three of them. Life had never felt so right, so perfect as when they were together.

And without them, it had never felt so wrong, so alone.

What a mess, Kevin thought now, staring at the office floor.

He picked up the curtains, which had been shredded by the creatures' claws, and tossed them out into the hallway in a heap. He righted the chair, then stood on it to hook the curtain rod back into its wall support. Then there were the books and the office supplies, and the matter of saving as much of the potting soil as possible. He replaced the spider plant on top of the filing cabinet, then dragged out the vacuum cleaner and went to work on the carpet, doing as well as could be expected from a tired man this late at night.

Once the room was livable again, he booted up the computer and sat down in front of the monitor. It took a minute for the operating system to come up. Kevin leaned forward, and dialed up the local telenet number: (213) 555-2251. The modem went through its high-pitched squealing, and the connection was made.

TERMINAL=

He entered his terminal emulation.

@

He typed: "C", then followed it with the network user address. The NUA was a private computer that changed its address every three days according to an advanced logarithmic formula agreed upon between Kevin and his contact.

The connection was made.

He typed: "Mail" then followed it with an ID number and a password.

An encrypted message came up on the screen. He decoded it. The message read: THE BIRD'S IN THE CAGE. THE CAT IS PROWLING. LITTLE ANTICIPATED RESISTANCE. SET FOR RELEASE IN TWO DAYS. CONFIRM.

His return message, before encryption, read: NEVER UNDERESTIMATE THE CAT. CONSIDER IT A GO. WOULDN'T MISS IT.

Kevin encrypted the response, sent it, then logged off telenet. For a time, he sat staring blankly a the desktop screen of the computer, his mind several thousand miles away, wondering how his mother-in-law was doing and if, in two days, he would be walking into a trap.

He trusted James Flynn, his contact, as much as he trusted anyone he had ever worked with in the Agency or the fringes of the Agency. But the sad truth of the matter was this: no one was truly, one-hundred-percent trustable. Not in the Agency. Not around the Agency. Not anywhere near the Agency. There were simply too many personal agendas, too many subplots playing behind the scenes.

So it was not improbable to imagine that Flynn had been turned by Hunter. Kevin didn't believe that was the case, but he would be foolish not to at least consider it as a possibility. Hunter did have influence. And influence inspired a following, even with the oddest of bedfellows.

He turned off the computer, stood up and stretched, then started upstairs for bed.

It would not be a restful night.

There was simply too much on his mind.

SIXTY-NINE

The eggs sit in the middle of the frying pan. Hash browns to the right. Sausage links off to the side on the left. The man flips the eggs one last time, then shuts off the gas. The flames *pop,* then disappear. He dishes the food onto a plate, adds a slice of buttered toast, and sits down at the kitchen table.

He has made a decision this morning. It is not an easy decision, and even as he takes a bite out of his toast—chewing slowly, meticulously—he questions himself again. The decision he has made is this: to dismantle Silas and the others.

Roland is still missing.

This is something that troubles the man to no end. He has no idea what has happened to Roland, beyond his assumption that the creature was somehow crippled—or worse yet, killed—during their last little enterprise into the real world. But even this is not certain. The papers have reported nothing, not a single word, about an attack or a murder that might even remotely be attributable to his creations.

Yet something happened.

Silas returned mutilated.

And Roland hasn't returned at all.

The man places the slice of toast on the edge of his plate, picks up his fork, and takes a bite out of his eggs. He returns the fork to its proper place. As he chews, he used a napkin to wipe the corners of his mouth. After he swallows the egg, he raises his cup and takes a sip of coffee.

Something happened that night. He has no way of knowing exactly what it was, but something brutal happened, and for a reason he cannot quite fathom, no one has raised a fuss about it. This is something that troubles him even more than Roland's disappearance.

He uses his knife and fork to cut a small portion off the edge of a sausage link. He returns the knife to its proper place, then takes the sausage into his mouth and savors its warm spicy seasoning. His father taught him to chew mercilessly. Thirty-two chews before he swallowed. As a child, he counted each movement of his jaw until he reached the prerequisite thirty-second before he swallowed. Counting, however, is no longer necessary. It has not been necessary for a good many years. Thirty-two is a number that is ingrained so deeply into his consciousness that it arrives without thought now. Not thirty-one. Not thirty-three. Just a perfect thirty-two chews before swallowing.

He is losing control.

That, perhaps, troubles him more than anything.

The creatures, his children, his creations . . . they ventured out on their own and they hurt people. Yes, it is true, it is true, that these people they hurt were the enemy. They were young and brash, without an ounce of appreciation for what had come before them, and they deserved to die.

The man replaces his fork next to the plate, surprised by the words that have just traveled through his thoughts. No one deserved to die. No one.

He has lost his appetite now.

He can't eat another bite.

My God, the words he has just permitted inside his head.

My God.

He pushes back the chair, stands up, then clears his place at the table. He places the uneaten food in a small plastic container and places the container in the refrigerator. Waste not, want not. He fills the kitchen sink with water, adds soap, then washes each dish thoroughly, with a close, discerning eye looking for any spots he may have missed. Then he dries each utensil, each dish, with great care and returns them to their proper places in the cabinets.

He wipes his hands off on the kitchen towel and returns the towel to its drawer.

Then he heads downstairs to the basement.

Silas is on the workbench, toying with a roll of masking tape. The cabinets are all open. The family is huddled in the corner, near the water heater, clinging to each other as they often do. Each of the creatures has its own individual personality, but the family seems to feed off itself emotionally. They are a skittish bunch, frightened by nearly everything.

The man stops at the bottom of the stairs, fighting with himself to keep his voice even and strong. "Good morning, my children. Good morning."

The other two creatures come out from the cabinets, where they have been sleeping. They climb down from the workbench to the cold concrete floor, only mildly interested, and play a game of tag that he has seen them play before.

Roland, though . . . he misses Roland.

He crosses the floor to Silas, and takes the masking tape away from him. "This is not a toy. It is not to be played with." He hangs the roll of tape on a hook attached to the side of the nearest cabinet, and closes the cabinet door. He pulls out the stool, then sits down.

Silas comes up to him, its eyes big and round.

Amazing.

He takes Silas by the arm and prompts the creature to turn to its left. It is so incredibly real. The golden, reptilian eyes. The large, carnivorous mouth. The claws. The high shoulders, and the way it moves on two legs, as if it were almost human.

Amazing.

He has created something absolutely amazing.

And *that* is the quandary he finds himself facing. How can he destroy something so magnificent, something so much of himself? How? He would be a father destroying his child.

The man sits back on the stool.

"You are something, you are."

Silas opens its mouth and lets out a deep throaty sound.

"I don't think I can do it," the man says. "I don't think I can."

SEVENTY

Kaufman arrived at work to find a note on his desk saying Captain Savino wanted to see him. It was light out, though the dawn was young and the sky had been purple and blue on his drive into the office. It had been an unusually peaceful drive. For a while the only movement he had noticed was the thin, reedy leaves of the palm trees stirring in a light breeze off the ocean.

He stood at his desk, staring at the note, feeling an uncomfortable itch at the back of his neck. This had something to do with the three homicides he had heard about on the radio coming in. One had been a drive-by. Gang related. Someone in the Southeast Area Crash Unit had already identified a suspect, according to the report. It was just a matter of tracking him down now. The other two, however, were right up his alley. One had been a home invasion in Hermosa Beach. An elderly woman had been murdered. The other had been an unidentified Hispanic-American male in his late thirties who had stumbled into an Exxon station with a knife sticking out of his gut.

Kaufman dropped the note on his desk. What he needed more than anything right now was a cup of coffee. He shed his jacket, which he hung on the back of his chair, then went looking for the filters. No one here liked making coffee. No one. It was a matter of will in the mornings to see who could hold out the longest. But he wasn't even going to try to pretend indifference this morning. He needed his coffee and he was willing to make the ultimate sacrifice to get some.

He leaned back against the wall, staring at the coffee-maker as if he were watching a particularly sexy movie on cable. Water flowed through the coffee grounds, through the filter, into the glass pot. When the process was finally complete, he took his coffee cup with him and went to see Savino. You can only put off the inevitable for so long before you finally have to face up to it.

Savino was sitting behind his desk. He had shed his jacket, too. His shirtsleeves were rolled up high on his forearms. He glanced up, over the top of his reading glasses, then put down the pen in his hand and removed the glasses.

"It's only temporary," Savino said. The rest was filled in silently. They had worked together long enough to understand the demands made on each of their jobs and how things sometimes had to go, whether they liked it or not.

"Which one?"

"Mrs. Eleanor Hammer. The home invasion."

"Who's got it?"

"Dixon."

"How long?"

"A couple days. A week at the outside. Until he has something solid. Then you can get back to your case." Savino stared at him, studying his face for a hint of what might be going on inside his head. "Sorry. The devil came out to play last night and left us a mess to clean up. Dixon's got two other cases he's trying to finish up. If you can help him out a little, maybe we can get things back to where they're manageable again."

Kaufman raised his coffee cup. "I'll talk to him. See how I can help."

"Thanks."

"All in a day's work."

SEVENTY-ONE

Most of the flowers in Kate's hospital room had either started to wilt or had already surrendered to an overabundance of fluorescent light and a sad lack of attention. Summer busied herself weeding out those that were either still salvageable or made from plastic.

If you didn't busy yourself in a place like this, you could go crazy. Thoughts start pushing their way into your head whether you want them there or not. She had managed a good night's sleep, and she honestly felt better able to cope with the sterile hospital surroundings this morning. Still, throughout most of the day, Summer's thoughts had wandered aimlessly and uncontrollably through the tricky terrain of her past.

Sometimes she wondered who she really was . . . the little girl who had tried so hard to keep the appearance of normality in her life, doing the grocery shopping, cleaning the house, putting her mother to bed after she had passed out on the living room couch from another long day of drinking. Or the girl caught in the system, labeled dangerous and manipulative, lost in the black hole where they send kids they don't know what else to do with. Or the teenager who had tried to please Samuel Hunter because least he seemed to see something of value in her. Or . . .

. . . or the young woman that she was becoming, still uncertain of herself at times, struggling to fit in because the people around her were good people, even if she wasn't sure that she was good enough to be a part of their lives. Just sort of lost, yet trying not to let on.

Not much different from Kate, she imagined.

The day already felt as if it had dragged on forever. Kevin had dropped her off, along with James—who seemed unusually quiet and withdrawn—hours ago, promising to be back before long. Then shortly before noon, Doctor Revell had arrived on his morning rounds. His initial optimism about Kate's recovery had been wilting day by day, much the same as the flowers. This morning had been no different. Revell came in, said his obligatory "Afternoon," then immediately went to Kate's chart. He read it without making a sound, then rolled the sheets up around Kate's ankles and tried to prompt a reaction by stimulating the bottoms of her feet. When that failed, he tried the palms of her hands. This, too, failed.

Revell had nodded absently, mostly to himself. "I'll be back around later this afternoon."

Then he had left.

Summer had been happy to see him go. She had given up asking how Kate was doing. The answer was fairly self-evident. Kate was not doing well at all. The fingers on her left hand had begun to curl inward so dramatically that the physical therapist had finally placed the hand in a brace to keep the fingers extended. Her body had curled into itself as well, and the therapy sessions had grown a little longer every day. Worst of all, though, was the diminishing sense of Kate's presence. Summer could feel her friend drifting farther and farther away, to the point now where Kate felt like a distant, flickering star.

Summer picked up a potted cactus plant Marie had brought in, and moved it into the sunlight on the windowsill.

"He didn't say anything," James said casually. He had been sitting across the room, in the corner, reading a paperback book by Peter Jennings called *The Century*. The book was closed now, abandoned on his lap, as he watched Summer busy herself with the plants.

"He never says anything."

"Maybe we should ask for a new doctor."

"They're all the same," Summer said cynically. "They come in, they look at her, they pretend they're actually doing something, then they leave. One's the same as another. It doesn't make any difference."

Kevin walked in, looking a little harried and flushed. He was wearing a long-sleeved, light-blue shirt, and he had the sleeves rolled up on his forearms. She had never seen him do that before. "What doesn't make any difference?"

"Who the doctor is," James said.

"I was just saying that it doesn't matter who the doctor is, they're all alike." Summer picked up a bouquet of dried flowers that had gone well past the dry stage and were now beginning to crumble. She moved it to the table, adding it to the collection of dying plants.

Kevin went immediately to Kate's bedside. He took her hand, held it in both of his, and stared down at her. "No change?"

"There's a change," Summer said. "It's just not for the better."

"The doctor tell you that?"

"The doctor didn't say anything," James said.

"He didn't have to. Trust me, she's not hanging around. I can't even tell if she's trying anymore. I used to get such a strong charge off her; it was like a shock. you know, like static electricity or something. But now, she's not even there. It's like she's off in some other place I can't even reach."

Kevin looked up from Kate, his face suddenly serious. "I know it's rotten timing, but something's come up and I have to leave town for a few days."

"Now?" James said.

"I'm sorry. I know it's a bad time. If I could put it off, believe me, I would. But it's something that needs immediate attention. There's a life at risk."

"It's Hunter, isn't it?" Summer asked.

Kevin nodded. "He's got my mother-in-law. He's using her as bait, hoping I'll either exchange you guys for her safe return, or I'll go looking for her and place myself at risk of getting caught."

"You're going after her?"

"I have to; I don't have much choice."

"By yourself?"

"No," Kevin said softly. "I'm not quite that stupid. There's a friend, still at the Agency. He'll be helping me."

"What if it's a setup?" James asked.

"It might be. I won't really know until I get there. That's a chance I have to take." Kevin shifted uncomfortably, then glanced out the window at the open space above the city. He seemed terribly ill at ease. His mouth was straight, tight, trying to give away nothing. "You have to understand, it wouldn't be right to ask someone else to do this. I need to do it myself."

"What about Kate?" Summer asked.

It was a question that seemed to make him even more uncomfortable. He looked at her, then at Kate, then cleared his throat. "I was hoping you and James would continue to look after her."

"That's all we've been doing," Summer said with a sudden fierceness that surprised even her. "What about you? When are *you* going to start spending some time here? You know, just some time, like you cared. Like it mattered to you."

"It does matter to me. All of you matter to me. You know that."

"No, I don't. You're never around anymore." She hated herself for what she was saying. She knew it wasn't fair. She knew he was doing his best, that he had always done his best for her and the others. But she felt like one of those pathetic Goth kids from school, sullen and withdrawn, always dressed in black, listening to The Sisters of Mercy and talking about their latest suicide attempts. She felt weighted down with the world around her, and Kate was the biggest weight of all, because Summer just didn't know how to help her anymore.

"I'm sorry," Kevin said. "I didn't know you felt that way."

He had an incredibly hurt expression on his face, as if she had taken a knife to his heart and given it a good, solid twist in the process. Which was exactly what she had done, Summer thought. She hadn't meant to hurt him, not at all, it was just that . . .

Her eyes began to fill with tears.

"Hey, it's all right," Kevin said. "I've got thick skin. Really, I do."

Summer shook her head. "It's not that. Well, it is, but it's more than that. You know? It's just . . ."

"Everything. I know," Kevin said. "Sometimes I feel the same way."

Summer wiped away her tears, then Kevin gave her a hug. It was the first time he had ever hugged her, and for a moment she felt like a little girl again, wrapped in her father's arms, protected and safe. It didn't change the fact that the world had grown heavier than Summer could bear, or that she felt a certain helplessness as Kate drifted aimlessly on the oceans of her coma. But for that one single moment, none of the rest of it mattered.

SEVENTY-TWO

Summer had looked worn out and a little down, so Kevin had offered to give her a ride home, which she had quickly accepted. For a while, James stood over Kate's bed, watching her, looking for some sign that she might be improving. Then the social worker, Maria Santos, had popped her head in for a few minutes. She asked politely how Kate was doing, then asked about Summer, and finally she asked James how he was doing.

Crappy, he thought. *Kate's not getting any better, and we're all doing a little crappy because of it.*

But he told her he was doing okay, that the long stay in the hospital was boring and sometimes he wished he didn't feel so useless just hanging around. She said that was a common feeling. It was always frustrating when you wanted to do more but there was nothing more you could do. It sounded like a line she had used before. Then she handed him a business card, as she had handed Kevin a card when they had first met. James figured it was an ingrained behavior. A card when you introduced yourself. A card when you were ready to say good-bye.

Then Maria Santos had excused herself.

James finally settled into a Koontz book, and he read for several hours, until he couldn't read any longer. He closed the book and set it aside, then stood and stretched, and spent a moment gazing out the window across the valley. Afternoon was beginning to move into evening. It was still relatively bright out, however, in sharp contrast to the way it felt here in the hospital room. Kate's downward spiral had started almost from the moment she had arrived in this room, and James had begun to wonder now if it was ever going to stop.

There was something else that he had begun to wonder about. It had been bothering him for several days now. It had come to him late one night, right here in Kate's room. The lights had been dim, the usual hospital activity rather still. He had suddenly come awake, out of a dream. In the dream, he had been walking down a long, dirt road, seemingly an endless road, back through his life, from adulthood to childhood, then to a previous life he couldn't recall now. One of the reasons Hunter had initially taken an interest in him was because of his ability in hypnosis, particularly as hypnosis could be applied to past-life regression. That night, as James had shaken off the last images of the dream, he had begun to wonder if the use of past-life regression techniques might be a way of bringing Kate out of her coma.

James gazed at Kate's reflection in the hospital window.

Revell had added a splint to her right hand this afternoon, to keep Kate's fingers from curling. She looked a bit like a burn victim, both hands bandaged, the respirator pumping oxygen into her lungs, tubes running every which way. It was getting harder and harder to look at her and remember the Kate that lay beneath the exterior. She seemed so far gone.

He turned around, thinking maybe he should read to Kate for a while, just as the evening nurse came into the room. Her name was Jennifer. She had long dark-brown hair that hung to the middle of her back and which she always kept braided. She was in her early thirties, he guessed. One of the few nurses who seemed truly interested in Kate.

"How's she doing today?"

"About the same."

"I see the doctor added a splint."

James nodded without saying anything.

"Did she do her physical therapy?"

"After lunch."

"Good." Jennifer checked Kate's vitals, then checked the IV drip, then the respirator, making sure everything was working the way it was supposed to be working. Then she pulled up a chair and took hold of Kate's hand. "Well, Kate, here we are again, just you, me, and James. We've got the whole room to ourselves, and nothing to do but talk."

James pulled a chair up to the other side of the hospital bed.

"Someone's been in here rearranging the flowers and plants, I see."

"That was Summer," James said.

"She's got the cactus over by the window, getting a little extra sun."

All of Jennifer's visits began in this fashion, with a description of the changes in the room, or what the weather outside looked like if you took the time to really notice. Then she would talk a little about herself, about what she had done since her last visit, what plans she had already made for later in the evening. It would be a genuine conversation, the kind she might have with a good friend, and it was the genuineness that James liked most about her.

"James looks like he could use a little extra sun as well," Jennifer said. "How long have you been in here?"

"All day."

"You're a lucky young woman, Kate. Having James here to keep an eye out for you."

She asked about Summer, then about Kevin, and it wasn't long before she guided the conversation to how warm the sun had felt today, and how interesting the smell in Room 213 was now that one of the patient's relatives had brought in some potpourri. She talked about music, about how Jewel's new song, "Hands," appeared to live up to her first album, about Garth Brooks and the Backstreet Boys, about a song her grandmother used to sing to her when she was a little girl. She would talk about anything that involved the senses. Because the senses, she believed, were what kept Kate connected to the world.

James liked Jennifer.

Kate was in good hands when she was on duty.

Finally, Jennifer apologized, wishing she could stay at Kate's bedside longer, but conceding it was time for her to get back to her rounds. She said good-bye to Kate, then leaned across the bed and gave James a pat on the back of the hand.

"She's lucky to have you here," she said. She favored him with a warm, mostly compassionate smile, then promised to be back later, and left.

James found himself alone again in the room, feeling empty inside.

He thought again of pulling out the Koontz book and reading to Kate, then thought better of it. Jennifer and the doctors had encouraged him to read to her, but it was one more thing that hadn't seemed to help. Maybe now it was time to try something new.

He went to the window and closed the curtains.

He turned off the lights, and closed the door.

Then he stood next to Kate's bed, patiently removing the splint from her right hand. When it was free, he cupped the hand in his own, and spoke in a calm, soft voice. "I don't know if you can hear me or not. I don't even know if you're still there. Or if you're ever coming back. But I need you to trust me right now."

There was no physical response. He hadn't expected one. Her eyes were closed, her head tilted to the right, away from him. Her knees were drawn up slightly, also tilted away. The skin around the hole in her trachea, just beyond the white tape that sealed the tube, was red and discolored.

"Just trust me," he said. He kissed the back of her hand, then reached out and turned off the respirator.

The steady, rhythmic sound that had become the heartbeat of the hospital room over the past few days, immediately ceased. In its place, deep at the back of Kate's throat, he heard the sound of air escaping. It was the most horrible sound he had ever heard in his life, and if it had gone on only a moment or two longer, he would have surrendered to it and turned the respirator back on. But somehow, magically, Kate managed to catch a single, labored breath.

Then another.

And another.

And soon she was breathing on her own again.

"Thank you," he said, addressing both Kate and

God together. He squeezed her hand, then let out a sigh of relief that had never felt so good. "All right. That's good. That's a good start. Now I need you to try something for me. I need you to think of time as a long continuous, uninterrupted line. Can you do that for me? Just think about it a moment. Picture it if you can."

For the first time in over a week, he felt an ever-so-slight point of pressure as she seemed to curl her hand.

"That's wonderful. That's really wonderful." He paused a moment to listen, to reassure himself that she was continuing to breathe on her own, which she was. His mouth had gone dry and cottony. He swallowed, but it didn't seem to help much.

"All right, Kate. I need you to float up above this timeline now. Float up above it, and look down on it. Take a good, long look, and try to notice where your future is, and where your past is. Can you do that for me now?"

Outside the door, there was some sort of commotion. A woman said something about dinner, something about how much longer it was going to take, or what was was supposed to be on the menu. James couldn't quite make it out.

"Have you got it yet?"

Again, he felt a very slight pressure against his hand.

"You're a trooper, Kate. Now I need you to go back into the past along this timeline. I need you to pick out the event, the single momentary event that brought you here to the hospital. Go ahead and see if you can find that for me."

Almost immediately, she squeezed his hand again.

"Okay, great. Now I need you to project that event up on a screen in front of you. Make it black and white. Keep it unemotional if you can, as if it were something that had happened to someone else. It's just a movie you're watching. An old black-and-white movie."

Something felt as if it had shifted slightly.

Kate squeezed his hand again.

"Now I need you to roll the movie forward one frame at a time. Very slowly. Taking your time. I want you to roll it until you come to the very moment that you held the clay in your hands, just before you passed out. I want you to find that single, solitary moment, and then I want you to freeze the frame. Can you do that for me?"

There was a stir in the air around him. James glanced up. He felt as if someone were standing over his shoulders, watching him. A chill passed through his body.

Kate made another gasping sound, deep at the back of her throat.

Her body convulsed forward.

Her hand clamped down around his fingers with surprising strength.

"Kate?" James had a vague sense of what was coming next and it scared him. "Let go, Kate."

Her grip tightened.

An explosion of light went off. The room disappeared from around him. James found himself standing at a doorway, a universe of stars across the horizon in front of him. Below the horizon, as if he were God gazing down upon an intimate little corner of the world, he could see where a small stream had etched a canyon out of the terrain. There was a steep, nearly-vertical wall on one side of the stream, lined with thick ferns that sparkled with dew. On the other side, a blanket of white clay covered the ground, its gentle hills and valleys barely noticeable against the absence of color.

At first, it appeared as if the clay were shimmering under a bright moonlit night. Then James looked closer, and he could see waves of grayish clouds rising out of the clay like winter steam rising out of a city drain. Only this wasn't steam. It was a churning, roiling funnel of souls, eyes huge and depthless, mouths twisted and distended and letting out a blustery, howling wail.

Before James could tear free of Kate's grip to cover his ears, he was struck by a force that sent him reeling backward. He slammed into the wall, striking the back of his head first, then sank to the floor.

The ghostly wails were still thundering in his ears as he temporarily blacked out.

When James woke up again, Kate was gasping for air.

He climbed groggily to his feet, feeling the first early pulses of an oncoming headache, and crossed the room unsteadily. It was the respirator. He had turned it off before trying to bring Kate back from . . .

. . . the image of those souls, tortured and wailing, came flooding in again. He turned the respirator back on, then watched until Kate's breathing appeared to even out again. Her hand was open, the brace forcing the fingers to extend, and for a moment he wondered how she had managed to hold onto him so tightly with the brace in place like that. Then James wandered back across the room, his thoughts jumbled and fleeting, and he sat down in the chair and closed his eyes. He wouldn't open them again until early the next morning.

SEVENTY-THREE

Late that night, Kevin drove back to the hospital, left the car in the lot, and placed the keys on the Koontz paperback next to James, who was sound asleep by that time. He kissed Kate on the forehead on his way out, disheartened when there was no response. Revell had assured Kevin that she would be fine. For a few days, his presence wouldn't be missed one way or the other. But the idea of leaving her still tied Kevin in knots. From the lobby, he called a cab and made arrangements to be picked up within fifteen minutes.

Marie and Dan had agreed to keep an eye on the kids while he was gone. Marie already had menus planned for a solid week, with a promise from both James and Summer to stop by in the evening around seven for dinner. As for the case, Dan told him not to spend a minute worrying about it. All his time was wrapped up in another case anyway, he said. When Kevin got back, they could try regrouping and maybe give it another shot. Then he wished Kevin the best of luck and told him to be careful. Marie gave Kevin a peck on the check. She assured him she

would keep an eye on the kids and not to worry.
They were in good hands.

It was almost midnight by the time the cab finally
arrived.

The trip to the bus terminal was a quiet, lonely
journey through the city, and Kevin lost himself in
his thoughts. He had always been close to Helena's
mother, even before they had married. But after Helena's death, the rest of the world had ceased to exist,
and for a time, he had come to depend heavily on
Ivy. She had depended on him, too, he imagined—
they had spent hours reminiscing—but without her,
Kevin thought he would have disappeared into his
own cocoon and never come out again. He was a little ashamed to admit it to himself, but Ivy had been
stronger than he had.

When he couldn't go home to face an empty house,
she found him an apartment to rent from one of her
friends. On Saturday nights, which were particularly
difficult for Kevin because those were the nights
when he and Helena and Christy had always made
time to do something special together, Ivy began to
invite him over for dinner. They didn't talk much.
There wasn't much to say. But he saw a little of Helena in Ivy's face, and eventually he learned to find
comfort instead of pain in that resemblance. He supposed there were pieces of Helena that were recog-
nizable in him as well, and that looking across the
table at him, Ivy was somehow able to hold onto her
own fond memories of her daughter.

Kevin watched a white stretch limo pass them by,
and wondered at the changes his life had taken.

Once he had made the decision to sell the house,
Ivy had used her background in real estate to arrange ·

the initial listing and help move things smoothly through escrow after an offer had been made. He didn't have the strength to sort through all their belongings (not then, less than five months after Helena's death), so Ivy arranged to have everything moved into storage for him. Months later, when he was feeling as close to whole as he would ever feel again, she spent a day with him, sorting through Helena's clothes and jewelry, through Christy's stuffed animals and music. The memories all came flooding back, as fresh and as painful as ever. He told Ivy about the time Christy had heard about a little girl who was in the hospital after a fire, and how she had insisted on taking her favorite stuffed Tigger to the hospital to give to the girl. He had been so proud of her that day. And Ivy had told him about Helena's fourteenth birthday party when Helena had fallen into the Koi pond at the Japanese Gardens and how she had cried because she was so embarrassed. Eventually, Helena had learned to look back at the calamity with a sense of humor, and it was that wonderful sense of humor, that never taking herself too seriously, that Kevin had come to love most about her. They were fond memories. All of them. Some brought tears, some brought laughter. But quietly that day, Ivy and Kevin had boxed them all up and finally put them away.

Kevin stared out the cab window, hating himself for having put Ivy in such a dangerous situation.

The trip to the bus terminal would be the first leg of a two-day journey back East. Several sets of false identification were tucked away in a light suitcase sitting on the seat next to him. A route, which would crisscross the country using rented cars and trains, buses and airplanes, was mapped out in detail in his head. No one was going to be able to trace his steps. Not to the East. Not back again.

God, he prayed Ivy was going to be all right.

SEVENTY-FOUR

James opened his eyes and found himself curled up in a chair at the hospital.

The morning nurse looked up from the bedside, where she was taking Kate's blood pressure. She smiled. "Well, look who finally woke up."

"What time is it?"

"Almost nine."

He sat up, feeling a variety of aches and pains from sleeping in an awkward position all night. He felt something else, too. The headache to end all headaches. It felt as if it were centered high at the back of his head, where he had struck the wall last night, but there was more to it than that. His eyes were having trouble focusing, and his legs felt as if they were weighted down with concrete.

"Are you all right?" the nurse asked.

He nodded. "I could use some aspirin."

"Headache?"

"Yeah."

"Tylenol okay?"

"Sure."

"I'll get some for you."

He tried to stand up, didn't like the way it felt, and

sat back down again. He had pushed himself too hard last night, trying to connect with Kate and bring her out of her coma. Today, and maybe for a few days to come, he was going to be paying the price.

James closed his eyes again.

He didn't open them until he felt the nurse tugging at his shirt sleeve.

SEVENTY-FIVE

The house was one block over and Kevin hadn't seen it yet. Nevertheless, he had formed a picture in his mind. Two simple words said it all: crack house. He didn't need to know any more than that to know that it was not a place where Ivy belonged.

The Ford LTD was parked at the curb. Kevin sat in the back seat, a walkie-talkie in one hand. He leaned forward and tapped the driver on the shoulder. "What time you got?"

"Five to eleven." The driver was a man by the name of Buddy Walker. Kevin had never worked with him before, though he had worked with Arthur Manning, the man sitting in the front passenger seat. The last man in this four-man team was James Flynn, who was one block over, making his way down the street, passing out political flyers.

Kevin's initial concern that this might all be a setup was far at the back of his mind now. If there had been a double cross in the works, they would have sprung it on him shortly after they had all congregated at the doughnut shop a couple of miles from here. There was no question that he was still vulnerable, he would continue to be vulnerable until the moment he left the area of his own free will. But the opportunities for a double cross had been numerous, and they had all passed without incident. That was one worry which he wasn't going to burden himself with now that it was getting close to crunch time.

The primary concern now was getting Ivy out of the house, and safely into their custody. He needed to remain focused if the operation was going to go as smoothly and as quickly as possible. He did not want to see her get hurt in the process.

"You guys ready?" he asked.

They both answered in the affirmative.

Into the walkie-talkie: "Status?"

"Next house. I'll give you a go. Count it out to twenty and we're on."

"Copy."

Walker started the engine.

There had still been no sight of Ivy. It was not a given that they would even find her inside the house. Flynn had been casing the place for nearly three days now. Dressed inconspicuously in sweatpants and a Raiders parka, a guard sat in a chair outside on the front porch twenty-four hours a day. Every eight hours, a shift would end and a new guard would rotate in. (Flynn thought Hunter's arrogance might be at work here, which would explain why they made such little effort to avoid the attention of neighborhood residents.) These were not men who were associated with the Agency, at least not in any capacity that Flynn had been able to determine. The only sure sign that this was a safe house at all, or that it might hold Ivy, were the daily visits by Hunter. He stopped by, usually in the mornings, stayed for five or ten minutes without ever entering the house, then departed. He had already made his daily visit earlier this morning. All the better that they didn't have to deal with his presence.

Kevin's stomach tightened into a knot as he waited for the go. His years with the Agency had been almost entirely dedicated to the PSI Project, where he essentially had played the role of skeptic. At no time during his association with the Agency had he ever participated in field duty. That fact was at the back of his mind, not haunting him, but reminding him to remain cool and make sure he did nothing that might place the other members of the team, or Ivy for that matter, at risk.

A burst of static came over the walkie-talkie.

Then the word: *Go!*

Walker shifted into gear.

"No! Wait!" Kevin started a silent, agonizing countdown. The moment he hit twenty, he tapped Walker on the shoulder. "Now!"

The Ford jerked clumsily forward, caught some momentum, then was away from the curb and rounding the corner within seconds. Manny pulled out a black Beretta 92F, pumped the slide, then released his seat belt and wrapped his free hand around the door handle. Kevin slid across the seat and prepared to jump out.

The tires squealed as the Ford rounded the corner.

Kevin sat forward.

He could see Flynn climbing the steps of the crack house porch, a stack of political flyers in his hand. Beneath the flyers, in his other hand, was an automatic pistol. Kevin couldn't see it, but he knew it was there. He couldn't see the wide, friendly smile on Flynn's face, either. But he had no doubt Flynn was shining one.

The house, an old dilapidated two-story structure with peeling white paint and a burned-out lawn, was set back from the street maybe thirty feet. The front windows were boarded, something that Kevin noted as the Ford came to a screeching halt and the three of them piled out. Boarded windows left them blind. Not a point in their favor.

Both Walker and Manning were screaming the official cover line of the day, "FBI!" as they ran up the walkway.

At the top of the porch steps, Flynn already had the guard handcuffed and lying on his belly. He motioned to the three of them to quiet down, then sent Manning to the left, Walker to the right. Kevin went up the steps. Flynn waved him to the far side of the door.

It was strictly by the book.

Flynn on one side, Kevin on the other, both with raised guns.

Kevin had been scared out of his wits the other night, faced with the creatures. But this was a different scare. This was the unknown. This was a faceless enemy, number unknown. On top of that, it wasn't only himself he had to worry about.

Flynn pointed at his own chest, indicating he would be the first one through.

Kevin nodded and braced himself.

Flynn stepped out, gave the door a solid kick near the lock, then went low as the door swung open. Kevin stayed behind him, high, covering the room right to left. It appeared to be a living room, or what had once been a living room.

Flynn nodded to the right, where an old sofa without legs and two missing cushions sat back against the wall.

Kevin moved across the littered floor, took a position next to the left of the sofa, and covered the room as Flynn entered to the other side. The windows at their backs were boarded, painting a murky, shadow-laced pattern across the floor, the walls, and ceiling. There was a single, open doorway centered in the far wall of the room, leading deeper into the house.

Kevin crossed the floor and stood to the right of the doorway.

Flynn moved into position at the left.

Beyond the doorway lay a short hall.

Flynn went first. He stopped at the near side of a doorway to the right.

Kevin followed.

They entered the room in the same order, following the same procedure. This was the kitchen. The appliances had been removed, but there was a countertop and a sink with some overhead cabinets along the far wall. They swept the room, then moved back into the hall.

The next room was a bedroom, on the left.

It was empty.

Kevin was beginning to worry that they might have the wrong place after all, that this might have been a decoy house. He followed Flynn to the next room. A bathroom. To the right.

Empty.

There were two more doorways. One on the left, open. One straight ahead, closed.

Flynn took a position to the left of the first doorway.

Kevin took the right.

As before, Flynn went first, low, sweeping from left to right with his gun. Kevin followed behind him, high, sweeping right to left. It was another bedroom. The carpet had been pulled up and the subfloor was exposed, littered with fast food wrappers, beers cans, old newspapers, and clothing. It had been a long time since anyone had lived in this house, though transients had certainly spent a good deal of time here. There was a stale, piss-and-beer odor that Kevin hadn't noticed at first but which was nearly overwhelming now.

He coughed and tried to minimize his breathing, which was deep and labored. His eyes watered. "What the hell is that?"

Flynn shook his head, then nodded toward the closet, which had no doors. On the floor to one side, buried in a stack of empty food cans, was a clump of fur. A dead dog.

"Jesus."

Flynn crossed his lips with the pistol, then motioned him out of the room.

There was only one door left. It was padlocked on the outside.

This had to be it.

They established positions on either side.

Flynn knocked on the door, and remained in character. "FBI. Is anyone in there?"

"Ivy?" Kevin shouted. "Are you all right?"

There was no answer.

"Ivy?"

No answer.

Kevin glanced at Flynn. There was only one option left at this point. "Ivy, step away from the door. Do you hear me? Step away from the door. As far away as you can."

Still no answer.

Kevin nodded.

Flynn stepped out and fired three quick rounds into the padlock. The burst was short, sharp, and accurate. The padlock snapped open. Flynn unlatched it, then opened the door and pushed it into the room. Again, they followed procedure. Flynn went through first, low. Kevin followed him, high.

The first thing he noticed was the soundproofing tacked to all four walls and the ceiling. Then he noticed the porta-potty in one corner, the mattress sitting on the floor in the other corner, and someone lying facedown and perfectly still on the mattress. It was Ivy.

He went to her, knelt next to the mattress and turned her over. Her eyes were open, sunk deep into their sockets, staring vacantly at him. A dull, pasty, ghost-like mask covered her face. A spot of spittle had dried at the corner of her mouth. She was unconscious, but she was breathing and alive.

Behind him, Flynn said, "The stairs."

"What?"

"The stairs to the second floor. Where are the stairs to the second floor?"

Kevin stared at him a moment, unable to grasp Flynn's point. What did it matter? They had swept the house, it was empty, and they had found Ivy. But what if it wasn't—

Outside, a sudden burst of gunfire tore into the quiet. The shot appeared to come from the rear of the house, sounding like exploding champagne corks through the open door, like someone snapping his fingers through the soundproofing.

"We've been set up," Flynn said, already on his way out. "Stay put."

"We need an ambulance."

"First things first."

Kevin raised Ivy into his arms, then sat on the mattress, his back to the wall, cradling her. "Come on now.

I know you've been through hell, but you've got to hold on. You've got to hold on."

Across the room, something moved.

Kevin watched a section of the soundproofing swing away from the wall, as if an invisible door had opened. Samuel Hunter stepped out from the fuzzy-gray shadows. He hadn't changed much. He flashed a smug, self-satisfied grin that Kevin had learned to despise, then flashed something else. A gun.

"Surprise," he said softly.

Kevin held Ivy a little tighter.

"I knew you would come."

"She needs help."

"How are the kids doing these days? Feisty as ever? Summer still headstrong and making life difficult?"

"She's going to die, you arrogant bastard. Did you hear me? She needs help."

"She might die. That depends largely on you." Outside, the gunfire had fallen silent, a fact that Hunter seemed to take as favorable. He leaned against the edge of the open door, waving the gun in the air as he spoke. "Tell me about the kids."

"There's nothing to tell. We scattered."

"No, you didn't. Nice try, but I know you too well. You'd never leave them on their own. You're too responsible." Hunter tapped his wristwatch with the barrel of the gun. "Let's not waste anymore of your ex-mother-in-law's time, shall we? I don't think she's got all that much to waste. Where are the kids?"

Ivy's breathing was so shallow, Kevin wasn't sure she was breathing at all. He brushed the hair back from her face. God, she was so pale.

"If I tell you, what guarantee do I have that you'll let us go?"

"I can assure you if you don't tell me, she's going to die right here, still in your arms."

"Jesus, Hunter, what kind of a monster have you turned into?"

"Where are the kids?"

"Alaska," Kevin said quietly.

"Where?"

"Alaska."

"You're kidding."

"It's far away. It's isolated. And it's too cold, even for the likes of you."

Hunter grinned appreciatively, then pulled a cell phone out of his jacket pocket. "Give me the number."

Kevin rattled off the first numbers that came to mind. Hunter dialed using one hand, then raised the phone to his ear. It rang half a dozen times before he hung up.

"No answer."

"Can we go now?"

"Not just yet." He dialed again. "What city?"

"Juno."

Someone picked up at the other end this time, and Kevin realized what Hunter had done. He had called information, using the area code Kevin had given him.

"Juno," Hunter said. Then after a short pause, "Seattle? Really? I'm sorry, I must have mixed up the numbers."

What happened next, happened in an instant.

Kevin was already frantic, trying to sort out a plausible explanation for the false number, when Hunter lowered the cell phone and a shot went off. It happened so quickly, so unexpectedly, that he thought Hunter had gone ahead and shot Ivy out of pure malevolence. Kevin flinched and fell back against the wall, trying to move her aside and cover her before another shot could go off. Hunter flinched, too. Kevin saw him fall back against the open door, his face wearing a clownish expression of surprise, and a crazy thought passed through Kevin's head: *My God, that gun has a kick.*

But it hadn't been Hunter's gun that had gone off. Flynn was standing in the main doorway, a puff of smoke rising into the air in front of him.

Kevin glanced from Hunter to Flynn, then back to Hunter again, in time to see his cell phone slam against the floor, shatter, and send half a dozen pieces flying in all directions. The surprise was still etched into Hunter's face, even as he somehow managed to use his backward momentum to hook his hand around the edge of the soundproof door and swing the door shut behind him as he disappeared back into the space from which he had originally emerged.

It happened, all of it, in the flash of a second.

"You all right?" Flynn asked.

"I think so."

Flynn crossed the room, and tore away the panel of soundproofing that had concealed the steel door Hunter had used to enter. He traced the outline of the door with the barrel of his gun, until he was able to confirm the obvious: there was no handle, no latch, no visible means of opening the door from this side.

"He thought it through, I'll give him that."

"Everyone outside okay?" Kevin asked, climbing to his feet. He picked Ivy up in his arms, amazed at how light she was, alarmed at how pronounced her shoulder blades felt.

"Yeah. They scattered as soon as we engaged them. I think they were largely diversionary." Flynn pushed Kevin ahead of him out the door and down the hallway. "We need to get out of here. The cops are going to be swarming this place. If they get you into custody, it won't be long before they figure out who you are."

"What about Hunter?"

"We don't worry about him. There's nothing we can do about him, and there's nothing he can do about us. Another day, another fight." As they passed by the door to the kitchen, Flynn nodded toward the far corner of the room. "There's your stairs to the second floor, by the way. Behind that door. It's a crazy floor plan."

Once outside, under the sunlight, Kevin was glad to see Walker and Manning were already in the Ford, with the engine running. The guard, who had been sitting on the front porch of the old house, was now sitting in the back seat, his hands in cuffs, his legs shackled. Walker climbed out of the driver's side, opened the passenger door, pulled the guard out to make room for Kevin and Ivy, and left him there. As they pulled away, the screaming sirens of police cars came into earshot for the first time.

"Have you've got a local ID?" Flynn asked.

"Yeah."

"We'll take her to the hospital. You can be the Good Samaritan, a concerned neighbor. When you went to check on her this morning, the first time in several weeks, you found her lying unconscious on the bathroom floor. So you immediately brought her to the hospital. Got it?"

"Sure."

"But you can't stay there long. Hunter's going to be looking for you."

"I just need to make sure she's going to be all right." Ivy's eyes were still open, still gazing vacantly off into the distance. The temperature in her hands had dropped noticeably, and Kevin imagined she had gone into shock. There was only so much a body could take. It seared him to think what she must have been through. "Can't we go any faster?"

SEVENTY-SIX

Ivy never made it to the hospital alive.

She was already dead by the time Kevin and Flynn got her into a wheelchair and into the emergency room. A male nurse took over from there, wheeling her into the chaotic throngs of patients and relatives, until she disappeared from sight and Kevin became aware that he would never see her again.

Flynn tapped him on the arm. "We need to get moving. I'm sorry."

Kevin nodded numbly.

The trip home was a solitary, soul-searching journey through bus depots, rental car lobbies, train stations and airports. It took two full days, and Kevin was grateful for the time.

Oh, Ivy . . . what a sweet, dear woman.

He didn't want to remember her the way she had died, the last days of her life spent alone, locked in a small, windowless room. He didn't want to think about the stain that Hunter had been on her life. In their younger years, he and Helena used to call her Dear Prudence behind her back. The name had come from a Beatles song filled with lines like: *The sun is up, the sky is blue: it's beautiful, and so are you.* That was Ivy.

She saw the beauty in everyone around her, in the world, in the children, in everything.

He should have been able to protect her from the likes of Hunter.

He had let Ivy down, and he had let Helena down.

Unable to sleep the first twenty-eight hours of his return trip, exhaustion finally caught up with him on the bus. He closed his eyes, still overwhelmed with sorrow, and when he opened them again, night had fallen and three hundred miles had passed. A small part of his sorrow, that which had been mixed with an unhealthy dose of guilt, had passed as well. Not completely, of course. But enough to make room for a deep, seething hatred for Hunter.

As he exited the bus, the hatred exited with him. It followed him into the bathroom as he relieved himself, then into the depot restaurant, where he ordered a cup of coffee and an egg salad sandwich. It followed him to the phone booth where he called a cab, and it followed him in the back seat of the cab to the train station. It followed him like a nest of angry yellow jackets, with a belligerent relentlessness.

Hunter had to pay.

With his life.

That was the buzz of the yellow jackets.

Kevin entertained the buzz as the train left the station, for hours as it crossed the plains, and might have entertained it all the way to its fruition if thoughts of the kids hadn't interjected themselves. Once the kids were inserted into the argument, he was forced to start examining his thoughts and emotions through more responsible eyes. He was forced to take a closer look at a bigger picture.

Hunter's turn would come.

But for now, it was more important that Kevin remain focused on keeping the kids safely out of Hunter's reach.

He stared out the Amtrak window, watching the beautiful countryside pass by, and continued to argue with himself, first to go after Hunter. then to protect the kids. Ivy and Helena both came to mind, and they both argued for the safety of the kids. Hunter came to mind and expressed incredible disdain for how gutless Kevin had been back at the house. If only he had . . .

He had never liked Hunter.

Not from the first day he had met him, when Hunter had told him right off that a psychic war was not only possible, but that it was Hunter's job to build the psychic army and lead them into battle.

It was no longer a personality conflict now.

It was no longer a philosophical difference.

It was personal.

Someday, Hunter was going to have to pay.

Until then, though, the kids had to come first.

SEVENTY-SEVEN

Kevin went directly from LAX to the hospital. It was midafternoon, approaching rush hour, which he had finally come to understand started around two and usually didn't end until well past seven. Traffic was a nightmare. He curled up in a corner of the back seat of the cab, physically drained, and closed his eyes.

He dreamed.

Ivy came to him, surrounded in a soft, white aura. She was wearing the same outfit she had worn the last time he had visited her at her apartment: a white, knitted sweater and green slacks. She smiled upon him, and reassured him that she was in a good place now, and she was all right.

"It was not your fault," she said. "I was grateful that you came for me. You're a good man, Michael Hastings."

Kevin felt overcome with emotion. Completely . . . exhaustively . . . overcome. A wave of sorrow crushed down upon his shoulders, burying him under the remorse, under the despair, under the devastation of what had happened. He felt as if he were ten again, at his grandfather's funeral, staring down into the casket and experiencing a sense of almost unimaginable loss.

"I was always proud to have you as my son-in-law."

Behind her, in the dream, something moved.

The background suddenly turned dark, then foggy.

The fog began to roil.

The image of Ivy began to fade.

Behind her, to the right, Kevin became aware of another figure. This was a vague, shifting form, dipping in and out of focus as if he were looking through a kaleidoscope.

Gradually, he became aware of the figure's identity. It was Kate.

"Help me," she said. "They're all around me."

Floating weightlessly in the murk, she appeared to be enclosed by a thin protective membrane. Hovering around the edges, poking their grotesque, misshapen faces into the lamina, stretching it, distorting it, were these . . . entities . . . these black souls . . . these demons.

"Please," Kate repeated.

Please.

Please.

"Come on, Mack. I ain't got all day here."

Kevin came floating back to the surface. He opened his eyes. The cab was parked at the curb in front of the hospital. The driver, a man who looked as if he hadn't shaved in a week, gave him a hard, cold stare. Kevin sat up.

"Nice nap?"

"Sorry, it's been a long week."

"Try driving a cab for a living."

Kevin paid the man, then climbed out with his suitcase in hand. As he entered through the sliding glass doors and made his way to the elevators, he shook off the last vestiges of the dream; and by the time he was on the second floor, walking down the corridor, the dream had nearly been forgotten altogether.

He noticed Summer first as he entered Kate's room. She was curled up on a chair in the corner, asleep. It looked like a terribly uncomfortable position. He wondered how long she had been like that and if she would be able to straighten up again once she awoke. James, on the other hand, was sitting in a chair at Kate's bedside, reading aloud from the newest Dean Koontz paperback, a novel called *Seize the Night*.

He looked up and saw Kevin. "You're back."

"I don't quite believe it myself," Kevin said, dropping the suitcase on the floor.

"How did it go?"

"Not well." He held her left hand, which was still in a splint to keep the fingers from curling, and was immediately reminded how much he disliked the slow, mechanical sound of the air being forced into her lungs. "What has Revell had to say? Anything?"

"He didn't sound too optimistic the last time he made his rounds. She's not brain dead or anything like that. But he thinks she's losing her will to live."

Summer stirred from her sleep. "I told you."

Kevin nodded, without looking up. "What do you think is happening to her?"

"She's just drifting. That's all it is. There's nothing for her to hold onto. It's like she's floating in the ocean, just bobbing along on the waves with no way to get back to shore. She's lost."

"You can't reach her?"

"I don't know how," Summer said. "It's not the same as what I've done before. This is like the entire universe has got its hands on her. I think I'd get lost, too. I think we'd both be lost."

He didn't entirely understand what she was trying to say, though in her own way, he supposed she was simply expressing her feelings of being overwhelmed. She wasn't alone. He felt very much the same.

Kevin gave Kate's hand a loving pat, then let it fall gently back to her side. "I think I need to talk to Revell."

SEVENTY-EIGHT

Lyle Henderson opened the door and stared out at Kaufman with that same jittery nervousness he had displayed the last time the two of them had stood face-to-face. He scratched at the stubble on his face, then swallowed hard, and said, "Oh, lucky day. You're back. What do you want?"

"Did some checking on you, Henderson. Seems you've got a bit of a temper."

"This is L.A. Everyone's got a temper. Haven't you been on the freeway lately?"

"Yeah, but you took yours out on a cop."

"That was a long time ago. I was drunk. I got sent to my room without dinner, and I've been a good boy ever since." He was dressed in a torn T-shirt, ragged jeans that were too large for him, and no shoes. He shifted his weight, then glanced nervously over Kaufman's shoulder, out toward the street, pulling at the loose skin under his chin. "That's the way the system works, right? You do the crime, you do the time, then everything's even? All's forgiven?"

"Not exactly. It's still on your record."

"So now I won't be able to work at the U.S. Mint.

So what do I care? Big deal. Why don't you just tell me what you're doing standing here wasting my time?"

"I'm waiting for you to invite me in, so we can talk."

"We can talk right here."

Kaufman grinned, curious now. Was it simply that Henderson was a prick who liked to make things difficult just for the fun of it? Or was there something he was trying to hide? "And here I thought we were old friends by now. Is there some reason you don't want to invite me in?"

"I'm not exactly Martha Stewart, you know. The house is a mess."

"You forget . . . I've seen the mess. But if you insist, I suppose I could stop by and visit a judge, see if he'll draw up an invitation for me, do it up all official like, and then come back. It shouldn't take me long. Less than an hour, I would guess. Though an hour's an hour, and I wouldn't be thrilled with having to waste one."

"Christ, you guys are all alike."

"Know a lot of us, do you?"

Henderson stepped back into the house, leaving the door open. "Come on in if you have to. You know where it is . . . straight ahead, first room on your left."

"Toss the papers on the floor. Yeah, I know," Kaufman said.

He stepped through the doorway.

SEVENTY-NINE

Kevin had a nurse at the nearest station page Revell, and it was a good twenty minutes before the doctor finally showed up. He looked as tired as Kevin felt. Dark circles under his eyes. His shoulders slightly sagging. His mouth tight and unforgiving.

They shook hands.

"Just get back?" Revell asked.

"Straight from the airport."

"Had a chance to see her yet?"

Kevin nodded. "What can you tell me?"

"Not much, I'm afraid. She continues to exhibit activity in the cerebrum, which is, overall, a good sign. But the fact that she continues not to breathe on her own, that troubles me. I'm wondering now if maybe there was some damage to the brain stem, something I might have overlooked."

"And if that's the case?"

"Well, let me put it this way: it's a path we hope we don't have to go down. There's no coming back once you wander down that road."

That was as much as Revell seemed prepared to say at the moment, and as much as Kevin supposed he wanted to hear. They spoke a brief time longer, mostly small talk about how tired each of them was feeling, and a little about the strain that was beginning to show up on the faces of James and Summer.

Then Revell received a page and excused himself.

Kevin went back down the corridor to Kate's room.

It seemed apparent now that he needed to do something, and he needed to do it soon. Kate was trapped in a state of limbo that only seemed to be dragging her deeper and deeper into its depths. If he stood around and watched much longer, she might never find her way up again.

He had already lost Ivy.

He couldn't bear the thought of losing Kate, too.

Summer was standing at the window, staring out across the smoggy layer that had settled over the area. James was standing at Kate's bedside again. He had closed the Koontz paperback and left it on the swing table next to a plastic cup with water that Summer had used to water the plants.

"Okay," Kevin said. "Time to get down to work."

He didn't know exactly what he meant by that, only that it was better to do something and fail than to do nothing at all. Kate had landed here because she had touched the white clay. And it seemed to him that if they could figure out where the stuff had come from and what qualities it carried, then maybe they might have a chance at helping her come out of the coma.

But he didn't want to leave Kate alone, so James volunteered to stay with her.

Summer, on the other hand, well, Kevin wanted Summer with him. He trusted her intuition. It was a struggle for him at times. He still had not been able to find a place for it in his worldview. Yet he had seen enough to know that Summer possessed a special gift most people did not. Beyond that, he felt part of the reason she had become so withdrawn and moody lately was because she had spent all her time here at the hospital. She needed to get out. She needed to feel as if she were helping to bring Kate back and not just watching her sink deeper.

First, though, Kevin wanted to stop by the house, drop off his suitcase, and freshen up.

EIGHTY

Something was different.

Kaufman didn't know what it was exactly, only that he had a feeling that something was not right.

He followed Henderson down the hall and into the living room, where he moved a stack of newspapers and sat down on the sofa. Henderson stood across the room, leaning against the television set with his arms crossed. He glanced to his left, out the sliding glass doors that opened into the backyard, then to the doorway, then to Kaufman, his eyes seemingly unable to settle anywhere.

"All right, you're in. You've made yourself at home. Everything's peachy. Now ask your questions and let's get this over with, so you can get back to catching the bad guys and I can get back to reading my newspaper."

"Still unemployed, I gather?"

"Still not a crime, I assume?"

"How are you getting by? Not being employed and all?"

"Didn't know you cared," Henderson answered sarcastically. He tugged at the loose flesh of his neck again, glancing sideways out the sliding glass doors. "I manage. A little unemployment insurance. A job here and there."

"You look like you've been losing some weight."

"A couple pounds. Why? Is that against the law, too? What the hell is this all about? You have a question that has a point behind it? I mean, how long do we have to keep playing this . . . this shitty game of good cop, oh, I really give a damn? This is shit, man. Pure shit. And you know it. What are you doing here? What are you looking for?"

Kaufman thought he might have already found what he was looking for. Henderson was irritable, nervous, hyper, talking incessantly. He looked like he hadn't slept in days, like he had been living in the same clothes, in the same squalor so long he wasn't even aware of what he looked like. To Kaufman, it seemed rather clear. He looked like a guilty man.

"You seem awfully edgy, Lyle."

"Wouldn't you be? I already told you I didn't know anything. But you're back, aren't you? Hassling me again because you don't know what the hell you're doing. You're shooting in the dark and you're shooting fucking blanks and you know it."

"Come on, Lyle, you're wasting my time."

"Hey, you got something to ask, you ask it. If you don't have anything to ask, then excuse yourself and get the hell out of here." Henderson stared at him a moment, then nodded and looked away, suddenly feeling a little cocky with himself.

"You done?"

"Maybe." He shifted uneasily. "I don't know. I guess. Yeah, okay. Yeah, I am. I'm done."

"What are you using, Lyle?"

"See? There it is. That's why I don't like talking to

you guys. You think you know everything. You think you can just look at a guy and peg him." He snapped his fingers. "Like that. Without knowing nothing. Nothing. Like he's no one in your eyes."

"Speed?"

He scoffed. "No."

"What is it, then?"

"Nothing, man."

"Oh, it's something all right." Kaufman had begun to notice the odor. It was faint, simmering just beneath the strong scent of ink from all the newspapers in the room. But this was a sour smell. It reminded him of the smell inside his grandmother's house when he was a kid.

"What's the smell, Lyle?"

"Oh, sure. Now the house stinks." He took a whiff of his right armpit. "Or maybe it's me. That what you're trying to say? I stink?"

It wasn't Henderson.

It wasn't the ink on the newsprint either.

Kaufman wasn't sure what it was, but it was familiar.

So damn familiar.

EIGHTY-ONE

It was a combination of things, Kevin assumed, that made their arrival home a rather subdued, wordless event. He was still dragging from the trip, of course. He'd need a couple days to catch up on his rest and start feeling energetic again. Then there was Ivy's death, which was still fresh in his mind, and still carried an emotional blow every time he relived finding her alone and dying in that barren, dilapidated old house. And finally, on top of it all, there was Kate, who seemed to be disappearing right before his eyes.

He opened the front door for Summer, who went through first.

"I'm going to use the bathroom," she said, heading upstairs.

Kevin wandered down the short hall to the kitchen. He tossed the keys on the table, then sat down, wearily. The house had begun to feel too big lately, too empty. It needed Kate back. It needed family here again. Everything was falling apart, and he was beginning to feel helpless to hold it together.

He got up, admonishing himself that doing nothing was worse than doing something that didn't help.

Dougherty had given him the number of the Minitu shaman, which Kevin had written down on a piece of scrap paper. He went rummaging through the kitchen drawer next to the phone, where he thought he had left it, and found the scrap of paper under a pencil and a couple of AA batteries.

The shaman was a woman by the name of Cecelia Haring. She was a soft-spoken woman with a young voice made even younger when she laughed. Kevin introduced himself, told her Dougherty had passed her name to him, and asked if he could have a few minutes of her time.

"How can I can help you, Mr. McConnell?"

"Dougherty mentioned a warrior burial ground. I guess you might call these *fallen* warriors."

"Yes. There is such a place."

"It's not mythological?"

She laughed. "To some it may be. To others . . . there is no such thing as mythology."

"I assume you would be the latter?"

"The place exists, Mr. McConnell. Whether or not it exists for you . . . that's not for me to say."

"I was told the soil there is white clay?"

"Yes."

"That's rather unusual for a burial ground, isn't it?"

"It serves a specific purpose."

"Is that to trap the spirits? To keep them earthbound?"

"Mr. Dougherty tell you that?"

"Yes."

"The burial ground is sacred. It's been many years since anyone has been buried there. However, it is true that the ground is white clay; and it is true that this is a place where my people chose to bury those warriors who had shamed their peers. It was believed, it is still believed, that the clay entraps these spirits and holds them to this earthly plane, where they cannot rise to higher spiritual planes."

"The clay, then, becomes sort of a depository for the spirit?"

"Yes."

Summer came into the kitchen and sat at the table. She brushed the hair out of her face, then stared quietly at Kevin, listening halfheartedly to the conversation. It had been a long time since Kevin had seen a smile on her face. The situation with Kate had hit her hard, and the longer it went on, the deeper Summer seemed to pull into herself.

"If I removed some of the clay—"

"That would be impossible," the shaman said.

"Why?"

"The burial ground is sacred. It's not permissible for anyone to remove the clay."

"Hypothetically, I mean. Hypothetically, if I removed the clay from the burial grounds, what would happen to the spirits?"

"Spirits buried in the clay would go where the clay goes. The clay is the body of the spirit. They cannot leave the clay."

"Interesting. Let me tell you a little bit about the situation here and why I called you," Kevin said. He leaned back against the cabinet, watching as Summer picked up the armature he had left leaning against the wall nearly a week ago now. Trying not to get ahead of himself, he proceeded to fill the woman in on the murders and the white clay samples that had been found at the crime scenes. Eventually, he arrived at the night when the creatures had appeared right here in his own house. He explained how they had captured one, and how they had later stripped the creature of the clay. Kevin never mentioned anything about the rubber band and the white clay. He didn't want to muddle the story any more than it already was.

"Is this leading where I think it's leading?" the woman asked.

"I don't know. Where do you think it's leading?"

She laughed again. "You can't even say it, can you?"

"What?"

"What you're thinking."

Maybe that was true. Kevin paused and took a moment to look at himself. He had to admit, he had definitely been resisting the one idea that seemed to keep popping up in his thoughts about this case. It was not something he had made a place for yet. Not in his personal belief system anyway. "Okay, fair enough. Here's what I've been trying to find a way around: somehow, this guy who works in the business gets his hands on some of your clay."

"It's not *my* clay. It belongs to the earth."

"Sorry," Kevin said. "He gets his hands on this clay, and he uses it to sculpt his models. And the . . . the . . ."

"Spirits. The word is spirits."

Kevin laughed, amused at how difficult this was becoming. "And the *spirits* inhabit these models. They animate them, bring them to life, make them real. Is that even possible?"

"Yes," she said matter-of-factly. "It is possible. Quite possible."

There was a long silence, when Kevin couldn't seem to absorb what he had heard.

"You were hoping I would tell you something different."

"I've always dealt a little better with the concrete."

"A man of science?"

"For the most part."

"What about God?"

Kevin had never fully reconciled his thoughts about God. Publicly, he had always maintained an atheistic position, fully advancing evolution and natural selection. Privately, he found himself in awe of everything from the delicacy of a flower petal to the mysteries of a black hole. When he thought about these things, he tended to feel a certain disdain for the idea that all these wonders were no more than happenstance. Yet how they all related to God and to what God might actually be . . . these were still unanswered questions for him.

"I haven't decided," he said, surprised by the shame he felt in these words.

"What about faith?"

"I cross my fingers."

She laughed again, that youthful sound. "It is possible that the spirit in the clay could bring life to your sculptures. Spirit is eternal. It never dies. The difficulty, however, is in obtaining the clay from the burial ground. This would not be a simple task. Not normally."

"I was told the grounds were in Hayfork. Northern California, right?"

"Yes, in a very remote part of the area."

"Difficult to find, I take it?"

"Impossible. Unless someone within the tribe were to take you there."

Summer had completely lost interest in his conversation with the shaman now. Her attention shifted solely to the armature, which she had set on the table.

She toyed with one of the joints—a knee joint, Kevin thought—extending it to its full range, then closing it again.

"Which may have been exactly what happened," the shaman said resignedly.

"Pardon?"

"There was a man who came to one of our members a number of months ago. He presented himself as an anthropologist. He claimed to be interested in studying our burial rites."

"Someone took him there? To the burial grounds?"

"He was shown the grounds, which he returned to twice over three days. There was a guide with him."

"Always?"

"Yes."

"And he wasn't permitted to remove any of the clay?"

"That would be sacrilege," the woman said. She paused this time, and Kevin imagined she was considering if she wanted to continue down this course of conversation or not. Then, softer, she added, "Though someone did remove some clay from the grounds, Mr. McConnell. This occurred several weeks later. I don't know if it was or not, but it may have been our anthropologist."

"Did he give you his name?"

"John Turner. It was not his real name."

"You checked?"

"Yes. After the clay was removed. I had my suspicions then."

"What did he look like?"

"On the short side, maybe five-eight. Late fifties, early sixties. He walked with his shoulders hunched forward, as if he might have a bad back. He had a good aura, healthy, blue-yellow. Passive, caring. Appeared to be a decent man."

"Something else just occurred to me. You're a shaman. Doesn't a shaman have healing powers?"

"God has healing powers. A shaman serves God."

"But you can heal, can't you?"

"If it's God's wish."

"I was wondering if you would do me a favor."

EIGHTY-TWO

The impression came to Summer suddenly, in a flash.

She stiffened. The armature slipped out of her hands, and crashed to the table.

Something wasn't right.

A strange charge ran through her body—a vibration or a hum—and she couldn't seem to move.

"What is it?" Kevin asked. "What's wrong?"

There was a bright flash, and suddenly Summer found herself floating, weightless, in a strange, ethereal state. She could hear Kevin's voice somewhere in the distance behind her, calling her name. And somewhere in the distance in front of her, she thought she could hear Kate's voice, though she couldn't tell what Kate was saying.

Summer tried to focus her energies on getting back to the kitchen, back to her body. But it felt as if the connection with her own body no longer existed, as if she were floating free through space, an astronaut without a lifeline.

Then there was another bright flash.

She found herself standing at the head of a narrow gorge. There was a mist coming down around her. The

sides of the gorge were covered with a thick blanket
of ferns and moss. A shallow creek with clear water
that appeared almost motionless snaked down the middle of the gorge. The banks of the creek on either side
were pure white clay.

Then another flash.

Summer opened her eyes and she was standing in
the corner of a dark room. A line of cabinets and a
workbench stretched along one wall. There was a man,
sitting on a stool, hunched over the workbench, his
back to her. He was a familiar figure. She stepped
around to one side to see his face.

"Summer!"

Kevin's voice.

"Can you hear me?"

She felt another jolt of electricity charge through her
body. Her muscles stiffened. The figure in front of
her disappeared. The room around her disappeared.
Her eyes opened to a sudden, blinding brightness. She
caught a deep breath.

She was back in the kitchen again.

Kevin was kneeling on the floor in front of her. He
had her by the arms, staring into her eyes. "Hey, you
back?"

She blinked, then nodded slowly.

"What was that all about?"

Her vision cleared. She shook the last remaining images out of her thoughts, then looked at him squarely.
"I think I know who it is."

EIGHTY-THREE

The smell that had seemed so familiar to Kaufman was cat urine.

His grandmother had loved cats. They were in and out of her house all day long. Some wild. Some her own. Some belonging to the neighbors. She fed them, gave them a place to sleep, and thoroughly enjoyed their company. And that was the smell that Kaufman remembered . . . that cat urine odor that seemed to stain every room in the house.

"You like cats, Lyle?"

"Cats? Christ, what are you talking about?"

"That smell. That's cat piss. So I figure if the place smells like cat piss, you must have cats. Right?"

"Maybe."

"Unless it's something else?"

Henderson's face went pale. He shifted from one foot to the other. His eyes darted again, from the doorway to the sliding glass doors, then to Kaufman. "It's nothing. What is it with you, man? You need to get a life. You've been playing cop too long. Everything's a crime. Everything's suspicious."

"Not everything. Just you."

"Well, you're barking up the wrong tree. I can tell you that."

Kaufman sniffed the air. "Doesn't smell like it."

He had a fairly good idea of what was going on here. It had taken him a while to peg the smell, but it all made perfect sense now. Henderson's nervousness. The clutter in the house. The cat urine.

Kaufman stood up. "You know. I still haven't received the grand tour. Why don't you show me around the place?"

"There's nothing to see."

"Sure there is," he said, moving out into the hall. He glanced to the right, down the short stretch to the front door, then to the left. "What's down this way?"

"The kitchen."

"See? I haven't seen the kitchen yet."

Henderson forced his way past him. "It's a mess. Believe me, you don't want to go in there."

"I've seen the living room. How much worse can it be?"

"Plenty. I'm telling you, you don't want to go in there, man."

Kaufman kept moving forward. Henderson kept backpedaling. Together, they ended up standing in the doorway. As hard as it was to imagine, Henderson had been telling the truth. The kitchen was worse than the living room. Half of the linoleum had been pulled up, exposing the black backing underneath. The sink and counter were littered with fast food containers. The refrigerator door had been removed, the shelves stacked with cans of ravioli and spaghetti, pork and beans, chili, and tuna fish. The gas stove, which was white enamel, was chipped and rusty. Cobwebs bridged the space between the back of the stove and the wall.

"Don't cook much do you?"

"Cute. Now you've gone and lost your invitation for Christmas dinner."

Kaufman grinned.

"Okay, you've seen the kitchen. Now will you finally excuse yourself and get the hell out of my house?"

The smell of cat urine was particularly strong here. It appeared to be originating from a door off to the right of the room. The door was closed. There was a padlock on it. Kaufman motioned in that direction. "Where's the door lead?"

"The basement."

"What's down there?"

"My work. I told you all this before. Every once in a while, I still do some model work, even some design work. And I like to play around with the mechanics and stuff."

"Mind if I have a look?"

"Yes. I mind. It's my *work*. I don't want some dumb, asshole cop messing around down there."

"That why you keep it padlocked? To keep out all the asshole cops that come nosing around?"

Henderson shook his head, like some dumb teenage kid who can't believe his father is putting him through so much agony. "What do you think?"

"Open it."

"What if I don't want to?"

"What if I give a call to the county and get an inspector over here to make a list of all the health code violations? Then we'll all get to look in the basement together. And when we're done there, we'll just condemn the whole damn house and toss you out on your ass."

"You can't do that."

"The hell I can't." Kaufman pulled out his cell phone, flipped it open and started dialing.

"All right. All right. Christ, you'd think I was Lee Harvey Oswald." Henderson stuffed a hand into the right front pocket of his jeans. He came out with a key chain. On one end was a small, plastic skeleton head with black, deep-set eyes. On the other end, half a dozen keys of various sizes and shapes dangled from a small metal ring. He stepped around Kaufman, found the right key, unlocked the padlock, and opened the door. Then he took a step back. "There's nothing down there, man. Just a lot effects shit."

Kaufman grinned, thinking how this was getting better all the time. He stood at the threshold and gazed into the darkness. "Where's the light?"

"To your left. On the wall," Henderson said. There was a crackle in his voice. "I'm telling you, there's nothing down there. Nothing even worth a look."

Kaufman found the switch.

The light went on.

He stepped onto the top landing of the stairway, shaded his eyes, and tried to look beneath the glare of the light at the bottom landing.

The last thing he remembered was not what he saw, but what he smelled. The stench of cat urine was overwhelming here.

Then he blacked out.

EIGHTY-FOUR

"Who are you? And what are you doing?" James asked. He had gone downstairs to the hospital cafeteria for a Coke and some chips to carry him through the afternoon, and when he had returned, he had found the stranger standing over Kate's bed.

She looked up, neither surprised nor concerned. "You must be James. My name's Cecelia Haring. Your father asked me to come."

"My father?"

"Kevin McConnell."

"Why?"

"He thought I might be able to help."

"I don't think anyone can help," James said. He crossed the room, dropped the Coke and chips on the chair next to the Koontz novel, then joined her at the hospital bed. Kate hadn't stirred, even reflexively (as the doctors liked to call it), in longer than he could remember. He took her hand in his own, protectively. "The doctors haven't been able to do anything, what made him think you could help?"

"I'm a different kind of doctor," she said.

EIGHTY-FIVE

Kevin knocked on the door, then took a step back on the stoop and stood next to Summer.

They had both arrived at the same conclusion almost simultaneously. For Kevin it had been spurred by the shaman's description of the man she had suspected of removing clay from the burial grounds. For Summer, it had been the impressions she had received after holding the armature in her hands.

"You all right?" Kevin asked.

Summer nodded and crossed her fingers. She still appeared mildly shaken. The color had not fully returned to her face. On the trip over, she had stared out the car window, not saying a word until they had come to a stoplight, when suddenly she had asked, "You think it's too late for Kate to come back?" The best he had come up with was the old cliché: it's never too late.

Victor Koenig answered the door. "A return visit? To what do I owe the pleasure?"

"Sorry to bother you again," Kevin said. "We were just wondering if we might be able to ask you a few more questions?"

"In regard to our previous subject of conversation?"

"Yes."

"I would be surprised if I could be of much more assistance, but please, do come in. It's always nice to have company." Koenig stepped back into the house and held the door open. "You remember your way?"

Kevin said he did, and Summer followed down the hallway close behind him.

The living room was in stark contrast to the brightness outside. The curtains were closed, effectively shutting out the sunlight. There was a slightly musty smell in the air, a smell that had been there on their previous visit, but which had not seemed nearly as vivid. Kevin and Summer sat on the sofa. Koenig sat in the recliner across from them. He let out a sigh, his breathing slightly labored, then he put a hand to his mouth and cleared his throat.

"Is there anything I can get for you?"

Kevin said, "No, thank you." He had tried to reach Kaufman, directly, without the pager, but Kaufman had been out in the field somewhere. So instead, Kevin had used the pager to leave a message letting his friend know where they would be, just in case anything went wrong.

"Ever heard of the Minitu?" Kevin asked bluntly.

"Pardon?"

"The Minitu. A Native American tribe in the northern part of the state."

Koenig stared off to the right, then shook his head. "No. No, I'm sorry. I don't believe I have."

Kevin nodded. "It's an interesting tribe."

"Is it?"

"They have this sacred burial ground . . ."

"In a gorge," Summer said. "With a creek running through it, and lots of ferns and moss."

"And a good deal of white clay." Kevin finished.

"Ah, the clay. This is what you asked about last time, if I'm not mistaken. This clay, this is important to you?"

"We know you were there. We know you presented yourself as an anthropologist, and after you were shown the burial grounds you returned and removed the clay." Kevin sat forward. "Did you have any idea what you were doing? Did you know what you had?"

"I think you're confusing me with someone else."

"The shaman remembers you."

"Does she?"

Kevin grinned. A slip. "Yes, *she* does."

Koenig sat motionless, realizing his mistake and collecting his thoughts. He looked older than he had the last time they had visited. The lines in his face were deeper. The life in his eyes dimmer. He removed his bifocals, rather mechanically, and used a corner of the afghan that covered the chair to clean them. He put the glasses on again, then sighed.

"It has not been easy," he said. "It's been a nightmare, actually."

EIGHTY-SIX

When Kaufman woke up, he found himself lying at the bottom of the steps, flat on his back. He sat up, felt an alarming shot of pain through his rib cage, then leaned against the cinder-block wall, and tried not to move unnecessarily.

The tumble down the stairs had left him feeling sore all over, but the worst of it was a rib on his left side. Either it was severely bruised or it was broken. Every time he took a breath or twisted just slightly in one direction or the other, there was another explosion of pain.

To top it off, there was a knot the size of an avocado pit growing out of the back of his head. He touched it, then winced, and vowed not to do that again. It hurt like the dickens.

Henderson, bless his little soul, had left the light on. The door at the top of the stairway was closed. Undoubtedly it was also padlocked again. Across the concrete floor, piled against the far wall, was an assemblage of odds and ends: half-a-dozen plastic containers of antifreeze, lantern fuel, a stack of coffee filter boxes, batteries, duct tape, cold medications, a number of clear glass beakers and containers. The crude makings for methamphetamine. In the far corner, several pounds of the substance had already been bagged and weighed, and were waiting to ship.

That explained the strong odor of cat urine.

And it explained Henderson's erratic behavior and incessant talking.

And it explained how Henderson was getting by on unemployment.

The basement was small, maybe fifteen by twenty. There were no windows here. The only door was the one at the top of the stairs. Under the odor of cat urine was a damp, musty smell, apparently caused by a water leak in the far wall, where mineral deposits had left a white, crusty trail down the cinder blocks.

No one knew he was here.

Except for Henderson, of course.

Under normal circumstances, he didn't think Henderson was the kind of man who would commit murder. He was a prick, as Kevin had so aptly described him, kind of a slimeball headed down a long road to nowhere. But a murderer? Probably not.

Of course, this was no ordinary situation.

The stakes were high.

The meth was probably worth a hundred grand on the street.

So it was easy to image what Henderson was doing now. He was upstairs, pacing, trying to decide if he should just pack his things and leave town before all hell broke loose, or if getting rid of the cop in the basement would save him all that trouble.

It could go either way.

And it didn't help that Henderson wasn't just manufacturing meth, he was using it.

Kaufman adjusted his position again, and winced,

this time at the pain coming from his ribs. As he settled back against the wall, he felt something in his left jacket pocket jab him in the side. With care, he opened the jacket and stuck his hand into the pocket. He couldn't believe what he came up with.

It was his cellular phone.

In his panic, Henderson had forgotten all about the phone.

Maybe the fact the man was on meth had actually worked in Kaufman's favor.

Kaufman flipped the phone open, dialed up the department, and waited. The connection was charged with interference, probably caused by the cinder blocks, but it wasn't so bad he couldn't be heard. He filled them in on the situation, the location of the house, and the fact that he was locked in the basement only a few feet away from a meth lab. Then he hung up and waited.

It was all a matter of timing now.

Who would arrive first? Henderson or the cops?

EIGHTY-SEVEN

Silas became aware of the intruders upstairs.

There had been a knock at the front door. The man had answered, and he had welcomed the visitors into the house. Initially, there had been feelings of curiosity and an odd gratefulness for the company. But those feelings had quickly given way to agitation, and the agitation had given way to fear.

Something new was happening now.

Silas could sense the danger.

The creature pushed open the cabinet door and jumped down to the workbench. Gradually, its eyes adjusted to the basement darkness, a darkness that suddenly felt electrified with emotions. It moved down the line to the adjacent cabinet, opened the door, then encouraged its fellow Protector to step out and join it. Then to the next cabinet, the next Protector.

These were their bodies now, where their spirits resided. Breathe in, and the man's fear filled every animated cell, every fissure, every thought, idea, form. The fear swirled in the air like an angry, turbulent storm, the way the man's bitterness had swirled around them before, calling them, begging them, enticing them to respond.

Silas gathered the creatures at the foot of the stairway, communicating through a series of odd, rhythmically-unbalanced *clicking* sounds generated near the back of their throats. They had been designed as warriors, to protect the alien family, but they had adapted, and now it was the man they were devoted to protecting. He was their creator, their God.

Silas raised its head in the air, filled itself with the imbuing fear, then started up the stairway.

The others followed close behind.

EIGHTY-EIGHTY

.

Cecelia was an intense, focused woman. After she had filled James in on her background as a Minitu shaman, she began to remove a variety of stones and talismans from a leather pouch. "Kevin ... he's not your natural father, is he?"

"We're adopted."

She handed him a feather. "This is an ówl feather. Normally, it is used to assist the flight of your soul while you sleep. It will help if you need to reach Kate."

"I've already tried to reach her," James said. On and off for the past four days, after he had tried to direct Kate to her timeline, he had continued to experience small, nagging headaches. They had been accompanied by an odd sense of detachment, as if everything were out of focus. This morning was the first time he had become aware that he was starting to feel normal again.

"I know," she said matter-of-factly. "You met them, didn't you?"

"Them?"

"The demons."

"That's what they were? Demons?"

"Actually, they're the spirits of disgraced warriors." She handed him a necklace made from a leather strap wrapped securely around a quartz crystal. "For protection."

"You're getting me worried here. What exactly are we going to be doing?"

"Retrieving her soul." Cecelia placed an agate on Kate's bedsheet. "This will help us discern the truth in the face of lies."

Another stone.

"Azurite. To help us communicate." She placed a third stone next to the others. "This is dravite. For protection."

"Guess you can never have too much protection," James said.

Another stone.

"Obsidian. To eliminate gullibility." She pulled the last stone from the leather pouch. "Tiger's eye. For clarity. To see things as they are and not as the demons would have you see them."

"Are we going to need all this?"

"Let's hope not." She didn't need to explain the next item she pulled from the pouch. James was already familiar with it. The white clay. She peeled the waxed paper away from it, then placed the small, open packet on the bedsheet between them.

"I've seen that stuff in action," James said. "You can't trust it."

"It's been cleansed in ceremony."

"What's it for?"

"To serve as a container for any demons that might escape."

"Great. Glad I asked."

"I believe we're ready now."

EIGHTY-NINE

"Please, you have to understand," Koenig said. "Such a thing was never my intention. I never imagined anyone would be hurt. Never."

"Did you know what you had?" Kevin asked plainly. "Did you know the clay was inhabited by the spirits?"

"No. No, of course not. I thought it was all a silly superstition." His eyes filled with tears. He bowed his head. "My God, what did I do? I wanted to work again, that was all. Just to have my work respected again."

"Three people have died. Husbands and fathers."

"There was so much bitterness inside me. A man . . . his thoughts get clouded . . . he loses his perspective." Koenig caught his breath, then sighed deeply. "I read about the burial ground in an article in a magazine. It mentioned this clay, this rich, moist clay, and I asked myself . . . what if this is something special? What if it's the first step in finding my way back?"

"So you pretended to be an anthropologist?"

"Yes."

"And when you saw the clay . . ."

"I knew right away it was special, and I had to have it."

Kevin had focused so intently, so entirely upon Victor Koenig that he had nearly forgotten Summer was in the room with them. But that changed when she quietly reached out and touched him on the forearm. He stopped and looked at her. She raised her head slightly, as if she were listening to something just beyond his range.

"What is it?" Kevin asked.

"They're coming."

"Who's coming?"

"The creatures."

NINETY

Everything seemed to happen all at once.

Summer had sensed their presence in the house, but she hadn't realized how close they were. No sooner had she warned Kevin they were coming when an incredible commotion erupted somewhere out in the hallway. There was a loud splintering sound. A wave rolled through the floor like an earthquake beneath Summer's feet.

Koenig looked up, startled, his eyes wide. "We'd better get you out of here."

The creatures were coming, and they were coming fast. The sound of their claws clamoring madly across the surface of the linoleum floor was like a drumroll before the fall of the gallows gate.

Summer stood up and backed away from the doorway.

Kevin stood and stepped in front of her.

All three creatures arrived in unison, scrabbling around the corner like a pack of wild dogs after a rabbit. They fought their way, shoulder to shoulder, into the suddenly small room, in a savage, furious rampage that left little time for Summer to do anything but fall back.

The first one through took to the air and struck Kevin just below his rib cage, knocking him backward into Koenig, who had remained seated. The recliner flipped over. Kevin went flying in one direction, Koenig in another.

The creature came down hard, smashing its head into the metal footing of the standing lamp. It landed only inches away from Kevin's face, then staggered to its feet, dazed from the impact. Before it could regain its senses, he wrapped his hands around its neck and held it at arm's length, safely away from his body.

Summer, who had managed to sidestep Kevin as he was falling back, was hit by the second creature through the door. It wasn't a clean hit, thank God. The creature flew past her as she twisted away. Still, its claws raked across her stomach, shredding the bottom half of the black T-shirt she was wearing.

She screamed, more out of fear than pain, but managed to maintain her balance.

Koenig crawled on all fours across the floor, until he reached the corner, next to the mahogany cabinet. He huddled into the space between the cabinet and the wall like a child who feared his father was coming with the belt. He had lost his bifocals in the scramble. His eyes looked like small, white pearls. He brought a fist to his mouth and bit down on a scream that was trying to break free.

Kevin barely had time to climb back to his feet. He had managed to keep the creature at arm's length, though in its struggle for release, its claws had already done some serious damage to both of his forearms.

Blood was flowing freely.

He hurled the creature across the room like a football. It collided with the wall near the center of the

Carnival of Souls poster, went limp, then fell to the floor in a ball of latex.

In less than a breath, the third creature attacked.

It hit Kevin low, raking its claws across the back of his calves in a now-familiar tactic to bring him down. For a moment, the pain was barely noticeable, just a cold sensation across the surface of the flesh. Then it exploded, and Kevin collapsed to his knees.

Across the room, the creature who had attacked Summer turned and went after her again. This time, she made no effort to move out of its way. Instead, she held her ground. When it arrived within range, she buried the toe of her tennis shoe deep into its midsection. It doubled over, and went flying across the room backward.

Summer turned her attention to Kevin just as he was falling to his knees.

The creature that had brought him down went after him again, tenaciously. It clamped its jaws around Kevin's right shoulder and dug deep into the flesh. He screamed, then fell forward into the side of the overturned recliner.

Summer cringed.

Something familiar began to boil inside her.

To her left, from out of the mahogany cabinet, Koenig brought out a long metallic cylinder that looked as if it had once held architectural plans or maybe a prized movie poster. He brought the cylinder down, flush, across the head of the creature at Kevin's shoulder.

There was a loud squeal.

The creature fell away.

Summer helped Kevin to his feet. Together, with

Koenig close behind, they limped toward the door-way.

The shortest end of the hall took them past a door that was hanging by a single hinge. It was the door that led to the basement. The creatures had at-tacked it so violently in their rush to break out, they had nearly torn it off its hinges. That had been the sound she had heard, the rumble she had felt beneath her feet.

The hallway opened into an expansive room. They had been here before. This was the room where Koenig kept his Wed clay, the room with twelve-foot ceilings, cabinets along one wall, and movie memorabilia along the other.

Summer helped Kevin across the floor to the cabi-nets, which offered some temporary support. He looked like the losing fighter at the end of the twelfth round. Blood was flowing freely from both forearms, from the wound in his shoulder (which was deep enough to expose the musculature underneath) and from the back of his legs.

He leaned against the cabinet doors, barely able to keep from collapsing to the floor. In a breathless whis-per, he thanked her.

"We need to get you some help."

"I'm all right. Don't worry about me." He nodded at the wall across the room, where the prop sword from *Jason and the Argonauts* hung on display next to the Frankenstein poster. "Why don't you grab that. It might be useful."

Off to the side, Koenig was pacing back and forth along the cabinets, his gaze cast toward the floor, on hand to his mouth. "I'm sorry. I'm so sorry. You have to know how sorry I am. You have to understand, I never wanted any of this to happen. Never."

From the hall, the sound of claws against the linoleum began to rise again.

NINETY-ONE

"This is going to be up to Kate," Cecelia said. The last item she had pulled out of her leather pouch had been what she called *colomsek*. When James had asked what it was, she explained it was wild sunflower root for purifying. She lit the root, let it burn for a short time, then blew out the flame.

"Someone's going to come in and get upset," James said.

"Why don't you close the door." She said a prayer while he closed and locked the door, then handed him the smoldering root. "Run this under the water for me, would you?"

"How do you get to be a shaman?" James asked, after he had dampened the root and handed it back to her.

"You're chosen." The root went back into the leather pouch. Cecelia looked up at him, then bluntly asked, "Is she strong?"

"As strong as they come."

"I hope you're right. She'll need to be." She rubbed her hands together, slowly at first, then gradually faster, until they had warmed, then she placed them over Kate's chest. "Turn it off."

"The respirator?"

"She needs to breathe on her own."

When the respirator went off, the room fell into an eerie silence, made all the more unsettling when it became apparent that Kate was not breathing on her own. James returned to her bedside, feeling intensely overwhelmed by the sense of déjà vu. He did not want to relive his experience of a few days earlier, nor did he want to leave Kate stranded in that dark netherworld.

Thirty seconds passed.

"We need to turn it back on," he said.

"Leave it be." Cecelia closed her eyes, and silently repeated a prayer.

One minute.

"It's too long."

"Patience."

The wait felt like an eternity. If it had dragged on for only a few seconds longer, James would have turned the respirator on with or without Cecelia Haring's consent. But it never came to that. Suddenly, Kate's head raised up off the pillow. She gasped for a single breath. Her entire body stiffened. Her head fell back to the pillow again. She swallowed, took another breath, then gradually her breathing began to fall into a comfortable, rhythmic pattern.

"She is strong," Cecelia said.

"What now?"

"Now we try to reach her. Give me your hand." She took his hand, then took Kate's hand and asked James to do the same, completing the circle. "It's okay to trust what you see, but trust what you feel first."

James nodded.

They closed their eyes.

*   *   *

Kate had been floating in an ethereal fog, a timeless wonderland with only a vague connection to the world she had left. She was aware that James had tried to reach her at one time, and that he was a good person, someone she cared for. She was also aware that this nebulous existence was not the result of an injury to her body. She was here because she had foolishly held the clay in her hands, and the clay had been inhabited by spirits. The spirits, desperate for release from their earthly bindings, had literally pulled her out of her body.

And now she was lost.

She wasn't supposed to be here, and she was lost.

Kate understood this as clearly as she understood anything here.

She also understood that if she wasn't able to connect with her body again soon, she might be stuck here forever.

Not for the first time in her recent consciousness, she became aware of a small pinpoint on the periphery of her perception. It appeared to be flashing, like a beacon marking a moment in time. She had watched herself gradually drifting away from that moment, untethered, since the birth of her experience here. Now, she wondered if that was the moment where she had entered into this strange and confusing world. And if it was, then wouldn't it also be the moment where she could escape?

There was something else taking form within the sphere of her perception as well . . . a roiling, grayish-black cloud. It was not the first time she had discerned this gathering mass, but it was the first time it had seemed so raw, so dangerous to her well-being.

With effort, she willed herself to move away from the cloud, in the direction of the beacon.

The malevolent presence expanded in pursuit.

A wail rose from somewhere behind her, the sound of a thousand voices howling in unison, the sound of souls trapped in eternal damnation, the sound of anguish and torment and . . .

Focus.

She struggled to push the sounds away from her thoughts.

Just focus.

NINETY-TWO

Summer pulled the sword down from the wall. It was a crude weapon, light, without much balance. The blade, though wide, was surprisingly short. A block of weathered wood served as the hilt. She swung it through the air once, silently praying it wouldn't crumble in her hands if she had to use it.

Then suddenly the creatures were upon them again.

The first one through went directly for Kevin, who barely had enough strength to keep his balance. He turned away from the beast as it sailed through the air. It landed high on his back, between his shoulder blades. He turned, trapped it between himself and the cabinet doors, then slammed his weight against it.

The creature squealed in agony.

Kevin slammed his weight against it again.

Another squeal.

The next creature through nearly lost its head as Summer raised the sword and sliced the air just above the beast as it went sailing past her. It ducked, then followed in the footsteps of its predecessor and went straight for Kevin.

He slammed the first creature into the cabinet one more time—another squeal—then managed to move to his left in time to watch the second creature crash head-first into one of the cabinet's framing supports. It fell to the floor, a gash opened in the top of its head where white clay oozed out in a gelatinous glob.

The third creature was neither as lucky nor as quick as the second. It arrived at the doorway just as Summer began to bring the sword around again. The blade sliced perfectly through the creature's neck, just above its high shoulder blades. Its head fell forward to the floor, making a moist, sickening sound as the clay was compressed against the linoleum.

The creature's body stumbled headlessly to one side, waving its arms in the air to help maintain its balance.

Koenig yelped.

He knelt next to the disembodied head, then picked it up, both hands gently cupping it as if it were a prized possession. He stared into its silvery eyes. His own eyes began to fill with tears.

Summer, keenly aware of the familiar boiling-over anger that was building inside her, watched this display of emotion with an odd detachment that was unlike her. It was almost as if she couldn't understand it, as if such obvious love were completely foreign to her.

Then Kevin let out an awful groan.

She turned in his direction.

He had fallen to his knees again. Both creatures were at him, one gnawing at his shoe like a rabid dog, the other attached to his right arm, just above the elbow.

Summer froze momentarily. Bile began to rise at the back of her throat. She lowered her head, narrowed her eyes. Her body began to quake uncontrollably. The sword slipped out of her hands and fell to the floor with a rather dull, far away thud.

It was coming now.

That familiar boiling anger that had always scared her.

In a last-ditch effort at defending himself, Kevin lamely kicked out at the creature at his feet. The blow struck the beast in the face, barely brushing it back.

Then suddenly Summer's anger erupted.

She felt a sharp pain tighten around her head. A violent shudder raised her off the floor an inch, maybe more, then dropped her back again.

The creature nearest her, the headless alien body stumbling blindly in circles now, exploded into flames. Its latex sheathing peeled away almost instantly. The white clay solidified around the armature freezing the joints until the creature finally fell forward onto the floor, helpless and unable to move.

Then the creature at Kevin's feet erupted into flames of its own. It wailed, then stumbled backward, waving its arms in the air in a futile effort to put out its own burning flesh. The latex peeled away in small lappets that fell to the floor like fiery scraps of burning trash.

Another fire broke out, this one at Summer's back: the Frankenstein poster.

Then an explosion at the far end of the room, where a fiery cabinet door tore off its hinges and went flying through the air. It came down on a detailed, miniature set, crushing the landscape and sending the alien terrain up in flames.

The creature at Kevin's arm released its hold.

It climbed to its feet, then turned toward Summer, as if it knew what was coming next. She lowered her head again. The force of flames that instantly erupted around the creature sent it wheeling back into the cabinet doors, a charred mass of latex, clay, and metal.

Another fire broke out, this one in the nearest corner.

Heat began to fill the air, mixing with the smoke in a deadly cocktail.

Another uncontrollable surge of energy began massing inside her. Summer glanced around the room for something else to destroy. Flames had begun to climb the walls now, like white hot ivy tendrils, up the walls and along the ceiling. Then suddenly one final, intense surge of anger exploded from within her.

The entire back wall of the room went up in a blaze.

Summer slumped forward, the anger finally dissipated, leaving her exhausted and drained.

"We need to get out of here," Kevin said. Though he was hobbling on one leg, he managed to get his arms under her to keep her from collapsing. With Koenig taking the lead—he had left the head of the creature behind, tossing aside whatever lingering connection he might have still felt with the beast—they clumsily made their way out of the room, back into the hallway.

Smoke was gathering in a thick blanket at the ceiling, working its way down the walls.

Kevin stayed as low as he could, still shouldering most of Summer's weight.

As they rounded the corner and reached the door to the basement, Koenig suddenly came to a stop. He turned to them. "You two go on. I'll catch up with you shortly."

"You can't go down there," Summer said.

"There's no time," Kevin added. "You'll never make it out."

"You don't understand." Koenig smiled with great sadness. It was a loneliness Summer had always known was there. "There are more of them. A whole family of them."

"In the basement?"

He nodded, then started down the steps. "These are my children. I created them. I have to try."

"We can't let him go down there," Summer said. Somehow, she managed enough strength to tear free of Kevin's grasp. "He'll die down there."

"So will you if you go after him. Let him go. There's nothing you can do." Kevin grabbed hold of the back of her shirt, pulled her away from the basement door, then pushed her ahead of him down the hallway. They stumbled out of the front door and into the sunlight like two battle-scarred war veterans after a horrific shelling.

Outside, a crowd had begun to gather.

A thick, black cloud of smoke reached seventy or eighty feet into the sky.

They helped each other hobble down the walkway to the car. Kevin leaned against the door, then slid down to the curb. Summer sat next to him.

Flames erupted from the roof near the back of the house.

Another angry plume of smoke rose into the air.

"He's not going to come out," Summer said quietly.

"I know."

"It's my fault. I killed him."

Kevin put his arms around her. "Listen to me. None of this, not any of it, is your fault. He fooled around with something he shouldn't have. Innocent people died because of what he did."

"He wasn't a bad man."

"I know that."

"He didn't deserve to die."

"It's not your fault. You don't have a bad intention in your body."

But I did, Summer thought guiltily. *For a few short minutes, I did.*

She watched the flames rise higher into the air, feeling a strange sense of detachment. Every once in a while she thought she could make out the face of some sort of twisted demon in the pyre, but the face would quickly disappear as if it had never been there at all. It would be hours before she would be able to find the strength to stand on her own two feet again.

Two days later, Victor Koenig's body was discovered huddled in the corner of the basement, his arms wrapped lovingly around a hardened, misshapen mass of clay, glass, and metal.

NINETY-THREE

Someone jiggled the handle to the door.

James opened his eyes.

"Concentrate," Cecelia said. "Don't let yourself become distracted."

He closed his eyes again. They had crossed the boundaries of the physical world into the same strange, nebulous netherworld he had experienced in his previous attempt to reach Kate. Cecelia was at his side, her eyes closed, her hands raised.

"What are we doing?"

"We cannot force a soul back into the body. We can only show it the way."

In the distance, he had a vague sense of Kate's consciousness. Closer to home, someone had began to knock at the door.

"This door shouldn't be locked." It was Maria Santos, the social worker. She knocked again, with more determination this time. "Is everything all right in there? James? Mr. McConnell? This door is supposed to remain unlocked. If someone doesn't answer me, I'm going to have to get security up here. Can anyone hear me?"

"What should we do?" James asked.

"Let it be." In the netherworld, Cecelia pointed toward a distant glimmer. "You see? That's her. She knows now."

"Knows what?"

"She knows we're here, and if she wishes, she knows how to come to us."

The pounding on the hospital door suddenly fell silent. James was smart enough to know that wasn't the end of it, though. It wouldn't remain silent for long. Maria Santos had gone off to get security, and when she came back, this time she would have a key.

Time was running out.

Kate continued her descent toward the beacon of light. Behind her, the malevolent presence had closed the distance between them and was now pressed up against a thin, invisible membrane that seemed to surround her. A face appeared out of the roiling blackness, embossing its distorted, ungodly self-portrait into the surface of the casing.

Kate turned away.

Focus.

Down below, she could sense two new spirits. She believed one belonged to James, though the other was unfamiliar. There were like rays of hope in a sea of desperation. She brightened as she realized they were making an effort to connect with her.

Focus.

Just focus.

Cecelia and James opened their eyes and returned to the physical world, only to discover that Kate had stopped breathing again. He held her hand a little tighter, hating the sound as she struggled for air, wishing there was something more he could do to help her.

The commotion at the door had started up again. In place of the pounding, he could hear the jangle of metal now. Someone from security was sorting through a huge disorganized ring of possible keys.

It had been nearly twenty-five seconds since Kate had taken her last breath.

"Isn't there anything we can do?"

"It's up to Kate now. We showed her the way."

Forty-five seconds.

A key was shoved into the lock, jiggled, then pulled out again.

James glanced up at the clock, then at the respirator. "What's taking her so long?"

"Patience."

One minute.

"What if she lost her way again? What if one of the demons has her?"

Seventy seconds.

Another key went into the lock. Security wasn't giving up.

Eighty seconds.

That godawful sound of air at the back of her throat.

Then suddenly Kate arched her back.

In an instant, the room filled with a blinding, grayish-white light that poured out of her chest and raced around the outer edges as if it were bird that had just been set free. With it, came an ear-shattering wail like nothing James had ever heard before. He covered his ears.

"What is it?"

"A demon," Cecelia yelled. She raised the small

square of white clay into the air and fell immediately into a frenetic prayer.

Kate finally swallowed a difficult breath, then fell back against the bed.

The key in the door lock clicked.

James ducked the swirling presence.

Cecelia raised her hand higher into the air, and as if it were incapable of resisting, suddenly the demon latched onto the block of white clay. The wail grew momentarily louder. Gradually, the grayish-white light was drawn out of the air and absorbed into the clay.

The door handle turned.

The room fell silent for a moment, then started to fill with nurses, orderlies, and hospital security.

Kate's eyes fluttered open.

"Welcome back," James said. "We missed you."

NINETY-FOUR

The door at the top of the stairway opened.

Kaufman looked up, feeling another attention-grabbing stab of pain across the left side of his torso. He winced and tucked his left arm into his body, which seemed to temporarily alleviate the pain.

Henderson stepped through the door, onto the top landing. He stared down at Kaufman, his eyes reflecting the overhead light. He seemed less agitated now, and Kaufman wasn't sure if that was a good thing or a bad thing.

"Made up my mind," he said.

"'Bout what?" Kaufman asked with another wince. No more unnecessary questions. Talking hurt too much.

"'Bout you. I've been giving it a lot of thought, you see. Because you've made a big fucking mess of things now. Take a look around you down there, and you'll see the predicament you've put me in. I mean, Christ, you weren't looking for what you found. You just sort of stumbled onto it by accident. Pure, dumb luck. But now I've got a problem and I've got to do something about it."

Kaufman wanted to ask him what he had in mind, just to keep him talking, but all he could do was take a breath. The pain wouldn't allow him any more than that.

Henderson started down the stairway, his feet making a clomping sound that seemed to contradict the man's light frame. "Looks like you went and hurt yourself. You can't be too careful around stairs. That's something I learned a long time ago. A loose handrail, a rotted-out step, and it's head over heels all the way down. Ooh, that does look like it hurts. A rib, isn't it? Those damn things can cripple a man, you break one of those."

He arrived at the bottom landing, only a foot or two away from Kaufman. He sat down on the second to last step. "Ever tried meth? Don't answer that. I know it's gotta hurt to talk. Besides, between you and me, we both know the answer. You're just too upstanding a guy for something like meth."

He reached into his shirt pocket and pulled out a plastic sandwich bag filled with white chunks. "You see, I'm not the nicest guy you're ever going to meet. Not by a long shot. Some people think I'm a bastard through and through, and that may be so. But I'm not a murderer. I just don't have it in me to knife a guy, or to put a bullet in his head. Just can't do it."

He waved the bag. "But an overdose . . . that's like an accident, you know. It's like something that just happens. No one's fault. Just a bad break."

Whatever was going to happen now, Kaufman knew it was going to hurt. There was no way around the pain. Either it hurt and he lived, or it hurt and he died.

Henderson stood up, still waving the bag in his face. "So you can take this stuff willingly and make it easy on both of us. Or I can whack you over the head again and stuff it down your throat. It doesn't much matter to me. The result's the same. Either way, it's one dead cop."

Kaufman waited patiently for an opening. He was only going to get one shot at this. If it didn't work, Henderson was going to go into a sudden rage, and that was going to be the final word of the final chapter.

"So what's it going to be, old buddy, old pal? The easy way or the—"

Kaufman struck out with his right foot. He aimed it perfectly and it landed nearly full force directly across Henderson's left knee.

There was a loud *crunch*.

The knee snapped, and the force of the blow sent it burrowing to a point somewhere far behind the back of the leg.

Henderson screamed.

He went down immediately, clutching at his knee, rolling on the floor.

Kaufman winced and adjusted his position again. It didn't hurt as much this time. In fact, it almost felt good.

Backup arrived less than a minute later.

NINETY-FIVE

They looked liked an old, ragged pair of war veterans.

Kevin wore his right arm in a sling to help alleviate the pain from the bite on his shoulder. And he still walked with a minor limp, though every day it was becoming a little less pronounced.

Kaufman wore his bandages under his shirt, so they weren't as obvious. The rib had, indeed, been cracked. He still winced whenever he moved a little too fast. Marie didn't like to admit to it, but it was obvious she had been smothering him with sympathy.

Two weeks had passed since the fire had destroyed Victor Koenig's house and all his worldly possessions. It seemed like a long time ago now. Kate was out of the hospital, almost back to one hundred percent, except for some minor weakness in one hand. Summer was her old self again, sometimes quiet and moody, sometimes obnoxiously outgoing. And James seemed as if he had finally come to feel comfortable in the midst of this family of misfits and outcasts.

Kaufman had managed to keep his captain gleefully in the dark about what had really happened. He wrote a report that properly named Koenig as the villain. But in the place of Koenig's creatures, he had pointed a finger at a pack of well-trained Rottwellers. It was easier to cast blame on the familiar.

Kaufman had also managed to keep his word to Mimi Van Mears. Unwilling to put anything in writing, he had called her one afternoon and told her the entire story, the whole truth, nothing but the truth, from beginning to end. She wrote the story just as he told it to her, the *National Insider* ran it, the readers loved it, and no one (including Mimi herself) believed it.

On the other front, Flynn had sent a message to Kevin that had arrived just yesterday. It seemed that Hunter had gone into hiding. He was feeling pressure from all sides now after what he had done to Ivy. Not a word had been heard from him in nearly three weeks. Eventually, he would resurface again, Kevin had no doubt of that. And eventually they would meet up again. But for the time being, Kevin found a certain degree of enjoyment in the idea that Hunter was now the hunted.

Kevin raised a glass in toast. He looked around the table, at the people gathered here near the back of Hugo's, and felt an appreciation for all of them. For Dan and Marie. For Summer and Kate and James. And for the new family that was unfolding.

"To good friends, and a loving family."

JULIE E. CZERNEDA

"One of the fastest-rising stars of the new millennium"—Robert J. Sawyer

The Trade Pact Universe
☐ **A THOUSAND WORDS FOR STRANGER (Book #1)**
0-88677-769-0—$5.99

☐ **TIES OF POWER (Book #2)**   0-88677-850-6—$6.99
Sira, the most powerful member of the alien Clan, has dared to challenge the will of her people—by allying herself with a human. But they are determined to reclaim her genetic heritage . . . at any cost!

Alos available:
☐ **BEHOLDER'S EYE**   0-88677-818-2—$5.99
They are the last survivors of their shapeshifting race, in mortal danger of extinction, for the Enemy who has long searched for them may finally discover their location. . . .

PRECURSOR

by C.J. Cherryh

The Riveting Sequel to the *Foreigner* Series

The *Foreigner* novels introduced readers to the epic story of a lost human colony struggling to survive on the hostile world of the alien *atevi*. Now, in the beginning of a bold new trilogy, both human and *atevi* return to space to rebuild and rearm the ancient human space station and starship, and to make a desperate attempt to defend their shared planet from outside attack.

☐ **Hardcover Edition**   0-88677-836-0—$23.95

☐ **Paperback Edition**   0-88677-910-3—$6.99

Be sure to read the first three books in this action-packed series:

☐ **FOREIGNER**   0-88677-637-1—$6.99

☐ **INVADER**   0-88677-687-2—$6.99

☐ **INHERITOR**   0-88677-728-3—$6.99

TANYA HUFF
VALOR'S CHOICE

"Readers who enjoy military SF will love Tanya Huff's
VALOR'S CHOICE. Howlingly funny and very
suspenseful. I enjoyed every word."
—*scifi.com*

Staff Sergeant Torin Kerr was a battle-hardened professional.
So when she and those in her platoon who'd survived the last
deadly encounter with the Others were yanked from a well-
deserved leave for what was supposed to be "easy" duty as
the honor guard for a diplomatic mission to the non-Confedera-
tion world of the Silsviss, she was ready for anything. Sure,
there'd been rumors of the Others being spotted in this sector
of space. But there were always rumors. Everything seemed
to be going perfectly. Maybe too perfectly. . . .

0-88677-896-4 $6.99

Prices slightly higher in Canada DAW: 149